The Heart of the World

Jane Doe

Copyright © 2023 Jane Doe

Cover art by 沫語

All rights reserved.

ISBN: 9798864019702

DEDICATION

I dedicate this novel to my family, friends, and all those who have ceaselessly supported my work and reminded me that it doesn't deserve to be stuffed in a drawer somewhere. Without you, I never would have written this novel.

CONTENTS

	Acknowledgments	i
1	The Island That Isn't an Island	1
2	A Man Named Wizard Lenin	12
3	The Thing About Clark Kent	39
4	The Heart of the World	59
5	The Plans of Mice and Men	84
6	Iff's Brave New World	97
7	The Fellowship of the MacGuffin	121
8	The Seven Labors of Lily	133
9	All That Glitters	145
10	The Origin of War	156
11	The Once and Future King	171
12	What Are We Going to Do About Rabbit?	184
13	Fate is Written This Way	196
14	The Blind Prophet	211
15	The Endlessness of Eternity	221
16	A Rabbit by Any Other Name	234
17	An Inevitable Betrayal	244
18	A Disquieting Redundancy	254
19	All Hail the Conquering Heroes	265
20	John's Bargain with the Gods	278

21 The Play   287

ACKNOWLEDGMENTS

Thank you to all those who supported me and were willing to look over this novel. Especially thanks to Vinelle. Without your tireless dedication, overwhelming amount of support, reminders, pep talks, and countless hours spent helping to edit this novel I would not be here.

1 THE ISLAND THAT ISN'T AN ISLAND

In which a young girl meets herself in the afterlife, discovers there is a death with a capital D, and decides to change her name.

Like all people born into this world, Eleanor Joan Tylor died.

If anyone asked, what had happened was that she'd climbed the tree in the backyard and hadn't thought about how she'd get back down. Gravity had taken care of that problem for her, but as she'd landed on her neck—

Ellie was going to take her very unfamiliar surroundings as a very bad sign for her health.

At first, she thought she was on an island, an island with gleaming sand surrounded by an unnaturally calm and dark sea. Except, when she looked closer, she saw that it wasn't water surrounding her. In the place of waves, there was an expansive, endless, night sky extending both above and below her, interrupted only by the distant twinkling of stars.

The island itself was covered in unfamiliar, glowing, plant life. Wildflowers swayed in a gentle breeze, blue pollen rising like embers with each small movement.

There was no sign of any people. There were no buildings, no ruins, no roads, no trails, no traps, boats, bridges—nothing. There were only the flowers, the grass untouched by feet of any kind, and an eerie feeling of emptiness Ellie had never encountered before.

She walked along the shoreline, found herself easily circling the island and returning to where she started. No part of it any different than the other.

Except for the pedestal in the middle of the clearing. It sat there, not unremarkable exactly, but like something that wouldn't have looked out of place in an over decorated garden. It looked shockingly new or else well cared for, the stone still white and unstained, not a hint of moss or mold on it. There were simple carvings on it, nothing more than a few vertical lines on each side to give it texture.

A single, dark, orb rested on it, its metallic surface reflecting the light from the plants.

Something about it though, beyond the fact that it was the only artificially constructed thing here, bothered her.

She forced her attention away from it, shoving her hands uncomfortably into her pockets.

"Hello?" Ellie asked the emptiness, her voice pitched loud enough that had she been at home the whole neighborhood would have heard her.

"Is something supposed to happen now?" she pressed when she heard no answer, not even an echo.

Still nothing.

Frowning, Ellie pressed on, deciding to start with the basics.

"My name's Ellie Tylor," Ellie said, trying to sound less lost than she was, "I'm five-years-old and—I don't think I did anything particularly bad. Haven't done much of anything, actually."

As she said it, she realized that might be the problem and quickly added, "But people have said I'm smart for my age. I'm also tall for my age, that's a good thing, isn't it? I've read thick books… Oh, and I've watched a lot of television! That's very impressive in some circles!"

No one responded.

Feeling a little annoyed, Ellie flopped onto the ground. She stared up at the tapestry of stars that looked identical to those beneath the island.

There was, she noted with a frown, no Little Dipper or any other recognizable constellation.

Ellie wasn't sure if this was just what death was like, if she was being punished somehow, or if this was better than most people got when they died and she should be grateful.

It wasn't unpleasant, but it was a little empty.

"Don't thousands of people die a day or something?" Ellie asked the emptiness, raising a challenging eyebrow, "Shouldn't it be, I don't know, a little bit busier here?"

Was Ellie really going to sit here for the rest of her—

Well, not her life, she'd gone and messed that up. Still, for the rest of forever, which sounded like it was going to be much longer than her life had been.

If she'd known life was going to be that short she'd have made sure to finish *Ghostbusters*, now she'd never know how it ended.

Just as she closed her eyes, though, there was an out of place crunching noise next to her.

She jerked upright, scrambled to her feet, and caught sight of a tall man who certainly hadn't been standing there before.

He was wearing dark clothing she didn't recognize, made from fabric she couldn't place, not only worn at the edges but notably faded. His cloak that might have once been blue had now been consumed by black, his tunic that looked red if she squinted was also near black, everything he was wearing was almost but not quite black.

Somehow more striking than his grim, oddly fantastical looking outfit was his face. His face—it looked uncomfortably familiar, easy to pinpoint too, if only because Ellie saw that same face in the mirror every day. She saw his sports car red hair, his traffic-light green eyes, his high cheekbones, nose, jawline, brow, and coloring in the mirror every morning.

While his hair was much shorter than hers, standing on his head like feathers, and there was a masculine something to his face that certainly wasn't in hers, it was decidedly her face with all the oddities she'd never seen elsewhere.

Just like her, it made him look unnatural, even with all the right parts in all the right places.

He wasn't looking at her, hadn't even seemed to notice her, but was staring out at the endless sky surrounding them. He seemed frustrated.

"Tree?" Ellie asked, breaking the silence.

His head whipped towards her, eyes burning bright, intense and unnerving.

"I fell out of a tree," Ellie confessed, rubbing the back of her head with an awkward laugh, trying to force her stomach to settle, "I just wondered if, I don't know, maybe this was the afterlife for tree-fallers."

She'd never heard of an afterlife for careless people who fell out of things, but if there was a Valhalla then there could be an afterlife for just about anything. The absence of trees, here, might be indicative of her punishment for climbing them.

He didn't say anything to that, and while his expression didn't change, she somehow knew he was debating leaving without a word.

"Wait, don't go!" she held up a hand to stop him, darting towards him only to halt before she could grab at his sleeve.

Unfortunately, this left her still awkwardly leaning forward, arm outstretched, feeling desperately unbalanced and useless.

(Ellie was hopelessly reminded that she'd never been all that good with people, even if she was only in kindergarten.)

Her heart thundered in her ears and her throat was tight as she blurted out, "My name's Ellie."

She waited one second, then two, wondering if that had somehow been enough to drive him off, and then he smiled.

His shoulders relaxed, no longer as straight or still as before, and his smile made his whole face soften and almost look—

Human.

Human, for all that he had a face that was supposed to be human.

"Hello," he said in response, his voice softer than she'd expected it to be, reaching out and shaking her outstretched hand lightly.

His hand was warm, she thought with some shock, only to wonder why she'd thought it would be cold. Well, that was a lie, like his face, his hand looked human enough but—there was something about it that just didn't look right.

He didn't offer a name.

Ellie waited, her hand in his, still leaning forward, feeling as if she was holding her breath until he said something.

A gentle breeze tousled both their hair, he remained silent.

"When someone says their name, you're supposed to say yours back," Ellie told him, as that was what she had figured out in kindergarten. The Tylors, of course, were very familiar with Ellie's name and not all that interested in it.

It was probably the wrong thing to say, Ellie had a bad habit of saying the wrong thing, but he didn't seem offended. In fact, he laughed. It was a small, short, laugh, not even a chuckle, but he seemed as surprised by the noise as she was.

"Sorry, people don't usually expect it," he offered, his voice still very soft but—the thing was she could hear it just fine, it wasn't quiet exactly, just distant somehow.

Yes, that was the word for it. Everything about him was distant, his voice, his smile, his very presence. It was like she only got to see the outer layer of him, what he was choosing to show her, and that something else, something very different, rested beneath it.

His smile, while amused and gentle, had a sad edge to it that didn't belong in human expressions.

He stared down at their joined hands for a moment while he contemplated his answer. Finally, after several long seconds, he said, "I've been called Death before."

Ellie stared at him dumbly for a moment, feeling the reality, or distinct lack of reality of her situation sink in.

Right, she was dead.

She was dead, had entered the afterlife of all those who didn't look before they leaped, and now she was meeting Death.

"I thought you'd be taller," Ellie said after a beat, "And—different."

She looked him over, from his very red hair, his too green eyes, his lean frame—the outfit at least was the right coloring (black and then more black) but even that didn't really fit what she'd expected.

"I once thought so too," Death responded, like this was a very funny joke.

She waited, wondering if this was the something she'd been waiting for.

Would she undergo some trials now? Be escorted to a different afterlife more fitting for all her accomplishments or lack thereof? She did think it was a bit unfair to be judged like this when she'd only just gotten to kindergarten.

She was about to point as much out when she saw he wasn't looking at her.

He was staring out at the stars, the ones that looked like a sea but weren't, his smile having dripped away from his face.

She felt herself start when he said, "It's the same."

"What is?" Ellie asked, looking out with him, frowning as she tried to see what he saw.

The view wasn't uninteresting, though staring too long did give her an uncomfortable feeling of vertigo. Still, despite the eerie way that down looked like up out there, the twinkling light sin the distance just looked like stars.

"This place is exactly the same," he sighed, then glared over his shoulder at the pedestal, "Even the Heart of the World is back in place."

Now that—

That orb, Ellie would agree, was downright unnerving even if she couldn't explain why.

"This isn't your first time dying?" Ellie asked, only to remember, "Right, sorry, you are Death, obviously you come here all the time."

She shoved her hands back into her pockets, thinking about that, "It's my first time dying, you know."

That got his attention.

He gave her a funny look, confused, even tilting his head to the side just a little like he was a bird.

Then Ellie realized what he might not have put together yet (though she was pretty sure she'd mentioned it right away).

"Oh, see, I'm dead," Ellie told him cheerfully (now having gotten used to the idea), "At least, I think I am. Suddenly ended up in this place after landing on my neck so—it's either I'm dead or this is what comas are like."

She supposed it wouldn't matter either way.

If she was in a coma and she woke up, or if it was all a dream, then nothing that happened here would matter. If it wasn't then it was best to go along with it.

Who knew, maybe this was reality now. Maybe it'd hiccuped when she hadn't been looking and instead of dying the universe had shifted a little. She wouldn't be surprised.

The important thing was that she wasn't supposed to be wherever here was and if she was—something bad had happened to get her here.

Death, however, was still staring, clearly thinking hard.

Then, rather than confirm Ellie's death, or tell her this was only a dream, or even tell her that this was just what the universe was like now, he asked, "Your last name is Tylor, isn't it?"

Ellie felt her smile fall, a chill racing up her spine. After a second's pause, she confessed, "Yes."

Death just nodded, as if it was all clicking into place, "You were adopted by Mike and Carol Tylor."

That was also true.

Ellie Tylor had started life without a name and with no real origins to speak of. The way local news had said it, she'd been found in a dumpster with no hint of a birth certificate or a guardian.

Mike Tylor had then been running for office, and had thought adopting a local child in need would boost his ratings in the polls. That hadn't worked out for him, but he had ended up stuck with the kid.

"Have you met them?" Ellie found herself warily asking.

Death asking after her adoptive parents couldn't be good news.

While Ellie had her issues with the Tylors, with their constant vanishing acts, they weren't the worst parents she could have. She could have ended up in a foster home, on the streets, or maybe even in an orphanage singing about food, glorious food.

Even if Ellie didn't always appreciate being ignored, she appreciated that she had a roof over her head, three meals a day, and—

None of that mattered because she was already dead, wasn't she?

Right.

"Yes and no," Death said, and it took a moment for Ellie to realize he was answering her question, whether or not he'd met the Tylors.

Ellie stared at him dumbly, wondering if she was stupid for not figuring out what that was supposed to mean. She didn't feel stupid, she never had, but she supposed she was only five and moments of stupidity could spring up on you without warning.

Rather than explain, Death nodded towards—a table and two chairs that had suddenly popped into existence. "We should sit," he said.

"Oh," Ellie said in a daze and followed him to the table. She tried not to blink when a pot of tea and two porcelain teacups appeared out of thin air.

"I'm you," Death said as he poured the tea, one for her and one for him.

"Sorry?" Ellie asked as she took a sip—she couldn't place the flavor. It wasn't apple, not orange, not peach, not cinnamon either but it was tinted with some very distinct flavor that she just couldn't place.

"Technically, I suppose I would be your brother," Death continued, as if he hadn't just confessed to—something that didn't make any sense at all, "However, for all intents and purposes, I'm you."

"How can you be me?" Ellie asked slowly, not even sure she was asking her question right.

This all felt very philosophical.

Ellie wasn't usually one for philosophy.

As someone who wasn't entirely sure her reality even existed, or if it was in any way consistent, trying to sit down and puzzle out whether it was all someone's dream, what the meaning of it all was supposed to be, or who she even was, left her stumped.

It felt a bit like entering a trivia contest where you just knew you were going to get every question wrong.

"My name, once, was Elliott Tylor," Death confessed, his expression grave now, "I was adopted by Mike and Carol Tylor, I lived with them until I was twelve, then—I suppose it doesn't matter."

Ellie opened her mouth to protest, because that sounded like it mattered quite a bit, but he continued, "I know that you're like me, that you must in some fashion be me, because only I can enter this place. When a human dies, this isn't where they end up."

"Well—" Ellie said, not sure what to say, only that she should say something, "Are you sure?"

For a moment, he said nothing, he only drank his tea while he stared at her with those eyes that—were her eyes that unnerving? She'd known they looked odd, that they were a bit too bright, but she'd never realized how unsettling they were.

"I also once thought I was human," he said quietly, "For many years, I lived like I was any other person, despite many indications that I was not. In truth, there had been signs all my life, sometimes small and sometimes quite glaring, that I was not what I thought I was. I had never realized, never guessed, until the evidence was so overwhelming I could no longer deny it."

His expression hadn't changed, neither had his tone, but something about the atmosphere had. The lights from the plants surrounding them had dimmed, the stars winked out overhead, and with each word he said the world seemed that much darker.

His eyes never left hers.

"I am telling you this because I wish that I had been told in the beginning," he continued, "There was no reasonable way for anyone to have known, for anyone to have guessed, but I wish they could have. I wish that I could have known and that I wouldn't have had false expectations. It's hard, Ellie, to try so hard, to be something you are not capable of."

He nodded towards their surroundings, "This place isn't the end for you, it will never be the end for you, because there will never be an end for you. If you wanted to, you could easily turn back the way you came, and reenter the world of the living. You're the Death of this universe, Ellie."

Ellie wasn't sure what to say to any of that.

She felt—

Well, that was a lot of information, for one thing, but it also felt uncomfortably personal.

"Well, I'm not sure I have any expectations," Ellie finally said, shifting in her seat, "And I also—"

She wanted to say that she wasn't Death, couldn't be, but something stopped her.

How did she know that?

Granted, it was a little peculiar that a stranger in another world was telling her what she was and wasn't, but she didn't know it wasn't true. There was also something, not something she could see, hear, or even smell, but something like a thread that extended out into the darkness.

She had the sudden, instinctual, certainty that if she followed that thread, she'd find herself at the bottom of the tree right as rain.

"Well," Ellie finished lamely.

Death laughed at that, pouring himself another cup of tea. She was glad one of them was laughing.

"But if you're Death then how can I be Death?" Ellie asked, there can't be two deaths.

"This universe," he said, an amused twinkle in his eyes, "I'm a different Death who is simply passing through."

"Oh," Ellie said, wondering if that was supposed to be a good or a bad thing or anything at all.

"You're from a different reality?" Ellie asked only to remember that he'd introduced himself as Elliott Tylor who was really her.

She supposed—he must have been from the world where Ellie had been born a boy. That, maybe, there were hundreds of millions of worlds each with their own version of Ellie Tylor, with only subtle differences. Each one, apparently, Death.

Except she had a feeling that Death didn't mean what she thought it meant. She didn't recall reaping anyone's soul or controlling who lived and who died or anything like that.

She didn't doubt he was something other, though, and that apparently she was too.

"Just so," he agreed with a hum.

Ellie tried to wrap her head around it.

She supposed—reality wasn't very consistent, she'd noticed that early on. It was entirely possible that there were other worlds, other Ellies, and that each Ellie was—whatever Death even was.

"Wait, if you're Death," Ellie said accusingly, "Then doesn't your reality need you?"

She supposed the world didn't have to need death, in fact most of what it caused was suffering, but things would certainly be very different, and she imagined a lot of people would be very confused.

However, Death didn't look surprised at all by the question, instead he looked—shuttered.

"No," he said, and then nothing else.

She considered that for a moment, then shrugged, "Well, I guess my reality doesn't need me."

It'd seemed to have gotten on fine without her before she was born and it'd probably do well enough now that she was wherever here was. Maybe that was a little strange, if she was supposed to be important, but she didn't think this Death business necessarily made her important.

"That's not true," Death protested, looking oddly vehement, even a little upset.

"When I say that they don't need me—" Death began, gripping his hands together and staring down at the table, "I meant it is because there is no one there to need me."

Ellie opened her mouth to ask but then closed it.

There was no one there to need him—that meant that everyone in his reality was already dead. There was no need for Death because everything was dead already.

She didn't ask what had happened, why, and if he'd done it himself. She didn't ask him if he'd chosen this place or if he'd just somehow ended up here.

He was—

By all accounts, he was a frightening figure, or at the very least eccentric. However, for as strange as this had been, he'd also been very kind. He'd been kinder, in fact, than anyone she had ever met.

He hadn't just stayed, poured her tea, but it looked as if he was going to stay for as long as she did.

And Ellie realized, staring at him, that she had never felt anything like this.

She didn't know what she was feeling, she only knew that she didn't want him to go.

"I don't see what's wrong with a world having two Deaths," Ellie blurted, "And I can't be very good at my job seeing as I didn't know I had one. You can stay here!"

He gave her a funny look again, red eyebrows raised dubiously.

"I mean, I should probably go back," Ellie blathered on, "There's things I still want to do in kindergarten and lots of movies I want to watch—and if you don't want to come that's fine—just—"

He didn't say anything to that, giving no indication of whether he intended to stay or leave, but he did smile.

Ellie felt herself relax.

"It will get better," Death told her suddenly.

She almost asked if he meant the tea, only to realize that he had to mean the world of the living. The Tylors.

There was an oddly, uncomfortably, knowing look in his eyes as if—

well, as if he'd lived the same life.

Ellie wasn't sure if she believed that but didn't say anything.

Instead, she thought over everything he'd said.

Was she Death?

She certainly felt like something but that didn't mean it was anything as exotic and terrifying as Death.

If she was Death, a different Death than him, what changed?

If she was Death now, then she'd always been Death, even when the Tylors had picked her up out of that dumpster.

She realized, with a growing sense of dread, that nothing would change.

She'd go back and when she did no one would be the wiser. There'd been no babysitter around to watch her fall, so there'd be no one to watch as she sat back up again. She'd just go back inside, flip through channels on TV, and continue to do what she did every day of every year.

No, something had to change.

Something must change, if only to be some small marker that something significant had happened.

"I need a new name," Ellie blurted.

She looked directly at him, daring him to protest, but he didn't. Instead, there was that entirely too knowing look again. (He hadn't introduced himself as Elliott, at first, had he?)

He smiled, a true but pained smile, and noted, "I was always terrible with names."

"Then—"

He interjected before she could finish, "My mother's, your mother's, name was Lilyanna."

"Lilyanna," Ellie repeated.

It was a bit of a mouthful, not a name she'd heard before either, it was only either Lily or Anna. She could be Lily, though.

It wasn't anything eye-catching, an ordinary name, but there was something about it she liked. It felt right.

"Alright," Lily said with a grin, "I'll be Lily then."

**

After leaving Death and the island, somehow vanishing the moment she truly thought about it, she found herself lying at the base of the tree with a kink in her neck.

Nothing seemed to be broken, and staring up at the sky, time didn't seem to have passed. The only indication that anything had happened were the broken branches above her.

As she'd expected, no one seemed to have seen it happen.

She doubted the Tylors would care even if they had miraculously been around to witness it.

She stood, brushed off her knees, and stared upwards at the tree.

Lily wasn't sure she'd ever see him again.

He'd still been sitting at the table when she left. He'd smiled fondly but his eyes had been distant and shadowed as he'd watched her go.

She was certain he was still sitting there even now, staring out into the abyss again but—

She wasn't sure how she knew, she'd never done it before, but she was certain she'd made a friend.

She stared at the tree for a long moment, watching, as if he might come walking through it like a door.

He didn't, but she watched all the same, a new tender hope sneaking through her.

She turned from the tree and walked back inside where, just as predicted, television and cookies waited.

Everything and nothing, she was sure, had just shifted on its slightly tilted axis.

2 A MAN NAMED WIZARD LENIN

In which Lily develops a dangerous pastime and meets a very peculiar man who lives inside of her head.

At least, everything and nothing should have shifted on its axis.

Two months had come and gone, and with it, Lily's patience.

Time was a funny thing. Objectively, she knew two months was barely the blink of an eye, but to a five-year-old two months was an eternity and a half. To an adult in another dimension, though, two months must have been next to nothing.

It also didn't help that it'd gone exactly the way she'd thought it would.

Everything was deceptively normal, that cardboard cutout soap opera sense of normal that Lily had known all her life. No one had realized she'd died and risen, the Tylors hadn't even realized there'd been a tree in the first place, and to anybody who paid any amount of attention (which had to be just about nobody) Lily was still the same old Ellie Tylor.

It was now Christmas. The decorations were out, the holiday specials on, and Lily was in formal wear at the first of the seemingly infinite parade of Christmas parties she'd be forced to attend this year.

Now, why Lily was at a Christmas party when Thanksgiving had only just ended, Lily didn't know. It was one of those infinite mysteries of life that you were never really meant to solve.

Thanksgiving aside, the Tylors liked parties, and if they were forced to interact with their only daughter then it was usually through a party where there would be ten other children to distract her.

The only problem, of course, was that Lily wasn't really a people person.

She tried, she was trying, she just—

"Barbie needs to go to the party."

Lily was sitting across from Annie, a familiar face from these parties, but an unfamiliar one from school.

More specifically, they were sequestered away in Annie's playroom, far from the adults and the cocktails and excused to go do whatever children did to entertain themselves.

Annie probably would have abandoned Lily long ago if she'd had other options. Unfortunately for Annie, she didn't, she had Lily.

Lily blinked at Barbie's frozen, forever too cheerful, grin and her dead painted eyes. Doll's eyes like a shark's eyes, Lily thought to herself grimly.

"Isn't Barbie already attending the party?" Lily asked, trying and failing to smile.

It didn't work.

"No," Annie scowled, "She needs to go to the party. We have to get her ready."

Barbie looked about as ready to party as she always did, in Lily's opinion. Her pink dress looked fashionable enough, her heels were pointed enough to cause damage if she stepped on someone's foot, and Lily couldn't think of anything more she could possibly need.

Still, best to play along, "Well, how does Barbie get ready?"

Annie's scowl turned into a puzzled frown as she considered both Barbie and Ken. Ken was already waiting in the pink plastic convertible with a far too cheerful grin of his own and equally dead eyes.

"She needs a fancy outfit," Annie concluded, 'These aren't party clothes."

Lily wasn't sure she agreed with that or with the need for formal wear at all. Her own clothes, her tights especially, were very uncomfortable and annoying.

Lily would hope that Barbie's identical looking friends with different hair colors wouldn't judge her.

Of course, that was all dancing around the root problem.

"Why does Barbie need to go to the party?" Lily asked.

Annie frowned once again, "Everyone's going to be there."

"Well, sure," Lily answered lamely, "But what's going to happen at the party? They're just going to sit, talk, and maybe comment on each other's outfits. Sheila over there might say something impolite, which will cause gossip, but I'm sure they'll be over it soon enough. Nothing will actually happen."

Lily was on a roll, now waving her hands about to emphasize her point, "I mean, Barbie might as well just stay at home. It's not much better, I guess, but at least she'll have TV."

Unfortunately, that seemed to be when Annie reached her limit, "You're mean! If you're not going to play then go somewhere else!"

Lily stared at her dumbly, hands still raised, but Annie didn't relent and Lily had the sudden, awkward, familiar feeling that she'd shown up on the set of the wrong play.

Lily offered her a strained smile, a small nod, then scrambled to her feet. She didn't wait for the part where Annie wouldn't take back her words and instead rushed out of the room. Annie didn't call back for her, Lily didn't expect her too, that didn't happen at school or at Christmas parties.

Lily sighed and started wandering through the hall, searching for the rest of the Christmas party. Like the Tylor's house, even the hallways were filled with furniture. Reproductions of famous paintings, photographs of the family including Annie, vases on tables with marble surfaces, and red carpets lining the floors. It was all very nice-looking save that, just like the Tylor's house, it was eerily empty of people.

Lily reached the edge of the main room and peaked in. There were too many adults to count, most of them red faced and holding wine glasses, all equally well-dressed for the occasion. The Tylors had disappeared somewhere into the throng, perfectly indistinguishable from the masses. None of them even glanced in her direction, most were laughing at some joke she couldn't hear over the dull roar.

All at once, the very sight of it was unbearable.

"This," Lily said to herself, "is not acceptable."

She wasn't sure what was acceptable, she expected she'd never seen it before, but it felt like the right thing to say.

She'd been hoping Mr. Death would come to her, that he would sail across the night sky in a little boat, but it looked like he was being difficult after all. She'd have to find a way back to him. It was a good thing, she thought with a bitter smile, that she knew the way.

She darted away from the party, her heart beating wildly, and a wild grin growing unbidden on her face.

**

One of the wonderful things about the Tylors knowing a lot of people with too many hobbies was all the potentially lethal hardware they kept in the garage.

After much searching, debating, and discarding various drills, hammers, and other blunt metal objects, she managed to find a lengthy and sturdy hose.

Now in the mysterious confines of these strangers' attic, she set about busily tying the knot, testing its strength and making sure that it would hold her weight.

When that was done, she stacked several boxes labeled 'Christmas Decorations', and stood on her toes to tie it through the rafters. Just as she finished, she fell off the boxes and onto the floor, only just rolling out of the way of the topmost box that had tumbled after her.

She wiped at her face, sneezing at the sudden plume of dust, and observed the silently hanging noose.

It looked foreboding, much more foreboding than the tree ever had for all it had killed her. She supposed that was because, last time, she'd had no intention of dying before.

It was a little nerve wracking this time around.

A very small part of her asked if maybe the reason Death hadn't come to her was because he wasn't actually real. Another Ellie (Lily now) in another dimension who said he was Death? That wasn't supposed to happen to people. That was the sort of thing that was on TV because it explicitly didn't happen to people.

Maybe, all that would happen if Lily killed herself, was that she'd just die.

She contemplated that for a moment, mulling it over as she stared at the noose.

"Well," Lily said to herself, "Then I guess I'd better write an obituary."

She searched around for pen and paper. Not surprisingly, she didn't find any, but just when she was about to give up, she suddenly found some next to her shoe.

She swore that hadn't been there two seconds ago.

Then again, she thought with a dull feeling of resignation, that sort of thing seemed to happen to her now and again. Items she swore she couldn't find would suddenly turn up in the place she'd looked two seconds before, broken objects wouldn't be broken after all, and people named Death lived in islands in other worlds.

Lily had decided a long time ago to not let it bother her.

She took up the pen and the paper, mulling over what to write.

"Lily Eleanor Joan Tylor—" she started.

Then she stopped.

That was a mouthful, wasn't it? What kind of person had four names? It just didn't feel right. Of course, the only real name in there was 'Lily' as all the rest had been foisted onto her before she could even remember. Except, if she just wrote that, then no one would have any idea who the obituary was supposed to be for.

"This is hard," Lily muttered in some frustration.

Sighing, she kept the name and started over, "Lily Eleanor Joan Tylor, daughter of someone who left their child in a dumpster for safekeeping.

Adopted daughter of Mike and Carol Tylor who were kind enough to take her in then leave her to her own devices for five years.

Friend of Mr. Elliott Death Tylor and—uh—"

Lily thought about that for several seconds before giving up, "Tolerated by everyone else. 1979-1984."

Lily wrote her signature with a flourish (a little bit wobbly, but pretty damned good considering Lily was only five) and then set the page back down.

Someone would find it, she was sure.

She stood there for a moment, staring at it, waiting for some grand epiphany to hit. Maybe this was the moment she was supposed to realize the meaning of life, love, friendship, anything at all. Instead, there was nothing, just the shadow of the hose-noose hanging behind her.

There was no reason to delay any longer.

Stacking the boxes once again, Lily carefully climbed up, stood on her toes, and stuck her head through the noose. With one final, shaking, breath, forcing herself to get control of her nerves, she stepped off.

A few jerks later the attic disappeared. A pristine beach that wasn't a beach, on an island that wasn't an island, took its place.

"I did it," Lily said in breathless wonder, wandering forward and just stopping short of tumbling over the edge and into the stars. Still, she grinned to herself, staring down at the water that wasn't water.

"I did it!" she cried out in jubilation, clapping her hands together. Her fingers were buzzing, her feet were buzzing, she felt like she could leap over buildings with a single bound.

It was here, it was all still here, just the same as he'd promised. And—

There he was, still sitting in the furniture he'd made out of nothing, staring out at the empty rolling hills with an equally empty expression. He'd taken off his gloves, his billowing scarf, and even his cloak. Without them on, he looked even thinner than he had before, as if the only substance to him was the shadows he wore and the red of his hair.

"Death!" Lily cried out, not even thinking to stop herself. She sprinted from the edge of the island towards him, paying no mind to the grass and flowers crushed underfoot, "Death! It's me, Death!"

He looked over at her, his expression changing to one of shock. He stood swiftly, in a strange, inhumanly graceful motion—the kind that seemed almost disjointed for how smoothly he'd done it—and began walking towards her.

"It's Lily," Lily continued, almost breathless as she slowed and then stopped a few feet in front of him, "Remember? We met a couple of months ago. I fell out of a tree and broke my neck, you just—showed up here somehow. We talked about all sorts of things like life, death, alternate universes, and—well, whatever else there is to talk about."

Her words trailed off, Death was still walking towards her.

He didn't stop until he reached her, he didn't say anything though, but instead put his hands on her shoulders, and inspected her from head to toe with a worried expression.

Lily suddenly felt self-conscious of her clothes, they seemed so much more out of place here than Mr. Death did, and was struck by that horrible feeling that she may have made a mistake.

This was more real than the party, than her world, and it always would be but—

But maybe she didn't belong in this place any more than she had Annie's playroom.

"Lily," Death finally asked, "What are you doing here?"

Lily tried to shrug, to be casual, "Well, you didn't come to visit."

Yes, as if it was his fault, and not hers at all for having misread the room.

"It's almost Christmas," Lily continued, "Well, I mean, it's Thanksgiving but 'tis the season if everyone else is to be believed.

"Anyway, it's almost Christmas, and I wasn't doing anything—Well, I guess I went to this party, but it hasn't been any fun. So, it wasn't like I was actually doing anything."

She stopped abruptly, wishing she had pockets she could shove her hands into. She felt a bit uninvited, very uninvited, and maybe it only counted when you accidentally died, or you died the first time.

"Anyone else come by?" Lily asked awkwardly, hoping to deflect from her sudden imposition on his island but—

There wasn't anybody, and from what he said last time, some instinctual knowledge she couldn't explain, there wouldn't be anybody either.

Death opened his mouth but closed it just as quickly. When he did speak, it was in a flat tone, one that spoke of stars burning out long before the universe lost memory of their light, "I'm sorry, but you decided to visit? How exactly did you decide to visit, Lily?"

Lily stared at him, trying to remember what she'd told him last time, what he'd seemed to know already.

"Well," Lily said, then decided there was nothing for it but to start from the beginning, "My biological parents are absent, you've probably met them, or I have—"

Lily still wasn't entirely clear on who was supposed to be Death and who wasn't. She figured he was picking up the slack as she hadn't remembered meeting any dead people before she'd gone and done it herself.

"Anyways, they left me, literally, inside a dumpster and I was pawned off onto Mike and Carol Tylor."

She kicked at the sand a little, trying to find a way to make that sound a little less personal, because it wasn't personal.

"And that's fine, really, I'm not ungrateful. They just—they have these expectations. I'm adopted, I mean, theoretically they can get rid of me. I'm not sure how that'd work exactly but it feels—possible."

She shrugged again, unable to look directly at him for too long, at his intense eyes and empty expression, "I'm doing fine, really, I think I'm doing a pretty bang-up job if I say so myself. I'm killing it in kindergarten, grade wise, I really am. It's just—hard sometimes, you know?"

She was sure, somehow, that he must know. At least, if anyone in the world could possibly know, then he had to know.

"You have to be smart but not too smart, not the kind of smart that makes you cringe and think of a horror film, but more like that kid who wins the spelling bee and you wish was your kid."

Lily wasn't good at finding the distinction between those two.

"Anyways, that's not important," Lily dismissed, realizing she'd gotten off track, "So, here I was, at this Christmas party right after Thanksgiving, and I was thinking of using a tree again but it's snowing outside. Plus, what if I landed on my legs or not my neck? Then I'd just be stuck there in the snow not dying. Then, I remembered that these people have a garage, so I dug through there, found a hose, took it up to the attic and hung myself."

It felt like a bit of an anticlimactic ending, but Lily supposed it was a fitting end to what had been an anticlimactic life.

She watched his face, trying to guess what he was thinking.

He looked, in that moment, like a tragic idol. It was like he was standing on a pedestal his people had built for him, staring down at the writhing masses, unable to conceive how he'd gotten so high off the ground in the first place.

Then his burning eyes dimmed, an ancient sadness creeping through them. He reached out for her slowly and pulled her into an embrace.

"I'm sorry, Lily."

She couldn't remember a time when she'd been touched with this sort of affection. Her earlier memories were blurry, so it was possible she just couldn't recall anything, but her adoptive parents weren't much for physical, or emotional, signs of affection.

It was an unfamiliar, but pleasant, feeling.

Eventually, she drew herself out of the hug with some awkwardness, looking back to the chairs Death had made last time. She pulled him over towards them and smiled at him, glad they had gotten this first part out of the way.

She waited until he was seated before she asked, "So, you never told me about your world. What were you doing there? What's it like being Death? What—"

She cut herself off when she realized he wasn't listening.

He was looking past her, tapping his long fingers on the table's surface.

He was silent for a very long, uncomfortable moment.

"Lily," he said without prelude, "I need you to understand something."

"Yes?" Lily blurted before she could stop herself, almost kicking herself for how desperate, needy, and stupid that must have sounded.

"What you did today was not—You can't hang yourself, Lily."

THE HEART OF THE WORLD

Lily waited one second, two, but he didn't add anything to that. He still wasn't looking at her.

"Well, I kind of did," Lily pointed out. It clearly was not only entirely possible, but easier than she'd expected it to be. She'd spent so many years not dying that she'd have thought she'd have to put some real effort into it.

"No, I meant—" Death finally looked at her, searching her face desperately before finishing, "You should not kill yourself, Lily."

"Oh," Lily said dumbly.

She wondered what she was supposed to say to that.

In theory, he was right, but in practice—

Even this conversation, stilted and emotional as it was, was real. He was real, even with his funny eyes and his too red hair. This was the only place that felt real and the only person she'd met who looked at her like she was a person too.

Even if she couldn't go back, then maybe that was the best outcome anyway.

Her thoughts must have been written on her face, because he was frowning, his fingers tapping faster as he searched for words.

"I know that it is difficult. More than you can possibly imagine, I know what life can be like. I can empathize, sympathize, more than anyone else. More than you can possibly imagine, I know what life can be like."

His voice softened as he said, "I know that it doesn't have to be violent, truly terrible, or—that being, feeling, so alone and unwanted can sometimes be enough."

He took her hands in his, his hands large and warm around hers, "You have to remember that it does get better. There is light in the universe if one knows how to look for it."

Lily stared at their hands, at the way his dwarfed hers so easily, the feeling of warmth seeping into hers.

Then she caught herself.

"Right, light in the universe, great," she blathered, laughing a little, "That's great. Actually, speaking of life in the universe, how about that universe? Was there space travel in your universe? Or Jedi? Or—"

He stared at her, stunned for a few seconds, before responding in a daze, "I can't speak to the Jedi but—yes, I suppose there was space travel, certainly by the time I left, but—Lily, was it truly that terrible?"

"Terrible?" Lily asked in turn, thinking the word over, "Not really, I guess. Boring mostly, but it's okay. We made Christmas cards in class the other day. I made one for you, but I wasn't sure how I'd bring it. Maybe I can find a way next time."

She brought her clothes, after all, so maybe if she just stuffed it in her pocket or something...

"Next time?!" Death spluttered, nearly falling out of his seat, "Lily, I—

Do you understand what you just did?"

"Came to visit for Christmas," Lily responded easily, that one was obvious, "I figured since it didn't look like you'd be visiting me that I'd have to come and visit you."

Then, a terrible thought struck her, "Unless you are coming to visit. Is Mike Tylor going to have a heart attack?" she asked, "The doctors are a little worried about his blood pressure."

"What—I—No—Lily!" Death spluttered incoherently, before gathering himself and beginning again, "Lily, killing yourself is a very serious thing and death is not to be taken lightly!"

"You do look heavy," Lily agreed as she looked him over, certainly much heavier than her for all he was very lean for a man his size.

"No, not death as in me," Death protested with wild hand gestures (gestures a little too familiar to Lily, as she often made them herself unconsciously), "Death as in the topic in general!"

"Oh," Lily said when it looked like he expected her to say something.

Death, however, wasn't done, "To even consider taking your life is not a game, or a hobby, or a whim! It is an irrevocable decision that cannot be taken back!"

He looked at her, clearly waiting for something, but whatever Lily was supposed to do she didn't do it because he added, "We do not kill ourselves so that we can visit strange men we met in purgatory!"

Lily considered that, tapping her fingers together, leaning back in her chair as she thought deep thoughts.

"You're not really a stranger though, Mr. Death," Lily mused, "I've met you twice now, that's more than most people greet the afterlife, and we all meet our maker eventually. To call Death a stranger is, well, I guess it's a bit naïve."

Death didn't say anything to that, he was instead giving her a very funny look, one where it seemed like he desperately wanted to say something but at the same time had nothing to say.

"Besides," she added with a grin, "Even if I really am dead-dead this time, I think you're way more interesting than my current batch of relatives!"

And if what he had said was right, then he was a relative of a kind—a brother who was also her.

She'd never had a brother before.

He seemed at a loss.

He stood for a moment, crossing his arms and staring past her, as if waiting for something to happen. When only a gentle breeze rolled through, a pot and two cups of tea appeared out of thin air again, one placed in front of Lily.

She took it gingerly, sipped at it, and noted the same peculiar flavor as last time.

"Lily," he said, nearly causing her to choke on her tea.

She recovered as fast as she could, "Yes?"

He spoke without any change of inflection or expression, "You wanted to hear about space?"

Not trusting herself to speak, she nodded vigorously.

"I don't like the word 'space' to describe it. The newer languages had better words. Space does not capture the light or the void. It was both the heavens and hells we imagined existed outside our own realm."

Death went on at length about the nature of his reality. Not about himself, so much, no mention of his mysterious life as Elliott Tylor, but about the very general overarching history of his world with very few details and very few players.

What he'd done there, who he'd been before he was Death, how he'd discovered he wasn't Elliott Tylor at all, but a man named Death—he didn't even hint at that.

He also didn't say why he'd left and why he'd chosen to come to this place.

Somehow, despite all her social failings, Lily knew there were questions you didn't ask.

In turn, he didn't bring up his disapproval of her visit.

He seemed to have pushed the topic beyond them, out into the glittering sea, where it would rest safely in the island's orbit.

***

With her first venture deemed a success, Lily began the questionable and dangerous activity of visiting Death every Sunday. She also planned on visiting him for Christmas Eve, Christmas, and New Year's, but he didn't know that yet.

Whether Death approved of this venture or not was hard to say. Whenever she arrived, he'd get this strange look in his eyes, as if he'd lost and gained everything all at once. He never tried to stop her or warn her against visiting, but it was in his eyes, something both disappointed and glad.

The hose noose worked well the first few times, but after coming back still hanging she decided that maybe it'd be better if she found some alternatives that didn't involve her accidentally dying twice.

She seemed to regenerate every time she came back, her neck was never broken and all her limbs seemed to work, but she didn't want to push her luck. Besides, hammering oneself to death sounded messy and she didn't think five-year-olds were permitted to buy firearms.

It was to be her fourth visit that Lily remembered Carol Tylor's sleeping pills that were never, under any circumstances, to be mixed with the gin that was hiding in the top cupboard in the kitchen.

No mess, regeneration should heal the damage to her intestines, and painless. It seemed like an ideal solution.

With flourish, she flipped open her notebook of obituaries. Skipping past the first few entries to the first blank page, she began writing her eulogy, "Here lies Lily Eleanor Joan Tylor, five years of age. She didn't really do much with her life. At all. That's about it. 1979-1984."

With that she threw back the glass of gin (nearly choking on the sudden bitter, horrible, taste), and then swallowed the pills.

Unlike the tree and the hose, it didn't happen right away, she wasn't suddenly on the island. However, it didn't take long for her to start feeling really, truly, awful.

Awful and fuzzy.

She remembered crawling under the bed, willing herself to curl up and prepare for death, but after that things got very hard to remember and think about.

When she did start being able to think anything, what she noticed was that she wasn't on an island.

She wasn't under the bed either.

She was instead curled up on the floor of somewhere very dark and oddly—flexible looking was maybe the term for it. The walls, if they were walls, looked a little wobbly. As if they'd only happened to form themselves into wall-like surfaces, but could collapse at any moment.

Squinting as she picked herself up, she noticed bookshelves lining the walls, filled with leatherbound books with no titles. There were no windows, no ceiling lights, and the only reason she was able to make out anything was because of the dying embers glowing in a fireplace across the room.

Just in front of the fireplace were two leather chairs, and in one of them, an unfamiliar man.

Even in profile, even given the unfamiliar surroundings, it was obvious he wasn't Death.

His hair was nowhere close to the right color, neither were his eyes, but even his face alone would have made it clear. Death's expressions were fluid, his expression changing from a human's to something else's in an instant. A mere glance, word, or thought and his face would shift. Death was only in the habit of acting human, he often forgot himself and played at being both human and not in the same moment.

This man was different.

He had a quiet intensity about him, something which drew the eye and demanded it stay there. The air about him was something both refined and raw at the same time. He lounged in the chair, long legs crossed, dark hair curling away from his face, pale blue eyes intent on the dying fire.

He looked as if he was on a set, in a pivotal scene in a play Lily should know but didn't, waiting for something to happen.

"Are you going to stand there all day?" he asked, still looking at the fire.

Lily started, stumbling backward a bit, and looked around for his fellow actor, or at the very least someone who would suit the scene. There was no one else, though, just the books on the walls, the chairs, and the fire.

He didn't ask twice, didn't turn to face her either, but Lily could almost feel his impatience.

Lily scrambled forwards towards the empty chair opposite his. When she sat in it and looked up, he had finally started looking at her. His expression—it wasn't as hard to read as Death's sometimes were, but it was different. Death, she felt like she just didn't understand whatever he was showing on his face, this man she felt was purposefully hiding it. While his eyes were intense, his expression was impassive, almost empty.

"Sorry," Lily offered after a moment, "I think—I got a little lost."

This felt very, uncomfortably, awkward.

She wondered what she'd done wrong.

Maybe the island wasn't the afterlife for all occasions, as she'd thought, but only the afterlife for those who broke their necks. That was what happened when you hung yourself, wasn't it? You didn't really asphyxiate, your neck broke first.

Now she was in the afterlife of—alcohol and sleeping medication, she supposed. She wasn't sure she liked it.

She looked at the man sitting there, now searching his features intently. The thing about Death was that he really did look exactly like her. He was a grown man, sure, but it was easy to peg him as being Lily except if she was a man instead.

This man looked nothing like her.

He was very beautiful, and that was the word for it, not handsome but beautiful. He just might be the most beautiful person in the world. There was something about the color of his eyes, his cheekbones, his brow, that made him seem otherworldly, ethereal almost–but not the way Lily was. There was nothing jarring about him, nothing that made you instinctively look elsewhere if you stared at him too long. His was just–a perfect face.

In other words, he didn't look like he was a different Ellie Tylor who was also, somehow Death, and had wandered into this very gloomy representation of the afterlife.

However, he wasn't saying anything, and if she didn't say anything—

Lily cleared her throat and decided to just bite the bullet, "You wouldn't happen to be—um—Death by any chance?"

A single dark eyebrow raised impertinently, his lips twitched into an amused, but cold, smile, "Can't say I haven't been called it before."

"Oh," Lily said simply, trying to interpret what that could possibly mean. Did that mean he was Death, an Elliott Tylor in some other world, but was simply being coy? She wished he'd just say it plainly.

He didn't.

"Nice place you got here," Lily said, eyeing the walls, trying to be polite.

That was clearly the wrong thing to say.

He was still smiling, but it was sharper now, and he looked—very angry. "Yes, isn't it just?"

Somehow, the way he said it, Lily got the feeling he was implying this was somehow her fault.

"Well, if it was a bit better lit maybe," Lily murmured, hopping out of the chair to stoke the fire. The flames didn't flicker back into life. The fire didn't die either, it just remained the same dying embers.

As she was stubbornly poking at the charred wood he said, "Haven't you had enough, Iff?"

Lily blinked, looked back at him in confusion, but he looked anything but confused.

"If," Lily repeated dumbly, trying to figure out what the rest of that sentence was supposed to be. Haven't you had enough if the fire won't start? No, that didn't make any sense either.

His smile that wasn't a smile only grew sharper, "Nice try."

Lily had no idea what she had or hadn't been trying. She tried to think it over then realized, the way he'd said it, Iff had been a name.

"Oh, is your name Iff?" she asked, "See, where I'm from, it's Ellie Tylor. I also met another one, you know, another Death, who said he was an Elliott Tylor. You look a few standard deviations away from the mean, though."

Iff Tylor, that was a bit of a strange name, wasn't it? She didn't think the Tylors would have picked out a name like that. Of course, it was possible that Iff hadn't been adopted by the Tylors at all, mind boggling thought that that was.

"No," the man who wasn't named Iff said shortly.

At Lily's dumb look, he said (looking like he was pulling teeth), "My name, Iff, is not Iff."

"Oh," Lily said. She wondered if she should go back to her chair or not. Somehow, the idea of walking back felt awkward.

"Well, my name's Lily now," Lily said, "I changed it when I died because—well, it felt like the right thing to do."

"Did it?" he asked, like Lily had made a very funny joke that was only funny for him.

Lily decided it was best to stop talking.

He, however, had not decided the same thing. He motioned to the chair again, "Sit down, Iff."

Lily opened her mouth to correct him again only to close it. He wasn't as objectively terrifying as Death, that man was terrifying just by standing in the same room, but there was something uncomfortably intimidating about him.

She walked back over to the seat and sat down.

Next time, whenever she got a chance, she would hang herself instead.

The man who wasn't Iff or Elliott didn't waste any time. As soon as she was seated he asked, "Why are you here?"

Well, wasn't that the question of the hour. How to put it politely...

"I took the wrong exit on the freeway," Lily said with a small, awkward, laugh. When he didn't smile in turn, she quickly amended, "Um, I hadn't realized that the way one dies matters. Sorry, again, didn't mean to interrupt."

It hadn't looked like he'd been doing anything but, well, she really wished she hadn't interrupted whatever he hadn't been doing.

It wasn't a bad conversation, per se, and it was the most engaging one she'd ever had outside of talking with Death. It was just so uncomfortable.

"What the hell are you talking about?" he asked and this—before, he'd sounded very controlled. Oh, there was certainly menace in his tone, lots of it, but he'd spoken very deliberately and like he was amused if anything by her attempts to say or do anything.

This was just impatient.

Lily eyed him dubiously. It struck her, suddenly, that he might not know.

She hadn't known until meeting Death, after all. So, it was entirely possible he'd accidentally had too many pills and gin and ended up sitting here without knowing why.

No wonder he was so upset, Lily would have been too.

"Oh," Lily said, wishing she could remember exactly how Death had put it. She decided to start with her own story, as that, surely, would trigger some memories on his part, "Well, I'm Lily, previously Eleanor Joan Tylor, and my parents left me in a dumpster."

She watched his face to see any hint of recognition. He certainly looked offended, maybe even a little annoyed, but it didn't look like he was having any grand sort of epiphany either.

"Your parents did not put you in a dumpster," was what he said instead.

Oh, lucky him, he hadn't been left in the trash. Now it was Lily's turn to be a little annoyed, wondering what he'd managed differently than her and Mr. Death.

"Well, somebody did," Lily snapped back, "Look, that's not really the important part. The important part is—turns out I can rise from the dead or something and when I die I meet—weird people in gloomy libraries. Alright?"

That, of course, didn't apply to Death but she was no longer in the mood to talk about him with this new, intimidating, rude Death. Even if he did, probably, deserve to know just what had happened to him.

He didn't comment on that though, instead, he asked, "Haven't they told you about me?"

"They?" Lily asked, mouth hanging open, "Who the hell are they?"

The Tylors? No, they barely talked to her at all, why the hell would they have told her about another Death that wasn't Death who lived in the world's worst library?

Finally, his face—it didn't soften, soften definitely wasn't the word, but it was like some of the fight had just gone out of him.

"It seems they haven't," he concluded, sounding annoyed if not a little bitter, "They must have written me off completely."

That didn't sound like the Tylors, Lily didn't think they felt strongly enough about anybody to go and do things like write them off.

"A reintroduction is in order," he commanded, glaring at her as if just daring her to try and leave the chair again, "We've never actually spoken before now, you were very young when we first met."

"Oh," Lily said lamely, wondering what 'young' was supposed to mean when she was only five.

"Given the circumstances, you may refer to me as the Usurper."

Lily stared dumbly. She wondered what circumstances possibly required him usurping anything. It also just sounded, well, either ominous or very stupid. There was something about calling yourself 'the' followed by an occupation that made it sound either very silly or very foreboding. The Baker, the Executioner, the Lawyer, and now the Usurper.

The man's eyebrow twitched, his lips strained in that pleasant smile that wasn't at all pleasant.

"Well," Lily said, trying to pivot, "Anyways, I'm actually looking for Death. Not you Death, obviously, or me Death but—he's on an island that isn't actually an island. Any idea how to get there from here?"

"Where in the world do you think you are?" he asked, his annoyed look hadn't disappeared but he seemed more flummoxed than he'd been before.

"The poison victim afterlife?" Lily asked after a beat.

He actually laughed at that, only to stop immediately, as if he hadn't meant to do it.

"We're inside your mind," he said quickly.

Well, that was a surprising turn of events. She supposed it explained the lack of Death and the island but—how could she get inside her own head.

As if reading the thoughts off her face he added, "I've been terribly curious how you got here."

"I got lost?" Lily asked, trying to wrack her brains for what could have possibly gone wrong.

She had to be dead, she just had to be, she knew mixing those things together wasn't good and that it must have killed her. Unless, of course, that was another, unspoken, broken thing about the universe.

"No, that doesn't cover it," he dismissed easily, "Are you very ill?"

"I don't think so," Lily said, looking down at herself, wondering now if she'd had a fever without her knowledge. She wasn't sure she'd ever been sick before, though. Illness avoided her as steadily as children on a playground.

"What were you doing before you arrived?"

Lily stared, "I thought I told you, I killed myself."

Now it was his turn to stare dumbly at her.

"I mean, I drank all the gin in the cupboard and took sleeping medication. That's supposed to kill you, right?"

"You were attempting suicide," he seemed somehow offended like this, as if it were a personal affront to him. Then, in sudden realization, he blurted, "And they shipped you off to Tellestria?!"

"That's a crude way to put it," Lily commented, "I think of it as visiting Death for Christmas."

She almost added that he was secretly her brother, sort of, but caught herself just in time. She also wondered what that Tellestria comment was supposed to be about. Lily had never heard of a Tellestria before, it sounded like a summer camp for nerds.

He stared at her for a long moment, as if waiting for her to relent. She squirmed uncomfortably in her seat.

Then, just like that, he said, "You didn't kill yourself."

"What?" Lily asked.

"You're dying, not dead," he dismissed, "That's why you're here. Your body must be giving out on you."

"Oh," Lily said. Did that mean if she just sat here long enough everything would work itself out? That didn't sound right but she supposed it was as good an outcome as any. Next time, though she'd make sure not to take the long way.

"You said you were visiting Death for Christmas," the man said dully, his British accent making it sound mocking somehow, "Do you often visit Death?"

"Every Sunday," Lily said, and immediately realized that wasn't the answer the man was expecting.

"Every Sunday?" he repeated dumbly.

"Well, for the past two Sundays. I accidentally visited a few months ago, but I've been consistent about it for the past few weeks."

She was very proud of that, actually, there were few instances where Lily really got to show her dedication to anything. She liked to think that Death knew Lily wouldn't give up on him no matter what had happened to his reality.

"You attempt suicide every Sunday," he said slowly, as if waiting for her to point out where he'd misheard.

"Oh no," Lily said brightly, eager to talk about it, "Not attempt, most times it works. So, I suppose a better way to put it is I do commit suicide every Sunday."

He didn't say anything to that.

She smiled charmingly, "You see, it's almost Christmas, and he's the closest thing I have to a relative who isn't a Tylor. I also think he's lonely. Not many people who visit stick around, if you know what I mean."

Lily almost added that the afterlife was shockingly empty just like this place, and that it didn't look anything like what she'd imagined, but she cut herself off.

Instead, laughing awkwardly, she pivoted, "My life's not that interesting, Mr. Usurper. What about you? It must be interesting in the bottom of my brain."

Even if the bottom of her brain was, apparently, a gloomy library.

He said nothing, just kept staring at her.

The walls surrounding them became transparent, through them Lily could see the faint flickering of her own thoughts.

"You aren't lying," he concluded emotionlessly, "You truly believe what you're saying."

Lily almost responded 'sorry' by reflex but stopped herself just in time.

"How many times have you visited Death, Lily?"

She wasn't sure she wanted to answer that question, not with that look on his face, but she found herself blurting it out anyways.

"Three times," she clenched and unclenched her fists, trying to think of a way to make that sound better, or else give him what he wanted to hear, "But it's really not important."

He didn't agree with that. She could tell just by looking at him that he thought, somehow, it was all very important.

Before she could say anything else, he stood, made his way over to the fireplace, and began jabbing at it with the poker. Just like for her, nothing happened, the flames didn't stir, and the room didn't change. He kept jabbing just the same.

Lily watched silently.

Now that she wasn't talking to him, she found herself unable to look away. It really was like watching television, like watching whatever a real human being was supposed to be, not one who just got drunk at parties but one who raged at machines and felt real, burning, anger that Lily had never encountered before.

It was fascinating.

Not for the first time, it occurred to Lily that there was something very wrong with the world she lived in.

It wasn't just because she kept dying and rising again, there was precedent for that and a whole religion about it, it wasn't about things appearing then disappearing either, but something about people.

According to TV, even TV with laugh tracks, people were supposed to be people. They were supposed to smile, frown, get upset, reflect on hardships, find true love and happiness, and do all sorts of things in a manner that required more than two dimensions.

They didn't though.

Until Death, and now this strange man, she'd never met a person like that. Instead, everyone she'd met seemed like little more than two-dimensional, pixelated, representations of human beings.

It seemed a dull but inarguable fact of life that humans were not sentient, but merely programmed to believe they were by some outside party. Probably the same party whose lack of foresight was responsible for the occasional glitches in reality.

Even Death, for all that he was, wasn't a person in the way that people were meant to be persons. He was something else, fully admitted it, and was at best a distant cousin of whatever humanity was supposed to be.

People weren't really people.

Except for this one in front of her.

Lily wasn't sure if that was a good thing or a bad thing. Exceptions meant a rule somewhere wasn't behaving as it was meant to but—

Well, maybe she didn't mind all that much.

To be honest, she'd been getting tired of reality. She wasn't sure she was ready to leave it behind altogether, but she didn't mind that it was breaking down.

Of course, she'd told Death all about this, but he hadn't seemed convinced.

It was her last visit; they'd been sitting at his table drinking tea. Death had seemed more at ease with her presence. His gestures had been more fluid, his expressions easier and more human. He had sat in his usual black wardrobe, legs crossed at the ankles, looking for all the world like there was no other place he could even think of being.

"Glitches?" he had asked, looking more puzzled than anything else.

Then his eyes had lit up and he'd smiled, "I suppose that's as good a way as any to describe it. I never thought of it that way, but I see where you're coming from."

"Oh, so you've noticed too," Lily had said, wondering why she was even surprised. Of course, he'd notice even if no one else ever did. He was Death, more, he'd once been in the Tylor's house too so he'd had to have seen it for himself.

"Well, yes," Death had responded haltingly, "Only, they aren't glitches."

"Not—" Lily had tried to interject, but he had continued.

"I know you're very intelligent, Lily, eerily so if we're being honest, but you are only five," he'd said with a fond smile, "That is, you only have five years' worth of experience in this world. That isn't very long, no matter what you might think. Things that seem strange or incomprehensible may be things you just haven't encountered yet, rules of the universe you haven't thought of," he'd paused then, clearly thinking on something or else the best way to put it.

"When I was young, only a few years older than you, I was introduced to magic. Everything that seemed strange was suddenly explained and had always existed, I just hadn't known it. I'm sure it's the same in your universe, there are many worlds, and some of them have magic," Death had finished, smiling cheerfully, and looking quite proud of himself.

Lily had only been able to stare back.

Death was the smartest, best, most awesome person she had ever met. Sometimes, though, she remembered he wasn't really human and couldn't be held accountable for the just plain wrong things he said.

Magic, that was a softer word than glitch, much friendlier and more familiar. It was the same thing, really, but by saying magic it became something a little less dangerous.

Death saw the signs, but he existed outside of time, space, and even his own reality. For him, the world wasn't ending, merely shifting. He'd left his own universe, too, there was no reason he wouldn't live on when her own collapsed.

The end didn't have to mean the end for him.

She wasn't even sure, sitting here now, if it had to mean the end for her.

She just knew that whatever other world he'd been talking about, she hadn't seen it, and even if she had, that had nothing to do with what she thought was going wrong.

"Iff," a voice jolted her out of her thoughts.

She looked around and saw the man, the Usurper, still standing there. He had stopped poking at the fireplace.

"Lily," Lily corrected him without thinking.

He just sneered at her.

He then turned back to face the fire, staring into it, only his back facing her. He was very tall, Lily suddenly noted. Taller than she'd expected him to be when he'd been sitting down. While he was lean, he wasn't as lean as Death, looked well built enough to strike an impressive and imposing figure.

"I'm going to assume they've told you nothing," he said to the fire.

Lily still wasn't sure who 'they' were supposed to be. She was now certain, however, that it definitely wasn't the Tylors.

It was true, though, that no one really told her anything. So, he wasn't wrong about that.

"I also assume you're in Tellestria," he added, sounding like he was trying to say it calmly but was two seconds from blowing his lid.

"Sure," Lily said after a beat. She'd still never heard of a Tellestria but it sounded like he needed her to say yes for his own sanity.

"You are," he told her, finally turning to glare at her. Lily almost agreed again out of instinct but held her tongue just in time.

Whatever a Tellestria was, she thought looking at him, it couldn't be good.

"There is a world beyond your own," he started, his eyes darkening as if a shadow had passed over them, "One where magic exists and is at the root of everything. I lived in that world and sought to overthrow the monarchy, to bring back a true understanding of magic, and to close the portals between the worlds."

"Sorry?" Lily asked, not sure quite what to say, because—what even was that? She felt like they'd just switched genres and he was now narrating the start of a movie she'd accidentally ended up watching.

He didn't seem to care, as he continued, "With loyal comrades among the elven clans and even the nobility, in only a few years, I had taken the kingdom and sacked the capital. I was not simply close, I was there, I had done it."

He didn't say anything for one second, two, then on the third he added bitterly, "Then there was the prophecy."

Oh, thank god, Lily knew that one.

"You killed your father and married your mother!" she interjected with a grin. The first part didn't sound much like Oedipus Rex but there was only one prophecy when it came to stories like these.

"No," he said shortly and—Lily wasn't sure, but she felt as if there was almost static electricity in the room, like her hair was standing on the back of her neck.

He continued, "It was prophesied that the next king would defeat me, solidify the kingdom, and unite humanity and the elven clans under his reign."

He kept staring at her as he said it, his eyes burning, and his mouth twisted downwards.

"Long story short, I couldn't have that," he sneered, "I entered the palace, slaughtered all those in direct line to the throne and more than a few besides. I murdered your father, your mother, your uncle, aunt, every single person who had a chance of inheriting the throne. Then, before I even got to the crown prince, I reached you."

He stepped towards her, leaned over her chair menacingly, forcing her to look nowhere but his sharp, awful, eyes.

"And I did kill you, just as I killed everyone else. Yet here you are alive and well, stowed away in Tellestria, and here I am a wraith, drifting through your subconscious. Tell me, Iff, why did this happen?"

Lily took in his story, blinking, then concluded, "So, you're basically Wizard Lenin."

"Do you honestly have no sense of self-preservation?" he asked coldly, his smile turning into something feral.

The library shifted too. It contorted itself into some unknown shape with the force of his rage. The walls began to collapse, the room stretched, the floor tilted, her chair started sliding backwards away from him, and the darkness crashed like a wave overhead.

Clinging to her chair, trying desperately not to fall out, she shouted back at his shrinking figure, "Why should I have one? I'm very preservable, like a pickle!"

The room stopped moving and she fell forward out of her seat and onto the floor. She hastily pushed the chair back towards the fireplace, ignoring the scraping sound against the floorboards.

When she reached him, the coldness had drained from his face, the smile had disappeared. A haggard expression had taken over his aristocratic features, and he was now leaning against the fireplace in exhaustion.

"I had forgotten for a moment," he explained to her with a tired smile, "You truly can't die, can you?"

A chuckle escaped him, then a cascade of laughter. Just like his smiles, his laughter didn't sound happy.

"I guess," Lily murmured, rubbing the back of her head, "I've not-died a couple of times, but that's not very conclusive. I also haven't been trying very hard to really kill myself, you know."

She'd thought about whether she could accept the consequences of it being permanent, but she hadn't tried to stay dead. That had to mean something, didn't it?

His laughter died down with that, and his somber, tired, look returned, "Your life isn't boring, Iff—Lily," he corrected himself for the first time, "I should like to hear about it."

"Oh," Lily said dumbly, and scrambled for something, anything, to say. He waited patiently, with a patience he hadn't shown this entire, odd, conversation.

For the first time, Lily felt glad she'd taken that detour. Maybe next time, she would poison herself, take a little extra time before meeting Death.

She launched into her observations about reality, about living with the Tylors, her mysterious origins, Death on the island, and even meeting him here.

He didn't interrupt and listened intently, even when one minute extended to five then to fifteen. It was the first time, she thought, anyone

THE HEART OF THE WORLD

aside from Death had actually listened to her for this long.
It felt—
She didn't know how it felt, only that it was all very exciting.
"I'd like to meet him," Wizard Lenin said when she'd finished.
"Who?" Lily asked blankly, before remembering the only person she'd mentioned worth meeting, "Death?"
She gave him a look, looking him up and down, trying to decide if this was a cry for help "I mean—look, I know I do it all the time, but I know I can come back. Is this library—"
Well, Lily had to say, this library looked pretty damn terrible. Lily could see why he was itching to leave it. Death was also good company, certainly better than nothing.
"If you come back, I'll come back," Wizard Lenin spat. "I exist, now, as a part of you and your mind. That cannot be easily undone."

Lily wasn't sure she liked the sound of that, but at least, looking at his face, he didn't like the sound of that either.
"So, you'll just—come with me then?" Lily asked, it was a very strange thought. True, she hadn't been visiting Death long, but she couldn't imagine just casually bringing another person.
Then again, there was something about this Wizard Lenin that—
He was definitely growing on her.
"Alright, let's go then!" Lily agreed with a smile before he could argue, hopping off her chair. She suddenly felt that it'd be quite easy to get there. Maybe her body out there in the real world, beneath the bed, had just been quietly hanging onto life so she could finish the conversation.
She started walking, grabbing Wizard Lenin's hand, and eagerly pressing on into the blackness.
At first, it was just dark, an endless darkness, but then little glittering stars appeared beneath her feet and in the distance a pale sphere winked into existence.
Lily stopped for a moment, staring at it dumbly.
"It really wasn't an island," she said, clutching at her hair, "It was a moon!"
It wasn't Earth's moon, and maybe it was a planet, but it was small enough and pale enough that it really did look like the moon. The sea, then, hadn't been the sea at all but the actual night sky with no sun or moon to interrupt it.
She'd been in space the whole time.
She looked up at him, expecting him to say something, but he didn't. He was staring ahead like he'd never seen it before either.
"Come on," Lily said, grabbing his hand and rushing forward again.
When they reached land, floating down onto it, Death was waiting there

in the clearing just as Lily had expected.

She rushed towards him, momentarily forgetting Wizard Lenin.

"Death!" she cried out, grinning ear to ear as she sprinted into his arms.

He caught her with a smile as always, ruffling her hair, but then he stopped a moment later. His one hand tightened on her shoulder.

"Lily, who is that?" he asked quietly.

Lily turned to see Wizard Lenin staring at the orb on the pedestal, jaw hanging open. He looked disturbed, just staring at it, seemingly unable to look away.

"That's Lenin," Lily explained, nodding towards him, "I found him in my brain on the way here. He said he lives there. Oh, and he said he murdered my parents."

That probably should have caught Lily's interest, she supposed, but for all she was an orphan she just didn't feel much connection with her parents. Maybe it was the dumpster thing but she just had no interest in them.

Most of the time, in fact, she'd rather not hear about them at all.

She supposed it didn't really matter, according to Wizard Lenin, he'd killed them and dead was dead for most people.

Death's grip didn't loosen. Quietly, with a hard edge to his voice, he said, "That's John Jones."

Lily almost corrected him to say that she thought Lenin was more fitting than John Jones or Usurper, as it certainly fit his zealous, revolutionary, and violent zeal, but Death wasn't looking at her.

He was glaring at the man, not a hint of the fond softness she was so used to in his eyes at all.

"Lily," Death said, "I need you to go sit in the chair. Don't move until I tell you to."

"But—"

"Lily," Death said, and it was clear that he wasn't asking, this was a command.

Lily nodded slowly. He let go, pushing her towards the chairs gently, and began walking towards the still distracted Wizard Lenin. Lily walked backwards until she reached the table, keeping her eyes on them both.

Wizard Lenin didn't notice Death, not even when he was standing right over his shoulder, staring at the orb with him.

"Mr. Jones," Death greeted cheerily and loudly into Wizard Lenin's ear, "I'm glad to see your interests haven't changed."

Wizard Lenin jumped, whirled, and moved backwards when he saw how close Death was to his face.

Death nodded towards the orb, "Of course, it's not the real Heart of the World. This place is only a metaphor, just the idea of scenery. So, if you're thinking of running off with it, I wouldn't bother."

Wizard Lenin blinked, his hands twitched as if he wished to raise them, but he kept them at his side. He took a breath then said, "You must be Death."

"Oh, did Lily tell you?" Death asked, not looking back at Lily. Lily in her seat stiffened, wondering if she wasn't supposed to have told him for some reason.

"Did she mention I don't make bargains?" Death asked meaningfully, "I got out of that business a long time ago. Nasty results every time."

That—by the look on Wizard Lenin's face, that had been something very personal, and something Death wasn't supposed to casually reference.

"No bargains, no chess, no nothing," Death continued merrily, "The best you'll get out of me is a game of Jenga."

Lily realized then, dumbly, that Death didn't like Wizard Lenin. He didn't just not like him but he seemed to loathe him. Lily felt something sink in her stomach, the excitement from earlier, the feeling of—was it making a friend? Whatever it had been, she felt it fading, disappointment setting in as whatever she'd been hoping for in bringing him here very clearly wasn't coming to pass.

"Do you know each other?" she blurted loudly, loud enough that both heard it.

Both turned to look back at her, Death frowning, his eyes tight. He hadn't wanted her to draw attention to herself, she realized.

He sighed after a moment, though, and looked tired again, "John Jones and I go way back. In fact, I knew him when I still thought I was human."

"Oh, he lived in your head too!" Lily said, feeling her smile return, hoping everything would get back on track.

"Yes and no," Death said, ignoring Wizard Lenin's hard stare, "There was a John Jones who was—paid to me in default, that's the best way to put it, but I was unaware of him for a long time. No, I knew the other John Jones. I consider myself worse for it."

Lily opened her mouth, closed it, and nearly bolted from her seat to properly join the conversation. She kicked at the dirt for a moment, thinking, then shouted, "Wouldn't that have been a different Lenin? That was your world, wasn't it?"

"Once you've met one John Jones, you've met them all," Death dismissed easily, waving his hand in Wizard Lenin's direction as if to brush him off the moon.

"And he's not even the real Jones," Death scoffed, nodding at the silent, fuming, Wizard Lenin, "He's a poor man's John Jones. A debt unwillingly paid off to higher powers."

"You have no idea what you're talking about," Wizard Lenin finally said. His voice was as quiet as Death's was and as dangerous as it had been in the library.

"I have every idea what I'm talking about," Death retorted imperiously, going so far as to cross his arms, "You're the one who has no idea when he's paid the same price twice. It's not my fault you think you're a real boy."

Death looked back at Lily again, his voice very clearly irritated, "When someone dabbles in ancient magic, in the very roots of the universe, making deals with entities beyond their ken, there is always a price.

"And, of course, trying to kill Death itself just sends everything to hell in a handbasket."

Death laughed then, shaking his head, and said, "Alright, since I'm here to spoil all the fun, I'll answer the question you haven't asked. The girl there isn't a girl, she's Death, the same way I'm Death, yes, John Jones, that same Death. I know you know what I'm talking about. Then you waltzed into the palace so very full of yourself, believing you had the power to defy prophecies and slay gods. What in the world did you think would happen? I've always wanted to ask you that."

Wizard Lenin looked stunned, shot her a look, but then just as quickly focused back on Death and shouted, "She wasn't even in the prophecy!"

"Wasn't she?" Death asked with a raised eyebrow, seeming to think that over, "Well, that's certainly strange. I'm sure the sun elves would have been very explicit about that. They certainly were in my world."

He then gave Wizard Lenin a funny look, "But if she wasn't in the prophecy then—Ah, right, I forgot, you're a murderous perfectionist. You had to go and kill the entire family tree, didn't you?"

Death started to walk away from him back towards Lily.

"Is that all you wanted?" he asked over his shoulder, "Not that I don't appreciate your company, but sociopaths slavering for immortality and magic are not my cup of tea."

Death sat across from her with a sigh, running a hand through his red hair.

"Lily, why did you bring a nuisance like John Jones here?" he asked, as if he was asking God why he'd made it rain today.

"I like him," Lily blurted, only realizing she meant it as she said the words, "He's interesting. I mean—he's nice."

"Earth must be a desolate toxic wasteland much earlier in your reality than it was in mine if John Jones was just described as nice," Death said with a small shudder. He summoned the pot of tea and the cups, pouring one for each of them.

There was no third cup for Wizard Lenin.

"And why Lenin, exactly?" he asked, eyebrows raised.

"He looks like a Lenin," Lily said, and when Death was about to point out he looked nothing like Vladimir Lenin Lily added, "I mean—he told me all about his revolution."

"Did he?" Death asked in a way that made it sound like—like he hadn't.

"Sure," Lily said, "He uh—has elf friends I think, and noble friends, and really hates Tellestria and a monarchy."

If that wasn't worthy of some revolutionary name then Lily didn't know what was.

"Oh, he certainly does have all of that," Death agreed, but didn't say anything else.

Lily looked back over at Wizard Lenin, he was still standing there and—the grass had somehow caught fire beneath his feet. Lily looked away again, deciding it was probably best to ignore him for now.

"You know, Lily," Death interrupted her thoughts, "Aside from slaughtering, and I do mean slaughtering, the royal line save for three people, he also spurred on the bloodiest war since the fall of Xhigrahi simply because he could. He tore his own kingdom apart, pitted the elves against the humans and each other, just because he could."

Death met her eyes, his own that burning, terrible, green again.

"This man is not your friend, Lily. He is incapable of friendship or any sort of compassion. He will destroy you, just as he will destroy anyone and anything else if given the slightest opportunity. He won't do it because he needs to, or even because he particularly wants to, but just because he can. That is the sort of demon that John Jones is."

Lily looked back at Wizard Lenin, still standing there, still—well, now he looked like he was on fire. The fire had spread up from his feet and onto his clothes. He didn't seem to mind at all, though, as if like everything else in this place the flames were only a metaphor.

"I like him," Lily declared to Death, "I know I just met him and all, but I do like him."

Death opened his mouth to protest but Lily beat him to it.

"He's the only person besides you who has ever listened to a word I've said!"

She was breathing heavily by the time she finished, waiting for Death to disagree, for Wizard Lenin to finally say something, but neither did.

Then Death said, "Who knows? Maybe you're right."

A third cup appeared and Death motioned for Wizard Lenin to join them.

"Put yourself out first, please," Death said before Wizard Lenin could take a step.

The fires disappeared. Wizard Lenin stood there for a moment, glowering and glaring, then walked over. When he reached the table, a third seat appeared, and he sat down to pour himself tea. He didn't look at either Lily or Death.

Lily's heart was still racing, she wondered if she'd offended him, if it'd only been Death who made him angry, and what he'd do when he was back in her head again and she was back in the world of the living.

She didn't want this to be the end.

Death slowly started to smile at Wizard Lenin, watching with amusement as he started drinking, "You're doing very well. The John Jones I knew would have tried to kill me by this point."

Wizard Lenin said nothing to that.

"Coincidentally, it's your favorite blend," Death added, "It happens to be mine too."

Wizard Lenin stopped sipping at that, looked as if he was very tempted to toss the tea aside, but he said nothing.

Death finally looked away from him and back to her, "John Jones aside, how are you?"

The conversation then calmed. Wizard Lenin sat stiffly, silently watching the pair of them as they discussed the latest and greatest in Lily's daily life.

Despite the earlier tension, there was a sort of glow to the conversation, one that Lily was sure would be engraved into her memory. She would remember this moment, and whenever someone asked her what happiness was, she'd think of this.

Soon enough, they were headed back into the real world, Wizard Lenin waiting impatiently while Lily and Death exchanged final words.

Death crouched down to eye level and brushed her hair back from her face with a sad smile, "Good luck, in everything, Lily. Remember, I will always be here."

He hugged her briefly then, for no longer than a heartbeat, then pushed her off towards Wizard Lenin. To Wizard Lenin, he only offered, "Try not to destroy the world in your miserable petty attempts to rule it."

With Wizard Lenin's hand in hers, Lily walked them back to the real world, where Lily was still lying under a bed.

3 THE THING ABOUT CLARK KENT

In which Lily is told her fantastical and mind-boggling origins, learns that Wizard Lenin's revolution didn't go according to plan, and stumbles into an evil alter ego.

"*Where are your parents?*"

It had been three days since Lily had almost but not quite killed herself, met the man in her head, then gone on and died anyway to meet Death with the mysterious and testy Wizard Lenin in tow. It was still Christmas vacation and the man in her brain, the Usurper and or Wizard Lenin, was still in her brain. He had also decided to become very vocal. She wasn't sure if anyone else could hear him, there was no one else around to confirm it, but he'd taken to nattering away when Lily was trying to watch TV.

Lily wasn't sure what she'd expected except that some part of her had expected him to stay safely in her head. Death, after all, stayed on his island-planet, it was safe to assume that Wizard Lenin would stay at the bottom of her brain unless she somehow wandered in there again.

Apparently, Wizard Lenin didn't content himself with that.

"*Would you stop calling me that?*" Wizard Lenin snapped, though there was no real feeling in it. When he'd first started talking (appearing with a pounding headache), he'd noted that he hadn't given her permission to call him Lenin.

Lily had pointed out that she hadn't thought names were all that important to him when he was going around referring to himself as the Usurper. If they had been, then he would have stuck with John Jones, wouldn't he?

Besides, he still felt like a Wizard Lenin. He clearly was some kind of wizard with all the talk of other worlds, magic, elves, monarchies, and whatever else he'd mentioned. Added to that his identity as an extremely violent revolutionary supporting the—whoever weren't the Tellestrians she guessed—and it'd seemed like the perfect name.

There was the now familiar feeling of someone else's profound irritation, and perhaps even rage, but it was smothered before Lily could dwell on it too long. Lenin was clearly picking and choosing his battles.

"They left you with someone, didn't they?" Wizard Lenin pressed, really stuck on the Tylors and their whereabouts. There was an image suddenly in Lily's head, probably the 'they' Wizard Lenin was referring to, but it was gone before Lily could think on it too long.

Only the afterthought of—

Quest burgers?

That couldn't be right.

Lily decided not to comment.

"Technically," Lily said in between bites of delicious ice cream.

"Haven't I told you not to speak out loud?" Wizard Lenin snapped, *"You look like a lunatic."*

"I'm five," Lily noted slowly, nobody paid attention to what she did or thought, it was one of the greatest things about being five.

There was another pang of irritation, one large enough that it gave Lily a stress-headache by association, and Lily took the hint.

"Fine!" she thought very loudly, as if she was practicing saying it out loud, *"Fine, I'll just—think things, I guess."*

That seemed to mollify him somewhat, for all that Lily couldn't help but add, *"You know, as a five-year-old, I get a lot of slack in the imaginary friend department."*

"I don't care."

Wizard Lenin, Lily had quickly learned, was a very blunt and very impatient man who didn't bother with things like pleasantries.

"Your parents, Lily."

"I thought you killed them," Lily said, forgetting herself and speaking out loud. She winced then corrected herself, *"I thought you said you killed them?"*

Lily supposed it was as good an explanation as any, for all it didn't explain how she'd ended up in the trash unless—

Had Wizard Lenin put her there out of petty revenge for her supposedly blowing him up?

"The question, Lily!" Wizard Lenin seethed, the idea of him being very offended at the very suggestion of his not simply killing her rattling about in their shared mind space.

Right, supposedly, he'd blown himself up, hadn't he? She wasn't sure she was entirely on board with his story, but if any of it was true then he would have been stuck in her head by that point. So, something else must have happened to get her to the Tylors.

She'd decided that it wasn't worth thinking about, she still had very mixed feelings about her parents.

"What about them?" Lily asked before Wizard Lenin could blow his lid.

"Where are they?" he repeated, and before she could ask why he cared he went on, *"It's been three days and I haven't seen a hint of them."*

"Yeah," Lily agreed, wondering what his point was here.

"You are five," Wizard Lenin said in slow disbelief, the feeling that there was something painfully obvious Lily wasn't grasping reverberating about in her head without her permission.

"Yeah," Lily repeated dully. She wondered, if she asked politely, if he'd let her continue watching her show.

Wizard Lenin was still very exciting, still very new, shiny, and full of potential and human emotion, however in the days since first meeting him she'd come to realize that he was a bit much. Oh, he was still fantastic, but she'd really like to watch TV.

"You've been watching TV for days," Wizard Lenin pointed out.

"Yeah," Lily agreed for the third time, for lack of anything else to even say at this point.

"My point, Lily, is that you are young enough that you should not be left to your own devices," Wizard Lenin said, his tone now—not charming, not exactly, but clearly hiding a world of displeasure, *"Why, just a few days ago, you purposefully poisoned yourself and ended up choking on your vomit under the guest room bed."*

The cleanup had not been fun. Lily had no plans to poison herself again any time soon.

"And since then, you've spent the past three days eating nothing but peppermint ice cream," he added.

"It's a seasonal flavor," Lily pointed out, she supposed to magic elf warlords from other dimensions that wouldn't mean much, but it meant she had to make the most of it before it was out of stock until next November.

"Look," Lily interjected before Wizard Lenin could say anything scathing about that, *"This is pretty normal Tylor behavior."*

"Are you serious?" Wizard Lenin asked.

"I am a very precocious and responsible young woman," Lily protested in the face of Wizard Lenin's damning silence, *"Also, they don't like to pay for babysitters."*

Worked out for Lily though, didn't it?

It might be nice to have someone to talk to, but she had Mr. Death and now Wizard Lenin for that. The way Lily saw it, everything was turning up Lily.

"How wonderful for you," was Wizard Lenin's waspish response, in his thoughts (rattling about in her head ever since he'd started talking) was the feeling that it was anything but wonderful for Lily.

"Yes, it is pretty wonderful for me," Lily agreed with a sniff, it certainly gave her full access to the television with premium channels, didn't it?

For a moment, she thought he might be content with that. He hadn't

THE HEART OF THE WORLD

exactly seemed content over the last three days, but he had been quieter. It'd felt like he'd spent the time taking everything in, trying to understand exactly who Lily was, where they were, where the Tylors were, what she was doing, pretty much anything at all seemed fascinating to him.

It was like he'd been looking for something that Lily wouldn't be aware of.

It seemed he wasn't done though, *"And it's just the Tylors?"*

"Yes?" Lily asked, wondering who else it was supposed to be.

"Someone dressed like they come from a renaissance fair," Wizard Lenin cut in dryly, the term being one he'd taken from her, when Lily had accidentally remarked that Wizard Lenin's bard costume needed a bit more red in it if he wanted to be a real communist.

He hadn't taken that well.

"Why would I meet anyone like that?" Lily asked dubiously. Sure there was Death, she supposed, he kind of counted. She supposed Wizard Lenin did too for that matter. No one here dressed like that though.

"Exactly," Wizard Lenin agreed, and by the tone in his thoughts she knew he'd have a wolfish smile if he was sitting across from her, *"They wouldn't be from Tellestria."*

"Oh," was all Lily could say to that.

He meant that other place then, the one he'd been talking about, that Death had been talking about too.

"That other place is your true home," Wizard Lenin corrected, *"It's where you were born, in case you missed that little detail."*

She supposed she had, it hadn't seemed that important.

"It's very important," Wizard Lenin retorted, *"Aren't you curious?"*

"I guess?" Lily asked, but her heart wasn't really in it. She supposed it was very interesting in theory, but it was just that, in theory. She'd seen enough of this world to guess that this new one wouldn't be any different.

"It is," Wizard Lenin assured her, *"Better in every way."*

It had better TV?

(Sadly, and Lily would be the first to admit as much, most things on television were not as interesting as their premises made them sound. If this new world had better TV then that was very tempting.)

"No, there's no TV," Wizard Lenin seethed.

Well, then it couldn't be better at all, could it?

Lily felt the prickling of yet another headache, this one more painful than the one before it, but managed to rub it away as Wizard Lenin got a hold of himself.

Except it seemed Wizard Lenin wasn't done, *"How are you not in the least bit curious?"*

"Dunno, I guess I'm just not that interested," Lily confessed honestly. Mr. Death and Wizard Lenin were one thing, but she just couldn't believe that

interesting people like them were easy to find. If they were, she would have found it a long time ago.

"You are descended from kings," Wizard Lenin told her, *"You are descended from one of the most powerful sun elves who ever lived. You could have been crown princess—"*

"You're kidding me," Lily snorted, now he was just going too far. Lily, a lost orphan magical elf princess? Was she supposed to be a person or a Disney cartoon?

"Oh, does that mean you think I'm lying?" Wizard Lenin asked and—she had the feeling he was trying to bait her somehow.

"I don't know, I just think—it's a bit much isn't it?" Lily asked, waving her hand despite herself, gesturing even without speaking, *"Magical orphan elf princesses don't end up in dumpsters for one thing."*

Let alone adopted by the Tylors, that had to be a wrench in the wheels, didn't it?

It was a fast thought, he clearly didn't want her to catch it, but Wizard Lenin privately agreed. He agreed that, under normal circumstances, she would never be in this house let alone this world. However, unlike Lily, he had a very strong suspicion of just who was behind it and why.

However, he didn't let her see that bit.

"Well, you'll never know unless you find out," Wizard Lenin hummed, as if it wasn't his problem.

Lily hated herself a little, but her curiosity was actually piqued. This was starting to sound like a real mystery, a real adventure, and her first adventure with Wizard Lenin or anyone at all.

There was just one thing she was wondering, though.

"What's in it for you?" she asked Wizard Lenin.

"Why should there be anything in it for me?" Wizard Lenin asked in turn, as if he had no ulterior motives whatsoever.

"You seem like a man with a plan," Lily responded, staring at the television with narrowed, suspicious eyes, *"And that plan doesn't involve doing anything for free."*

She wasn't even sure that Wizard Lenin liked her, truth be told. She liked him, even when he was angry, but for his own part so far, he just seemed to sort of tolerate her existence if not fume about it.

For a moment, he clearly considered lying to her, but then seemed to give up.

"I want out of your head," he confessed dully.

Oh, well, that made sense she supposed. She didn't want to live in anybody else's head either, especially if it had as poor lighting as it'd seemed to.

"The only way I can possibly manage that," he continued, clearly bitter about this, *"Is if we go back home."*

When she didn't say anything to that, to either agree or disagree, he added, *"And, at the very least, I'd like to find out what really happened."*

She thought they'd covered that with Mr. Death. Though, she supposed that had technically been whatever happened to his John Jones, it could have gone down differently for this one.

There was just one problem though.

"I have no idea how to go to other dimensions," Lily pointed out.

She'd been to two other places so far, the moon of dead people, and her gloomy brain. Neither of those seemed to be what Death or Wizard Lenin were on about.

As far as she knew, other dimensions were the things of television and not actually supposed to happen to real people.

"If it was that easy, all of Tellestria would know about it, wouldn't they?" Wizard Lenin snapped.

Lily could only stare at the television.

Finally, hating to admit it yet again, she pointed out, *"I'm five."*

Lily wasn't allowed to ride the train by herself, she wasn't crossing dimensions.

"That doesn't mean you have to be useless!" he retorted, which she supposed was true but—

It didn't sound right.

"Relax, the work's already been done for you," Wizard Lenin sighed, *"There are tears in the fabric of reality. It's just a matter of finding one. Luckily for you, I know where to start looking—"*

Lily started, falling off the couch, *"There are tears in the what?!"*

"Fabric of reality," Wizard Lenin repeated as if he was talking about the weather, *"Think of them as portals."*

Lily was thinking of them as tears.

Didn't that bother him? Wasn't reality not supposed to have tears in it? Didn't that sound inherently bad? Lily had thought she was cavalier about the world ending but this guy was giving her a run for her money.

"Oh, don't get in a snit," Wizard Lenin sniffed, *"The world's not ending. They're a naturally occurring phenomenon."*

They didn't sound natural.

"Imagine that human destiny is a wheel," Wizard Lenin explained, and in her mind was the sudden image of a wooden wheel, *"It rotates as it crosses through time and space, and as it does so, it sometimes leaves notches in the road, small divots, irregularities, that can be found and exploited.*

"Portals appear in places and times with significance to mankind. Places that are the center of significant thought, feeling, and imagination," he finished with the mental equivalent of a shrug as well as the thought that, if they could time it during the right time of year, they could enter through Stonehenge.

That still didn't sound natural.

"I also can't get to England," Lily pointed out before he could protest.

"It doesn't have to be England," he said, *"There's bound to be some near here, it's just a matter of looking hard enough—"*

Lily had the sudden, horrible, feeling that he'd make her walk around a city for days, weeks, until she managed to find one of these things.

"What about magic?" Lily blurted despite herself.

"What about it?" he asked dully, very clearly thinking that from everything he'd seen Lily knew next to nothing about it.

"Well, you're a wizard, aren't you?" Lily asked.

"Mage," Wizard Lenin corrected, and a damn good one went unsaid in his thoughts.

"Right, wizard," Lily nodded in agreement, *"Why can't we just use magic to make one?"*

Wizard Lenin took that as a clear sign that no one had ever spoken to her about magic.

"A single person, no matter how powerful, cannot tear reality," he said slowly, reminding himself it wasn't poor Princess Iff's fault that she knew nothing about anything. Even if he did see it as very convenient for certain people, very inconvenient for him, and however irrational it all was, he felt like blaming said people anyway as if they somehow knew he'd be inconvenienced by it.

"Why not?" Lily asked.

"Because magic is fueled by many people," and she could almost feel him gritting his teeth, like he hated having to explain any of this to anyone, *"Memory, mythos, the collective imagination, thought, feeling, and culture of sentient beings is the direct fuel of magic.*

"This has been obfuscated for ease of use and mass production, and many don't realize what they're working with, but the facts remain the same," he continued, clearly having very strong feelings about this, *"No single person carries with them enough—karmic destiny, enough power, to tear through space and time."*

He had no idea if Lily would be powerful or not, though he had a strong suspicion she would be, but this was something simply beyond even the greatest mage's limits.

"Have you ever tried?" Lily asked, because if these were so natural, then it should be something anyone could do if they just tried hard enough.

"Many have tried—"

Lily bet they didn't try that hard.

"Well then, why don't you prove all of us wrong and give it a go yourself, if it's that easy," Wizard Lenin said sweetly.

Lily stopped at that.

It was one thing to propose Wizard Lenin, a self-proclaimed wizard ghost, do magic, it was another thing to sit there and try to do it herself.

Well, why couldn't she?

He seemed to think she'd be able to do something, if not open portals to other worlds, and he could supposedly do this magic thing. Why couldn't she do it?

It felt wrong, though, to try to purposefully bend the laws of reality like that. It wasn't just like she was breaking the rules when nobody was looking, but purposefully doing something she knew would have very bad consequences down the road.

It also felt exhilarating.

It was like doors that she'd never realized were there had been flung open.

She rubbed her hands together, deciding to do it, and trying to decide how to go about it.

How did you tear reality?

Was it just a matter of wanting it enough? That was what Wizard Lenin had basically said, wasn't it? That tears appeared because humans did—whatever humans did about something, because they all wanted the same thing at the same time.

So, maybe, if she wanted it badly enough then it would happen wherever she was. She would give wherever she happened to be the significance the universe was looking for.

She stuck her hands out in front of her, exhaling, and tried to focus on tearing something apart. Not the air in front of her, for all that got in the way, but something deeper than that.

At first, there was nothing, but then the air rippled.

Except it wasn't the air, it was something underneath the air. The more she stared, the more she could see something, maybe light itself, bending out towards her. It bended, then began to take shape, starting to resemble fabric being torn from the center.

It stretched, the TV in front of her looking thinner and dimmer with every passing second, and then disappearing entirely. She found herself facing a single, jagged, hole where the TV should have been.

Lily let her arms fall to her side, staring at it in dull horror.

She'd been right, it didn't look natural.

Wizard Lenin was oddly, ominously, quiet in her head. It was as if she'd gone back in time to before she'd known he existed at all.

She stepped forward off the couch, brought her hand up in front of it, and tried to touch the edge. Her finger disappeared, as if it'd been eaten by the hole. She hastily dragged her hand out and found that it was still there.

"This is a portal, right?" Lily asked carefully.

"Lenin?" she prompted when he didn't answer.

"How did you do that?" he asked, and he was oddly breathless, even a little fearful in a way that didn't suit him.

"You told me to do it!" Lily pointed out, *"And, I don't know—I tried what you*

said, wanting it enough."

"That's not how this works," he said, sounding a little more irate but still not his old self either.

"Well how would I know how it works?" Lily asked, still feeling flustered and uncomfortable.

"Just because you don't know how it works doesn't mean you can change the rules!"

Well, they weren't very good rules then, were they?

Then she realized that maybe she was getting a little too hung up on this. She'd known this would happen, didn't she? The universe was failing, why had she expected it to fail cleanly, neatly, and consistently.

If magic was on the table, then Wizard Lenin could use whatever rules he liked, while Lily could just do whatever she wanted.

Wizard Lenin wasn't feeling nearly so assured but he didn't want to say as much.

Instead, he concluded, *"Waste not, want not."*

"What the hell is—"

"It means since you've already demolished your living room you might as well dive in."

Well, when he put it like that.

Lily stared at the hole uncomfortably, wondering if it really would go where he thought it would go.

She supposed there was only one way to find out.

She took a breath, closed her eyes, and leapt through.

***

"Lenin, I am filled with regret," Lily wheezed, clutching her ribs and staring numbly up at the sky.

The good news was the black hole had led to somewhere else.

The bad news was she'd fallen on top of a roof, had barely managed to stop from rolling off, and everything felt bruised.

Wizard Lenin was so in shock that she'd made it, he didn't even berate her for speaking out loud.

The sky wasn't overcast, not the way it'd been at her house. Instead there was a clear, blue, sky splattered with puffy white clouds. Bright sunlight shone through the brisk air, making it so she had to squint upwards.

The portal had already disappeared.

Lily wondered if she was about to meet Death.

This was turning out to be a very short adventure.

"You're not dying," Wizard Lenin sniffed, apparently over whatever had been bothering him, *"You're just a little bruised."*

She felt very bruised.

Nevertheless, she sat upright, trying not to wince.

The orange shingles she'd fallen on were broken in several places, the roof itself was circular and very steep, like it was the rooftop of a tower rather than a house.

She moved to the edge, peeking down, and blanched when she saw just how far off the ground she was.

The people below looked like ants, barely visible even with their bright clothing, she had to be as high as a skyscraper right now.

Across from her were towers made of a white, gleaming, stone with the same orange shingled rooftops as the one she was lying on. In the center of these, on a hill, was a building with even higher towers made of what looked like moonstone. It didn't just glitter in the sunlight, it glowed, blindingly reflecting off sunlight in every direction.

It looked, in other words, like a world that had magic.

"You were right," Lily breathed in wonder, unable to believe it. There really had been another world there this whole time. One that had magic, elves and—apparently princesses too.

God, did that make Lily some kind of knockoff Clark Kent? It didn't sound like she'd been sent away by her dying parents in the midst of a war, but she had been shipped off to Earth and apparently did have fantastical powers.

She'd never felt superpowered before. She'd never felt any kind of empowered before.

"I'm glad you're so pleased," Wizard Lenin said, sounding anything but pleased, *"Now, why don't you get yourself down?"*

Lily looked over the edge again.

She wouldn't survive that.

"Well, why don't you just use magic again, since you're so good at that?"

That didn't sound like a suggestion made in good faith.

Right, she probably wasn't supposed to be able to do that. Whether 'that' was flying or else floating or something that wouldn't end in her certain death, she was pretty sure he didn't think it was in her repertoire.

On the other hand, what else was she going to do?

The worst that would happen to her would be she'd see Mr. Death a little sooner than planned.

She worked up her nerve for the second time, squeezed her eyes shut, and rolled off the edge of the roof.

For a moment, she was plummeting to her certain death, then, about halfway down, Lily's latent magical talent must have kicked in. She was suddenly floating, very gently, down past the rooftops and streetlamps until her socks hit cobblestone pavement.

Lily gave a startled laugh, tapping her feet against the ground just to make sure it really was ground, then gave a laugh again.

She could get used to this.

People around her had stopped to stare.

They were dressed like Wizard Lenin, she noticed, all brightly colored tunics, trousers, and cloaks in place of jackets. The difference was the oddly brightly colored hair, several sporting navy blue, strangely colored eyes including gold of all things, some with pointed ears.

Lily barely noticed them, though, still in wonder over her spontaneous floating abilities.

"Did you see that?" she asked Wizard Lenin.

Wizard Lenin, however, did notice the growing crowd.

"Leave," Wizard Lenin commanded.

"What?" Lily asked.

"You just fell out of the sky!" Wizard Lenin hissed, now beginning to panic, *"And you're clearly—not even just a sun elf but your mother's daughter!"*

"What?"

"Get out of here before they call the guard!" he hissed.

Lily quickly darted into an alley, ducking under laundry left out to dry, over flowerpots, and away from the onlookers who had started staring after her.

She found herself in an empty street, heart pounding, a smile growing on her face.

Oh, this was exciting, wasn't it?

It felt like everything was happening all at once.

She'd met Death, then Wizard Lenin, then only three days after that she was in an entirely new world that had magic of all things. More, she was in a magical world, on a magical quest for a strange man with a dark past.

It was like she'd stumbled into one of her books or TV shows.

"Where to?" she asked Wizard Lenin in growing excitement. She had no idea what he'd say, what it would be, but she couldn't shake the feeling that it'd somehow be even more exciting than getting here had been.

Yes, she was glad she'd met him.

"Nowhere," he said coldly, *"Not looking like that."*

Lily looked down at herself with a frown, taking in her sweatpants and the holiday sweater, *"Like what?"*

"Like the only sun elf come down from the mountain," he said wryly, like this was some great joke she was too stupid to get.

"What?" Lily asked again.

"You're too easily recognized as Princess Iff," he told her.

"Who?" Lily asked, feeling very stupid.

"You, you are Princess Iff, Lily, Iff is your real name," he said, before continuing, *"And Iff is going to be just about the only person in this damned city with that hair, those eyes, and that face."*

Well, wasn't she this princess then?

"We don't want the whole bloody world to know it," he hissed.

Why not?

"Has it not occurred to you that someone purposefully left you in Tellestria?" he asked, for all he knew that it hadn't. *"Has it not occurred to you that someone could be very upset were they to find you here in the capital?"*

Oh, that she hadn't thought of.

By the way Wizard Lenin made it sound, something very bad would happen to her, ranging from imprisonment to execution.

"Aren't I a princess?!" Lily squawked, didn't that mean people were supposed to like her?

"Not the princess anyone would have chosen," was what Wizard Lenin said to that, and nothing more, very unhelpfully.

Lily inspected her hair, it was a very distinctive red, she'd always known that. However, she'd never tried to hide either. Maybe she could do something about the red but the eyes—

Closing her eyes tight, she tried to will her hair into turning colors. When she opened them, her hair was pitch black. Curling a lock around her finger, she couldn't help staring at it, wondering what she even looked like with hair such a different color.

"That's what you choose?" Wizard Lenin, apparently, wasn't nearly as impressed.

"What's wrong with it?" Lily asked.

"You're in a reindeer sweater and you look like a night elf," this was, according to Wizard Lenin's passing thoughts, the lowest of insults he could hurl at her.

"Yeah, well, I'm a very festive night elf in holiday disguise," Lily said, shoving her hands into her pockets. She'd just discovered magic, after all, he had no room getting up in arms about it.

Wizard Lenin reluctantly concluded that it wasn't worth getting up in arms about, she wasn't recognizable as Princess Iff, and that none of this was his problem even if he was mortified by association.

"Right, where are we going?" Lily asked.

"The gold elves," Wizard Lenin said with a very dramatic sigh, *"They specialize in money lending among other things."*

That didn't sound very exciting.

"Money makes the world go round," Wizard Lenin quipped, *"To find out what happened, we're going to need money to pay off informants if not to simply buy whatever histories were published in the past five years."*

Wizard Lenin didn't know where the informants he knew of would have scurried off to in his absence, he doubted his old connections were hanging about unscathed, but he did expect to find something mildly useful in the academy bookstore.

Lily felt her excitement dull at the thought that, apparently, her grand adventure was going to be meeting stuffy elf bankers and buying books.

Then Lily realized, *"I don't have any money!"*

She doubted they'd take the good old American dollar, for all she didn't have any of those on hand either. Oh, so sad for Wizard Lenin, they'd have to go on a real adventure after all and do all this book buying stuff later—

"You're a princess," Wizard Lenin cut in, *"Even if nobody wants you, they'll be inclined to give you something in expectance of payment from the monarchy."*

"But I thought I dyed my hair so—"

"The gold elves keep their mouths shut and their politics neutral," Wizard Lenin informed her, *"They certainly won't turn down free information like the whereabouts of lost Princess Iff. That alone is worth money to them."*

Wizard Lenin didn't like it at all, not one bit, but he liked the idea of trying to somehow convince them that Lily was actually just John Jones back from vacation even less.

Wizard Lenin hadn't said as much, but per his own thoughts, he'd never actually gotten on that well with the gold elves. They'd done business with him, but it'd always been very grudging, and they'd never signed up to fight the good fight for all he'd asked several times.

"Stop gawking and start walking," Wizard Lenin commanded.

With a frown, Lily started walking forward as commanded.

She didn't pay much attention to where she was going, following Wizard Lenin's directions as he called them out, and instead spent her time looking at her surroundings.

It really was fascinating.

It looked a lot like Earth, for one thing, surprisingly so considering it was supposed to be an alternate dimension. The stone pavement, the towers, the carved outer walls of the city, they all were things she'd seen here and there on Earth if never slapped together quite like this.

There were fountains everywhere, every other street would lead to a central plaza where there would be a fountain. They were all carved from white and an oddly gold looking marble, featuring humanoid figures with water spraying from their fingertips, surrounded by unfamiliar wildlife.

The buildings themselves all looked like they were made from marble and granite, all perfectly spotless, looking less like a city that people walked about in and more like a temple that was meant to look untouched.

There were old-fashioned streetlamps on every corner, each looking identical.

And the people, of course, were everywhere. They were walking quickly, clearly trying to get out of the cold, but were all dressed in cloaks, hats, and boots that looked like they'd gone out of style centuries ago. Most looked normal enough, but the further she kept walking, the people started looking more and more fantastical. She started seeing things like pointed ears and blue hair that didn't look like it came out of a bottle.

THE HEART OF THE WORLD

And all of them, no matter what they looked like, did a double take at her.

"*Stop here,*" Wizard Lenin finally commanded.

They were on a street overshadowed by the city wall, on the very edge pressed up against it. Everything still looked nice, perfectly clean, but Lily couldn't help but notice it was a little less ornate than the center had been.

The buildings were small, one-story, and rectangular with no artistry to them. The windows were all boarded shut.

There were no fountains here, no flowers in window sills, and no people walking about either.

The street was eerily empty.

"*You don't come here for a day trip,*" Wizard Lenin agreed, it wasn't a bad part of town exactly, but it wasn't a good place for humans to mill about.

This was, apparently, where the elves lived.

The closest to the edge of the city, the first in the line of fire if there was a siege.

"*It's that hole in the wall right in front of you,*" Wizard Lenin said instead of expanding on that.

This was not a metaphor, Lily thought to herself. Well, there was a doorway, but there was no actual door. Instead, there was a thin sheet of fabric hanging there.

"*Move it.*"

Lily moved forward, trying to smile in case anyone was watching, and pushed her way past the fabric.

She immediately stopped inside.

The first thing she noticed was that while the outside hadn't looked like much the inside was a different story.

There had to be about a thousand rugs on the floor, each dyed in bright colors with embroidered edges. The walls were all covered with ornate, incredible, tapestries picturing what looked like great battles and festivities. A gold chandelier hung from the ceiling, supporting a hundred burning candles, and just underneath that was a polished wooden table.

It wasn't like the Tylors' or any of their friends, but it was what they wanted to look like if they could, thousands of nice things in every direction.

There was a man sitting at the table on a floor cushion, some kind of game board in front of him, clearly intent on his next move.

She'd only had a chance to glance at the people on the street, and they'd all been bundled up and moving quickly, so it was her first chance to get a good look at somebody.

She could believe he was an elf.

It wasn't just the pointed ears, metallically golden hair, or the bright red tunic that could have been purchased at a halfway decent costume shop.

There was a strange, fey, quality to his face that was human enough to be recognizable but inhuman enough to have her do a double take. It was that same, similar, something that was in her own face, in Death's face, and even somewhat in Wizard Lenin's face that she hadn't been able to place before.

Something that made her take the concept of elves, of real elves, seriously even when she would have laughed before.

He looked up at her, perhaps sensing her presence, and stared.

They stared at each other for a very long moment.

Then Lily realized, in growing horror, that standing there wasn't good enough. She was going to have to confess, with real words, that she was a magical elf princess returned from having been thrown into a dumpster in another dimension.

And that she also wanted money.

Lily took a breath to steal herself, praying it would go smoothly, but before she could open her mouth he got up and disappeared behind one of the tapestries.

"Hello?" Lily asked lamely.

He didn't come back.

"I can't believe it," Wizard Lenin said slowly, *"They denied you service. You look too pitiful for even the gold elves."*

According to Wizard Lenin, the gold elves made a point of never denying anybody service. If you had money, even if you were a night elf, they'd do business with you.

Unless, of course, you were Lily in a reindeer sweater.

"What's wrong with the reindeer sweater?!"

It was comfortable, dammit.

Before Lily could make a fuss out loud, demand service in spite of her sweatpants, the man was back with a different golden-haired, golden-eyed, elf in even fancier clothing.

"They're sending in the clan head?" Wizard Lenin balked, then immediately started to panic that the royal family was somehow involved or else that bastard advisor Questburger.

"Jones, it's been some time," Mr. Clan Head said, staring directly at her with a very flat expression.

He did not look happy to see her. He didn't say he was happy to see her either.

He sat down at the table, motioning for her to do the same. The first elf nodded his head then disappeared behind the tapestry again, running so fast he nearly tripped over himself in his haste to leave.

Maybe Lily should have listened to Wizard Lenin about the sweater.

The man was staring at her, folding his hands together, looking her up and down in clear contempt.

Jones, hadn't he called her Jones?

Wasn't that what Death had called Wizard Lenin, John Jones? Lily hadn't paid much attention, as it really hadn't suited him, but she was sure that had been his name.

"It's not me," Wizard Lenin interjected, only to correct with an oddly nervous note to his voice, *"John Jones is me, your friend wasn't wrong about that, but there's another Jones—"*

"I assume you're here to discuss your accounts," the man cut in.

"Uh, right," Lily said, as she was sure that was what she'd come here to do.

For a moment, the man said nothing, and although his face didn't show it she was sure he was irritated by what she'd said.

What he did, eventually, say was, "They've been doing well. Your assistant knows all the particulars."

"That's—good," Lily finally settled on, well was good, wasn't it?

"Yes," Mr. Clan Head said with a very thin, strained, smile, "Was there anything else you wanted, Jones?"

She wanted to ask if he knew that John Jones was inside her, if he thought he was possessing her, but she held her tongue.

"Um, withdrawal," Lily said instead, "I'd like to withdraw today—not much just—for some books and things."

She walked out in a daze, minutes later, with a literal bag of gold in her hands.

That had been entirely too surreal.

They'd never asked for her name, never questioned her being John Jones or not, just got her the money then ever so politely (but very quickly) shoved her out the door again.

Well, mission accomplished, she supposed.

"We may pay dearly for this later."

Or not.

Lily began walking down the street, shoving the bag into her pocket, trying to ignore the feeling of eyes on her back, *"Pay for what?"*

"You stole from Lily Jones," he said, as if that should explain everything.

"Who?" Lily asked.

"Jones isn't me, it isn't just me," he corrected, *"There's one other Jones in this place."*

Lily wasn't sure how she felt about that.

"Terrified is how you should feel about it," Wizard Lenin told her, *"Lily Jones is the head of a gang of night elves, the only one in the capital, because she's murdered off all her competition."*

Even Wizard Lenin didn't trifle with her.

Lily also didn't think she looked like a gang leader.

"She's known to appear as a young girl with extremely dark hair. You have the right look," Wizard Lenin said, now deeply regretting Lily's choice of hair color

(this would never have happened if she'd just picked a sensible brown).

"Well, maybe I am this Lily Jones," Lily thought to herself, as the likelihood of there being two Lily's, and Lily being mistaken for her immediately, just sounded like too much.

Lily was already secretly an elf princess, why not a gangster?

"Surely you realize how stupid that sounds," Wizard Lenin said slowly.

"Well, those gold elves didn't seem to have a problem with it," they'd had a problem with something, but not with giving her money, *"So if they say I'm Lily Jones then I'm probably Lily Jones."*

Wizard Lenin did not agree.

However, he let the subject drop after that.

Instead, he said, *"We should get moving, I want to get to the bookstore before it closes and it's a long walk."*

***

As Wizard Lenin had promised, it was quite a bit of walking, all the way back across the city, until they found the bookstore that Wizard Lenin was looking for. It was down the street from a large, Renaissance-looking building, with expansive gardens enclosed by large fences he'd called the mage academy.

This street was filled with what looked like high end if old-fashioned shops. There were bookstores, jewelers, a store selling only parchment, another ink and pens, as well as a few restaurants.

"It's for the staff and students," Wizard Lenin explained, *"It's an easy, if expensive, place to shop for supplies."*

And the only place that sold magic tomes as well as histories in the city.

Heading inside the bookstore Wizard Lenin directed her to, she found herself directed down an aisle, towards the front, and then told to pick up a book, *History of the Realm: Twelfth Edition*.

"The last edition I saw was the tenth," Wizard Lenin explained as she started flipping through, *"Given it's been five years, this should have the basics of what happened."*

It was a very thick book, Lily thought with some intimidation, with only a few pictures here and there. None of them were photographs, either, but looked like etchings of people and places she wasn't at all familiar with.

It was also hard to read. At first, at a glance, the characters had looked nothing at all like English. It'd only been squinting at them desperately that they'd started to behave themselves and look like the usual Latin alphabet.

"Stop there!" Wizard Lenin commanded, right on a page where there was a picture of the capital on fire.

Right.

That would be the obvious place to stop, wouldn't it?

Lily focused and tried to read.

There was a brief, surprisingly short considering the length of the book, description of who the Usurper had been, a man of unknown origins believed to be descended from the mind elves, who had appeared out of seemingly nowhere and quickly won over several of the elven clans. He'd wanted to overthrow the divine, glorious, monarchy (their words, not Lily's) in what sounded like evil mustache twirling schemes. As almost an afterthought, it noted his goal of sending the Telletrians home.

There was no mention, however, of what a Tellestrian was. The author just assumed that Lily, the reader, obviously knew. She supposed she should have put it together herself by now, but she wasn't sure she had.

Wizard Lenin certainly had dropped the word a lot but he hadn't defined it either.

"Oh, for god's sake, Tellestria is Earth," he said in exasperation, wondering if she was being purposefully slow, *"Tellestrian is anyone, any human, who comes through a portal from Earth to this dimension."*

Oh, oh, that was very different than what she'd been imagining.

"Do I even want to know?"

She'd thought it was a word Wizard Lenin made up to avoid dropping the f-bomb in polite company.

"It's amazing that you think I consider you polite company," Wizard Lein spat back, *"Now, shut up and keep reading."*

Right, get rid of the Tellestrians, lots of elves, overthrow the monarchy—

"Wait, I thought you said you had human supporters," Lily noted, he had said that, hadn't he? That he'd had supporters among the nobility. She supposed that could have been the elves but the way he said it had made it sound like they were different.

"Obviously, they're not going to mention them," Wizard Lenin scoffed, *"Given it looks like the monarchy's alive and well, the capital's been rebuilt, I'm going to go out on a limb and say that the status quo wasn't overturned. Anyone who did support me would have cut all ties and blamed the elves."*

That, apparently, was the done thing.

Wizard Lenin wasn't thrilled about it, considered it cowardly and filled with the kind of sniveling privileged ambition he despised, but he wasn't surprised. If any of those families were to survive, as the monarchy had survived, they'd bury the evidence and buy off whoever came looking for them.

Not to mention that this history was the product of a well-known propaganda machine. It was sanctioned by the royal family, sold in a shop catering to the mage's academy, and had some guy named Questburger's implicit approval.

By the look of it, Questburger had decided a united, human, front was in order.

"*That's not a real name—*" Lily scoffed but Wizard Lenin wasn't having it.
"*Keep going.*"

Right, right, she was reading.

Evil Usurper, lots of elves, anti-monarchy and anti-Tellestrian, no humans whatsoever, attempted to topple the monarchy, dire threat to the kingdom, blah blah blah, the Usurper was an unnatural warped human who made evil deals with evil demons like an evil person, blah blah blah, many brave heroes and mages fought against his forces and oh look there were all their names, blah blah blah, the Usurper swept through the kingdom and sacked the capital, blah blah blah, and then—

There it was, the paragraph that accompanied the picture, the one describing Wizard Lenin's grisly end.

All but three any reasonable distance from the throne had died. Crown Prince Theyn, Princess Iff, and some distant cousin named Wheyn who was now king regent were the only survivors. The Usurper himself had blown up along with half the palace in what the author described as, "God's unquestionable declaration of Crown Prince Theyn's divine right to rule".

In the aftermath, Iff was sent away for protection and had yet to be brought back into the kingdom, while Theyn was being groomed for his role as king and protected by what remained of the royal guard.

The book then quickly pivoted to talk about how the mage academy had been rebuilt, the early years of Wheyn's reign so far, and what had happened to the elves who had supported Wizard Lenin.

Lily set the book down.

She suddenly felt very overwhelmed and a little numb.

Wizard Lenin had been right, she really had been Clark Kent the whole time, and it wasn't her parents who'd had anything to do with where she'd ended up but someone she didn't even know.

All this time, she'd lived her life like she was just anybody, and it turned out she'd been from another world entirely.

And she'd only found out because she'd happened to poison herself and happened to agree to take Wizard Lenin to this place.

Lily was a magical elf princess who'd been named after a conjunction.

She felt like she'd been hit by a sledgehammer.

Wizard Lenin, however, did not feel like he'd been hit by a sledgehammer.

"*Keep reading.*"

Lily flipped open to the page she'd left at but—

There really was nothing else. They were close to the end of the book now, and there weren't many details on what had happened to Wizard Lenin, to Iff, or even to Wizard Lenin's comrades in arms. It was like this one page had been sacrificed to devote itself to this subject but not a word more would be spared.

"Lenin, I think that's—"

"There must be something else!" he snapped.

Lily flipped a few more pages only to find herself at the end of the book. There was no index, no glossary, just a blank page and then the cover.

That was it.

Just a single page in a book.

"Well, you got more words than I did," Lily said after a beat, and she was supposed to be a princess.

Wizard Lenin didn't say anything to that, didn't say anything to any of it, but in her head she could feel his growing rage, rage and—something else, something more despairing but just as angry.

He knew it was irrational, knew that for all anybody knew he was dead and buried, knew that the price of failure had been oblivion but—

He'd been reduced to a page in a book.

Lily brought the book to the counter, buying it despite the human clerk's dubious look, and walked back out onto the street. Wizard Lenin didn't tell her to enter a different bookstore, or go to the pen store, the parchment store, or any of the restaurants either.

"Lenin?" she asked.

He didn't say anything to that either.

He didn't say anything the whole way home.

4 THE HEART OF THE WORLD

In which Lily becomes very worried about Wizard Lenin, receives an ominous warning from Death, embraces the dark side, and hears a story that sounds as if it will be important later.

"Lily Jones?" Death asked with a frown, "I would have heard of her if she had existed in my dimension. Jones isn't exactly a common surname on the other side."

Upon arriving back home still in a daze, Lily had decided there was nothing for it but to visit Death and tell him everything she'd found out. At the very least, it might help her process some of it.

As before, Wizard Lenin had shown up with her, however rather than sit with her and Death he was trying to light the orb on the pedestal on fire. So far, he'd burned down all the plants surrounding him, and taken out large chunks of the earth. The orb miraculously remained undamaged.

Death had taken her story in stride, surprised by none of it, which Lily supposed meant that he'd lived it all already. Even with his comment, his attention was on Wizard Lenin, watching him with a frown.

"And what happened to him?" he asked.

"Lenin?" Lily asked in turn, "I don't really know, he hasn't said much since we got back."

"He's acting more violent than usual," Death commented, "Well, maybe not more violent, but more erratic."

Lily wouldn't know as she really hadn't known the guy that long.

She would admit that all of this was a little uncomfortable.

"Well, he was fine all day," Lily said, thinking it over from the beginning, "Really he was fine up until the bookstore where I—oh—I think he's upset that he's dead."

That was when he'd started acting funny, after all.

But he'd known that! He and Death had spent that whole enigmatic conversation talking about the fact that he was dead or had paid some damages to Lily who was Death or something. Lily hadn't thought any of that was a surprise.

Death also looked unimpressed.

"I mean, I guess for normal people, being dead is upsetting," Lily said, "I mean I'm not sure I'd care that much, but Lenin here sounded like he had a lot of things he wanted to do. Now, he's stuck in my brain."

Death gave her a funny look at that but turned his attention back to Wizard Lenin soon enough.

He crossed his arms, tilted his head, and observed the man as he lit even more things on fire.

It really was very dramatic looking, Lily had to say, like she was once again a silent observer to whatever movie Wizard Lenin happened to star in.

"Of course, he doesn't want to be stuck there forever," Lily informed Death, "The whole plan was to somehow get him a body back and find out what happened. We found out what happened but—we really haven't started working on that body part."

He'd kind of forgotten about that.

"Of course," Death said, looking neither impressed or surprised.

"Of course?" Lily asked.

"He has many terrible qualities as a human being," Death explained dryly, "But the worst of all might be how damn stubborn he is. And now he's roping you into it."

"I'm not being roped into anything," Lily huffed, "Look, if he's unhappy inside my head then I can't exactly blame him, can I? I don't think I'd like to be a voice in someone's head."

Death gave her yet another look, "It shouldn't be about what he wants."

"Why not?" Lily asked.

"Because what he wants is always, without fail, deplorable," Death explained, "Better for everyone if you keep him out of harm's way."

Lily blinked, blinked again, then blurted, "You mean I should leave him in my head?!"

"I'd strongly consider it," Death said.

For a moment, he just sat there silently, staring past her. Then, he sighed, the fight going out of him.

"Lily, I'm not going to tell you what to do," Death said, "To be frank, I'm not sure how much I should tell you at all. Your world is parallel to mine, but there's no guarantee that anything transfers over, this Lily Jones character is proof enough of that. It's your life and I strongly believe you should live it without being biased by me."

She supposed that explained why Death had been so tightlipped about

Lily's origins. He could have told her she was a magical elf princess long before Wizard Lenin had let the cat out of the bag.

She wasn't sure if she agreed with Death's philosophy or not but didn't have much time to consider it as he continued.

"However, nothing good comes from associating with John Jones or letting him loose on other people," he said, "And from everything you've told me about your little field trip, that much hasn't changed."

"So, I should just imprison him for what he might do?" Lily asked, because that's what it was. It wasn't being stuck in her head if she was purposefully keeping him there, it was keeping him imprisoned and swallowing the key.

Death seemed old then, and very tired. He sighed as he looked out at Wizard Lenin, "If he can cause this much destruction in a world that doesn't exist, what will become of the real world?"

He didn't ask like he expected her to answer, just continued to look grimly at Wizard Lenin's shadow dancing against the flames. Lily found she couldn't turn her eyes away from Wizard Lenin either, not even to respond to Death's question.

"It doesn't matter though," Death said quietly, "He won't be able to do it without help."

"What do you mean?" Lily asked.

"Even the most powerful mages can't fashion something from nothing," Death said quietly, "They can't raise the dead, they can't create vessels to house themselves, they can't extract their essence from gods either, they can't truly pervert the laws that govern the worlds they live in. There are rules and they are bound to them."

"Oh, come on," Lily said with a laugh, "There can't be rules for magic, that's just—"

"He'll try to cheat the system, he's done it before," Death continued, "But he won't manage it again, not without a miracle, and he knows it. He's going to run you ragged trying to find a way out and there will be nothing for it.

"That's why he's so upset," Death finished with a smile, looking darkly amused by it.

Lily didn't say anything to that for a long moment, just drank her tea, and watched Wizard Lenin.

"So, you're saying it's impossible," she finally concluded.

Death frowned, "He'll have a golden opportunity in a few years' time, if your world really is aligned with mine."

Lily looked back at him, wondering if it was the right moment to tell Wizard Lenin the good news. Years wasn't great but it was a whole lot better than impossible. Maybe if he knew he had a way out, if he just had to be a little patient, then he'd be fine again.

They could focus on other things until that opportunity, whatever it was, came knocking and they could just—Lily had no idea, sit around and watch every movie Lily had ever seen, suffer through school together and make Christmas cards, write their own TV show about space elves, reminisce about how the Tylors were never around, anything.

She could live her life with a private audience and someone to talk to.

However, Death continued, "If I were you, I would do everything in my power to keep him from taking advantage of it."

"But—"

"You have time," Death said quietly, "It won't be for several years. I'm sure, by that time, you'll see what he is and agree with me."

He didn't explain what those ominous words meant, whether he was speaking about Wizard Lenin's violent revolutions, his apparent pyromania, or something else entirely.

It was some time later that the fires burned out and Wizard Lenin stalked back towards her. He didn't take the cup of tea Death graciously offered.

"You okay?" Lily asked quietly.

In his pale blue eyes, she could see the ruins of the island reflected.

"I'm fine."

***

He was not fine.

It didn't take long for Lily to figure that out.

They got back to the Tylors and it was just like before, when he hadn't talked, and she'd had no idea he was there. Every time she thought something at him, even said something aloud, there was no response.

The house was empty of both the Tylors and now Wizard Lenin's caustic commentary on everyone and everything.

In her dreams, she'd find herself wandering into his library, but he would never look at her. He'd just lean over the fireplace, holding a poker in one hand, not even bothering to stoke it.

On the island, he would wander off from her and Death, disappearing for hours on end, only reemerging when Lily called out to him and told him that she was leaving.

Christmas passed, Lily opening gifts left by the Tylors along with a brief apology/note that they'd had to be somewhere else for the day, and then Lily was back in school once again.

There was no comment on her pitiful attempts at artwork, on the trials and tribulations of learning the alphabet, on anything at all.

He didn't ask to leave her head, to make a body, or even to go back to the other side.

He didn't ask for anything.

While Lily, of course, was now a magical princess who wasn't a magical princess at all. Unlike Clark Kent, Krypton wasn't gone, it just didn't seem to care what happened to her. It made her almost wish she hadn't found out at all, as then she'd never have to wonder why she was sent here, what she was supposed to be doing here, and if anybody would ever realize she was gone.

Lily felt a growing heaviness inside her, from both her and him, as winter began to melt into spring.

Whatever had been driving them both until this point, whatever hope had been burning inside them, it was gone. Only a pervasive hollowness now remained.

Except, Lily didn't want to be a hollow person.

She didn't know who she wanted to be, maybe she did want to be a heroic figure with a destiny, it'd been exciting for the few hours it had lasted in that other place. Maybe she didn't need that much, maybe she just needed something to do, some mountain to conquer, but she was beginning to recognize she needed something.

She needed people, yes, Death and Wizard Lenin, but she needed something more than just that.

She needed a path.

And whether Death liked it or not, Wizard Lenin's path, his goal, getting a body for himself and some autonomy—it wasn't just noble and romantic, but it was the only path that had ever made itself known to her.

Lily had no reason to be here, Wizard Lenin did.

That had to mean something.

Without consulting Wizard Lenin or Death, she returned to the other side.

This time, she appeared not only on street level, but right outside of the mage academy bookstore she'd visited last time. As before, the portal had disappeared as soon as she'd exited, and she was left standing in the middle of the road looking as out of place as last time.

She hastily transformed her hair to the expected color and, this time, changed her clothes from her jeans and sweater into a tunic, cloak, and boots like what she'd seen everyone wearing time.

She felt ridiculous.

However, when she entered the bookstore, while the clerk gave her a long stare, he didn't say anything.

Neither did Wizard Lenin.

She sighed and made her way to the books. There really were a lot of them, and while Wizard Lenin had seemed to know exactly which to pick last time, Lily had no idea what she was looking for.

She picked one off the shelf at random, flipped through, and—

Was that a diagram of someone dancing and song lyrics? That couldn't be right, but she couldn't think what else it could possibly be. Frowning, she placed that book back on the shelf and reached for another one.

She flipped it open and—

"Oh, come on," Lily said to herself.

It was the same damn thing.

Alright, the poem was a little different, and so were the dance moves, but it was the same damn thing.

She didn't even know what she was looking for, she supposed maybe something that would tell her how to conveniently make a body, anything, but she knew she wasn't looking for the macarena.

"Alright, universe," Lily said with a sigh as she replaced the book, staring at the bookshelf and trying to speak quietly, "I'm not really a patient person. I've also never really asked you for much before, so I think I'm good on credits here. If you could give me a little help here, just this once, I'd really appreciate it."

Neither the universe nor Wizard Lenin answered.

Lily threw her hands into the air and exited the shop, a little bell tinkling behind her as she made her exit.

"Alright, think, Lily," she commanded herself, "What can you do here?"

Books were nice, and all, but Lily had no idea what she was supposed to look for. She could try to talk to people, but she had no idea who she was supposed to talk to. She guessed there was that gold clan head guy but he hadn't seemed to like her much and she didn't want him to necessarily realize he'd given money to the wrong person.

Death wasn't going to tell her anything that would help Wizard Lenin, he'd made that abundantly clear, and while Wizard Lenin was probably a fount of information, he wasn't being cooperative either.

She supposed she could try to just magic Wizard Lenin a body or something, the way she'd done the portals but—

But that just meant he'd leave, didn't it?

Lily didn't want to admit it, especially not when she had already come all this way, but while she wanted to help him, wanted to do something, she didn't actually want him to go.

It'd only been a few weeks, a few days where he actually spoke with her and played any real part in her life, but going back to the time before him seemed painful.

She could just imagine sitting on the couch again, watching daytime TV, because daytime TV was all there was when you were Lily. It was all scripted, pre-recorded, television starring people who didn't really exist. The real world, of course, was somehow even worse. Wizard Lenin wasn't that he was–dynamic, interactive, he was a person in a way she'd never experienced before.

Ideally, she'd find a solution, whatever solution Death had hinted at, and it'd take years and years to do anything and by the time it happened Lily would be mentally prepared for it.

Who knew, maybe Wizard Lenin would even agree to be her pen pal or something or even take her on his adventures with him.

If he left now—

With a sigh, she sat down on a fountain, and glumly stared out at the plaza.

People were avoiding her, she noticed. Some walked past her, dressed in what clearly was some kind of military uniform, all royal blue with golden buttons, looking too busy to loiter near a fountain. Others, though, took a look at her, frowned, and quickly walked in the opposite direction.

Lily would wonder what gave, if it was something about her clothes or her hair but wasn't in the mood.

That just felt like par for the course.

"I could really use your help here, Lenin," Lily said out loud to no one.

No one answered.

That was it, she'd bother that gold elf guy, even if he didn't have useful information, Lily pretending to be that Jones person would at least piss Wizard Lenin off enough to get some kind of reaction out of him.

That would teach him.

She marched determinedly down the street, in the direction she'd thought the gold elves had been, and was immediately certain she'd taken a wrong turn. It didn't matter though, because she'd find it eventually, and if she didn't find it then Wizard Lenin could just get upset that she'd managed to get herself lost in this place and was walking around looking like an idiot.

It was about a half hour later, still marching through back alleys and side streets, that her path was blocked.

A tall, unnaturally pale man with hair as black as hers, stood just at the exit of the alley. Judging by his pointed ears as well as his ruby red eyes, he must have been an elf.

They stood and stared at each other, each waiting for the other to say something, or perhaps move out of the way.

Neither did.

She didn't know why, exactly, but something about him reminded her of Wizard Lenin. It wasn't just the dark hair or the clothes for that matter, but he looked like—that was it, he looked like a watered-down version of Wizard Lenin. He looked dangerous, even when he was just standing there, but not quite as dangerous and definitely not as charismatic.

It was like if she'd somehow caught Wizard Lenin walking down the street, looking and trying to act like he was a normal person, the kind of person who didn't light islands on fire.

"I guess you're back from vacation," the man finally said.

THE HEART OF THE WORLD

He didn't really sound like Wizard Lenin either, he lacked that inherent gravitas that Wizard Lenin's voice had, that quality that forced you to pay attention even when he was saying nothing at all.

"I guess so," Lily found herself responding.

He didn't say anything to that, just kept standing there, so did she.

She wondered if she could get around him somehow or if she could go back the way she came. Maybe she could ask him for directions—

"Didn't you want to ask something?" the man asked, crossing his arms, giving her an expectant look.

Well, that was creepy, wasn't it?

Lily laughed awkwardly and decided to just go for it, "Well, do you happen to know how to make a body?"

He didn't say anything to that.

"I have a friend who has—misplaced his, you know how it goes, and he'd really like it back," Lily continued, trying to gauge how he was taking it, "Rumor has it this isn't really possible, not without a lot of help or something, but I thought I should look into it anyway."

The man burst out into laughter.

He actually threw his head back and laughed, like he was absolutely delighted.

"That's what you ask first?" the man asked, "Boss, what in the world are you up to?"

"Nothing," Lily hastily said, not wanting to admit to trying to resurrect what that book had made sound like a warlord.

"I don't believe you," he said, but he sounded more entertained by that than anything else.

Lily laughed awkwardly, wondering if he'd thought she was joking. Except—it didn't look like he'd thought she was joking.

"Come on," the man nodded behind him to where he'd come from, "A lot has changed since you've been away."

Had he—did he know she was Princess Iff? Wizard Lenin had seemed to think she was unrecognizable. It was that or he'd been following her around last time, had somehow known who she was and what she was up to.

She hastily darted after him, he didn't seem to mind and even smiled as she bumped into him.

"It's been a mess since you've been gone," he was explaining, nodding towards the buildings surrounding them (which looked perfectly fine to Lily), "You missed a whole civil war, you know. I hope you enjoyed the beach because it was no picnic here."

"Are you alright?" Lily asked after a long pause.

"Please, we're fine, we kept our noses out of it," the man said with a laugh, "Even those sad Xhigrahi hangers-on kept out of it, too much pride to fall in with a human. Had to move shop when he sacked the capital, but he didn't stay long."

"Oh," Lily said, realizing that he was talking about Wizard Lenin, about what that book, Wizard Lenin, and Death had all mentioned—the time Wizard Lenin had sieged this city.

"It looks alright now," Lily mused.

"It's a façade," the man said knowingly, a wry smile on his face, "They commissioned the gold elves to reconstruct everything. It's why it glitters so much. Half the buildings are empty, half of the noble families have died out, and the mage's academy is a laughingstock."

The man was talking like Lily had very strong opinions about all of this.

She hoped Wizard Lenin was paying some, any, attention as this was the sort of information that he would love to have.

"I think we should take advantage of it," the man mused to her, causing Lily to jump somewhat, "I'm not sure how, not exactly, but the time is ripe, and it won't be forever."

"Are you sure that's a good idea?" Lily squawked in her panic, thinking of Wizard Lenin and the fact that—was that what he wanted? He hadn't said anything, but she assumed this body thing was a means to an end, and then he'd pick up right back where he'd left off.

Hopefully without killing her or the rest of the royal family, though, she thought he could skip that bit.

The man raised a dark eyebrow but didn't protest.

Instead, after a moment, he sighed, then bitterly said, "It's the Xhigrahi problem."

At Lily's questioning look, he explained, "After a thousand years of nothing, we're still infighting, and the rest will band together at the slightest hint of anything. Humans have short memories, but the others don't, and they hate us more than they hate them. Even if we get Xhigrahi to fall in line, which we won't, we'll be hopelessly outnumbered."

"Well," Lily said after a beat, "That does sound like a problem."

The man nodded, still looking bitter.

Lily looked about and noticed—

There was no one on the street again.

The same as last time she'd passed through this area, there wasn't a single person on the street, not a hint of anybody.

She'd thought it was strange last time but now—

Now she was starting to think she was being avoided.

"Jones didn't have that problem," the man said out of nowhere, startling Lily again. At Wizard Lenin's name, she started focusing again, trying to put what he was saying together with what she'd heard so far.

"The upstart who started the uprising," the man explained, "No one calls him Jones, though, he didn't advertise it and—well—that's a

Tellestrian name. They'd rather call him the Usurper."

Oh, was that how that had started? Lily supposed that no one had told her yet, that she'd just assumed that of course Wizard Lenin had some ominous alter ego title but—

This sounded complicated.

"He was very charismatic," the man said, "Got nearly every clan on board, except the obvious ones. I really thought he was going to manage it. Well, I suppose I didn't, thanks to you."

Lily wanted to ask but held her tongue just in time. It was best, she felt, to pretend she knew what he was talking about.

"You look younger," the man noted after a beat.

"Thank you," Lily said with a smile, as if she was flattered.

Before she could pivot away from that, say something else, Wizard Lenin, after weeks of silence, emerged from the hole depression had thrown him into.

"Lily, what the hell are you doing?"

Lily tried to contain her smile, aware that the man was still looking at her, *"You're alive!"*

She'd thought he was, hoped he was, and seeing him every time she died and every night in her dreams had certainly helped. Still, some part of her had doubted it every second he was silent, wondering if she'd made him up out of lonely desperation.

But he was alive and vocal again.

"What are you doing?" he asked again, his tone strained and clearly angry.

"I decided to get you a body!" Lily confessed, nearly bouncing with the fact that she was doing something, making progress, and that now Wizard Lenin was noticing, *"That's what you really want, right? Death seems to think it'll take years but I thought I'd try to look myself and that maybe you'd—"*

"I know that!" Wizard Lenin snapped, which was entirely uncalled for, *"I haven't gone blind and deaf! I meant, what the hell do you think you're doing?"*

Lily glanced at the man next to her, who seemed to be waiting for her to say something. God, what was she doing? She was pretty sure she'd had a plan but now that she was walking along she had no idea why it'd felt like a great idea.

"Following this guy?"

"Lily," Wizard Lenin said with conviction, annoyance, and a genuine trace of fear that he rarely showed, *"That man is a night elf."*

Night elf.

Wizard Lenin had mentioned them before, hadn't he?

She supposed she could see where the name came from, what with the hair but—it wasn't very imaginative, was it?

Not that gold elf had been very imaginative either.

"It means he feeds on human and elven blood. He is essentially what you'd call a

vampire," Wizard Lenin spat, and with this projected the man next to her dressed as a classic vampire, Dracula mustache, cape, and anemic woman dangling from his arms.

Before Lily could respond to that (or say something to the man next to her, who was starting to give her a very odd look), Wizard Lenin added, *"Not only is he a night elf, Lily, he's one of Lily Jones's night elves. He is, in fact, the night elf."*

She could almost see Wizard Lenin speaking through gritted teeth as he concluded, *"Now, I can't imagine why, but he seems to think you're Lily Jones. If he finds out you're not Lily Jones, and believe me you are not Lily Jones, then he will cut us both into pieces and feed us to his coworkers!"*

Lily was plagued with the sudden, graphic, vision of someone's cut up remains left on the street.

Lily swallowed.

"We don't know I'm not Lily Jones," she tried to reason slowly, *"The gold elves thought I was, they didn't even ask. This guy seems to think I am."*

He hadn't asked either, had just greeted her like she was—well, she was supposed to be his boss, though it felt more like an old friend.

"If you're really Lily Jones, then I will have no choice but to believe your ridiculous theory about magic being a side effect of the end of the world."

"But that one's true," Lily protested.

"The point is, Lily," Wizard Lenin continued caustically, *"That you are five, can barely talk to people, and are haphazardly trying to impersonate one of the most ruthless people I've ever heard of. This is a terrible idea."*

She was mildly surprised that Wizard Lenin wasn't claiming the title of most ruthless.

"When they first sent mages to arrest her," Wizard Lenin said, *"She took one look at them and told her gang of night elf thugs to eat them raw."*

Well, that was one way to take care of a problem, Lily guessed. Waste not want not, if you were into that sort of thing.

From the feeling in her head, that wasn't the impression Wizard Lenin had been trying to leave her with. Rather than give up, however, he gave it another try, *"While I won't pretend to appreciate being trapped inside your head, I do appreciate that there is a head for me to be trapped in."*

Well, now he was just overreacting, he knew as well as Lily that she was immune to death.

"Have you tried being digested before? Eaten alive?" Wizard Lenin asked, knowing that the answer was no.

"Let's not push it, Lily," Wizard Lenin concluded, sweetly if it weren't for the murderous undercurrent running through her mind.

It was too late though, the man next to her had stopped, as they must have reached their destination.

They were in front of a building at the end of an alleyway. It was the only building whose windows weren't boarded up, the only one with any sign of anyone at all living in it.

The most surprising thing about it though wasn't the flowers in the windowsill, or even the gleaming doorknob, but the sign over the door.

"Jones Inc," Lily read slowly, "Abandon Hope All Ye Who Enter Here or Just Leave it at the Door for Later"

Someone liked Dante.

"I've never understood that," the man next to her confessed wryly, but didn't wait for Lily to explain before he stepped forward, pushed open the door, and motioned for her to go inside.

Lily hoped she wasn't about to be eaten, that would be very awkward to explain to Death.

Mustering her courage, trying to look like she knew what she was doing, she stepped inside.

She blinked at her surroundings, not sure what to feel or even think, it had—well, it had just about everything. There were *Star Wars* posters on the walls, tacky lava lamps of every imaginable color on every available surface, the owl from *Blade Runner* staring out with glowing eyes from a wooden perch in the corner, the red bicycle from *E.T.* leaning against the wall, and in the center, a recreation of the Wizard's intimidating head, Oz the Great and Powerful, from *The Wizard of Oz*.

Lily felt a smile growing on her lips as well as the realization—someone else liked movies.

The night elf, for his own part, was rushing behind a green curtain in the corner. She was sure he was fiddling with dials, desperately cutting off Oz before he could start.

"I forgot about the head," Wizard Lenin grumbled.

Despite his apprehension, Lily had the distinct feeling that he was annoyed.

"You've been here before?" Lily guess he'd never implied he hadn't, but he'd made it sound like he didn't know what Lily Jones looked like either.

"I've never met her, but I have been here," Wizard Lenin corrected, *"I came here when I was beginning my—revolutionary movement, for lack of a better term. I was short on funds, and I needed something more than talent to convince the nobility. I figured it was worth a shot asking Jones to pitch in."*

It was funny, she thought, but she'd always just assumed revolution was his main occupation. The idea that there had been a Wizard Lenin, a John Jones, before all of whatever had happened was an anathema to her.

"So, what happened?"

"She was on vacation," Wizard Lenin said bitterly, *"I got lucky in that, for some bizarre reason, she'd left a note decades earlier telling them to fund me and collect when I died. The idea being I'd cause so much chaos that I'd bring in clientele desperate to protect themselves from me or stab each other in the back. I always thought she was mocking*

me—"

It'd turned out, in retrospect, that she'd been right.

Wizard Lenin hated that.

"I got it!" the man behind the curtain, Night Elf Magoo, cried out. He reemerged, wiping his hands together with a grin, looking very proud of himself.

"Well done," Lily couldn't help but congratulate him, only to nearly bite her tongue as she wondered if a cannibal elf gangster would say that.

He didn't seem to notice, though.

"Right, where were we?" he asked instead, moving towards another door in the back of the room. Lily followed and found herself in what looked like an ordinary office, complete with paperwork and even a personal computer.

"John Jones," Lily said without missing a beat.

"We loaned him money, good call by the way," the man said as he took his seat behind the desk, "I had no idea one human could cause so much chaos. He died, as you also predicted, struck down by the power of God if you'd believe it."

"No," Lily said as she took a seat, out of instinct more than anything, "I can't believe it, can you believe it?"

The man gave her a funny look.

"What is wrong with you?" Wizard Lenin balked, *"Find a way to leave!"*

"No one really knows, of course," the man said after a long pause, "Certainly lots of rumors, the humans have been pushing that it had to do with the prince, even though he was nowhere near the prince at the time. More convenient in these trying times, everyone loves a fully human prince."

The man shrugged as if it had nothing to do with him. He then gave Lily a searching look, more searching than it'd been before.

"By the way, I've always wanted to ask, Jones isn't a very common name," the man said, eyes roving her face, "Is he a relative?"

"Nope," Lily said quickly.

The man didn't seem surprised by that, he shouldn't as they looked nothing alike, but he did say, "I always wondered if he was trying to recruit us through some connection through you. He never tried to claim he was a relative though."

Internally, Wizard Lenin was seething at the accusation of nepotism and relying on someone else's bloody reputation.

Apparently, that wasn't his style.

He'd rather be John Jones, or just the Usurper, than stand in someone else's shadow.

"Not much more to say about him," the man shrugged, "He's been dead for five years now."

As if he was over, finished, just like Wizard Lenin had feared.

"What about bodies?" Lily blurted, unable to help herself.

"Lily!"

"Bodies?" the man asked dully, "Oh, that thing you asked about earlier."

"Yes," Lily insisted, moving to the edge of her seat, staring directly at him as she waited for whatever he'd say next.

"Can't be done," the man dismissed easily, waving his hand as if to brush the idea off the table and onto the floor.

"Oh, come on," Lily said but the man just shook his head.

"Well, I don't know what you can do, boss," he said with a casual shrug, looking hopelessly out of place in his modern office chair behind his intimidating office desk, "But the rest of us peons only have so much juice in us. Even if I was at the top of my game, high on the blood of the universe itself, the best I could do—well, I don't even know, but no one in Xhigrahi ever brought back the dead or made life before, and they were rolling in power."

Lily felt her heart sink in disappointment.

"If it was that easy, don't you think I would have done something about it?" Wizard Lenin snapped.

"You people manipulate glitches for a living," Lily reminded him, *"Raising the dead should be a cake walk, I do it on a weekly basis!"*

"Not all of us are you, Lily," he sounded very bitter about that.

"There's got to be something—" she trailed off in horror as she realized she'd never caught the man's name. A name that she would probably have known if she was really Lily Jones.

The man stared at her for a moment, head tilted to the side, blinking owlishly.

Then he seemed to catch on.

He knew that she didn't know his name.

Well, it seemed she was about to get eaten after all.

Before she could dart out of the building, or else make herself a portal back to Earth, he said, "My name is Gwendlrarjunikartzin."

Lily stared.

He was looking at her expectantly, with something that might be called hope, even grinning across at her with teeth that were a little too sharp.

Lily—

Couldn't remember what he'd said. Not by a long shot. She couldn't ask him to repeat either, not without revealing that—well—she'd never met him before.

In her panic what slipped out was, "You're hilarious, Frank."

"You deserve to die, Lily, there is no helping you."

Lily stared across at him, watched him staring back, waiting for him to realize—

He laughed, shook his head, and said, "You got me, I really—I really thought for a minute there—"

Lily laughed, a very forced laugh, as if she'd made a very funny joke that she understood.

"I'm really funny, Frank," Lily insisted, winking at him.

"You really are," Frank agreed, still looking pained.

(Inside her head, Wizard Lenin had decided to wash his hands of her fate, he'd ignore the fact that his life depended on her remaining alive and well and look the other way. It was the only way for his sanity to survive this encounter.)

"But there's got to be something, Frank," Lily said, repeating the name, as if to somehow convince the man that his name really was Frank and had always been Frank.

By some miracle, he was either convinced or didn't mind, as he thought her words over.

"A bit of a strange thing to ask for, isn't it?" Frank mused, "I suppose there's always business in raising the dead, just the same way humans chase after immortality."

He paused then, as if caught by some thought, "Well, there is always that, isn't there?"

"What?" Lily asked eagerly.

"That unknown thing resting at the edge of everything," the man said, a knowing smile growing on his lips, "The Heart of the World."

Lily's mind flashed to the orb on the island, what Death had called the Heart of the World, what Wizard Lenin had first gawked at and then later tried to destroy in his nihilistic rage.

"The Heart of the World?" Lily asked.

"Even the humans know about that one," Frank said with a grin, "Though, to be fair, most don't seem to know all the details."

(Wizard Lenin, who was still pretending to be above this, mentally nodded in agreement that he'd certainly heard of the Heart of the World for all he didn't consider it immediately interesting.)

Lily decided to take a leap of faith and told the man, Frank, "Pretend I don't know anything."

He looked a bit bemused but didn't seem to find this odd, "Well, it's a bit of a long story, and not exactly a happy one. I'm not even sure if it's true or not—just a convenient explanation to explain why everything is the way it is."

"I've got time," Lily told him, crossing her legs on the chair and settling in.

He smiled at that, looking pleased (as if he'd wanted her to ask), and said, "I suppose the first thing I'll say is to not pay any attention to the humans. They're so busy spinning their own histories, painting the world the way they want to see it, that they've forgotten the truth."

Well, that wasn't hard given Lily had no idea what the humans were saying either. She hadn't had the nerve to open that history book she'd bought, not when Wizard Lenin had been so absent in her head.

"You know that there are only seven elven clans?" the man asked with raised eyebrows.

Lily felt herself wracking her brain—

Wizard Lenin hadn't given a number, had he?

"There are more than seven, but it's debated," Wizard Lenin cut in, *"Products of intermarrying between clans, generally frowned upon, not to mention dallying with the humans, though most of the genes are recessive in that case. The ones beyond the seven— they're not worth mentioning."*

Though, apparently, if you needed a good shoe, the shoe elves were your guys.

Lily wasn't going to comment on that.

"Sure," was what Lily said to Frank.

"The gold elves, moon elves, love elves, mind elves, happiness elves, night elves, and sun elves, in that order, always," Frank listed off, counting them off on his fingers.

—Those didn't sound in any way more legitimate than the shoe elves.

(Wizard Lenin couldn't believe Lily was getting away with anything when she clearly, blatantly, didn't even know the seven major clans.)

"We each have our great strengths," Frank continued, eyes glowing in the darkened room, "As well as our great weaknesses."

Wizard Lenin—

Was surprised that this man was talking about this, at all, with anyone. Wizard Lenin had had comrades among the elves, some he'd felt fairly close with for all they had never truly known him, and they had rarely if ever talked about their strengths and weaknesses.

It was generally known, though not in detail, that the elves were fantastic at branches of magic associated with their clan and positively terrible when it came to anything else.

This was why human mages were noteworthy, they didn't excel the same way as the elves, not unless they were exceptional, but they were well-rounded in a way elves simply couldn't be. It was that generalized nature that gave them the edge the elves had lacked.

And the elves had paid for it.

"The Heart of the World is a bit of ancient history," Frank said, "All the original parties, if they even existed, are long dead. They all killed each other, or so the story goes."

He paused, face turning towards the light shining through the blinds. For a moment, he looked more profound than he had any right to, his face painted gold and red and eyes distant as he looked out towards the sun.

For a moment, Lily really believed he was immortal, that he could be thousands upon thousands of years old.

That maybe Frank really hadn't suited him.

Then he started, "They say it was thousands of years ago, earlier than our earliest records, before magic was a known thing."

He looked back at her, "They say that this world was empty, a wild place, and that there were no elves and no humans either. It was mankind who crossed the border from Tellestria, without magic or immortality to aid them.

"There were seven men, unrelated, who started a village with dozens of others. They looked beyond their meager housing to the wild hills, forests, and seas and all the wonders that could possibly await them. They left their wives, everything they'd known and built for themselves, and together faced seven trials beyond the mountains.

"Each trial was more harrowing than the last, requiring the talents of each member, but they survived and after weeks and weeks found themselves in a clearing filled with light.

"There, in the center, was a single pedestal with a dark orb resting on it."

Lily flinched, immediately thinking of the orb, the orb she'd seen in person every time she died, the orb she knew this man was certainly talking about—

"It was ordinary in every way," he said, "Except for the perfection of its shape. By its very nature, it was something unnatural, and each of them knew it. They also knew, just by staring at it, that it contained a power they couldn't begin to imagine.

"But it was not unguarded.

"There was a man standing beside it. He was dark-haired, tall, thin, and while his features were handsome, they looked like they'd been painted on. Like he was wearing an artfully made, perfectly shaped, mask that no being would have for a real face."

Frank leaned forward, staring her in the eye, and said, "They say his eyes were the most unnatural green that could ever be seen in eyes."

Lily reached up, as if to touch her own eyes, but stopped just in time.

Frank grinned.

"When he opened his mouth," Frank continued, "His voice was just like his face, it was beautiful but featureless, genderless, a voice that only mimicked a person's.

"He introduced himself as the creator and destroyer of this and all other worlds, that people called him Death, because they always remember the end more than the beginning."

Lily's mind flashed to Death in the station, Death who had red hair like hers, who had a face that was her face, who was tall but not taller than

Wizard Lenin or this man and certainly wasn't—

"He said that he had been watching them, had invited them into this world, his final world, in the hopes that he might understand the single greatest gift they possessed.

"Sentience."

Frank stared at her, waiting for her to process, but even when she didn't say anything he continued.

"The seven men, having suffered through their trials, were offended.

"They brought up everything they had suffered, their journey to this world, their journey to this clearing, their mortality, and one went so far as to ask that if this man really was the creator and destroyer of every world, then why had he made it so terrible?

"The man considered that, aghast, as if he hadn't realized the extent of the ills of the world.

"After a long pause, he admitted that though reality was beautiful, its creation had been an abrupt, ill-timed, and contentious thing. The world had been made before thought was a concept, the very idea of a world, of anything, had been unnatural at the time.

"Destruction, he explained, was regretfully inherent in its creation.

"In repentance, he offered each of the men a wish, to transform themselves and grant some measure of the immortality they craved."

Frank lifted his first finger, the finger he'd used to count off the gold elves earlier.

"The first, like each of them, had been poor in the old world. All his life he'd felt the burdens of poverty, until it had driven him out entirely. Even here he felt it with his small village hovel and was terrified he'd return from this worthless journey a poor man.

"He asked for wealth, power over gold, precious metals, jewels, and all artistry. He would never want for a trade, never want for work or employment, he would find precious material no one else could, and would never hunger again.

"With his wish, the man's hair turned golden, his eyes metallic, his ears pointed, and his face fine.

"He was blessed with instinctive magic that could shape, find, and mine precious metals, ores, and jewels. He could craft them as he pleased, better than any smith ever could, and he and his descendants would build their dreams out of gold.

"That," Frank concluded, "Was the gold elves."

Frank lifted a second finger.

"The second was a warrior, stronger than the rest, and had taken pride in his ability to survive in the harsh wilds of this new world. However, the trials had challenged him, and he would not have survived on his strength alone. There were times he'd become injured and grown very close to death, while he had survived, it had shaken him.

"He asked for a keen eye, swift hand, and unmatched power in his blade. He would never be bested in combat, never lose to a beast, his arrow would always fly true, and so long as there was prey he would never hunger.

"With his wish, the man's hair turned as pale as the moon, his eyes became a wolf's yellow, his ears pointed, and his face fine.

"He gained an instinctive mastery of the blade, unparalleled among all others, along with a stamina that far surpassed what he'd had before. No weapon would disobey him, no shot would miss, and in physical fighting he would always win.

"And that," Frank said, eyebrows wriggling with a smile, "Was the moon elves."

He lifted his third finger.

"The third had once been a learned man, he was proud of that fact, proud of the fact that he'd been far more learned than the others. It was his knowledge, more often than not, that had seen them through one task or another. He was driven by curiosity and pride, not any desire for strength, riches, or even glory.

"He asked for knowledge, all knowledge, and the ability to surpass all his fellow men when it came to intellectual pursuits. You see, he wanted to always be the wisest in the room.

"With his wish, the man's hair turned a dark shade of blue, his eyes a clear gray, his ears pointed, and his face fine.

"He gained a memory that could store all information he could hope to learn, an intuitiveness that had previously escaped him, and innate understanding of the minds of others. It would never again surprise him, how others thought, and why they thought. Illusions, dreams, they became nothing to him.

"And that," Frank nodded towards her, "Was the mind elves."

A fourth finger.

"Which brings us to the fourth man," Frank said with a grin, "Now, he was vain. He wasn't particularly bothered about money, about strength, or knowledge, but he had always been a good-looking man and proud of it. It had gotten him his beautiful wife in the village, it had gotten him all the attention he wanted, and he'd been very pleased with the fact that he'd been by far the best looking one on the journey. Until, of course, he wasn't.

"He looked over and saw three men, all more beautiful than he was, and couldn't help but remember how the journey had scarred him more than any of them.

"He asked for beauty, for adoration, for every head to always turn in his direction to covet and envy.

"With his wish, his hair turned the color of wine, his ears pointed, and his face was even finer than the first three.

"There was this innate beauty to him, unexplainable, where every eye would always turn towards him and every expression he made could be read as an enigmatic invitation."

"That was the love elves."

Five fingers.

"The fifth considered himself, in a sense, wiser than the first four. On the journey he'd come to realize that glory, wealth, beauty, and even knowledge meant little at the end of things. In the end, what men truly strived for was simple happiness that could defy the poor as well as the rich.

"He asked for happiness, the kind of happiness that a child has when receiving a gift or having had a wonderful meal. The happiness that men have searched and died for.

"With his wish, his hair became a softer shade of brown, his ears pointes, his face fair, and there was a sudden sense of contentment in him that spread to his companions, as if by simply standing next to him they could taste the happiness that had eluded them.

"Which of course," Frank concluded, "Was the happiness elves."

Here, Frank paused, as if trying to see what she'd made of the story thus far. Lily was again struck by how timeless he looked, different than he'd been in the alley, and even when he'd stepped foot into this building. It wasn't like what he'd been was a charade but more like some veil she hadn't noticed had been lifted.

She wondered what it was he saw when he looked at her.

He continued before she could ask, raising his second hand, and the sixth finger.

"The sixth man was my ancestor, cleverer than the others had been. He had more of a grasp of what magic really was. He'd listened to what the stranger had said, watched their transformations, and kept careful track of what exactly he'd envied about them.

"He didn't ask for money, strength, knowledge, beauty, or even happiness. He asked for life.

"And this time, the stranger hesitated," Frank said, smile growing cold, "He warned my ancestor that what he sought was divine, that his line would be forever altered by this great and terrible gift.

"Nonetheless, the stranger cut the palm of his hand, his blood a bright, radiant, white light like stars magnified.

He offered it to my ancestor, who swallowed it."

Frank leaned forward over the desk, rested his hands on it, "They say that with just that first taste, he burned his tongue. His hair burned too, became black as cinders, his skin white like ash, and his eyes crimson like fire. Like the others, his features became fair and his ears pointed, and for a single moment a god's blood ran through his veins. He gained mastery over the immeasurable, incomprehensible, force of life itself.

"And that was the night elves."

Frank sighed, stared down at his hands, he didn't lift them again,

Instead, quietly, he said, "Then there was the last, the seventh, that enigmatic ancestor of the likes of Princess Iff, Lilyanna the elf queen, Ilyn the butcher, and too many to name. You see, it was important that he went last, because he saw all the gifts and all the mistakes the others hadn't even known they'd made yet. Like the sixth, he realized that it was the stranger who was important, unlike the sixth, he asked for something else.

"I want your eyes, was what he said, so that he could see what the man saw.

"Like my ancestor, the stranger considered him, leaned forward, and whispered something in his ear. Some say it was a warning, some a plea, and some say he asked for some further price. Whatever it was, the seventh agreed, and watched as the stranger gouged out his own eyes then replaced the seventh's.

"The moment they were in his skull, his hair turned the color of sunrises and sunsets, and his face and ears changed just like the others. They say that when he opened his eyes, he could see the shape of the world, the past as well as the future, all of it as if it was a simple path extending unobscured ahead of him.

"That was the sun elves," Frank concluded bitterly.

"The stranger, now eyeless, yet somehow unbothered, escorted them out of the clearing. The clearing sealed itself behind them. The Heart of the World, he said, would wait until a worthy party could come for it. Just like that, he disappeared into thin air, as if he'd never been there in the first place.

"So, they traveled back to their homes and their wives. They had children, and their gifts were inherited, and for a while they were all quite pleased with themselves. That didn't last.

"The first five gradually discovered that they were weak. Their magic, their gifts, were tied to their wish and the material world. Everything they had was in gold, battle, knowledge, beauty, and simple contentment. They were incapable of miracles, of truly powerful magic, and grew envious of the night and sun elf whose power seemed immeasurable. For all their immortality, they were still mortals, while the other two were not.

"The night elf, on the other hand, faced the gruesome realities of his new existence. Unlike the others, though he had tremendous power, he and his children began to fade. Oh, they were still certainly immortal, but their bodies began to wither into husks. The taste of a god's blood, passed to his descendants, demanded payment in kind.

"Then there was the seventh. He was quieter, with his strange new eyes, but seemed to have no weaknesses or consequences, despite having the same power as the night elf. He and his children seemed to have paid no

THE HEART OF THE WORLD

price at all, and when questioned only offered that his price was that peace would never last between the seven of them."

Frank paused yet again, tapped his fingers against the death, then bitterly continued.

"My ancestor, they say, in desperation stole the seventh's first-born son, drained him of blood, and consumed his flesh."

He grinned wolfishly at Lily yet again, "And that was the start of the war, the war that lasted thousands of years, until Xhigrahi, the night elf empire, conquered them all."

Frank sighed, his smile dimmed and became something more tired than amused, and the fight seemed to go out of him, "It's only a legend. If they existed, they died in the early days of infighting. As far as I remember, and my father remembered, and his father, we've been fighting over land, magic, resources, blood feuds, and just about anything else you can name forever. At least, until the humans showed up with their mass-produced, cheap magic."

Lily waited for him to continue, enraptured, but it seemed he was finally finished. That that was that, all there was, and all there ever would be.

"Did the man, the stranger, give a name?" she asked.

"Just Death," Frank said, "Some say he's only Death, some say he really is both death and the creator like he'd said, depends who you ask."

Frank waived his hand in dismissal, "He's a common figure, really, he pops in and out of stories if you know where to look."

Lily's mind was still racing, it couldn't have been Death, they didn't sound like they looked similar at all but—there was that pedestal on the island, Death having called himself Death and calling Ellie Death, it felt like it should mean something.

"What about the Heart of the World?" Lily pressed.

"An object of mystery," Frank told her easily.

"But it can make a body?" Lily pressed.

"I don't see why not," Frank said with a shrug.

Lily's smile fell, "You mean—you don't know."

"No one knows," Frank said with a knowing smile, "No one's ever fetched the damn thing."

"What's that supposed to mean?"

"It's been tried before, and no one's ever made it," Frank said with a shrug, "The sun elves, if you listen to them, have said that it'll never happen until the conditions are right."

"When are the conditions right?" Lily asked.

"That would be too convenient, wouldn't it?" Frank asked with a huff of laughter, "Nobody knows, except that they haven't been right in thousands of years."

He then gave her another look, "It's just a story, Lily. It's a nice way of explaining why the sun elves are such lucky bastards, why the others like to believe they have useful talents even when they were overwhelmed by human parlor tricks, and why my own people have the shortest end of the proverbial stick. That's all it is."

Lily poked at Wizard Lenin with a proverbial stick, waiting for him to say something.

He'd never heard this particular story, what he'd known of the Heart of the World was that a party of elves had seen it but had been unable to retrieve it.

Like Frank, he thought it sounded like a good story, the kind people used to explain things that otherwise didn't make any sense. Drinking the blood of a god would get you cursed, Wizard Lenin thought wryly, it was a nice story to tell yourself that you were being punished for someone else's stupidity.

"The great human trick, the mass production he's describing," Wizard Lenin noted, *"Was to bind the cultural cornerstones of the clans, all their ancient poetry, prayers, and sags, into tomes that they could then print en masse. Because humans believe the spells work, because they're so deeply rooted in the memories of the elves, they do, and they now have a cheap reproduction of the original elven magic which they used to build this grand kingdom you see today."*

Lily felt a little stunned.

She thought about what she'd seen of this kingdom so far, how put together it had seemed, and thought—

There was a long, complicated, history that she knew nothing about.

***

"Now that you're not depressed," Lily said when they'd returned to the empty Tylor residence, *"How do you plan to get a body."*

"I am depressed," Wizard Lenin responded with a sniff, *"And I don't know."*

"You don't know?" Lily asked, wondering at how he'd admitted it so easily.

"The Heart of the World isn't an option," Wizard Lenin said, *"Neither is any other ancient artifact nor trying to barter with a god. I am out of ideas, in other words."*

Lily supposed that was good for her, she loved having Wizard Lenin around, but that didn't sound very good for him.

"If it was easy, everybody would be doing it!"

Lily thought about that, she supposed that, generally, most people didn't get stuck in people's heads or make bodies for themselves.

"What about an exorcism—"

"I don't believe in those."

"What about a shaman—"

"I don't believe in those either."

"What about if we make a robot—"

"No."

Lily frowned, moving to turn on the TV, trying to think of something he might accept.

"Well, what about if I just do it?" Lily asked.

At this, Wizard Lenin paused, wanting to dismiss it and feeling an eerie sensation of dread rising in him.

"You can't," he said after a pause that was a little too long.

"Why not?" Lily asked challengingly, *"I do it all the time."*

"You shouldn't," Wizard Lenin amended, and before Lily could ask explained, *"You haven't the slightest idea what you're doing and whatever your results, I'm the one who pays for it."*

That didn't mean she shouldn't try.

She searched around, trying to find inspiration. She glanced at the TV and saw a magician on stage, not the old-fashioned kind in a tailcoat and top hat, but one of the newer ones who could make an elephant disappear.

That didn't matter, though, because with a grin, thinking hard, she held out her hand where—

Yes, there was a top hat.

"That's terrifying," Wizard Lenin commented, *"Please stop that."*

Lily held it out, felt the fabric, even put it on her head, *"Looks like a perfectly good hat to me."*

"Oh, well, I'm so glad you managed a hat, Lily," Wizard Lenin bit out, *"Truly, I'm inspired."*

Before he could go on telling her to knock it off, Lily grinned, hopped off the couch, and held the hat out in front of her as if there was an audience right there.

"Don't you dare," Wizard Lenin said, guessing at what she already had planned.

She jammed her hand inside, reached into the nothingness, reached past the hat entirely, and with appropriate panache pulled out a white, dark-eyed, snuffling rabbit into the world that Lily sometimes dared to call real.

Lily bowed to the imaginary, ecstatic, clapping.

"Oh, thank you, Lily, I'm so relieved since you've made a bloody rabbit! Truly! I have no doubts left! I've always wanted to be a rabbit!"

Lily dropped the rabbit with her sudden headache, wincing, and trying to rub it away.

"The rabbit's a metaphor, Lenin," she said out loud, hobbling her way back to the couch.

"For what, your stupidity?"

For his body, and he knew it too, for all he wasn't saying it.

"The rabbit's not the point!" Lily shouted at the TV, "The point is that I can do this!"

Maybe not right now, she didn't want him to leave right now, but the point was that she could, she would, do this and he just had to realize that. He could leave anytime he wanted, all he had to do was ask, and there was no need to worry at all.

"Why is it still here?"

Lily opened her eyes, stared at the floor where there was the rabbit right where she'd dropped it.

Its eyes were staring back at her—eerily dark.

"Was it supposed to disappear?"

It wasn't supposed to exist at all.

You couldn't make something from nothing. Even if you could, even if you could make something like a hat, then you certainly couldn't create life, even if that life was only a rabbit.

If it had existed at all, even for a heartbeat, then it should have disappeared by now.

It hadn't.

"I don't know," Lily said, leaning forward to look at it, *"It looks like a rabbit to me."*

She clapped her hands, a loud, startling, sound that should have sent the rabbit jumping.

It just sat there.

"Get rid of it," Wizard Lenin commanded.

Lily wasn't sure she liked the idea of that, it was a thing now, and getting rid of it would essentially be killing it. It hadn't asked to be pulled out of a hat to prove a point.

Frowning, Lily first caused the hat to disappear. In the blink of an eye it was gone, nothing but air left in its place.

She turned her attention to the rabbit, took a breath to steel herself, telling herself the rabbit wouldn't even know it'd never existed, reached out to dismantle it and—

It was still there.

Lily blinked, it didn't blink back, and she tried again.

Nope, still there.

"You're not making me a body," Wizard Lenin concluded.

Lily reached forward to pick up the Rabbit, trying not to feel unnerved, and quietly agreed, *"I guess I'm not making you a body."*

5 THE PLANS OF MICE AND MEN

In which time passes, someone finally comes looking for a lost princess, and a house is lit on fire.

Destiny was not a subtle thing.

The funny thing was that Lily had thought it was.

Oh, her life had suddenly flipped on its head when she was five, and in the following months she'd made a host of fantastic discoveries about herself and the world she lived in. The trouble was she'd been the one doing the flipping. Lily had accidentally met Death, accidentally met Wizard Lenin, found the other side, then stumbled across Frank. She was the one who'd done all the work, and since then—

A whole lot of nothing had happened.

At first, she thought that was just how it was supposed to go. It was a bit much, discovering you were a half-elf magical princess who moonlighted as a vampire gangster, and there'd been Frank's story about elves and the orb but—

Nothing had ever come of it.

Wizard Lenin certainly hadn't given up on getting a body, he'd remind anyone who listened, but he'd put it on the back burner.

"I don't see the point in wasting my time on solutions I know won't work," he'd spat out when she'd brought it up.

(He was still a little miffed about the Rabbit experiment. To be fair, Lily wasn't sure that could be called any kind of success either.)

Since then—

He was best described as a running commentator on the sad reality that was Lily's life.

Lily, for her own part, ended up splitting her time between one side and the other. She'd hop over to Jones Inc. at night, see what Frank was up to and stop him from getting any meaningful work done, and during the day she went to school as Ellie Tylor.

She supposed she could commit to one side or the other, that maybe she really should commit to being this Princess Iff person who had to be a whole lot more important than Ellie Tylor, she just couldn't find it in her though.

Nobody asked about Iff any more than they did Ellie, nobody seemed to be looking for her, and if she decided to stay full-time—it'd make it all seem a little less real, wouldn't it?

That was the last thing Lily wanted.

So, she just—

Bided her time until something important happened.

And asked Wizard Lenin a lot of questions he didn't want to answer.

"What if you don't get a body?" she'd asked one night when she was dreaming, the library in her head having shifted into a tropical beach complete with virgin margaritas that Wizard Lenin had refused to touch out of sheer pettiness.

(Lily had never been on a real beach vacation before, the Tylors never took her, but she liked to think she'd imagined a pretty damn good one.)

"I'm getting a body," he'd said curtly.

"I'm serious," Lily had said, lowering her sunglasses to look at him, "You're the one who said you didn't have any ideas. What if you never do it?"

"I'm doing it," he'd spat back.

"So, you have some kind of a plan—"

"I'm waiting for an opportunity," he'd cut in, and even though he'd been wearing his own sunglasses she was sure he was glaring.

"I have all the time in the world," he'd said, "I'm not going anywhere, even if you are. Something, eventually, will make an appearance."

"What do you mean you're not going anywhere?" Lily had asked.

"I made sure of it," he'd said, and nothing else.

(Wizard Lenin liked doing that. He liked dropping just enough hints to intrigue you, to hint at something large, but then refused to expand on any details.

Lily had gotten used to it.)

"But hypothetically—"

"Then I suppose I become a figment of your imagination!" he'd interjected, finally removing his sunglasses and turning towards her fully, "I become a footnote in a history book, a paragraph, and nothing more than a clown in your cosmic slapstick routine."

He'd stared at her, daring her to say something, anything, but Lily had realized by that point that anything she'd say would have sounded—cheap.

But she hadn't been able to help herself, "I don't think you're a clown."

"Oh, shut up," he'd said, leaning back in his chair, replacing his sunglasses, and staring up at the sun.

"What about me?" Lily had asked.

"What about you?" he'd asked in turn with a sigh, clearly wanting to be done with this.

The trouble was, Lily wasn't entirely sure what she'd meant either, just that it felt like the right question to ask.

Like she was supposed to be doing something very important, but had forgotten what it was when she'd gotten up that morning.

He'd sighed at Lily's lack of answer and asked, "What about that pseudo-brother of yours? He certainly doesn't have any grand ambitions."

Yes, but Death's role was very clearly over. He'd had a story, somewhere, somehow, and he was now in the epilogue. Lily had known that the moment she'd seen him, for all he hadn't said it, and Wizard Lenin did too for all he wouldn't admit it.

Lily's story couldn't be over before it started, could it?

"I'm a princess, aren't I?" Lily had asked him, "Shouldn't that mean something?"

Wizard Lenin had laughed at that, as he always did whenever she brought that up, "Oh, but Iff, you're not the princess anyone wanted. I'm not sure they ever intend to bring you back."

"What's that supposed to mean?"

"It means your father made a very controversial decision when it came to his bride," Wizard Lenin had said, still laughing, "And everyone's reminded of it the second they look at your face."

He hadn't explained that either, he never did, like it was a joke she was supposed to have understood from the start.

"Chin up, Lily," he'd said, "Most of us don't have a destiny."

Lily wasn't sure she didn't have a destiny, too many things had happened for her to easily shake it off, but she had come to believe that destiny was a lot slower, smaller, and less grand than she'd thought it would be.

It turned out she'd just been impatient.

***

Lily was twelve when it happened.

It was an ordinary summer day, in what had been so far an ordinary summer, after a series of ordinary years. She'd been out in the Tylor's' yard, under the blazing sun, trying and failing to get Rabbit to do anything.

"I really wish you'd get rid of it," Wizard Lenin said for what had to be the billionth time in his life.

"I tried that," Lily responded for what had to be the billionth time in her

life.

The rabbit, Rabbit, had been a point of contention since its sudden appearance. After seven years, it still hadn't disappeared. It hadn't disappeared and it hadn't died despite its lack of consumption of any food or water. It never did anything, exactly, it'd just—sit there, watching, unblinking.

It also possibly ate things out of reality.

Oh, she had no proof, but sometimes things, people, or even ideas would disappear as if they'd never been there.

Carol Tylor used to go to bridge club, now the date was still marked every month on the calendar, but bridge club wouldn't actually happen. It was just, for some reason no one could explain, marked on the calendar by some unspoken agreement. An agreement that didn't involve playing any bridge.

And she couldn't prove it was Rabbit, but it'd started happening only after he showed up and refused to leave.

She definitely didn't think it was a rabbit for all it was rabbit-shaped, more some—she didn't even know, eldritch monstrosity from the dark side of a silk top hat.

"Alright, Rabbit, today we're going to hop," she told Rabbit.

Rabbit, of course, did absolutely nothing as usual.

Lily had been doing this for years, now, ever since Rabbit had refused to leave her plane of existence. She'd bring him out onto the grass and try to get him to do something, anything, she'd even accept unusual behavior for rabbits.

She'd tried putting him on his back and rubbing his belly, pulling out hamster wheels, frisbees, rope toys, those fishing poles with birds on the end that cats liked.

But nothing every single time.

"It's not a dog," Wizard Lenin groused, again, not for the first time.

"It's not a rabbit either," Lily refuted, staring across at the uncooperative not-rabbit.

"Hop, Rabbit."

Rabbit did not hop.

It did not even snuffle.

"I didn't say it was a rabbit," Wizard Lenin said, *"Have I ever once said it was a rabbit? It's some—thing you made from nothing."*

He just thought it was a product of poor craftsmanship. Rabbit was what happened when you tried to create something out of nothing.

Lily didn't disagree that trying to get Rabbit to do anything was an exercise in pointlessness, it was just she was so bored.

Night elves, it turned out, slept during the day and she didn't have anything else to do on the other side. She'd already wandered through all the bookstores, done a scavenger hunt to find all the fountains, loitered outside the mage's academy and tried to peek inside. She hadn't just done it this summer, she'd done it every summer since she was five, she'd already done everything, and she was all out of ideas!

"Why don't you watch TV?" Wizard Lenin suggested, his voice dripping with derision, *"Doesn't that usually keep you entertained?"*

Lily was also out of TV shows and blockbusters.

It was in that unassuming moment, where she'd been ready to admit defeat, that destiny decided to strike her over the head with a baseball bat.

She happened to glance down the street and there, walking down the middle of the road, staring down at some kind of pocket watch, was the most ridiculous looking man Lily had ever seen in her life.

He was tall, thin, legs and steps long and filled not necessarily with confidence but with a brash and overbearing determination that by its very nature filled anyone who watched his approach with a sense of unease.

He wore a bright blue, militaristic uniform with golden buttons, the kind Lily had often seen on the human mages near the academy. Clashing with this, though, was a bright, tattered, rainbow scarf that bled from gold into pink, wrapped loosely around his neck, as well as thick strawberry-blonde hair, tied away from his face in a single braid with only a few loose curls framing his face.

Though he was every inch an elf, with his pointed ears, pretty face, and brightly colored hair, there was something unkempt about him that made every part of him clash with some other part. The thickness of his hair clashed with the thinness of his hands, the impatience of his feet with the serenity of his cheekbones, and the discontent carved into his face contradicting everything else. He looked like a jigsaw puzzle that had been forced into fitting after a fit of rage.

There was none of the easy elegance of Wizard Lenin. Despite having every reason to be good looking, this man somehow wasn't.

And then, almost as an afterthought, Lily picked up Rabbit, realizing that she was watching an elf walk down the middle of the street in her suburb, on Earth, as if he had every right to be here.

"Ilyn!" Wizard Lenin cried out with an alarm that rivaled Lily's running into Frank for the first time.

"Gesundheit," Lily responded.

"No, Lily, that man is Ilyn," Wizard Lenin spat.

Had Wizard Lenin ever said that name before? She didn't think it had ever come up, but then, most things didn't come up with him.

"He was a comrade in the war, a sun elf, and he was—"

The word Wizard Lenin was looking for, apparently, was terrifying.

Dead, butchered, bodies filled Lily's mind's eyes, villages set on fire with a single word. Pale jade eyes, her color but diluted tenfold, stared out at the burning world with utter indifference. In Wizard Lenin's memories, he'd been wearing the same scarf over a brightly colored tunic, the kind that only belonged on the other side.

"Oh," Lily said, holding Rabbit a little closer as she noted that the man seemed to be headed directly to her.

"What could he possibly want?" Wizard Lenin hissed, then, taking in the uniform, asked, *"And how did he get drafted into the kingdom's forces?!"*

Then he seemed to remember where he was and whose head he was stuck in, *"Forget all that, we need to leave, now!"*

It was a little late for that.

The man came to a stop directly in front of her, unnaturally still even as he lifted his head to look at her. Just like Wizard Lenin remembered, those were her eyes. Her eyes diluted and made opaque, a green so light they were almost white.

He stared for an unnaturally long time, his face expressionless and eyes unreadable. Then, he looked at the house behind her, empty on this fine summer's day, and without another word lifted a hand and made the slightest of gestures.

The Tylor's house promptly burst into flames.

"Holy shit!" Lily exclaimed.

Before she could even think about putting the fire out, Ilyn grabbed her free wrist, pulled out his pocket watch again, and began dragging her down the street.

"You just lit my house on fire!" Lily accused.

The man spared her a wry, withering, wordless glance.

"Why did you light my house on fire?!" Lily asked.

He didn't even twitch, there was no indication he heard at all. He just continued to pull her down the middle of the road, as if this were all perfectly natural. Never mind that the neighbors were streaming out, calling 9-1-1, and shouting to get hoses.

It was a small miracle that the Tylors, as always, were out and about with only Lily herself in the house. Otherwise, judging by how fast the flames were spreading, she doubted they'd have made it out in time.

For a moment, she wondered if Ilyn had already known they weren't inside, or he simply hadn't cared.

"The latter," Wizard Lenin answered easily.

After they'd walked through half the neighborhood, Lily uselessly digging in her heels, Ilyn finally answered in a voice that was softer than it had any right to be, "Its existence offended me."

And that was apparently that.

Lily gave up, allowing herself to be pulled forward, reconciling herself to the fact that the house had probably burned to the ground by now. Lily would have to do—she didn't even know, something. Rebuild it, sure, but maybe she could somehow erase everyone's memories and make it seem like it hadn't happened. She hadn't done it before, but it couldn't be that hard, could it?

Of course, she wasn't going anywhere for a while.

She glared up at the man petulantly, he didn't look at her. Taking a breath, she said loudly, "Well, my name's Ellie Tylor and you just burned down my house."

Not a word to this.

"And you're kidnapping me," Lily continued.

Not a word to this either.

"Can you at least tell me where we're going?" Lily asked.

"Home," Ilyn responded.

It appeared Ilyn was a man of very few words, and that even getting those words was like pulling teeth.

Home, that had to mean the other side, didn't it? He hadn't said as much, but with those ears and that fashion sense there was only one place they could be going.

"You're not supposed to know that!" Wizard Lenin's panicked voice rang through, *"You're not supposed to know any of this, remember? They left you in Tellestria!"*

Moreover, Wizard Lenin had always been very leery of letting anyone find out that Iff had managed to wander in by herself. That, apparently, wasn't done.

He'd rather have her mistaken as Lily Jones than recognized as Princess Iff, and that said a lot.

"Lily, this is not a man to trifle with," Wizard Lenin cautioned.

She'd guessed as much, what with the wanton destruction of the Tylor's property.

"Lily," Wizard Lenin continued, oddly earnest as he whispered into her mind's ears, *"If you know what's good for you, for us, now's the time to start acting."*

Acting, oh, well, she'd never been a very good actor.

She felt herself flush and pale in turn, as she tried and failed to picture what a Lily who wasn't Lily would act like. An Ellie Tylor who, presumably, had never fallen out of a tree.

"I've never been kidnapped before," Lily said, probably a bit too loudly, "I expected more white vans and strangers with candy."

Ilyn said nothing, continued to pull her down the street, steps always the same measured length that Lily had to stumble to keep up with.

"So, I guess I want to ask where 'home' is, exactly," Lily said, still too loudly, and her smile too strained, "Is it a pit in your basement?"

She rambled on, mind in a tailspin as she tried to come up with something, "Is this where you tell me that I put the lotion in the basket, or I get the hose again?"

That finally got his attention.

He stopped dead in his tracks and turned to look at her, his expression stunned.

After a pause, he said flatly, in that lilting voice that tried and failed to be steely, "I have neither lotion nor a hose."

Lily considered this, considered him, then asked, "Do you have an interest in my virgin flesh?"

"Why do I put any faith in you?" Wizard Lenin asked, *"Why?"*

He deeply regretted not simply having fed her lines from the start. He hoped that however Ilyn chose to kill her, he made it quick.

Ilyn however, seemed to have broken. His hand finally released her wrist, rising with shaking fingers to grip the bridge of his nose, as he let out a long sigh. Finally, haltingly, he said, "I was sent by the monarchy, your cousin, to collect you from Tellestria."

"Oh," Lily said, trying to act very surprised and very clueless, "What is a Tellestria—and a monarchy?"

He blinked, blinked again, then seemed to have a sudden realization dawn on him. In that moment, it was clear that he'd had no idea that Lily had had no idea what the hell was going on. Or, rather, he'd had no idea that Lily wasn't supposed to know what the bananas was happening, since she wasn't supposed to have died or had Wizard Lenin rattling around in her head.

Lily belatedly realized she'd just embarrassed herself publicly for nothing.

Stiffly, with an awkwardness that suited his voice even less than the steel had, he explained, "You are a princess of the monarchy I currently serve, Princess If, and you were sent here to Tellestria for safekeeping many years ago."

"Safekeeping?" Lily prompted.

Despite herself, and the surreal terror of the situation, she felt a growing curiosity. All the books had only ever said the same thing about Iff, that she was sent away for safekeeping somewhere. Frank had been oddly ambivalent about Princess Iff's fate, neither appearing overly interested nor entirely disinterested, and had theorized she was probably dead. Wizard Lenin had his own theories for why she was here, but he'd refused to talk about them.

There was something missing between the Point A of Lily's childhood as a princess and Point B of Ellie Tylor that she'd never been told properly.

Maybe, just maybe, this man would give it to her.

"A man burned down the palace."

Or not.

"You just burned down my house," Lily couldn't help but angrily point out.

Ilyn didn't seem to care about that.

"So, we're going back to my home planet," Lily said irritably, to which the man neither nodded nor shook his head, "Of which I was a princess this whole time."

Would they really have just left her here for twelve years? It was one thing when she hadn't thought they were ever coming, that made sense in its own way, but showing up after twelve years?! She could have been doing something important for all they knew!

Seeing that they were done, Ilyn started to move again, grabbing her wrist once more.

"Wait!" Lily said, digging in her heels, "You didn't say where we were going! I mean—you didn't say how we were getting there!"

A portal, obviously, but given the fact that Lily had never actually gone looking for one and never managed to find one, she had no idea where he thought he was going.

He didn't answer, but he didn't have to, because Lily realized it herself.

He intended to walk down the middle of the highway to get there, wherever there was, obliterating any car or truck that dared to cross his path, leaving miles of destruction in his wake.

–He'd probably done just that to get to her house.

"Oh, sweet Jesus," Lily quietly exclaimed.

She had to find some way out of this, not just because she didn't want to walk for days, but also because she had to mitigate some of the collateral damage.

"Don't even think about it," Wizard Lenin hissed, reminding her silently, once again, that nobody created portals except for Lily because she broke all the rules. The moment she started doing that in front of Ilyn, he was bound to take notice.

Lily looked around wildly, trying to find something, anything. She dug her feet in and pointed at a house identical to all the other houses around it.

"Oh look, it's that very famous house that everyone loves," Lily said loudly, "God, people really do think about that house all the time. I'm um—pretty sure there's fifty sonnets just about that sweet, wonderful, house."

Ilyn stopped to stare with her, not looking puzzled necessarily, but at least not still walking.

"Wow, that is such a house, all houses are that house, it's like—the cultural cornerstone of houses," Lily continued, unable to gesture holding Rabbit as she was.

She didn't dare to look and see if Ilyn was buying it.

"You can't think this is going to work—"

"Oh my god, what is that thing?" Lily cried as, through the power of imagination, stubbornness, and panic, she tore a hole in reality right in front of them.

"Mr. Ilyn," Lily said, turning to look at him, "Do you see that thing? It's right in front of that very important house! Oh my god, I've never seen anything like it!"

Ilyn said nothing, she didn't look at him, didn't dare. She felt sweat rolling down the back of her neck, her heart pounding, waiting to see what he'd do.

She couldn't help but glance out of the corner of her eye where—he was looking down at that goddamn pocket watch! All that work, and he wasn't even looking!

She opened her mouth to ask if this was boring for him, but before she could, he started pulling her into the hole.

Then, two seconds later, they were on the other side. He started pulling her towards the central hill, where the palace was. He didn't even give her a second to take in the scenery.

"What is his problem?" Lily asked Wizard Lenin.

"Oh, he's always like this," Wizard Lenin dismissed, not quite at ease but deciding that either Ilyn had bought Lily's act or he hadn't, there was nothing for it now.

"Always?!" Lily asked, trying to imagine it.

"Well—" Wizard Lenin considered that, mulled it over, then said surprisingly softly, *"You remind him of your mother."*

He didn't explain that.

He didn't have a chance as finally, finally, Ilyn was speaking.

His eyes were still locked on the compass, he still wasn't looking back, but he was speaking just loudly enough that she could catch what he was saying.

"You're to be enrolled in the mage academy, to work on magecraft with your human peers."

Lily, in the mage academy? She'd never thought about that, it'd never really seemed like an option for her. She'd passed by it often enough, but it'd seemed like a world she hadn't been given an invitation to.

And here he was, just telling her that not only could she go, but she would be at the drop of a hat.

"More, my clan has said that the Heart of the World can now be retrieved."

"The Heart of the World?!" Lily blurted despite herself, that was—that was actually huge news. She couldn't believe she hadn't heard anything through Frank yet.

Even Wizard Lenin paid attention to that part.

And what did that mean, 'can be retrieved', did that mean it would or it wouldn't, and what did that have to do with Lily?

However, despite her outburst, it seemed Ilyn was done.

She opened her mouth to prompt him again, but Wizard Lenin cut her off.

"Don't bother, he won't answer," Wizard Lenin scoffed.

"What do you mean he won't answer?" Lily asked.

"I don't know if it's stubbornness, pride, or just a defect in his personality but he only says what he believes he has to," Wizard Lenin said, not so much to comfort Lily but to explain what was even happening, *"I never even got him to explain why he'd shown up to fight for the cause."*

And Wizard Lenin had tried many times.

Wizard Lenin reflected back on what he knew about Ilyn, what he knew didn't amount to much. Ilyn had been private in all things, except for his friendship with Lily's mother, and that was only because that had been obvious to anyone with eyes.

"You know, it's funny," Wizard Lenin said with dark amusement, *"Funny, and I suppose the nature of sun elves, he was the one who told me how she'd die."*

(There was the implication there, that somehow, this had been what had caused her and everyone else to die.

If he'd kept his mouth shut, then it wouldn't have happened, but then again, being a sun elf, he'd known that he wouldn't.)

It was a beautiful day on the other side and she was now closer to the palace than she'd ever been before. Just like the first time she'd seen it, it sparkled in the sunlight, stone a glittering transparent looking marble that she'd never seen on Earth, sculpted into high arcs and decorated with gold and precious jewels.

The gold elves, Frank had once said, had made the entire city and the palace. They'd been told to make the palace the most beautiful building that anyone could imagine.

And while it looked as if it had stood forever, had always been so resplendent, she knew it could only be a decade old at most.

They entered through the great, gilded, gates that led to the palace, passing by human guards in the same uniform as Ilyn. They nodded at him and then looked at her, their eyes lingering on her hair, her eyes, and her Tellestrian clothes.

On the wall of the gateway, in gold and jeweled tiles, was a mosaic of some great battle of magic. In one corner was a group of night elves, cowering at the edge of the mosaic, attempting to flee from triumphant human forces led by a golden-crowned human king.

Lily had no time to linger, to look for familiar faces in the tiles, before she was pulled further in. They walked through a courtyard overflowing with gardens, in full summer bloom, filled with trilling birds, colorful flowers, and children running after butterflies in rich, colorful clothing. Their eyes, as the guards had, lingered on Ilyn then Lily as they passed.

Then the gardens were gone, they were inside, and she was being pulled down mirrored and gilded corridors. In the walls, she caught sight of her stunned reflection, a girl who could have been Ilyn's daughter for the similarities in their faces.

Then he pulled her into an office and without a word pushed her into a seat.

He took the seat across from her.

Lily let her eyes wander the room. It wasn't barren, there was furniture, but something seemed utilitarian about it. Every piece of furniture in the room looked like it had a practical purpose. The shelves were filled with a select few leather books, the walls taken up by maps, and the sole window had been left slightly ajar to let air in.

There was nothing personal, no hints of the owner's likes, dislikes, or even identity.

"So—" Lily started, watching as Ilyn's eyes flicked to hers. She let whatever useless thing she'd thought up die on her tongue.

He said nothing.

Outside, likely from the gardens, Lily could hear children's playful shouts.

"Good luck," Wizard Lenin offered dryly.

"So," Lily started again, forcing the words through her lips, "Why am I—Why am I here?"

"The regent demanded your return," Ilyn explained.

Except, it didn't sound like an explanation, more like a rote answer he'd memorized but no longer thought about.

"Regent?"

Another clearly regurgitated, rehearsed, line, "Your older cousin, he holds the throne until your cousin, Theyn, is of age."

Theyn, yes, she remembered that. There'd been her, Wheyn, and then Theyn the crown prince. She hadn't thought too much about him or the regent, for all she was a princess it hadn't seemed to have much to do with her.

"Why did he want me here?" Lily asked.

The man considered this, finally thinking about his response. His fingers tapped a steady rhythm against the desk.

Finally, he said, "It is politically expedient, for humans."

Now, Lily had thought she'd been doing very well.

She'd had the upper hand of having some idea of what was going on, why she was here, what was really happening, but at this she lost it, "Kidnapping me was politically expedient?!"

"For humans," he repeated, like that made any sense to anybody.

"Can you tell me why it's politically expedient for humans?"

She had the terrible, awful, feeling that he'd just say 'no' to that and stop talking. However, he must have been getting tired too.

THE HEART OF THE WORLD

Instead of remaining silent, he said, "You were going to be brought back when you were sixteen. However, the stars are in alignment and the Heart of the World can be fetched."

"So?" Lily blurted.

"Without you, it cannot be retrieved," Ilyn said flatly.

She blinked, tried to read his face, but he looked deathly serious.

The Heart of the World.

According to Frank, it might be able to make Wizard Lenin a body. It was an object she'd long since associated with Death, with the island, with a place humans weren't meant to reach. Nobody was sure what it did, but they all agreed on one thing—

It was an object of power.

"And why does the—uh—monarchy want it?" Lily asked, putting two and two together.

"Human politics," Ilyn supplied, and here, at last, was some expression of derision and contempt, "The regent has been led to believe it will solidify his claim on the throne."

Something clicked for Wizard Lenin that certainly hadn't for Lily.

"What, what is it?" she asked, knowing she wasn't going to get the answer out of this guy.

"It's politics," Wizard Lenin said with the equivalent of an amused shrug, *"As Theyn gets older, or even you for that matter, the regent's hold on the throne will become shakier. Not to mention that Questburger's very obviously favoring Theyn. He needs some great triumph to keep his hold on the throne."*

Such as fetching some mystical, all-powerful, mysterious object.

"Will it?" Lily asked out loud.

Both answered the same thing at the same time, "Doubtfully."

Lily sat back in her chair, trying to take it all in, "So—To clarify, I am on this MacGuffin quest, of which I must be a part or it's doomed to failure because reasons, all to make sure my cousin who I've never met stays king instead of my other cousin."

"Yes," Ilyn said easily.

Wizard Lenin was too entertained to make some catty remark, but he thought this was just like the monarchy, and he found it delightfully stupid.

Lily suddenly wished she'd been allowed to stay home.

She picked up Rabbit from where she'd deposited him on Ilyn's desk, placing him back in her lap, where he remained a warm, motionless, emotionless bundle of white fur.

"Can I go home?" she finally asked.

"Home?"

"You know, Tellestria," Lily clarified, stressing the word Tellestria slowly, to make sure he understood.

Ilyn just looked at her blankly, his eyes filled neither with remorse nor pity. For a moment, his was the cold, unfeeling, relentless face that destiny chose to wear as it looked down at her.

"How can you?" no smile, no hint of any expression at all on his face, "I burned your house to the ground."

6 IFF'S BRAVE NEW WORLD

In which Lily meets a man named Questburger, makes the acquaintance of her cousin the crown prince, Frank wins a bet, Wizard Lenin despairs, and Death asks Lily to keep a secret.

Lily wished she could say she stood up and walked out after Ilyn dropped that bomb on her head.

Unfortunately, she didn't.

Instead, Lily sat there like an idiot, staring at him while he stared back, both of them waiting for the other to do something first. At least, Lily was waiting for something, she couldn't speak for Ilyn.

If it wasn't for the occasional blinking the man could be a statue. A gangly painted statue by some student sculptor that a patron hadn't wanted to pay that much money.

Lily broke first, "Can I go now?"

"No."

God, he didn't even have to think about that, did he?

Lily waited one second, two, but he didn't add anything to that monosyllabic answer.

"Why can't I go now?" Lily pressed, after a pause she added, "I'm not going home, in case you were wondering, since you burned my house down."

That wouldn't have stopped her if she'd really wanted to, of course, but Ilyn didn't need to know that.

As it was, she wasn't sure what she was going to do next, what was even happening, all she wanted was time out of this room to think.

"My superior wishes to speak with you," Ilyn said stiffly, not looking particularly pleased or displeased by that fact.

"Oh," Lily responded.

One second, another, then she broke and asked, "Couldn't your supervisor have come to pick me up from Tellestria?"

"No."

Lily grit her teeth, shifted Rabbit back onto the desk, and tried to contain her temper.

She failed, "Don't you have better things to do with your time?"

The man just gave her a very unamused look in response.

It was clear from the look on his face that picking up Lily had been a chore right up there with mowing the lawn or taking out the garbage.

She was about to make some comment on how she'd never asked to be kidnapped, had never asked to be a part of this mysterious quest or be a mysterious princess, when the door opened.

She turned in her seat and watched as a man walked in.

He was undeniably human in the same way that Ilyn was undeniably an elf. He was one of those old men who hadn't shrunk just yet, who still struck a broad and intimidating figure, the kind that must have been even more impressive in his youth. His eyes were dark and steely, and as he stepped into the room in a uniform more put together and impressive than Ilyn's, Lily almost felt compelled to turn and look at him.

The man looked first at her, only for a moment, and then over to Ilyn, "Thank you, Ilyn."

Ilyn wasted no time. He stood in a fluid motion, vaulted over the desk, and was out the door in less than a blink of an eye, slamming it so hard behind him that the glass on the window rattled.

Well, he certainly knew how to make someone feel like chopped liver, didn't he?

"Questburger!" Wizard Lenin snapped, clearly meaning—the man.

Lily blinked once, blinked again, trying to match what she was seeing with the name Questburger.

Oh, she'd heard the name before. Wizard Lenin had mentioned the name more than once, never in a good context, and there'd been something or another about him in that history book she'd bought ages ago. She'd never seen a picture though and—well—hadn't spent much time thinking about a man named Questburger.

That was even worse than the Usurper.

Questburger was busy making his way to the seat that Ilyn had vacated. He spared only a glance for Rabbit, but he didn't ask, and instead looked across at her.

Lily suddenly felt—

She hadn't been prepared for this, not by a long shot, and her shorts, flip flops, and tank top were not what she'd have ordinarily worn to meet with any kind of political official.

"Tell him nothing," Wizard Lenin instructed.

However, before Wizard Lenin could add anything else, the man had started to speak. He offered a small, apologetic smile, "You must forgive Ilyn, he's a man of many talents but few manners."

"Right," Lily said dumbly, not sure what else to say.

The man reached out a hand, clearly intending for her to shake it across the desk, "I am Quion Questburger, a royal advisor."

Lily shook it, still feeling dazed.

She kept waiting for this to flip on its head. Maybe he'd light her shoes on fire the way that Ilyn had lit her house on fire, maybe he'd report knowing that she moonlighted as Lily Jones and throw her in the brig, maybe he'd throw her out the window.

She didn't need Wizard Lenin to tell her that nothing good was going to come out of this meeting.

These people had not just left her to her own devices for years but had only dragged her back when they needed her. If they'd wanted to make a good impression, then Ilyn wasn't the person to do it.

So, whatever this was couldn't go well.

"I understand you must be very confused," Questburger continued, "Tellestria, to my knowledge, has no knowledge of our world or magic in general. Until this morning, you were living a very different life, and I am sorry it took this long for this moment."

He looked as if he expected Lily to say something to that.

Lily's mouth did open, but it closed again just as quickly, as she somehow couldn't find the words to string "twelve years", "the Tylors", and "dumpster" into a sentence.

The man either took pity on her or had a pressing appointment, as he continued without prompting, "The truth of the matter is that you are not Tellestrian. You are not from the world you left this morning. You are from this one.

"You were born the only daughter of the late king's brother, Whye, and his wife the sun elf Lilyanna. You are a princess and second in line to our throne after your cousin, Theyn, and your name is Iff."

"Everyone calls me Ellie—" she blurted without thinking (truly without thinking as there were a lot of people these days who didn't call her Ellie Tylor either) and the man offered a kind, if amused, smile.

"Your souvenir from Tellestria," he said, not without sympathy, "I'm afraid you'll simply have to get used to Iff."

His expression turned grave then, "In ideal circumstances, you would never have had to bear two names at all. You would never have been sent to Tellestria in the first place."

And here—

Lily felt herself begin to listen despite herself. The decision to send herself away had been referenced by more than one person but had never truly been explained. A part of her couldn't help but wonder just how they were going to explain it.

"The decision to send you to Tellestria, to be raised beyond our borders and protection, was not an easy one," he began with a long sigh.

"There was a rebellion, ended by nothing short of a miracle, but it took a grave toll on our forces. The city was sacked, the kingdom in ruins, and even the palace had burned to the ground. We were left without a king or a queen, only a crown prince, who would not be ready to rule for many years. We were left with few surviving guards and even fewer mages."

He paused, as if to assess how Lily was taking this. The trouble was, Lily wasn't sure how she was taking it. This was much more detailed, frank, than that history ook had been. Oh, it'd acknowledged that things had gotten bad, everyone did, but it had glossed over just how bad.

And he hadn't gotten to the part where a decision was made.

"As your cousin, the crown prince, was to someday take the throne, he needed to fully understand his culture, people, and history in a way that could not be done outside the capital. We had enough guards for him, however, we did not have any to spare," Questburger explained.

He motioned towards her, not in an insulting manner, but more as if to silently redirect the conversation back to her, "Due to your mother's infamy, your heritage, and your proximity to the throne there was no safe place in this world we could send you. The elves, many of whom had made up the Usurper's rebellious forces, would have sought you out to use you against the kingdom."

"What do you mean?" Lily asked, brow furrowed.

The man stared at her as if he hadn't even realized then, with a dawning look on his face, said, "Your mother was an elf, that was—not ideal."

And Lily realized—

She'd heard as much before. Wizard Lenin had said it, Frank had said it, the books had said it, she'd known that she wasn't just a princess but a half-elf magical princess. The idea of being a princess had been so hard to swallow she'd never stopped to think about the elf part.

However, from what this man was saying, from the little bits Frank and Wizard Lenin had dropped, that was a real problem.

What he was saying was that because Lily wasn't fully human, because of her mother, elves like Frank would want to use her. It was true, too, that every time Frank brought up the monarchy, he brought up Iff, not her human cousin.

If Iff was an elf—

That could be important, or troublesome, for a lot of people when it was supposed to be a human ruler.

"Tellestria was safest for you," Questburger concluded, clearing his throat in an attempt to move past his previous sentence, "When you were an adult, when Theyn was ready for his corination, then you would have been retrieved and introduced back into our society."

Lily stared.

The thing was, it sounded reasonable.

She wasn't sure if it was because it was reasonable or Quesburger had made it somehow sound reasonable. He hadn't brought up the dumpster, hadn't brought up the Tylors, hadn't brought up the fact that Lily had died on multiple occasions with great flourish, but—from what he'd said Tellestria, Earth, hadn't been a terrible idea.

The way he spoke, sending her to Earth might have been the only thing they could do.

"It's convenient is what it is," Wizard Lenin spat, *"Don't be taken in, Lily. That man could make a cluster of hamsters opening a lemonade stand sound like the most reasonable thing in the world.*

"I'll tell you what he's really doing," Wizard Lenin continued, beyond incensed at Questburger's sheer gall, *"He wasn't protecting you; he was removing the competition. The longer you stuck around, the more some of the noble families might have remembered that your father should have been king, and if he had, then you'd have been first in line for the throne. Questburger here was only planning to bring you back when you were no longer a threat."*

"However, something unexpected has come up," Questburger said, jolting Lily from her thoughts, "There is to be an expedition to retrieve the Heart of the World, an item of legend and great power. You were designated to join this expedition and had to be retrieved much earlier than anticipated."

"Oh," Lily said lamely, still caught on what Wizard Lenin had just said.

"When you return from your journey," Questburger continued, "You're to be instructed in magic at our finest academy, just like your cousin, and claim your birthright from this world."

He folded his hands together, relaxed, and shifted. It was a sign that he'd reached the end of whatever it was he'd wanted to say, "Do you have any questions?"

It was, she suddenly realized, the first time anyone had stopped to ask if she had any. Usually, whoever gave her information either assumed she knew what they were talking about or else didn't care to explain anything.

She was drowning in the questions she wanted to ask.

One though, more than any of the others, had to be asked, "Was Tellestria really the only option?"

His face softened, became sympathetic, and he nodded, "I'm afraid it was."

He sighed again, a weary look on his face, "If we'd had the strength to spare, if we hadn't been recovering, you would have been raised here alongside your cousin. However, as much as it pains me to say, the Usurper decimated our forces. We've regained strength in these years since his disappearance, his demise, but it has taken all of those years and we are still frightfully weak."

His eyes sharpened and he leaned forward, making sure she was looking nowhere else, "No matter what anyone might say, no matter where you grew up or what you were told, you will always be a princess."

It was strange.

Some part of her was relieved.

Lily hadn't realized it, but some part of her must have been holding its breath for the past seven years. First, it'd been the idea that her parents hadn't wanted her, hadn't even bothered to remember her existence, throwing her away in the most insulting manner they could. Then, it'd been the idea that while her parents had died, Lily had still ended up in that place anyway. She'd still been thrown out, even as a princess, even as someone who was supposed to matter and—

Questburger had just given her the reason she'd never allowed herself to ask for.

It didn't mean Lily liked it, that she was okay with it, but it was something.

And he'd gone out of his way to do it too, she realized. He could have left all of this to Ilyn, who'd wanted to give her less than nothing. He could have done less than even that.

This man was a royal advisor, he had to be busy, and he'd still made time for her. He'd come into this office, which clearly wasn't his, and sat down to answer Lily's stupid questions about things everyone was supposed to know.

Then she remembered how she'd been picked up this morning.

"Why did you have my house burned down?" Lily asked.

He looked at first surprised, then, impossibly, sheepish, "I'm afraid that I told Ilyn to, if necessary, persuade you to return to your home country if you had reservations. I see he decided to resort to his old methods."

Somehow, Lily was not shocked by that.

Questburger quickly moved the conversation along, "I know this is all very new to you, I realize I have undoubtedly not explained nearly enough. This was not how I imagined your introduction to our world, but I'm afraid we're pressed for time. After you return from the expedition, I'll see to it you have the resources you need."

He smiled at her, not quite grandfatherly, but not cold either, "My office will always be open to you."

He didn't take the words back.

Lily sat, stared, but he didn't start sweating, looking away, or look like he didn't mean them.

His door would be open.

She thought about the fact that Wizard Lenin, Death, even Frank had never said those words to her. If there was a door, she'd always had to force her way through, always, through belligerence, lies, and even violence.

It hadn't struck her, until this moment, that it didn't have to be that way.

***

There was more after that.

Questburger detailed that the expedition, now that all party members had gathered in the city, was to leave as soon as possible. After a ceremony in the public square outside the palace, they would leave the next morning, meaning that Lily had to be packed tonight. Supplies had been set aside for her, along with clothing, but if Lily wanted any input on what to bring she'd best get to it.

Lily was then escorted through the hallway to her new, extravagant, quarters that really did look fit for a princess and supervised the packing. Mostly, she just ended up nodding at whatever they stuck in there, until only a blue uniform just like what Ilyn had worn was left out on the bed for her.

And then she was left to her own devices.

She sunk down on the bed, placing Rabbit next to her, trying to wrap her head around everything that had happened.

After seven years of knowing about it, seven years of mildly joking about it, she really was a princess.

They hadn't forgotten her after all, not for a second, and with what felt like a snap of their fingers she wasn't Ellie Tylor anymore. Ellie Tylor's house didn't even exist, she might never see the Tylors again, and—

And someone had offered her an open door.

"Need I remind you that he left you in a dumpster?" Wizard Lenin asked.

And Lily's mood soured.

"Questburger," Wizard Lenin started in, with malicious, vindictive, glee, *"Is a ruthless, heartless, power hungry, egomaniac who loves to call the kettle black. He has slithered his way as high into power as he could possibly go and will rule the kingdom through your sad little cousin the same way he's ruling it through your incompetent older cousin."*

"He didn't seem the slithering type," Lily noted dubiously, but Wizard Lenin wasn't having it.

"You've been won over in two seconds," he scoffed, *"You, who thinks all human beings are made from cardboard."*

"I haven't been won over," Lily retorted, crossing her arms, "It was just—look, it was cool of him to do any of that, alright? He didn't have to sit there for that, and he didn't have to offer an open door either. I appreciate it, that's all. Besides, he probably didn't know that some underling just left me in a dumpster—"

"Well, it wasn't as if he bothered to check," Wizard Lenin cut in, *"For all he knew, you could have been run over by a carriage and it'd be one less problem for him to worry about. The fact that you have died biweekly really tells you his priorities. After all, with a dead Iff, the elves are kept in line and the nobility kept happy. Everybody wins."*

"It's not like that!" Lily protested.

"How would you know what it's like?" Wizard Lenin balked, *"You have no context for anything. The best you have is what I tell you, what that tight-lipped pseudo brother god tells you, and what your vampire minion tells you. He can tell you whatever he likes and give you an 'open door'!"*

Wizard Lenin stopped, as if hit by something very heavy, *"You have no context for anything."*

He seemed struck by that thought, as if he'd never properly realized it before.

"Lily, take a nap," Wizard Lenin commanded.

"I don't have time for a nap!" she protested. God, if she was leaving this morning—did she fix the Tylor's house? Did she visit Frank and tell him not to expect her for a while? Did she hit the Blockbuster and rent every VHS she could? There were so many things to do and so little time to do them in.

"Make time," Wizard Lenin hissed.

She knew enough to know he wasn't going to take no for an answer.

"Alright, alright, fine!" Lily snapped, flopping back and closing her eyes, *"I'll make time."*

She hoped this wouldn't take too long.

Luckily, the bed was comfortable, maybe even unnaturally so. Perhaps she really was that tired, or maybe it was something about the bed, but she found herself drifting off before she knew it.

And, like typically happened in dreams, she found herself yanked somewhere else.

This time, it was an old-fashioned school classroom, the kind with wooden desks, a blackboard, and Wizard Lenin as a teacher standing at the front.

His usual tunic was gone, replaced, instead, by tweed and a pair of thick glasses. He looked like a sad, nerdy, far too good-looking professor.

Lily felt something in her die just looking at him.

"It's become apparent that I have severely neglected your education," Wizard Lenin said as he wrote on the board in large letters, "History 101/Questburger is a Prick".

Lily was still staring.

"Because you lack the context for everything, and judge the world based solely on television, you're liable to make grave mistakes."

Lily grimaced, wishing she could just will herself awake already, and asked, "Is this really necessary?"

"As I live inside your head," Wizard Lenin raged with all the fury of Thor, "Your lethal mistakes become my mistakes. I will not be killed a second time just because you think Questburger is Father Christmas!"

"I never said he was Santa—" Lily tried to cut in, but he wasn't having it.

He'd already turned back to the board and started drawing, circling three different words: Tellestrians, Elves, and Humans.

He turned back to her and pointed to the "Tellestrians" bubble with one of those long wooden sticks teachers used. It made an audible, sharp thwack against the board.

"As you know, Tellestrians are those humans who originally came from Earth," he began, "They are people who, often by accident, wander through a portal to this world and cannot or will not find their way home. Though, sometimes, you'll hear natives refer to those more than one generation out as Tellestrian."

"What about the rest of the humans?" Lily asked.

"They've been here much longer," Wizard Lenin said, "There have always been humans in this dimension, though they used to be a minority compared to the elves. Native humans consider themselves quite different from Tellestrians."

Here, he drew an arrow between "Tellestrians" and "Humans".

"The native human population tends to be either neutral or outright hostile to the Tellestrians. If the Tellestrian population were small, if it were only one or two that stumbled through a portal every few years, no one would notice. As it is, they're a sizable minority of the human population. As the population on Earth boomed, so did the Tellestrians."

Lily supposed that made sense, having never found a real portal herself, she hadn't thought much about accidentally stumbling through one. With so many people on Earth, though, she supposed it had to happen quite a bit.

"For much of their history in this world," Wizard Lenin continued, "Tellestrians often became vagrants and were left to fend for themselves. They were given no introduction to this world, no basic education, and no support. As a result, they were often seen as a stain on human society and inherently lesser than those who grew up in this world.

"Around fifty years ago, the king before the last king, your grandfather, created a set of policies to address the Tellestrian crisis. Those who wandered in from Tellestria are now educated, trained in trades, and if young enough and showing enough promise sent to the mage academy."

Wizard Lenin then drew a frowny face over the arrow between the two words.

"This was not a popular set of policies.

"Education costs money, tax money that Tellestrians often cannot pay for until they're fully trained, which meant that the native population shouldered the bill.

"Admission to the mage academy takes slots away from the locals. It likely takes a slot away from the nobility, as few if any commoners were ever able to attend.

"With more Tellestrians every year, and the belief that Tellestrians possess no magic or otherwise useful talents, a good portion of the native humans chafed at their kind treatment."

Wizard Lenin then offered her a fox-like grin, "Which, of course, was exactly what I took advantage of to recruit wealthy humans to my cause. They balked at the idea of my being backed by the elves, but the idea of tearing down a monarchy that had supported Tellestrians for fifty years, of actually closing the portals, well, it was too good to resist."

"Wait," Lily spluttered, "You don't even believe in Tellestrian scum?"

"God no," Wizard Lenin dismissed, as if it was that easy, "Humans are humans. If your friend Frank is to be believed, even the elves are humans. We all came through portals at one point or another. A Tellestrian is just as likely to be as intelligent, hardworking, and even magically gifted as anyone from this place."

"But what about all your passionate revolutionary zeal?!" Lily exclaimed, arms flailing, trying to reconcile Wizard Lenin's confession with the proud revolutionary who'd been living in her head for the past twelve years.

"Well," Wizard Lenin said, mulling it over, "I had to have passionate revolutionary zeal about something."

"But, then, why—" Lily started.

"Oh, I did want the monarchy out of power," Wizard Lenin clarified easily, "It's a corrupted, bloated, self-important machine fueled only by nepotism and greased by myopic ambition. If I had to continuously rant about how much I hated Tellestrians to do it, then so be it."

"But you ranted about it to me!" Lily pointed out.

That was the first thing he'd done when they'd met.

He went on this giant, scary, rant about how he was the Usurper, Crusher of Tellestrians, Closer of Portals, and the guy who set her parents on fire.

By the look on his face, Wizard Lenin had forgotten about that.

"I have a reputation to maintain," he offered after a long pause, "If you must know, it's not that I love Earth and all its wonders, I like to think I'm contemptuous of all things equally."

Lily couldn't even. She just couldn't.

"What does this have to do with Questburger?" she asked, rubbing at her head.

Wizard Lenin smiled brightly, as if Lily had asked exactly what he'd wanted her to, "Given the fact that you've now lived so long in Tellestria, picked up its culture, and never been educated here or had access to any magic, many will view you with more contempt than they otherwise would have. You, essentially, are Tellestrian. It will make you a much less appealing option to place on the throne.

"Questburger has systematically guaranteed you will never take the throne."

That seemed like a lot of work given Lily wasn't supposed to inherit anyway.

Wizard Lenin, however, didn't bother to look at her dubious expression.

"Which brings us," he said as he began drawing a line between "Elves" and "Humans, "To the elves.

"Human society goes back as far as the elves, but until a thousand years ago, was hardly prosperous. Everything before then was brutally controlled by the night elf empire, Xhigrahi. Only the elven clans posed any real (if minimal) threat to the ruling power, humans weren't even flies on the rader. Humans only took power after the fall of Xhigrahi, when they started practicing magic, and the human kingdom has controlled elven territories ever since.

"As a result, humans view themselves as better than both the Tellestrians and the elves. Humans have forgotten that once, a long time ago, they weren't even worth bothering with. They don't like to be reminded of that fact."

He gave Lily a pointed look, "The idea that an elf, worse the child of an elf and a human, could rule over humanity isn't just a joke but a grave insult. I guarantee that more than one person was inclined to throw you into that dumpster at the first opportunity and I guarantee Questburger was fully aware of this."

Lily was starting to wonder if there was a point to all this.

She also wondered how long Wizard Lenin could keep going for.

"As for the elves," Wizard Lenin said, motioning to the third circle, "They're a very diverse group, as you've heard from Frank, but the long and short of it is that they hate each other and dislike humans almost as much. Thousand year grudges between the clans are not easy to overcome. As for the humans, after the fall of Xhigrahi they just filled the power vacuum left behind, tearing away any hope the clans had for freedom, and using the clans' own spells to do it."

"Wasn't that Questburger's whole point?" Lily cut in, "The elves hate humans, putting me anywhere near the throne is bad news bears because of it. I probably would have been kidnapped by the elves before I hit two and there'd be rebellion everywhere."

"You'd think so," Wizard Lenin said, as he made a small frowny face above his latest arrow, "But that's not the case."

Wizard Lenin began writing the seven major clans down on the board,

"The love elves might have tried to find you, except they were my staunchest allies and loathe the human monarchy almost as much as they do the night elves. They'd have sooner killed you to make a statement.

"The moon elves rarely think that far ahead about anything. With the fighting over, they probably couldn't even be bothered.

"The night elves would simply eat you. If the sun elves haven't shown up yet, they're not going to. The mind elves never bother with anything outside of their studies, the happiness elves are a joke, the gold elves are too dependent on the stability of human society, and the other clans are so small and magically incompetent they don't even deserve to be mentioned."

He turned back to her, "The truth is the elves are just a convenient excuse everyone can believe in, designed to dump you in Tellestria and cement the nice human boy's claim on the throne while reassuring the nobility that the monarchy does not take Iff seriously."

Wizard Lenin dropped his chal and backed away from the board, surveying it at a distance, "The truth is that Questburger's the sort of man who would gleefully stab you if he thought it'd serve his purposes. You think that door is open, Lily, I just dare you to try it and see where it gets you."

Lily looked at him, then at the board.

That board might just be the saddest thing she'd ever seen.

"I'm going to see Frank," Lily announced before he could ask her anything else.

***

It was somewhere between midnight and three in the morning by the time she got to Jones Inc. It was that ungodly hour where either magical adventures began or nothing good could possibly happen to you.

Lily, having been kidnapped only that morning to another dimension, was arguably experiencing both.

She stepped into the building with a sigh, exhausted, holding more VHS tapes than she should have been able to carry. Unable to spend time picking after she'd run home to fix the Tylors' house, she'd ended up taking the entire store with her. She could only hope she'd taken the good ones.

"Frank!" she shouted as one of the tapes began to slip towards the floor, stopped only by Lily's blatant manipulation of reality, "I could use a little help here!"

Wizard Lenin was disgusted.

"Shouldn't you be focusing on the journey ahead?" he asked, as having apparently gotten his Questburger rant out of his system, he was all ready for adventure.

"If what Ilyn and Questburger say is true, if the Heart of the World is coming into

play, then this is our chance," the opportunity, in other words, the one Wizard Lenin had been waiting seven years for.

Everything suddenly seemed to be an obstacle for him, even Lily stopping at a Blockbuster, just one more thing standing between him and the real world.

She was glad he was happy about all of it, because she was kind of miffed.

Oh, she'd thought about leaving Earth, she'd wondered why no one had come to pick her up, she'd just wished it'd been on her terms. She'd thought she had her whole life to decide, to weigh one against the other, or even pick neither. Instead, her opinion hadn't mattered at all.

She supposed she could go home and wait for Ilyn or whoever to show up again but—

It seemed as if a great door had slammed shut in Lily's life and there was no reopening it.

Frank stuck his head out of the back office, blinking at her wearily, even when it was the middle of the day for him, "Yes?"

Rather than say anything, Lily nodded down at the massive pile of VHS tapes in her hands.

He looked at it in confusion, but exited the office, and walked over to take some of the load off her hand. He looked for space in the already cluttered building.

Finding nothing, he escorted her over to a closet, set the tapes down, then dug around in a corner until he'd retrieved what looked like a hatbox. With a muttered word, a small motion of his hand, he opened the box and revealed a great black pit inside. Gratefully, Lily placed the tapes one by one into the box, watching their colorful covers disappear into the void, where they floated gracefully like falling leaves until they disappeared from sight.

Then he closed the lid and wrote over the top in looping, fancy, barely legible writing, "Boxes".

"VHS tapes," Lily corrected.

He crossed out "Boxes" and wrote "VHS Tapes" without a word. Then the box was back in the closet.

And Lily, for the first time in hours, breathed a sigh of relief.

"You do realize you forgot the VCR, right?"

"Goddammit, Lenin!"

The worst part was that he could have said that much earlier, when she'd still been on Earth, but he'd chosen not to just to be petty and vindictive.

"If I am petty and vindictive it's you who made me that way," Wizard Lenin sniffed with an ingrained feeling of superiority.

Somehow, she really doubted that.

Wizard Lenin was many things. However, being not petty and not vindictive were not any of them.

Lily tried to ignore her sudden headache, sighing as she noted to Frank, "I'll have to pick up a VCR later."

"What?" Frank asked.

"For the tapes," Lily said, nodding towards the closet.

By his blank smile, once again, Frank had no idea what she was on about.

Lily stared at him for a long moment, thinking of every interaction she'd ever had with Frank over the years. She thought about the moment she met him, all the times she'd barge in without warning, and even now when she showed up in the middle of the night with what to him had to be mysterious relics.

"Frank, do you just do everything I tell you to?" Lily asked.

There was a long, daming, pause.

"No, of course not," Frank said with that same blank smile.

Lily decided that she was going to let that one lie.

She guessed that meant it was time for the announcement, as much as she really didn't want to make it.

Lily never had seen too much, or any, of Lily Jones's other night elf goons. Normally, it was juts her and Frank, but they deserved some parting speech or an explanation of why she wouldn't be around for weeks, months—god, it wouldn't be years, would it?

Not to mention the whole plan to dump her in the mage academy. That was going to eat up a lot of time, wasn't it?

"Even if there was no quest," Wizard Lenin said, hesitating and shuddering at the word 'quest', which he felt made the whole thing sound silly, *"You would still be put into the mage academy. Even the most hopeless of the royal family are sent there. Given your aptitude for magic, whenever they decided to come for you they'd have thrown you in without question."*

Lily, he thought, would become a tool of state warfare. She'd be the black sheep due to the embarrassment of genetics, but gleefully sent out to quell elven and human rebellion alike.

There was some thought here of Wizard Lenin's own childhood and young adulthood, of wars and rebellions not his own that he had defended the kingdom against, but it was shuffled over too quickly by darker thoughts to see.

All she could make out were his eyes, so pale and blue, the great fires, and the blood.

"Lily?"

Lily turned to see Frank looking at her.

"Things have—changed," Lily settled on, "Drastically and very recently, a meeting's probably in order. You know, with everybody."

Frank looked at her for a moment, red eyes bright and burning in the dark, but he silently nodded and snapped his fingers. Shadows bloomed like a flower between his thumb and index finger, rising upward and outward in plumes of smoke. It rose to the ceiling then dripped down in the forms of six other night elves.

They were all equally Frank-like in appearance. All tall, dark haired, pointy eared, red-eyed, with the same delicate features that Frank had.

Still, of all of them, it was somehow Frank who stood out. Maybe it was his shorter hair, cut shorter than most in this dimension, or maybe it was the fact that she knew his face and saw him so often. Maybe he looked just a bit more tired than everyone else, overworked and haggard, but always ready to take on one more task.

She didn't know what it was, but something separated Frank from the herd.

"You called, Frank?" a woman, Faghiehagne or something Queally unpronounceable that Lily had never gotten around to memorizing, asked with a leering grin. Emphasis on Frank, there, as if the name itself was some delightful insult that never got old.

Lily waved, cutting Frank off before he could tell her off (looking strangely more intimidating than he ever did when talking to Lily), "Nope, I called."

All their eyes turned to her.

It really was intimidating, Lily thought, uncomfortable in a way she hadn't thought this would be. She summoned a soap box for herself to stand on, clearing her throat as she looked her audience over, and tried to look authoritative even with a rabbit balanced on the top of her head, "I—uh—have very recently been kidnapped by the government."

You could hear the sound of a pin dropping.

"Why must you be yourself at every opportunity?" Wizard Lenin asked.

Lily ignored him, "The government has told me that I'm going to be going on a quest to fetch the Heart of the World, with—people I haven't met yet. It's going to be exciting. I was then told I would be shipped off to the mage school when I get back. So, if you're wondering where I am—that's probably where I am."

"Wait," said one of the men, whose name was also an unholy conglomeration of consonants that Lily had failed to memorize, "The monarchy decided to kidnap you, Lily Jones, to send you to fetch the Heart of the World, then dump you into the mage academy?"

"Yes," Lily said.

They stared at her in dubious silence.

Lily broke with a wince, figuring there was nothing for it, "They um—also think I'm Princess Iff, not Lily Jones, for some reason."

You could hear the sound of a speck of dust softly landing on the floor.

They stared, jaws slack, eyes wide, no expression at all on any of their faces as they just tried to process her words.

As a group, they had lost all capability of speech.

"Lily, what is wrong with you?" Wizard Lenin asked.

"Oh come on, there's a celebration in a town square, they were going to—"

"What have I told you every time you have set foot in this godforsaken building?"

"—Stop being an idiot?" Lily asked, as that was really Wizard Lenin's catch phrase if there was any.

"Don't let them know you're not Lily Jones!"

She hadn't said she wasn't Lily Jones. She'd just said that the monarchy, for some inexplicable reason, thought she was Princess Iff.

"You walked in with red hair, you dolt!"

And that reason was because she really looked like Princess Iff, funny how that happened.

Lily opened her mouth again to mitigate the damage, deflect somehow, but she noticed Frank grinning. Grinning slyly, like someone about to devour a savory, well-earned, meal that he had been anticipating for years.

"I guess this means I win the bet," he said gleefully.

The spell was broken. Instead of descending on Lily like flies on a corpse, they were raging at Frank, cursing and yelling at him en masse.

"Goddammit, you sneaky bastard!" one of them cried, "She probably told you herself!"

"Oh come on," Frank said, smug beyond belief, "It wasn't that hard to figure out. She left a bloody note saying he'd be disposed of. Now, she could have left that to chance, or she might have gone and done it herself then disposed of the girl."

Lily was very confused. She supposed she should be grateful that none of them seemed concerned that Lily Jones was claiming to be a much younger girl.

Frank, still looking absurdly pleased with himself, pulled an old leather-bound book from his cloak and began flipping through pages.

"Now, let's see, I have written here that you, Jaekhaenig, had a substantial bet riding on spontaneous combustion. Faghiehagne and Kalinahrihga are down for God itself breaking thousands of years of silence to strike the man down in his prime," Frank's red eyes skimmed further, "And, well, there's all these other explanations I'm sure you remember. I really do like the resurrected Emperor Yaghiroshnik, by the way, completely incorrect but so patriotic."

Frank closed his book with a sense of finality, "So, the way I see it, I won the entire pot—and no one agreed with me. Such a pity for the rest of you."

"You're such a whipped piece of shit, Frank!"

This was followed by an eruption of arguing voices, vulgarities that would make a sailor blush, thrown objects, and a very cheerfully smiling

Frank.

Lily waited for Wizard Lenin to chime in and explain what was happening.

He was usually so good at that.

"They made a betting pool—" he said almost dazed, followed by a horrible anger, *"They made a betting pool off my demise?!"*

Apparently, he wasn't going to explain what was happening.

"Congratulations Frank," Lily offered, as if she completely was in on the joke, then added, "What's happening exactly?"

Frank gave her an odd look, "Well, boss, it appears you assassinated Jones, assassinated the princess, and are planning to infiltrate the royal family."

Oh.

Oh—Lily could see why they'd come to that conclusion. Princess Iff dies in a horrible accident, is sent away where no one sees her, then guess who shows back up suddenly as Princess Iff.

She didn't dare correct them.

"Yeah, I'm really sneaky like that," was what she ended up saying with a small laugh.

"Pity she didn't pick the boy," one of the others said, "Then she'd get the crown."

"Well, he's one small accident away from losing that position," another one commented with a meaningful look towards the other.

"So many plans," Lily hastily interjected before they started plotting her poor cousin's murder right then and there, "So many plans and so little time to do them in. Oh, this has been great. Really great."

"I told everyone," Frank said with a sniff, ignoring the way they glared at him, "Well, not about Iff, but I told them that Jones's death wasn't natural. The man didn't seem the type to set himself on fire."

Before another round of arguing could start up, Lily clapped her hands and said, "Great talk, everybody! So glad we got together for this!"

They seemed to realize they were dismissed, because they slunk back into the shadows, sinking through the floor and out of sight to wherever it was they loitered when she wasn't looking.

Then it was just Frank and Lily.

Frank was still smiling to himself, looking pleased as punch. When he caught her looking his smile softened slightly.

"At least this time," he said, "You had the decency to tell us where you're going."

At first, she almost asked when he was talking about, but realized he must have been talking about the real Lily Jones. The real Lily Jones who had disappeared and hadn't come back.

"Do I not usually?" Lily asked.

"No," Frank said quietly, "No, the first time you said you'd be back in a few years. You didn't say where you were going or why. You just disappeared then showed up again. The second time, though, you looked at me and said—you said you were taking a holiday."

"A holiday?" Lily asked.

"Just that, a holiday," Frank confirmed, "Then you walked out the front door."

He paused, looked over at her with eyes that were warm for all their eerie crimson glow, "But you did come back. It took decades, but you came back."

Decades ago, Lily Jones had stood in this spot, in this room filled with merchandise that would then have been out of place and time, and she'd walked out the door. Then Lily, decades later, had unwittingly taken her place so easily that not a single person had ever questioned it.

Suddenly, Lily was struck by a feeling of ill omen, as if this was a sign of—of something, something she should pay attention to, and yet something she had no power to change.

"A decade here, a decade there," Frank continued with that same smile, "It doesn't mean as much to us as it would to a human. Go to your human academy, if you think you have to, though god only knows you don't have to. We'll be here when you get back."

Lily could only nod, still struck by that strange feeling, as she made her way out the door and decided to walk her way back to the palace.

Hands in her pockets, she tried to pinpoint the source of her feelings. When that failed, she found her mind wandering back to the quest.

They really hadn't given her much of a turnaround, and that seemed to be intentional.

Maybe it was just Lily, but for all Questburger's assurances, she didn't think Wizard Lenin was entirely wrong. She got the feeling that Princess Iff wasn't wanted here. Waiting until sixteen might have been the plan, but nobody had been begging for her to come back either, and nobody besides Questburger had made time for her since she'd arrived.

These same people had once lobbed Lily into a dumpster at the soonest opportunity.

Something was wrong here, some intrinsic thing that she didn't know enough about to pinpoint.

'I told you, your mother was an elf,' Wizard Lenin reminded her, along with the silent thought that Lily's very existence was a national embarrassment, as the then crown prince, her father, had wedded and bedded the last person in the world he should have.

Maybe, probably, Wizard Lenin would know more about that than she would. Still, where did that leave her? Twelve-year-old Ellie Tylor—no, twelve-year old Iff, summoned for this great quest to find the Heart of the

World along with a band of trusty fellow adventurers. It really was like *The Lord of the Rings* or *Indiana Jones*, wonderous artifacts in a land filled with magic and mystery.

It was hands down more interesting than anything she'd been doing as Ellie Tylor.

Except, no one would ever call her Ellie Tylor again, not any more than they'd think to call her Lily. She was only twelve years old and already she had three different names to go by and only one used at a time.

The streets were quiet, empty of people this early in the morning.

Looking up, the stars were bright and glittering even with the moon's light diluting them.

Lily stared upwards as she walked, skipping from cobblestone to cobblestone, past fountains, temples, marketplaces, and storefronts until she made her way past the guards guarding the palace.

The sun would be rising soon, the quest would begin, but until then, it was just Lily trying to piece it all together.

Or at least, it should have been.

Halfway through the first set of palace gardens she stopped, blinked, and realized she wasn't as alone as she should have been. Here, in the magical hour between midnight and three in the morning, was someone who wasn't a vampire or a kidnapped princess, but a young unassuming boy sitting on one of the benches with a thick leather-bound tome in his hands.

The thing was that unassuming really was the word for him. Even with his uncomfortably stiff posture, his finely made clothes, there was nothing about him that caught the eye. In a world with a rainbow of hair colors, his was an ordinary, even mousey, brown. His face, though pleasant enough and hardly ugly, edged on being plain. There was nothing good, bad, or defining about him to draw the eye and keep it there. His eyes, even at a distance, were also the kind of brown you saw in nearly everyone's eyes.

In a world where people could look like anything but human, here was a boy who would look right at home on Earth, one of the faceless adolescent masses who'd grow up into a faceless adult.

Staring down at this book, he seemed hopelessly lost as he mouthed syllables, searching fruitlessly for something he just wasn't seeing.

Then, maybe feeling the weight of her eyes, he looked up.

"Ah!" he cried, fumbling with the tome and dropping it onto the grass. He frantically picked it back up, wiped off the dew, even as he blathered, "Sorry, I'm so sorry, I didn't think anyone would be up and I didn't mean to alarm anyone and—"

He paused, looked at her again, squinting in the dark to make out her features. An entirely different expression crossed his face, one of curiosity, anxiety, and wonder, "Iff, you're Iff! They said you would be coming today. Or, well, tomorrow and—"

He tucked the book under one arm and made his way over to her. He shook her hand with a little too much hesitance and vigor all at once, "Sorry, I'm Theyn, your cousin. We've never met, I know, and I think there's some official ceremony tomorrow or something. I've always wanted to meet you—"

He kept talking, or at least, his lips kept moving but whatever he was saying was drowned out by a ringing in her ears and Wizard Lenin's sudden irrepressible rage.

"This sniveling creature is the crown prince?"

There was a thought, almost hidden, that there was something very important about Iff's cousin that demanded Wizard Lenin's attention. Whatever it was, though, was hidden from her, shut off by a thick wall of memory, and so she could only stare at the prince and listen to the thought that he was nothing like what Wizard Lenin had been promised.

"—And then Ilyn, my tutor, told me that he was going to get ou today for the journey and I just couldn't help but think—Well, I don't really know, except I hope—" he cut himself off, a touch of concern and self-doubt in his expression, "I hope you don't find me disappointing."

He seemed to be waiting for an answer to this one. Lily gathered herself and lamely supplied with what she hoped was a reassuring smile, "I find you—um—loquacious?"

The blank look on his face told her that he didn't know the word, his eyes silently moved to Rabbit then back to Lily, "Is that good?"

"It's—um—not bad?" Lily winced, not great she supposed, but it wasn't the worst thing in the world.

Even if Theyn could have cut everything he'd said down into two sentences rather than twenty.

He grinned and said with genuine feeling, "I'm so glad you're here."

Lily could only stare.

Questburger had been polite, courteous, but he hadn't said he was glad to see her or acted like it. Death never said it out loud for the obvious bittersweet reason that her visiting him was her own demise. Wizard Lenin was stuck with her whether he liked it or not. Frank thought Lily was a different person entirely. Everyone else, especially the Tylors, barely tolerated the fact that Lily was in their lives.

Yet, here was this plain boy, this stranger she'd met from another world, who meant every word of it.

"Thank you," was all she could say.

He paused at that, maybe expecting more of a reaction, but soon enough smiled and pulled her to the bench. He started jabbering away, grabbing Lily's hand like it was the most natural thing in the world.

"I'm sure you have so many questions," he said quickly, "Ilyn's a great tutor, he even teaches a few classes at the academy on elemental mage craft, but he doesn't exactly talk much—"

"They have Ilyn teaching children?" Wizard Lenin asked in quiet horror.

There were vivid flashbacks of his own violent revolution and Ilyn's starring role inside it. He tried to equate the bloodstained elven war god he knew with someone who taught children magic.

Even having spent one afternoon in his presence, Lily had to agree with Wizard Lenin's baffled and horrified assessment.

"Anyway," Theyn continued, "If you have any questions, I'm sure I can answer some."

"Right, the quest thing," Lily said as she sat down next to her cousin, "Why are we going on this quest thing again?"

Ilyn had barely given an answer, might as well have grunted, and while Questburger had gone into a little more detail he'd danced around the actual topic. They'd both said Lily had to go on the quest, neither had said why.

Theyn paused, considered this, and said, "Well, I suppose it's because the sun elves finally said it could be done."

He nodded over at her, seemingly without realizing it, "Ilyn, he's a sun elf, says that the sun elves have always been able to see things better than the other elf clans and humans, the future especially is their domain. All the prophecies come from them, and for forever, they've said nobody could fetch the Heart of the World."

The sun elves, Lily remembered suddenly, had been given the gift of Death's green eyes. Her own eye-color…

"People tried, of course, but it never worked out," Theyn said with a shrug, before glancing at her with a small, almost wondering, smile, "Then, all of a sudden, they're saying that it can be done if you take the right people. You're one of the right people."

"Me?" Lily asked, motioning to herself, feeling that feeling of overwhelming destiny again. Theyn nodded earnestly.

"Wheyn, our older cousin, thinks that it might be because you're half sun elf. He thinks it's—um—a ploy by the sun elves for publicity or power or something. Everyone argued for a very long time, half the noble families didn't want you back at all just to prove a point. In the end, they decided it was just easier to take you along than risk it. So, here we are."

It really had been political?

Ilyn had said it, Wizard Lenin had said it, even Questburger had hinted at it but—she hadn't thought it'd be that political.

She hadn't thought much of the politics of this place at all. It'd always just been the other side, the place Wizard Lenin came from, and then the place so fantastical, colorful, and foreign it looked like it should have come out of an animated television show.

When Lily came, it was always to play her almost televised role, either as an elf gangster or now a half-elf princess. She hadn't realized that this was a real place that had real politics just like anywhere on Earth.

Even though Wizard Lenin had said it, multiple times, she hadn't realized Princess Iff was such a controversial figure.

"It's not as if, for some reason, we needed Questburger to get it through your thick skull," Wizard Lenin said scathingly.

She ignored him as she thought about the fact that there had been a debate, a very heated debate she'd nearly lost, over whether to bring her back at all.

"Of course, all this just means that I can't sleep and am trying to memorize more spells than I can hope to remember," Theyn admitted with a self-deprecating smile, nodding towards the thick tome next to him.

Quickly enough he brightened, smiled, and nodded towards it again, "Would you like to see one I've been working on?"

Looking at his eager face Lily had the feeling 'no' wasn't an answer.

She was kind of curious.

Lily had perused spell books, but never been able to make much sense of them. Everything she'd wanted she'd been able to do herself, anyway, and with Wizard Lenin always nattering about rules and things the practice of magic had just sounded exhausting.

The only real magic she'd seen had been from Death, in a world that didn't exist, Wizard Lenin inside her head and the world beyond death, Frank, and just this morning Ilyn.

She'd never seen a true blue human perform magic before.

Theyn quickly glanced at the book for reference. He stood, lifting both hands out in front of him, and started to gesture slowly and stiffly. He spoke in a voice that tried too hard to be solemn, "Oh bright eternal flame within my soul and the soul of my people, flow through my blood and body and out through my fingertips. Blind and burn the unworthy and unwanted who gaze upon me without soul, heart, and mind!"

At the end of this rhythmic over dramatic chant, a small pitiful orange flame the size of a candle's flame emitted from the tip of Theyn's index finger.

He looked down at his hand in disappointment then turned to her.

"That was—" Lily trailed off, not entirely sure how to politely finish that sentence.

"Pitiful," Wizard Lenin finished for her, *"And embarrassing, embarrassing for all of us."*

"At least there was fire this time," Theyn said weakly, with a small shrug. He looked over at her and asked the worst possible question, "Would you like to try?"

Oh, oh no.

"Come on," he said, pulling her to her feet. He placed the thick book in her hands, pointing to the words he'd just said at the bottom of the page. Like all spells, it was accompanied by a diagram of the hand motions he'd been trying to follow.

"If you're going a quest you're going to need to know a little magic," Theyn said to her, "I heard there aren't any mages in Tellestria, it's going to be really hard to catch up outside the walls and—"

Lily felt her eyebrows raising. She knew he didn't mean it, he sounded sincere, but she had the distinct feeling she was being talked down to.

Without a word, without any hand motions, she sent for a great inferno from her own soul. It weaved its way up and out of her body, towards the sky, in a great pillar of fire.

Thyen gaped, staring upwards, and for a moment Lily wondered if she'd gone too far.

Then he laughed, a desperate but amused laugh, as he cried out, "Of course you'd be better at magic than I am!"

He collapsed onto the bench in hysterical giggles. Lily stared as he lost it, just lost it. It took him several seconds to calm down enough to admit, "I've always been an awful mage. I've no talent for it. Everyone knows it, even if Ilyn's the only one who will say it to my face."

His smile fell somewhat as he shrugged again, "Except, because I'll be king, because of—because of the Usurper, I have to be good. So, we all just pretend and—and I'm expected to become some kind of mage-king when I can't master the simplest spells."

He smiled over at her, and while it was a sad thing there were no hard feelings in it, "I'm glad one of us has the knack for it."

***

Rather than sleep, she took what might be her last chance to visit Death.

There was so much to explain, too much, and it'd only occurred to her after she'd gotten back to her new room that, being on a quest, she might not have the time or space to kill herself without being noticed.

Wizard Lenin had wandered off, having no patience to sit and recap what had happened to Death. That, and Lily suspected he was still upset about Questburger. He'd get over it sooner or later, he always did.

In the meantime, it was Death and Lily at a table with tea.

"I was beginning to wonder if they'd come for you," Death said, an oasis of calm familiarity on a world that had been flipped upside down for Lily.

"You were?" Lily asked, "You could have warned me."

"Your world isn't always like mine," Death responded easily, "I didn't know if it would happen."

Lily frowned, but she supposed he had hinted at something like this.

Hadn't he said he'd been a few years older than she'd been at five when he'd discovered magic and another world? A few years could have been seven, which would have made Elliott Tylor twelve years old.

"It will be better than the Tylors," Death insisted, "You'll make friends in this world, wonderful friends, and it'll be like home in no time at all."

That was a tall order. Though, Lily supposed there was Theyn, not only close to her age but—nice and open.

Death smiled at her, reached out and ruffled through her thick red curls, "Quests have a way of bringing people together."

"Fair enough," Lily agreed, unable to help her own smile in response.

She then took his hand in hers, squeezed it, and decided to press for details, "What about this Heart of the World business. You went on this quest, didn't you?"

Maybe the Heart of the World that existed in this place was one that, somehow, Death had brought with him.

Death's smile dimmed, his eyes drifted from hers to trace the Heart of the World in the clearing. After a long moment, he said, "Lily, the Heart of the World is something that has no right to exist. It only attracts violence and death. By its nature, it's a thing of creation and destruction."

He turned back to look at her, "When you find it, you must destroy it."

Lily felt his hands slip from hers.

She thought about Wizard Lenin, about his body, about this being the only thing that might do it in seven years of looking.

"This is what Lenin's looking for," she said carefully, "Death, he's been waiting for years for this, ages, I can't just—"

"I will not lie and say I know this man, your Lenin, as I knew the Usurper in my world," Death said, taking her hands again and gripping them tightly, "I don't know what wonders or horrors he's capable of, but I'm afraid of the power the Heart of the World would bring him."

Death's eyes, as he stared at her, were filled with stars burning so brightly as they destroyed themselves in the vast emptiness of space. In them, Lily could see the consequences of a decision she had yet to fully consider.

Death had once hinted Lily would have an opportunity to restore Wizard Lenin's body, he'd told her she should take it, that if she did the world would burn for it.

She wondered how much she believed that.

There was a faint possibility, one she'd never really dared to consider, where Wizard Lenin didn't leave simply because she didn't want him to. Lily had always existed with Wizard Lenin, once he left, there was no guarantee she wouldn't suddenly transform into either Ellie Tylor or Princess Iff.

There had been no question that she would help Wizard Lenin leave, do everything she could, and even if she'd wondered if it would ever happen she'd believed in her heart of hearts that he'd manage it. He would return to his revolution and the world, she'd be—somewhere else.

That was how it was supposed to go.

Except, now, Death asked to put Wizard Lenin on one side of a scale and everything else on the other.

"You cannot give it to him, Lily," Death insisted, his words either a prayer or a note of warning.

Except, the thing was, it wasn't Death's world. He'd left his world, come to this place, and he was only a guest here. He had no right to its future, and had said as much himself.

He should have remembered that.

7 THE FELLOWSHIP OF THE MACGUFFIN

In which Lily catches a glimpse of her carefully chosen quest companions, listens to several speeches filled with both pomp and circumstance, and unwittingly plants a cruel and terrible seed.

"It's hot out here," Lily noted to Wizard Lenin as she stared out at the crowd.

They were gathered in the grandest square in the city, the one just outside of the place. A stage had been erected and Lily had been pushed onto it along with several others who seemed to have more of an idea of what they were doing and why they were here.

So far, she'd just been standing here, listening as what looked like important people gave speeches about—something.

It was so oppressively hot and humid that Lily was having difficulty paying any kind of attention to any of it.

It hadn't been as bad the day before, in part because she'd been in shorts and flip-flops. However, the uniform they'd given her, while certainly flashy and aesthetically pleasing, hadn't been designed for this kind of weather. The dark color absorbed all the heat, the thick fabric alone would have trapped the heat in, and all she could think about was the sweat rolling down the back of her neck and dripping inside her leather boots.

You'd think with all the manipulation of reality flying around, that somebody would have figured out fans, air conditioning, or anything. However, according to Wizard Lenin, that was advanced or else verboten, and Lily had to be as miserable out there as everyone else in case Questburger was watching and taking notes.

Maybe, if it'd just been hot, she wouldn't have minded so much. Oh, sure, placing Rabbit on her head hadn't been one of her greatest ideas, and maybe her feet were killing her, but if it'd at least been interesting then she would have been alright.

It wasn't just hot though; it was also unbelievably boring.

The current minister was speaking very eloquently about something. It was probably something that had to do with the quest, the kingdom, and maybe something else except that had been exactly what the last minister and the minister before that had talked about.

Standing up here, all that Lily could think was that she wasn't seeing why she'd been so vital to operations that they'd kidnapped her for it. Anyone could stand here and listen to this.

"That's because you don't realize how monumental this is," Wizard Lenin sniffed and—god, was he actually interested in any of this? The Heart of the World, sure, but the way everyone had talked yesterday there was a ways to go before that.

"The seven great clans, Lily, have been brought together to retrieve a divine object," Wizard Lenin explained, *"You'll never see the likes of this again."*

Well, it was Lily's personal opinion that she wouldn't have been missing out on much.

Lily side-eyed her new companions, trying to pick out who must be who.

Well, Ilyn standing right next to her in the same clothes as yesterday, looking as bored and miserable as Lily herself, had to be the sun elf representative.

Next to him was a stunningly beautiful woman, the kind of woman that had belonged to Hollywood's golden age and certainly not on this stage. With wine-red hair, purple eyes, and a strange almost hypnotic air about her Lily was going to guess she was the love elf.

Next to her was a sneering, stoic, muscular man who screamed trained warrior in all directions. He had a multitude of weapons strung across his back, in case one wasn't enough she supposed, along with shockingly white hair and yellow eyes.

That had to make him the moon elf.

Next to their resident expert in arms and future quest meat shield was an oddly diluted looking elf. His hair, his eyes, everything about him looked opaque, almost pastel, and he stared out at the audience with a contented smile that made it seem like he didn't have a single idea what was going on. In fact, he looked like he never had any idea what was going on and didn't care that he would never have an idea what was going on. Everything about him was haphazard, his clothes like they'd just been thrown on, his pack only half-packed, and his hair put through one terrible haircut.

Probably the happiness elf.

Then of course, the familiar Mr. Gold Elf Clan Head, who was looking even more impressive than usual in his regal attire. Of course, he hadn't looked as impressive when he'd caught sight off her and nearly fallen off the stage in shock. He now spent every few seconds staring at Lily as if waiting for her to jump into the crowd and start eating the townspeople.

Lily did feel a little awkward about that. She wasn't sure how to clear up that misunderstanding without admitting something she didn't want to, but she also didn't want him to suffer a heart attack over this.

Lily skipped over the blonde, seemingly human, little girl standing next to him. The girl was staring out resolutely into the crowd with a defiant expression on her young face. She looked as if she was trying to convince someone that she had every right to be in this dysfunction conga line that had been assembled.

She seemed to be taking herself very seriously.

Lily also skipped over the man next to her, not so much out of secondhand embarrassment but—she didn't know, something about him made her uncomfortable, like she really didn't want to look directly at him.

Then there was Theyn, of course, in the center of them all, standing just in front of the rest of them. He looked unbelievably nervous, thankfully, they hadn't made him talk.

Then her eyes landed on the last two elves.

The first had dark hair that in direct sunlight was that weird blue color that Lily kept seeing floating around every now and then. He was dressed a little more plainly than the rest, fabric dull colors that didn't draw the eye. His small pack was stuffed to the brim with rectangular objects that were undoubtedly books. He stared out at the audience with abject boredom, though not just boredom, but more—a look that easily said all of this was beneath him.

With his gray eyes, based on what Frank had said, the guy had to be the mind elf.

Which left, last but not least, the night elf.

Just like the others she'd met; she looked like Frank but she didn't look like Frank. They shared the eyes, the hair, maybe even a few facial features but that was where the similarities stopped. Her clothing was extremely different from Frank's. As much as Frank belonged to a fantasy world filled with elves, where tunics were the go-to fashion of the day, this woman was clearly better dressed than he ever was. Frank didn't look bad, but he didn't have silver embroidered into his clothing, and the fabric of his clothes didn't look the way hers did. She looked almost as impressive as Mr. Gold Elf Clan Head did, and that was saying something.

She didn't work for Lily Jones, though, at least Lily had never met her, and Frank hadn't seemed to know about this quest before Lily had told him. They must have pulled her from somewhere else, though where else you could find a night elf—Lily had no idea where they'd even look.

"That they invited her shows how serious they are," Wizard Lenin said as Lily studied the night elf.

The woman, who seemed to have noticed Lily's eyes, was pointedly not looking in her direction.

"*Why's that?*" Lily asked. If everyone else had been invited then it made sense that the night elves would get an invite too. She didn't see what made this woman special.

"*No one invites the night elves to anything,*" Wizard Lenin scoffed, "*They're cannibals, demons, and the only thing any of the elven clans have ever agreed on was the total annihilation of their dark empire.*"

Wizard Lenin reflected that there was likely some clause in the prophecy which had demanded the reuniting of the seven major clans, Lily's own presence, and maybe the crown prince's, the little girl's, and the man's. Wizard Lenin was a little more doubtful of the humans, as it seemed too convenient, and suspected that had been universally demanded by the kingdom so that humanity had more legitimate representation than a half-elf Tellestrian princess.

"*Frank's a really nice guy though,*" Lily protested, getting them back to the original argument.

Wizard Lenin laughed derisively, "*He's nice to you, Lily, but he is what he is and has gladly admitted it on multiple occasions.*"

This wasn't untrue.

It was perhaps one thing that Frank lived on a diet of blood, he couldn't help that, but the fact was that that blood came from debtors who were usually addicted to either gambling or else narcotics, both of which were peddled by Jones Inc.

Lily had supposed that everyone had to make a living, and Frank had drawn the cannibal straw, which meant that there really was no legitimate way for him to get his meals. As it was, Lily had a lot of respect for him having been able to run a business like that for so long.

"*He's a gangster, Lily, not an entrepreneur,*" Wizard Lenin said slowly, "*And need I remind you that he eats people.*"

"*Just because Frank is doomed to eat babies and live off the blood of virgins doesn't mean he can't be a perfectly pleasant guy,*" Lily retorted.

Wizard Lenin paused for a moment too long, then said, "*I want you to think very carefully about what you just said and then tell me what was wrong with your sentence.*"

"*Oh stuff it—*" Lily tried to respond, but Wizard Lenin had already moved on. He had a lot more to say about night elves, scapegoats, boogie monsters, and whatever ridiculous thing Lily might say in Frank's defense next, but was more interested in getting the measure of the regent.

The man was sitting directly behind the speaking minister, burdened with layers upon layers of robes and a gilded crown whose elegance and intricacy made Lily suspect that it was yet another product of the gold elves. He stared into the crowd with an expression that was trying to be both majestic and intimidating but failed at both. He, like Theyn, had this ordinary human look about him that was at odds with the authority he was trying to give himself.

"It's telling that I never heard of him before," Wizard Lenin agreed, *"He must have been very distant to have avoided the fires, perhaps not even in the capital at the time, and would have been just young enough to have escaped my notice."*

Most of the important faces that Wizard Lenin remembered from before he'd blown himself up were missing from both the stage and the crowd. All the mages he'd fought were gone, as were his compatriots, as was most of the royal family. Now there was only Ilyn and Questburger, who Wizard Lenin was starting to think of as cockroaches, able to survive even the end of the world.

Lily readjusted Rabbit, lifting him of her head a moment, taking a moment to crack her neck before placing him back again.

"I can't believe you brought the rabbit," Wizard Lenin groused, distracted from his political analysis as he took a moment to lament Lily's ruined image.

"Of course I brought Rabbit," Lily retorted, *"Can you imagine the consequences of leaving him unsupervised?"*

Entire states, countries, maybe even an entire world could disappear.

"Well, maybe you shouldn't have made it in the first place."

Lily couldn't believe he'd just tried to use that to win an argument.

Rather than respond to that, Wizard Lenin told himself to be the better man, and continue thinking about Wheyn. He wondered what would happen if this all went according to plan (which of course it would not). When he had the Heart of the World in the vaults, unable to use it due to the lack of knowledge and talent, would he kill off Prince Theyn and even Princess Iff for good measure? It would be the wise thing to do, if he wanted to keep that throne, and all he'd have to do was pin it on the night elf.

"Pin it on the night elf?!" Lily balked, unable to help looking back at the woman on the other side of the stage. A woman who, according to Wizard Lenin, was about to be framed for Lily and her cousin's murder.

"It's a time-honored tradition," Wizard Lenin explained with a mental shrug, *"It's the age-old excuse for murder, the night elves broke into my home and did it. Even when I was alive, taking credit for my own work, half of it was blamed on the bloody night elves."*

It'd taken a while for Wizard Lenin to solidify his reputation in battle if only because they kept thinking his victims were left behind by hungry night elves.

Wizard Lenin thought further on the woman, and Lily could see the mental equivalent of a smile curling in his thoughts, *"That's why she's really here. We'll be off to retrieve the Heart of the World, but somewhere along the way Prince Theyn and Princess Iff will have an accident, and there's the night elf who must surely be very hungry."*

Wizard Lenin was almost impressed, almost willing to reevaluate Wheyn's intelligence and ruthlessness.

Well, now not only was Lily hot, bored, and her feet killing her, but liable to be assassinated for a giant metal orb.

Her eyes unwillingly slid to Theyn, who she hadn't talked to since last night. She wasn't sure if he could handle the prospect of death as easily as she could, she'd had years of practice. Something about the thought of his demise made her uneasy.

Finally, with a few more bloated words, the minister appeared to be wrapping things up.

"Oh, thank god," Lily sighed in relief.

He stepped aside only for Quesburger to stand and take his place.

Goddammit.

Lily wanted to cry.

Was this day ever going to end? Were they ever actually going to start? Or was she just going to listen to this for the rest of her life with a rabbit on her head?

At least it was Questburger. Wizard Lenin could think what he liked, but he didn't seem long-winded. He hadn't been long-winded yesterday even when there'd been a lot to explain.

Just as in the office, the man had this commanding presence to him, one that made everyone hang on his words even before he started speaking.

"Greetings, most of what I would have said has been said far more eloquently than I could manage by our ministers," Quesburger said, nodding to the lineup of ministers who had spoken before him. They all looked quite pleased with the praise, pleased and sweating profusely due to the ungodly heat.

"However," Quesburger continued, "I will say that for the first time in thousands of years, the sun elves have informed us that a window is open. A brave party, one representing all the elves as well as our great kingdom, has the chance to succeed where all others have failed."

He motioned to the quest representatives, a grand and slow motion as if to make them look more impressive than they were, "We have gathered here members of the designated elven clans, our most promising academy student, a representative of the monarchy, our beloved crown prince, and even Princess Iff from Tellestria."

Lily wondered, with her matted hair, her sweaty face, and a rabbit on top of her head, if she looked like she lived up to any kind of title right now.

She wished he hadn't said her name last.

"I do not simply believe we will succeed," Questburger continued, "I know we will. God, after all, favors the royal family and always has. The Heart of the World will belong to the king and his successors, retrieved by none other than the crown prince's hand."

There was much cheering, and for the first time, Lily noted that the crowd was distinctly human. She couldn't spot a single elf out there, not even on the edges.

Theyn bowed stiffly at the noise, his smile strained, and his muscles clearly tense. He still didn't dare to utter a word.

And just like that, Lily realized the speech was over, the words linger far longer and with far more weight than they should have. For a moment, before he stepped back to his seat, Questburger's eyes met hers. Lily stiffened under them, holding her breath, until his attention turned back to his empty chair then to the audience in front of him.

Unfortunately, the end of Quesburger's blessedly short speech did not signal the end of standing there, yet another minister of something or another stepped forward to speak to the crowd.

As he started to blather, using equally as long and obscure words as the other ministers, Lily couldn't help but glance at Ilyn. Of all of them, except perhaps Lily, he looked the closest to committing homicide if it would get them out of here already.

He was also the one standing closest to her.

"How many of these do we have to go through?" Lily whispered to him.

He started, stiffened, then looked down as if he couldn't believe she'd just talked to him. After yesterday, she couldn't either, but beggars couldn't be choosers.

He seemed to realize how miserable he was, as he actually answered, "Too many."

"That's not a helpful answer," Lily hissed back.

She knew why she had no idea what was happening, they hadn't told her, and they'd only pulled her in the night before. She considered herself lucky that she'd even known there was a ceremony.

Ilyn had no excuse.

"They're human," Ilyn said with a sigh, "Their time is precious to them. If not, then sooner or later, they'll die."

"That could take decades!" Lily spluttered.

He wasn't serious, was he? Did he really think they'd be standing here for years? Even a few hours sounded awful. Lily wouldn't be able to handle a day let alone years.

Normally, Lily would have expected some blasé holier than thou response of how decades were nothing to an immortal being like him. That was just how elves, at least all the elves Lily knew, which was admittedly very few, talked.

However, at the idea of decades, Ilyn started to look a little ill.

He didn't seem to have anything to say to that.

Lily didn't either.

God, she was so miserable.

She spared Ilyn another glance. She didn't like him, and not just because he'd burned down her house, but if it was a choice between getting something useful out of this and ignoring him—

Lily would rather get something useful out of this.

"Can you at least tell me who's who?" she asked.

"Who's who?" he repeated, sounding like he'd never heard the phrase before.

"These lovely people," Lily said, nodding down the line of quest participants.

He looked over as well, frowning. He stared at them for a very long, very unnerving, moment, then said, "I don't know."

"You don't know?" Lily balked, "How can you not know?! I thought you were important!"

Once again, she had her own reasons for not knowing, but Ilyn had to know, didn't he? Unless, somehow, Lily had ended up standing next to the entirely wrong person for this.

At this, he did look a little annoyed, maybe even affronted, but nodded down the line as he started to explain, "The love elf is of no importance, I do not know her. She will be entirely useless if not an obnoxious hindrance."

The love elf was standing right next to him, had clearly heard every word he said. She valiantly didn't look over at them.

"I do not know the moon elf, except I'm certain he thinks with his sword rather than his head," Ilyn said, loud enough that the moon elf in question certainly heard it. Unlike the love elf, the moon elf glared back, going so far as to bear his shockingly pointed teeth.

Ilyn didn't even look at him.

"Happiness elves are indistinguishable from one another and are always of no importance."

The happiness elf—didn't even blink. He had no reaction; he was still smiling. He'd been smiling the whole time they'd been standing here. It was always possible he hadn't heard Ilyn but—somehow, Lily thought she had, and this was just his response to everything.

"The gold elf is Nhoj, the clan head," Ilyn said, nodding at Nhoj and—that one actually wasn't bad. Lily found herself genuinely surprised.

"The little human girl is Elizabeth, an academy student, more talented than most, but here to make our human overlords feel better about themselves. That they couldn't find anyone older makes them deeply nervous."

The little human girl in question, Elizabeth, very clearly heard the man and was visibly gritting her teeth and curling her hands into fists. It almost didn't matter that she wasn't saying anything, because what she was thinking was so clearly written on her face.

Lily regretted asking Ilyn anything.

"The man is Annde, a friend and advisor to the regent, I expect him to meet his gruesome death shortly."

Oh, did he? Just because? Lily tried to look at the man, to see whatever it was Ilyn must be seeing but—she just couldn't seem to look him in the face. Something about him made her feel so uncomfortable.

"The mind elf has likely spent millennia in some tower or another wasting his existence away over academic trifles," Ilyn continued, adding, "I don't know him" like that was even important at this point.

"And all night elves are flesh-eating demons unworthy of names," Ilyn finished, saving his worst insult for last.

Well, that was impressive.

He must be a great hit at parties.

"Lily," Wizard Lenin said, sounding almost stunned, as if he was feeling so much it couldn't come through his voice properly, *"Why are you gossiping, on a stage in front of the entire kingdom, with Ilyn?"*

God, she hadn't even meant to, it'd just somehow happened.

"Well," Lily said for want of anything else to say, "That was terrible."

Ilyn's lips twitched, as if he wanted to smile, but it'd been so long that he'd forgotten the muscle memory. He ended up sporting an awkward grimace.

"How so?" he asked.

Lily stared.

When he didn't say anything, she started listing them off, "You said the love elf is useless, the moon elf thinks with his dick, happiness elves are clones, and that the night elf is a flesh-eating demon."

"All true," he said with confidence, going so far as to look puzzled, as if asking her to silently explain how he was possibly wrong.

"Well, I wouldn't know," Lily said, motioning to herself, "It's not like I was just kidnapped here yesterday after my house was burned down!"

It was a good thing she hadn't expected any contrition, because she didn't get any.

She huffed, crossed her arms, and stared back out at the audience. Probably time to move the conversation along.

Though she supposed there was something bothering her. She'd never thought about it much, since she'd spent most of her time on this side of the border with Frank, but it was starting to bother her.

"Aren't you elves kind of ganged up on?" she asked after a moment, "I mean, theoretically, wouldn't it be better for you if you banded together somehow? Rose up against, well, these people?"

Lily supposed they could like the monarchy, Frank maybe wasn't representative, but Ilyn hadn't sounded all that fond of them for all that he seemed to now work for them. It just seemed a little strange that humans were so easily in control of everything.

By the look on his face, this idea was completely and utterly alien to him. It also looked like it was a non-starter.

They fell into a tense silence where they both stared out into the crowd.

Lily lasted two minutes.

"What's the deal with the human guy anyway?" Lily asked.

"Who?" Ilyn asked in turn, brow furrowed.

He seemed utterly oblivious to the attention that they were now attracting, not just from the audience Lily realized, but from the others on stage. Everyone except the man in question as well as the girl were looking at them.

Though the girl didn't look oblivious so much as resolutely determined to ignore their conversation.

"You know," Lily said, nodding down the line, "That guy."

"Annde?" Ilyn asked, and Lily supposed that was the guy's—what was it with the names here? She'd thought it before, but there really was some weird, awful, theme going on.

"He spent time in Xhigrahi and had a run in with night elves," Ilyn explained.

By which, of course, he explained nothing.

"Night elves?" Lily asked, trying and failing to look at him directly. It was—it wasn't like staring at the sun, but more like there was a magnet that repelled her eyes from looking at him.

She tried to imagine three or four Franks chasing after the man. Maybe she was rating Frank too highly but—she would have bet on Frank.

"Wait, wouldn't they just eat him?" Lily asked.

Lily winced when the night elf glared at her, but Ilyn didn't seem to care.

"Usually," he admitted with a shrug.

"But he's—still here," Lily said slowly.

"Perhaps he warded them off with human mage craft," Ilyn said with yet another shrug, though by the look on his face he didn't believe it either. It was just that he didn't care.

Lily was about to argue, but the speech finally ended. Trumpets then blared, drums rattled, and there was great applause. To her shock, as well as great relief, it seemed to really be the last one.

Before she could collect herself, though, she was practically shoved off the stage. She found herself scrambling to keep up as the group marched down the street, heralded on all sides by cheering civilians, towards the outer gates that Lily had never been through.

Off in an alleyway, in the shadow of a building, Lily caught Frank's eye. He smiled at the procession, offered her a slight wave and salute as she passed by. Lily tried to wave back, grinning, but he was out of sight in the blink of an eye, obscured by the faceless mob.

Then, just like that, they were out of the city. The iron gates closed behind them with a loud, jarring, thud.

Outside there was nothing.

Rolling hills of wheat and a single dirt road stretching into the distance until it disappeared into white-topped mountains. Compared to the city, always gleaming perfection, it looked oddly barren and undeveloped.

Before Lily could ask Wizard Lenin, though, the others were already walking forward, as if every one of them knew exactly what they were doing and where they were going.

"Wait!" Lily cried out, holding Rabbit to her head as she caught up, "Is that it? It's over? The quest is on?"

"Did you expect something else?" Wizard Lenin asked unsympathetically.

The group stopped and turned to look at her, not a single one looked sympathetic. The elves looked at each other with raised eyebrows, Ilyn looked just as stoic and unreadable as he had burning down her house, Theyn sheepish, and the girl Elizabeth annoyed.

It was the man, Annde, who came to their rescue, "Well you see, Your Highness—"

It was the weirdest thing.

There was nothing wrong with his voice in theory, it sounded like any other voice. However, with every word he spoke, she heard an increasingly loud ringing in her ears, loud enough to easily drown out every word.

By the time it stopped, she realized he'd finished ages ago, that she'd been standing there dumbly for god knows how long.

"Sorry," Lily offered, hitting the side of her head, "Something in my ear."

God, what even was that?

Either something was seriously wrong with her or else seriously wrong with him, and she couldn't decide which.

Maybe that was how he'd survived the night elves, for all she still couldn't believe it.

That seemed to be their signal to keep walking, as if Lily had been a pest for holding them up for two seconds.

"Is he cursed or something?" Lily asked Wizard Lenin.

"It's possible," Wizard Lenin acknowledged, not sounding very invested, *"It's not outside the realm of possibility."*

He probably didn't have long to live if that was the case. Something terrible would soon happen to him, that was the way these things worked. That, or given the others' lack of reaction, this was entirely in Lily's head and the price she paid for her bullshit powers.

"I don't pay prices for my bullshit powers," Lily groused, at least she hadn't before today.

There was just—

There was something really wrong with that guy.

Or maybe something else was bothering her.

Wizard Lenin had said everything was blamed on night elves, then Ilyn had gone and blamed whatever was wrong with this Annde fellow on night elves even when that made no sense at all. They just said night elves and no one, not even Wizard Lenin, questioned it.

"It's true that they'd more likely eat him," Wizard Lenin said, *"And that Xhigrahi is certainly a very dangerous place to travel. However, it's not impossible this is the night elves' doing."*

That wasn't the point.

The point was, even if Annde's story wasn't fishy (and it definitely was), night elves weren't just the age-old excuse for murder and a time-honored tradition, but a constant get out of jail free card that had been brought up twice today and counting.

It was a miracle that they blamed the Usurper for anything at all.

"Don't even joke," Wizard Lenin said, *"I worked long and hard for my reputation."*

That was exactly her point!

He was making her exact point for her!

The night elves were blamed for everything, especially if they didn't actually do it. Mr. Gold Elf Clan Head was always terse, at best, with Lily Jones. She'd always assumed it was just a personality clash or something, or because Lily Jones was a gangster, but it seemed like it was just because she was night elf adjacent. The night elf, per Wizard Lenin, had barely even been invited when everyone else had gotten an invitation.

She just thought—

If the night elves were going to get blamed for everything, even things like this Annde person, then they might as well do everything.

Frank was always talking about expanding, about getting out of the city and into the provinces. What he wanted to do, exactly, wasn't always clear but most of the time it sounded like he wanted an independent state, one fully outside of the monarchy's control.

He always said something about politics getting in the way, about the other elves, the night elves themselves, things Lily hadn't known enough about to follow.

Well, if he couldn't do it, then maybe Lily could manage something.

Lily sped up to catch up with the night elf, who was walking in the back, several feet from anyone else.

Lily cleared her throat.

The woman didn't look at her.

She cleared her throat again.

When that failed, Lily started in, "I—um—have a proposition for you.

I've been thinking, and I think it's time Jones Inc. stretched its wings. I think we should call it N.E.L.F., the Night Elf Liberation Front."

8 THE SEVEN LABORS OF LILY

In which Lily learns some of the trials that await her, admits to her illegal hobbies, and feels a sense of doubt she can't quite shake.

"Jones."

Lily had been expecting this.

They were three days into the quest and the gold elf had finally separated her from the herd. Not that this was that hard, considering Lily was always the last in the group and, when she wasn't, she was trying and failing to badger the uncooperative night elf into doing something.

Lily supposed that it wasn't any of the woman's business, she and Lily didn't even know each other, but she'd thought bringing up something like that would spark some interest or at least a response.

Instead, Lily had gotten nothing, and had had to huff and glitch a letter onto Frank's desk. Not that the letter said much, just that she thought Frank should branch out of the city after all. She didn't know if he'd take her up on it, but Frank usually was a man with a plan, at least when it came to logistics and that sort of thing. He'd come up with something, she was sure.

She'd just thought—

It would have been nice to get this woman on board with it.

But she wasn't, and it didn't even seem to bother the woman that no one else would even look at her. Lily at least tried to talk to her, engage her in conversation, but she acted like Lily was beneath her.

Not that the others were great conversationalists either.

Ilyn seemed to be moody, terse, and uncomfortably silent by nature. Whether it was burning through your house or marching through fields and abandoning the road, he was always the same.

The others stayed out of each other's and Lily's way, purposefully not speaking to one another, and most of the time barely even looking at one another.

Which left the man, Annde, who Lily still couldn't look at for some reason, Theyn, and the girl.

Theyn was fine, and it felt like he'd tried to talk to her, but every time he did he was called off either by Annde or the girl who, for some reason, seemed to have a real problem with Lily.

Lily was used to that, she'd never really been a people person, but she'd never seen anyone come on so suddenly and strongly before. Usually, Lily got a chance to stick her foot deep into her mouth before she started getting those looks. The only thing she could think of was the ceremony, but Ilyn had been the one to talk about her, not Lily, and it'd been miserable and boring for everyone.

No, she'd intensely disliked Lily from the start.

It was like Lily, somehow, had done something to personally offend her.

The oppressive silence, constant walking, and sheer discomfort of it all had driven Lily to wander to a nearby stream in the early morning before they set off again.

She was trying to remind herself that this was a quest, that soon, it would be incredibly exciting and important. Forget the pompous speeches, forget her sudden arrival, this wasn't just a thing that could get Wizard Lenin a body but an actual magical object that she'd seen glimpses of since she was five years old.

If anything was important in Lily's life, if anything was real, then it had to be this quest.

She shouldn't be disappointed that a certain amount of walking and uncomfortable company came with it.

Unfortunately, while she was sitting there enjoying the scenery, the twittering of birds, the gold elf clan head had taken advantage of the opportunity.

Because he had known her for the last seven years as Lily Jones, night elf gangster, drug lord, and all-around menace to society.

"Jones," the man hissed when Lily gave no response, "What game are you playing at?"

He was more formidable looking than she remembered him being. Maybe she'd been too young then, hadn't seen the regent yet, but there was a certain something to him that the regent and even Theyn just lacked. Frank had it, Wizard Lenin had it, Death had it, Questburger had it, maybe even Lily had it, and now this man did too.

Maybe Theyn would grow into it, maybe he just needed a bit of time, but she wasn't sure it was something that came with age and height. She also wasn't sure what it meant that he wasn't the same, even when he was the one who was crown prince.

She let her attention drift back to her surroundings.

Lily had never been one for camping, the Tylors would have had to invest time and money in that, but it really was beautiful. Outside the city walls, the path had crossed great fields, and then entered thick forests, and from there the foothills of the mountains.

Theyn had hastily told her, before he'd been called away by the man, that they served as the border between the kingdom of men, all the provinces and even what was left to the elves, and the wild untamed lands of the north.

There were no maps past the mountains, no one had ever gotten that far.

The pines were tall and uncut, towering in a way Lily hadn't realized trees could, and the sunlight filtered through patches of green to catch brightly on the surface of the gurgling stream.

Nhoj, however, didn't seem to appreciate the scenery. He was still glaring at her, clearly preparing to do something drastic if she didn't fess up to something.

"Look," Lily offered with a sigh, "It's not exactly like I volunteered for this."

Oh, she would have come, she had to so she could get the Heart of the World for Wizard Lenin. It was more than that, though. It did feel very exciting to be purposefully invited on a quest. The fact that she'd been named specifically meant—well, she didn't know, but it felt like for the first time in her life she had a reason to be anywhere or do anything.

Lily had always been improvising when it came to her life, making it up as she went along. True, they hadn't wanted her here, it'd all been a bit rushed, and so far no one was talking to her but that didn't change anything.

Except that it made her secret identity as Lily Jones a little awkward.

"They thought they were bringing the missing Princess Iff," Nhoj said. His eyes didn't seem gold as he said it, but instead molten. It was as if rather than being made of a flat, solid, substance they had been forged from a churning, glowing, liquid.

His shoes along with the grass beneath his feet began to char and burn, sparks of fire were dancing upward, threatening to catch the fabric of his trousers.

Lily had a sudden, horrible, feeling that he wasn't going anywhere. He wasn't going anywhere, and he wouldn't let her go anywhere until she fessed up.

(Well, she'd told Frank already, hadn't she?)

"Funny story," Lily said, wincing and hating herself a little, "In my spare time I am also a princess."

He looked ten seconds away from exploding into fiery molten globs.

She hastily turned her hair from red, to black, to red again.

"See? Just like that."

Although Rabbit sitting on top of her head probably made that look less convincing.

"Just like that," he repeated.

"Just like that," Lily agreed with a nod, "So—yeah, that's the story."

She opened her mouth to ask advice on N.E.L.F., on how he as a dignified leader with lots of real-world experience would plan the whole thing, but he was already walking away.

What was left of his shoes fell off his feet and he left a set of burned footprints behind him.

Lily stared after him, all too aware that it was just her, Rabbit, Wizard Lenin, and the scenery once again.

She hoped the quest would start being quest-like soon.

"Aren't you going to say something?" Lily prompted Wizard Lenin, who was notably not chastising her on revealing her stolen secret identity.

"I've come to realize that you'll simply never learn unless you have the opportunity to reap what you sow," Wizard Lenin responded, which of course meant he felt Nhoj the gold elf had made Wizard Lenin's point for him.

"He'll keep it to himself," Wizard Lenin added with a sigh, *"The gold elves have always been painfully neutral."*

That wasn't the term she'd have used to describe the man she'd just talked to.

Proud, angry, afraid, and with an innate sense of command, he certainly hadn't seemed 'painfully neutral' about anything.

"It's how the gold elves have done so well," Wizard Lenin explained, *"They arguably flourished, or at least survived, under the rule of the night elves and now humanity. They've sacrificed pride for utility and patronage. Even if the idea of you anywhere near the human throne offends him, concerns him, he won't do a thing about it."*

Just as the gold elves had apparently done nothing to stop Wizard Lenin's revolution.

"Get back before they leave without you," Wizard Lenin reminded her.

Lily sighed, her feet really were killing her. She supposed there might be a way to magically stop that, but she couldn't think of one, and Wizard Lenin hadn't offered any suggestions.

It felt wrong though, that they could leave her behind. Oh, she believed they would, they definitely would, but she was supposed to be in this prophecy.

Maybe she was thinking of it the wrong way, she thought in a moment of cynicism.

After she'd processed the fact that there was a prophecy, that she was in it, she'd started coming around to the idea. It wasn't how she would have chosen to leave Earth, to fully embrace being Princess Iff, but it was an indication that she was meant to do something with her life.

Nothing said, though, that Lily had to be the central figure in this prophecy. No one had ever said what it said exactly, how she'd come up, just that they couldn't retrieve the Heart of the World without her or the elves.

Maybe Theyn was the main figure of the prophecy, or Wizard Lenin, or someone else entirely who wasn't her. Maybe she was just a vital member of the supporting cast, only there as a part of someone else's story.

She didn't know how she'd feel if that ended up being the case.

Well, it wasn't conclusive yet. She hadn't heard the prophecy and the quest hadn't even really started, they'd been walking until—well, until she assumed something would happen.

This was just the prelude.

***

They were right where she'd left them.

Ilyn was already standing, his few supplies packed, staring down at his watch in intense concentration. The mind elf was still flipping through one of his many tomes, utterly unconcerned by anything going on around him. The love elf was staring out at the horizon with impatience, the moon elf sharpening his blade, the night elf looking dead to the world and miserable, the happiness elf—staring contentedly at the trees, the man Annde—Lily still couldn't look him in the face, and—

"Iff!"

Lily turned.

There was Theyn, smiling at her with clear relief, "Good, you're back. Elizabeth is nearly packed and—"

The girl, Elizabeth, cut him off with a hard glare. She continued to ever so neatly pack her clothes and sleeping gear, "Elizabeth, Your Highness, is not the one holding us up."

This last was said pointedly to Lily, just in case Lily had missed the implication.

Lily could only stare at her dumbly and note, "I'm already packed."

It was true. Thanks to the universe's constant bullshit, Lily never had to worry about things like not having enough space in a bag. Lily easily fit everything she wanted in there and easily retrieved it when she needed to.

Elizabeth flushed, her skin flaring, but then the flush was gone, and her pride and dignity were back like she'd never lost her emotional footing in the first place.

This was probably her preferred state, Lily thought with raised eyebrows.

THE HEART OF THE WORLD

Everything about her was put together to the extreme. Her uniform looked pressed, even days into the quest. Each of the brass buttons on her uniform glinted in the morning sunlight, clearly having been polished. Her hair was done up in perfect French braids, not a single hair out of place.

Standing next to Lily, who perpetually looked like she'd rolled out of bed, Elizabeth looked that much more put together.

In short, once again, Lily couldn't help but conclude that Elizabeth was trying to get someone to take her very seriously.

"Really, you're just going to leave that rabbit on your head again?" she sniffed, diverting the topic back to Lily.

Lily was sure she'd never be caught dead wearing a rabbit for a hat, if only because it'd clash with the miniature librarian look she seemed so fond of.

"Well," Lily said, lifting Rabbit off her head to look into his dark, soul-sucking beady eyes, as if they could provide her an answer, "What else am I supposed to do with him?"

"Leave him at home," Elizabeth said contemptuously, carefully folding the last of her things, and determinedly avoiding the dull eyes of their elven companions (who looked as if they did not have time for this bullshit.)

"That's a bad idea," Lily said.

Realizing that wouldn't be enough, Lily sighed and explained, "He's not really a rabbit, he's a something else—I don't know, maybe some eldritch abomination or something. When I leave him unsupervised, he devours things from reality. He only looks like a rabbit because—I actually don't know why he still looks like a rabbit."

It'd been seven years, you'd think Rabbit would have gotten tired of being a rabbit. Lily supposed that required the capacity to get tired of something, which Rabbit didn't seem to have.

He really was more like a furry lump than anything else. He just sat wherever you put him like an occasionally blinking throw pillow.

The girl stopped, hand still in her bag. She turned to look at Lily fully, and by the look in her dark eyes she had no idea what to make of it. Finely, primly, and properly she said, "You can't be serious."

"Perfectly serious," Lily responded easily, not quite sure what else to say.

Elizabeth opened her mouth, face red again even as she closed her bag tightly shut, clearly about to say something, but was cut off by Ilyn, "Elizabeth, don't make me regret tolerating the monarchy's decision to send a twelve-year-old Tellestrian."

Elizabeth's head whipped towards him, dark eyes now wide with fear and shame.

She bit her lip, stood, and slung the bag over her shoulder with shaking hands. She looked down at the ground, so that you could hardly make out her wobbling mouth or watering eyes.

After a very long moment, she said in a firm and desperately controlled voice, "Sorry, sir."

And that seemed to be that.

Either they'd been waiting for Lily to return or Elizabeth to pack her things, because in the next second Ilyn was striding off again, the rest all hurriedly putting away what they'd kept out to catch up with him.

Lily, as usual, found herself quickly falling behind the herd.

She wished she'd done more hiking before this.

She kept her eyes on Elizabeth who—it wasn't clear if she'd recovered or not. She was walking with her head held high, keeping up with Ilyn better than Lily was, but something about the way she was moving looked a little stiff, a little too tall, like she was masking what she was really feeling.

"Was that as bad as it sounded?" Lily asked Wizard Lenin.

"Oh yes," Wizard Lenin said, he still couldn't believe anyone let Ilyn near children.

Tellestria was Earth, Lily realized with a blink. She was from Earth, just like Lily—

"She is not like you," Wizard Lenin corrected before Lily could follow that thought, *"She was unfortunate to wander into a world where she doesn't belong. She may be clever enough to know all her posturing, studying, and talent can't disguise where she came from.*

"Some humans, Lily, are more human than others," Wizard Lenin reminded her, meaning of course that humans like Theyn who'd always lived here and humans like Elizabeth were very different. It wasn't just being human that mattered but coming from the right side of the metaphorical tracks.

"Sorry about Elizabeth."

Lily almost jumped out of her skin, barely keeping hold of Rabbit on her head.

"Theyn!" she exclaimed, noting his sudden presence next to her.

When the hell had he gotten there?

He sheepishly smiled back at her, rubbing the back of his head, and ignoring the way Elizabeth glared over her shoulder at the pair of them.

"She doesn't mean anything by it," Theyn continued, "She's not a bad person."

"I didn't think she was," Lily said in confusion, had she implied as much?

"Oh, good," Theyn breathed in relief, "She's just—She's the best in the academy, you know, the most promising mage in years. She deserves it too; she's had to fight tooth and nail for everything and—"

He cut himself off, glanced at Lily awkwardly, and in a more hushed tone said, "When they first announced this, the expedition, she was chosen above all the other, older, students. We thought for a bit it was just going to be her, me, and Annde. We—It took them a while to decide you should come."

What the hell did that have to do with anything?

There was a hideously loud sigh inside her mind and the metaphorical sound of Wizard Lenin's head hitting a wall. With great exasperation, he explained, *"The girl thinks she's in competition with you."*

What? Why?!

Wizard Lenin sighed again, clearly thinking Lily was being willfully dense, *"She's worked all her life to be the best, beating out those born to far more privilege than herself. Then you waltz in, like you always do, without a care in the world, and are given the same opportunities that she's taken years to earn for herself.*

"As far as Elizabeth is concerned, you're usurping her position."

"Opportunities?!" Lily mentally spluttered, *"I was kidnapped!"*

"Somehow, I don't think she cares," Wizard Lenin said dryly, *"Try to remember she's twelve."*

"What's that supposed to mean?!"

"It means she's a myopic, self-centered, ambitious, ungrateful ass who thinks that because she can pass an exam or two and read a textbook, she deserves to be the smartest person in any given room. If she's lucky, she'll grow out of it."

Unspoken was that some people, many people, were not that lucky.

That was—an oddly specific insult.

Insulting people was Wizard Lenin's great hobby, but usually he knew the person personally if he went on a roll like that.

"Are you speaking from personal experience?" Lily couldn't help but ask.

It felt like a nail was just driven through her head, which meant, of course, that that was a question Wizard Lenin had not been willing to field.

"Iff?" Theyn asked in concern.

"Hm, oh, sorry—" Lily said, dropping her hand away from her face, searching for some kind of excuse. Her eyes landed (which is to say they didn't) on Annde, "Andde—um—gives me headaches."

"Annde?" Theyn asked, brown eyes comically wide as he glanced over at the man. He, Lily couldn't help but notice, seemed to be able to look directly at him just fine.

"He's—" Theyn stopped, winced, then said, "He hasn't always been like this, you know, a few months ago he was perfectly fine."

Lily opened her mouth to ask what, exactly, was wrong with him. Ilyn had said something to, but Lily had never been able to actually look at him and see whatever it was everyone else saw.

He just felt—innately wrong.

Theyn fell into deep contemplation, thinking over Annde's unfortunate fate, whatever it was, that may or may not have been caused by night elves. Lily let her attention turn back to the landscape.

To her surprise, they were making visible progress. They were steadily climbing upwards, the incline steep enough that the foothills seemed to be behind them.

If she turned, she would likely be able to see the capital city, high towers gleaming in the sunlight far below them.

Lily felt some of her previous excitement and energy return.

"Where do you think we're heading?" Lily asked Wizard Lenin.

"North through the mountains," Wizard Lenin answered easily, *"It's a place filled with magic and mystery, even the elves left it alone when the world was theirs. It's there, on the other side of the mountains, that the Heart of the World is almost certainly resting."*

And in his mind was the island, Death, and the Heart of the World that wasn't a Heart of the World resting there.

Lily was ready, too ready, in fact, as she asked Theyn too, "Theyn, do you know exactly where we're headed?"

He blinked once, twice, then flushed in embarrassment, "Did nobody tell you?"

Lily laughed a little awkwardly, wondering if she was supposed to feel like this was a personal failing when someone really should have given her a brochure, "I guess everyone was busy."

"To get to the Heart of the World, we have to face trials, with each of the clans having the ability to get through it," Theyn said, motioning to the elves ahead of them, "The first is through the mountains, the gold elves' trial."

Lily frowned, thinking about that, about the fact that he hadn't said what her role was in it.

"Just how long was this prophecy?" Lily found herself asking. If it described what the elves all did, in order, and then said something about Lily—it had to be a lot wordier than 'you'll kill your father and marry your mother'.

"Well, there are plenty that are longer," Theyn said uncomfortably, clearly not sure how to take that question.

"The sun elves generally don't say much," Wizard Lenin concurred, *"But when they do, they bloody well make the most of your attention."*

"Your Majesty, Theyn," Annde's voice rang out, immediately summoning that awful ringing in Lily's ears, "Can I have a word?"

"Sorry," Theyn gave her an apologetic look, "I should go."

Lily was too busy trying to fight down her sudden, irrational, queasiness brought up just because Annde had said a few words.

Theyn darted to the man's side, looking up at him with eager eyes, like he was actually looking forward to anything he'd say.

Maybe it was Lily but—god, she just couldn't imagine willingly talking to him or even being in his presence.

"I doubt he's important either," Wizard Lenin thought with a mental shrug, still writing off Annde's weird state as something that wasn't his problem,

"He's old enough that I would have made a point to know his name."

Wizard Lenin believed that his revolution had left slim pickings for key positions, Questburger had then all but confirmed as much to Lily when he'd said why they'd sent her off to Tellestria. In another world, Annde wouldn't have been first choice for anything.

Yet here, thanks to Wizard Lenin, he wasn't just gainfully employed but sent to represent humanity to fetch the Heart of the World.

Lily tried to look at the man again and—oh, oh no, she nearly vomited.

Right, she was just going to pretend he wasn't here, and he could do the same with her. Everyone would be happy.

***

It was nearly sunset by the time they reached their destination.

It didn't disappoint.

There was a pair of gilded gates carved directly into the face of the mountain. While they had been carved from the mountain itself, out of a dark granite, they were inlaid with gold and precious stones. Shimmering patterns, swirls, stars, trees, and flowers glittered in the dying light, almost blinding in the sunset.

Lily found herself looking to Ilyn, wondering if he'd declare that they stop to make camp before they started. So far, they'd always promptly ended at sunset, giving them just enough time to make camp in the dying light.

He didn't say anything though, had even stowed his pocket watch into his uniform, and was instead looking with opaque eyes at Nhoj.

Nhoj, in turn, was staring expressionlessly at the door.

"You do know how to open it, don't you?" the mind elf asked with a raised, dark, eyebrow and an unbearably smug expression.

Nhoj didn't respond to that. He just stood there.

Elizabeth opened her mouth, clearly concerned and about to say something, but shut it before a word could come out.

"We should press on," Ilyn said when it was clear that Nhoj was just going to stand there, "We can't make camp here or in the caverns. Our best choice is to get through to the other side."

"The fastest route takes twelve hours," Nhoj said, his voice oddly flat, in a way that Lily had never heard it.

She'd heard him tersely polite, filled with dislike, and even filled with blatant rage but never flat.

"Then it takes twelve hours," Ilyn responded, either oblivious or indifferent to the way Theyn's face blanched at that news.

Twelve hours? God, they'd already been walking for twelve hours. How were they supposed to keep walking all night? She felt her enthusiasm begin to dim again, certain that whatever task happened, she wouldn't be much use if she was dead on her feet.

Before she could say that maybe they should make camp after all, finding some way to miraculously create enough space for them to do it, Nhoj reached out for the door. With a single push, as if the doors were made of nothing at all, they swung inward and opened.

Inside there was nothing, just a pitch-black tunnel.

Nhoj didn't turn as he commanded, "Don't fall behind and don't stray from the path."

One by one, they filed in through the door, and once inside it shut behind them with a terrible thud. For a moment, they stood there in total darkness, until with only a whisper a small flame appeared in Ilyn's hand.

Lily hastily followed his lead, conjuring her own bright flame to hover in her hand.

Without a word, they all looked to Nhoj, who was already walking forward into the darkness.

It quickly became clear why Nhoj was taking the lead.

There was no hesitation in him as he turned corner after corner, taking them through a meandering pathway only he seemed to know, and know well enough that it might as well have been etched onto the inside of his eyelids.

And one wrong turn, Lily thought, could prove deadly when the safest path stretched over a great crevasse. Nhoj had gone confidently ahead, crossing over a thin bridge of stone. Ilyn had followed, then the rest of them one by one.

Walking over it now, the last to cross just behind Elizabeth, Lily was feeling an awful sense of vertigo even with her immortality. There was something particularly awful about staring where the ground should be and finding only a black pit beneath you.

"What spell is that?"

Lily wobbled precariously, foot nearly slipping, and looked up to find Elizabeth glaring back at her.

Seriously?

Was now really the time for this?

"What?" Lily asked as she focused on regaining her balance and walking again. She was already last, and she had the terrible feeling that if she didn't keep up then Nhoj wasn't kidding about leaving her behind.

"What spell is that?" Elizabeth repeated impatiently, still stopped, glaring daggers at the light floating in Lily's hand. "You didn't go through any of the standard conjurations for light."

"The what?" Lily asked, readjusting Rabbit to keep him from toppling into the pit, trying to shift slowly forward.

"The tome books, you've seen them before," Wizard Lenin noted, *"They contain*

the standard, human, conjurations of mage craft. Every spell considered basic, or on the easy side of advanced, is written there with explicit instructions on exactly how to perform them."

"*And?*" Lily asked.

"*And you just blew past it without even blinking,*" she could almost see Wizard Lenin sneering, "*Humans don't do that, Lily.*"

"The standard conjurations," Elizabeth hissed, "The spells that each of us spend years perfecting!"

"Sorry?" Lily asked, looking down to make sure one foot was going in front of the other, "Look, I'm a little busy at the moment—"

"A little busy?!" Elizabeth balked.

"Elizbeth, Iff, please—"

Lily looked up to see that Theyn had edged back towards Elizabeth, reaching out an arm to pull her ahead. Lily, in turn, had now almost reached Elizabeth, was about an arm span away from her.

In retrospect, Lily should have seen it coming.

Elizabeth moved towards Lily, finger pointing in accusation and closing the gap between them. At the same time, Theyn moved forward and reached out for Elizabeth's shoulder to pull her back.

Unfortunately, Theyn lost his footing and slid forward into Elizbeth, who in turn was thrown off balance and tipped over the edge of the bridge. Her hand caught on the edge of Lily's uniform, causing Lily and Rabbit to fall with them.

Someone shouted after them in alarm but soon they were falling fast enough and far enough that Lily couldn't see or hear anything at all.

9 ALL THAT GLITTERS

In which Lily sees Elizabeth from an empathetic angle, Wizard Lenin advocates homicide, and tells her that a choice must be made.

Lily only just caught them in time before they hit the ground and cracked their heads open like melons.

She scrambled to her feet, picked up Rabbit, and looked up. They were so far down that Ilyn's light couldn't be seen at all, there was only the glimmering ball still in Lily's hand.

Lily was hit by a sudden, profound, sense of exhaustion as all the hours she'd spent walking finally caught up with her. She sank to the ground, laughing, thinking about just how far they'd fallen.

"We're off the path."

Lily looked over, trying to stifle her laughter, and caught sight of Elizabeth.

She was curled on the ground, holding her knees, and burying her face in them. She was choking on her own words and repressed tears, "We're off the path."

She took deep, shuddering breaths, her whole frame shaking even as she clutched her knees tighter.

Theyn rubbed the back of his head, sitting upright, blinking and clearly trying to regain his senses. He looked like he was still waiting to hit the ground.

One of Elizabeth's breaths was suddenly, startlingly, louder than the others. It was a deep hiccup, a prelude to a sob, that she tried and failed to stifle against the fabric of her uniform. A uniform that was wrinkled, dirty, and just a moment before had looked as if it'd never left the dry cleaner.

Lily's light wasn't quite bright enough, but if she looked closely, she could make out the dark stains Elizabeth's tears had left on her knees.

Lily suddenly felt like a voyeur.

Elizabeth was still the girl from this morning, but that veneer of confidence and even arrogance was gone, leaving a terrified child in its wake.

Lily couldn't ever remember crying, not like this, not anything like this.

Even when she'd died, that first time, and found herself in an empty world that just had to be the afterlife, there'd been no thought of tears.

Why should there have been?

There was nothing Lily could have said or done to change anything.

Elizabeth though, wasn't going to stop.

"What do I do?" Lily asked, only to be confronted by the mental equivalent of Wizard Lenin shrugging.

He neither knew nor cared.

"Try slapping her," Wizard Lenin suggested, voice dripping with sarcasm, *"Isn't that what they do on TV?"*

Lily took a breath, stalked over to Elizabeth, and set Rabbit aside. She held up her hand for a moment, judging the distance, then slapped her across the face with a resounding crack.

Elizabeth stopped muttering, and a hand reached up to the bright red mark growing on her face. She looked up at Lily through crocodile tears as if she hadn't realized she was there.

"I know we're off the path," Lily said, lowering her hand and rubbing her stinging fingers, "Saying it won't change anything."

Elizabeth said nothing for a moment, just swallowed, but then her eyes narrowed. When she spoke, a bitter anger had entered her voice, "Do you even realize what's happened?"

"We fell off the bridge," Lily summarized.

Elizabeth just shook her head, that bitter smile not leaving, "We're dead, Princess."

She let out a bitter laugh, threw her arm upwards, "You don't fall off the path, you don't stray from it, not here! There's a reason only a gold elf could get us through here!"

Lily blinked, looked upwards, then noted, "We're not dead yet."

"We'll be dead soon enough!" Elizabeth spat back.

Theyn stumbled between the two of them, holding out his arms, smiling and gesturing for peace.

"Come on, guys, there's no need to fight, really," he looked mournfully up from where they'd fallen, "Not after all this."

All three of them looked up, searching for a light, some sign of rescue, but the sky remained black and empty.

Lily suspected rescue would not be forthcoming.

"A human wouldn't have survived such a fall," Wizard Lenin agreed, *"They're too reliant on spells and tomes for anything that might save them from falling off a cliff."*

In other words, it was only because Lily had fallen with them that they were alive at all. Worse, nobody up there would realize that Lily had had the means to save them.

"What are we going to do now?" Theyn asked, voice wobbling as the reality of it all hit him.

For a moment, no one answered.

Then, staggering to her feet, Elizabeth moved to her pack that had fallen a few feet away. She removed book after book, carefully laying them on the ground, then reaching out and flipped through one.

"If we look through the gold elves' spells they might have left some hint of how to navigate this place," Elizabeth said, eyes furiously studying the page.

"Oh Lord," Wizard Lenin said with a small, disbelieving, moan in her head, *"She really is desperate to please, isn't she?"*

The spells, the prayers and poetry stolen from the elves a thousand years ago, had been for very specific tasks and purposes. Not everything had been handed over to humanity, the elves hadn't been that desperate, each clan had kept something to themselves. He highly doubted the gold elves would have handed over the secrets to navigating their ancestral homes. He'd certainly never come across it, and he'd read all the same books.

She kept flipping through pages with a single-minded focus, muttering to herself as she swiped strands of blonde hair away from her face, "Maybe this one. No, this one only works above ground. This one, maybe—"

And Lily was struck by the awkward knowledge, that neither Theyn nor Elizabeth knew, that she could solve this problem easily.

Lily didn't know how she did what she did, Wizard Lenin always complained about it, but she liked to think it was the fact that she just didn't believe in the rules. Lily had never tried before, but she was sure that she could find a way to teleport all of them from here to where the rest of the party was.

If that didn't work, for whatever reason, then she could at least get them to the top of the cliff.

"Look—" Lily started, but Elizabeth lifted her eyes, glared, and cut Lily off before she could start.

"Let me work, please," Elizabeth said, the 'please' tacked on with a surly pout.

"I'm serious—" Lily tried to protest, but Elizabeth just threw one of her other books at Lily's head.

Lily could take the hint.

She threw her arms in the air, picked Rabbit back up, and moved to sit against the wall. She could use some sleep anyway, she'd give Elizabeth a few hours, and then when she was ready to talk Lily would miraculously get them out of this place.

This wasn't Lily's problem, not when she had a way out any time she wanted.

It was, however, a poor excuse for a quest.

She'd thought—

Well, she'd thought something, but it looked like her only role in this was getting herself thrown off a cliff. Anyone could have done that.

At least there were going to be seven of these, that meant the next one had to be better than this.

There was a sigh, rustling, and Lily looked over to see Theyn sliding down the wall to look next to her. He gave her an exhausted smile, "I'd only get in the way."

Lily gave a hum of agreement at that and looked back over to Elizabeth. She was back at it, still muttering to herself, foot tapping erratically against the ground as she tried and failed to find the answer.

Lily idly wondered if she'd give up on the books or if she'd just look through them again when they didn't work out for her.

"She'll find something, don't worry," Theyn assured her quietly, "She always does."

"And if she doesn't?" Lily asked quietly.

Theyn tried and failed to smile, trying to pass off his response as a joke, "Then I guess we die down here."

As if Elizabeth not having an answer meant no one could.

Lily looked over at him, assessing, trying to see through her cousin. He looked uncomfortable under her gaze but didn't look away either.

She listened to the water drip down the walls somewhere, then asked, "You don't think I could?"

He opened his mouth, closed it, and clearly bit his tongue to stop from blurting the obvious answer. After swallowing, he said, "Iff, Elizabeth is— She's really good at this, she's been practicing mage craft for years, she's been taught by the very best. You're—"

He cut himself off, just motioned to Lily in all her glory, as if that was all he needed to say.

"He wouldn't be wrong ordinarily," Wizard Lenin chimed in, *"You don't understand what an aberration you are. That you are not only better than the girl, the best mage they have, but better than every human and elf mage who has come before you with no formal training of your own is inconceivable.*

"What you are, in all your facets, is nothing short of miraculous."

For all this world thrived on magic, immortality, and a half-forgotten god, there was no room for miracles here.

"She figure it out," Theyn assured Lily, "I promise."

She wouldn't, but they didn't need Lily to tell them that.

"There's a lesson to be learned here," Wizard Lenin concurred, *"One that is very difficult and painful."*

THE HEART OF THE WORLD

"What's that?" Lily asked.

"There is always someone better than you."

In her mind, in those memories that must belong to Wizard Lenin, Lily caught a flash of elusive red hair. There was an impression of a child, one that felt and looked like Lily, and a feeling of desperate inadequateness.

"The world is a series of interconnected ponds, each smaller than you suspect," Wizard Lenin continued, voice distant with nostalgia, *"Where for a time you may fool yourself into believing you are the largest fish."*

He paused, his thoughts on Elizabeth hunched over her books, the best there was at such a young age, *"I was fortunate enough to have that lesson forced upon me when I was very young."*

He could easily imagine the girl wandering the halls of the academy, books in hand, performing her spells and meeting the eye of each of her teachers and peers, *"Even with someone like Ilyn staring her in the face, she's too young. He's not a peer to her, not a competitor, and so she's blind to where she truly stands. She's allowed the monarchy to define her competition and has thrived on it."*

The likes of Theyn, whoever else was in that school with her, would never match up against the great mages of the elven clans.

"And then I showed up," Lily finished for him.

"And then you had the nerve to show up."

Wizard Lenin sighed, pushing nostalgia aside for the reality of the situation, *"Well, I suppose it's all for the best. I wasn't a fan of the crown prince anyway. Leave him and the girl to die and catch up with the rest of them."*

Lily started, drawing Theyn's attention, but tried to keep her surprised horror from showing on her face.

Had he really just suggested—

But why?

Wizard Lenin was a heartless man, a cruel one, and she knew that. He didn't hesitate to kill people, she knew that too, but there was a difference between that and just leaving them here for no reason.

Elizabeth would give up eventually, maybe in a few hours, and in the meantime Lily would get some sleep and convince the pair of them when all hope seemed lost anyway.

There was no need to—

She couldn't believe Wizard Lenin had even suggested that.

"I'm going to sleep," she told Theyn, falling over onto her side, "You might want to also."

"Oh, right," Theyn said with a start, as if realizing that they could be stuck here a while. He looked worriedly at Elizabeth, but she wasn't paying any attention to them. He flopped over as well, curling into a ball as he tried to stay warm.

As soon as she closed her eyes, she found herself facing Wizard Lenin.

He was wearing modern clothes, the kind from Earth and not from this place, and he was sitting in the Tylor's living room. There was no hint of the Tylors, not even of Lily, as there were no pictures on the walls anymore, only stock artwork.

The clothes looked good on him, the red in his sweater matched his namesake.

"Did you pick this place?" Lily asked with a smile as she looked around.

God—

She didn't miss it, couldn't really, but a part of her almost did. It'd been a simple place, if stifling.

He wasn't smiling, he was giving her a shrewd look.

"What is it?" Lily asked.

"She won't listen to you," Wizard Lenin said, of course meaning Elizabeth, "I know the type, she'd rather die than accept your help."

Lily laughed; she didn't believe that.

"That's ridiculous," Lily dismissed as she flopped onto the couch, "She'd rather die?"

Lily could die and come back, and she wouldn't rather die than accept help if she needed it. Just because she never had, didn't mean that she never would have if it'd come to that. Dying for your pride was a very silly thing to die for.

"Yes," Wizard Lenin said with that easy confidence he wore so well, "She's a self-made girl. She must stand on her own two feet or perish; those are the tenets she's made for herself."

"Well, I don't believe that," Lily said, "And even if I did, I can just knock her out and tell her she did it."

Lily wasn't above that; she didn't need the credit even if it'd be nice to have. If Elizabeth wanted to believe she'd miraculously saved them from certain death, then good on her. Lily would shout the news from the mountaintops.

This, of course, meant that this wasn't Wizard Lenin's real issue.

"Look," Lily said with a sigh, "I don't like her either, I'm not her greatest fan, but that doesn't mean she should go and die. Theyn certainly shouldn't, he's got nothing to do with any of this."

Lily didn't quite understand how he and Elizabeth were friends, but she supposed if Theyn was friends with Lily, then he was the type who could befriend anybody.

"Theyn is the problem," Wizard Lenin said, his voice ringing through the room.

Lily turned her head to look at him directly, he was looking away from her, glaring at the TV.

"I don't care about the girl," he continued harshly, "Do whatever you like with her, it makes no difference to me. The boy though—"

"What's wrong with Theyn?!" Lily blurted, sitting upright, feeling her heart race at the thought of Theyn, smiling Theyn, meeting any kind of unfortunate fate.

And Wizard Lenin—

God, the look in his eyes, that was pity.

"One day he will be your enemy," Wizard Lenin said.

"What?" Lily laughed, trying to even imagine it.

Wizard Lenin didn't take his answer back, he wasn't joking.

"He's my enemy by nature," Wizard Lenin explained, "I threaten his very existence, the future of his kingdom, even its legacy as my victory would bring me the power to rewrite its history."

Lily stared at him in dumb horror.

Wizard Lenin had wanted to overthrow the monarchy, he always had, and he'd never stopped mentioning it. She hadn't realized—hadn't stopped to think—that meant Theyn.

"But he's not king yet," Lily said quietly, "He's just crown prince."

And that wasn't if the regent claimed power for himself and officially disinherited both Lily and Theyn.

"He's the legitimate heir," Wizard Lenin said, "Questburger's been pushing the theory that he's responsible for my death. Even if he doesn't come into power, I would have to get rid of him."

"You can't—"

"That's what war is," Wizard Lenin said coldly, "What revolution is. The royal family dies and that is the end of the story."

Lily didn't say anything about that, she didn't know if that was true, but what was more important was that Wizard Lenin seemed to believe that was true. More, she thought of Theyn and—

"I don't think you'll have to do that."

"It's not about what you think," Wizard Lenin told her, "What matters is that he can die now, right here, in an unfortunate accident before he knows war or bloodshed, or he can die later, in humiliation and defeat."

She didn't believe that.

Wizard Lenin couldn't see the future, it didn't have to happen like that, Lily would find a way where it wouldn't have to happen like that. There would be, had to be, some other way to get Wizard Lenin what he wanted.

"What do you mean he'd be my enemy?" Lily pressed.

He smiled, as if he'd been waiting for her to ask that, "Sooner or later, lines will be drawn. I'll get my body back, people will notice, and they will watch to see what you do."

He pointed at her, "Simply by tolerating my presence, by failing to move against me, you'll fall onto my side. Questburger will suspect you, he'll whisper in Theyn's ear, and they will eliminate you as the vermin you are."

Lily laughed but Wizard Lenin cut her off.

"Leave him to die, Lily," he commanded, "Or you will forever look back on this moment and wish you had."

Did Lily believe that?

She couldn't picture it, not Theyn, polite, earnest, talentless Theyn who always kept an eye out for her.

Maybe, though, things would change. Maybe, somehow, lines would be drawn and there was nothing Lily could do about it. Maybe the seeds of friendship she thought existed between her and Theyn would sprout into weeds.

But she couldn't regret saving him.

"Lenin," Lily said, staring down at her feet and not looking at him, "I refuse to play the role of executioner to someone who may or may not betray me."

Lily wouldn't choose the path that would force the enemy Theyn into existence.

Right now was what mattered, right now, he was just a boy, timid, shy, deeply out of his element, and never quite living up to expectations. The man he would be didn't even cast a shadow yet.

And Lily believed that he could become her friend.

"You'll regret this," Wizard Lenin sighed, losing his fight and retreating back into the caustic cynicism that had kept him sane for all these years stuck in her head.

"I promise, I won't," Lily said.

He didn't believe her, she knew that, but he didn't have to.

What mattered was that Lily believed it.

Her real eyes opened and she was back in the cave. She turned her head to look at Elizabeth.

As Wizard Lenin had promised, in however long Lily had been asleep she hadn't given up yet.

"I told you," Wizard Lenin couldn't help, but Lily wasn't paying attention.

He was right, of course, she could see that now.

She had thought it was a silly thing to do but—Elizabeth was going to die before she gave up.

Maybe there was something courageous in that.

Desperate, yes, arrogant, certainly, but Elizabeth really believed their collective fate rested on her trembling shoulders and she hadn't buckled or even flinched.

She was doing everything she could to live up to the role that she believed she'd been assigned, no matter the opposition and doubts, either from herself or from Lily.

This was probably what Elizabeth was in every moment of her life, both in and out of her element. She fought against all expectations held against her, and so far, earned victory against the odds every single time.

She wouldn't falter now because she hadn't faltered then, because she could never afford to fail.

"You're giving her too much credit," Wizard Lenin scoffed, but he was looking at this too narrowly, skewed by the cold cynicism he couldn't shed.

What was important was that she was trying.

She wasn't blaming Lily for their circumstances, blaming herself even, or giving into any kind of rage or despair, but actively trying in every single moment.

Because, like Lily, she'd learned that no one would ever come to solve the problem for her.

Lily stood with a sigh, startling Theyn into waking up. She passed Rabbit to him, "Hold him for me."

"Iff," he whispered with large eyes, "Where are you going?"

Lily didn't answer, but instead walked until she was standing directly over Elizabeth. She cast a shadow over Elizabeth's books, making them impossible to read. Elizabeth looked up with tired, baleful eyes, "What is it?"

She clearly hadn't slept at all, not once since they'd left camp.

Lily crouched down so she was at eye level and held up the light in her hands.

"It's okay not to know the answer," Lily told her.

"What?" Elizabeth asked angrily.

Slowly, gently, Lily put her hands over Elizabeth's and closed the book, "It's alright, sometimes, not to know the answer."

"What makes you think—"

"You've always known the answer," Lily cut her off with a knowing look, "You've always had enough time and resources to find one."

"Sometimes, though, you'll fail even when you think you can't afford to. Sometimes, you'll fail even when everyone expects you to."

"Who do you think—"

"I think," Lily cut her off again with a smile, "That you and I have more in common than I thought."

For a moment, Elizabeth said nothing, eyes searching Lily's, then bit out, "You don't know anything about me."

"I know you're the best," Lily said easily, watching as Elizabeth sucked in a shocked breath at the admission, like she'd been kicked in the stomach, "I know you're more foreign than anyone gives you credit for, that you try to be more than the best because of it. I know that you wonder if it even means anything to these people."

Elizabeth didn't say anything, didn't dare to look away or even breathe.

"I know that this quest was the recognition you were waiting for, when I hadn't been waiting for anything at all."

Lily's smile became tender, stolen from Death and all those meetings they'd had over tea. She could see him saying these words, perhaps not to her, but through her to this girl that by all rights Lily shouldn't know at all.

"I know more than I should, Elizabeth," Lily finished, "But I also know that life can be unfair, and sometimes, it's not you who has the answers."

Elizabeth's hands shook, she set the book down onto the cold hard earth, and for a moment could only take in shuddering breaths as if she was just barely holding herself together.

"But if I don't find it," Elizabeth said breathlessly, "Then we'll be stuck down here forever."

Lily grinned, "I can do it."

You could hear the sound of a pin drop.

Whatever moment there had been was gone, washed away by Lily's declaration, leaving both Theyn and Elizabeth in numb disbelief.

"You can do it?" Elizabeth asked, eyebrows raised, unable to believe Lily's audacity.

"Iff, it's alright," Theyn decided to cut in, "Elizabeth knows the tomes better than anyone and—"

"I can do it," Lily repeated firmly.

There must have been something in her eyes, some unnatural glow, that gave Elizabeth pause.

"How?" Elizabeth asked.

"I am a thing of miracles," Lily said with appropriate hand gestures, stealing Wizard Lenin's line.

(He loathed that, and he wished he'd never said it.)

Elizbeth looked as if she dearly wished to disagree, Theyn as well, and inside her head Wizard Lenin was dying in embarrassment.

"Must you, Lily?"

If he didn't want her to quote him, then he should be less quotable.

"You don't have to do this," Wizard Lenin reminded her, thinking of the years to come, years down the road and all the pain and misery this would bring them both.

"I can do it," Lily insisted, holding out her hands to both of them, "I promise."

"Iff—" Theyn started, stopping when Lily kept holding her hand out.

"What does it hurt to have a little faith?" Lily asked them both.

They looked at each other, stared as if trying to decide on expressions alone what to do. With a grimace, Elizabeth hastily packed her books into her bag, then slapped her hand into Lily's.

"Don't make a fool of yourself," Elizabeth said, a daring look in her expression as if she'd hold it against Lily forever if this didn't work. There was a glimmer of something else in there, something beyond the unbridled arrogance, something genuine and true.

As always, Elizabeth was trying too hard.

Theyn winced, passed Rabbit back to Lily, and placed his hand softly into hers, "If you're sure, Iff."

He laughed, grinning over at Elizabeth, "I guess you're right, it doesn't hurt to try."

Lily only smiled in turn, squeezed both of their hands, and gave one last thought of reassurance to Wizard Lenin.

"It'll work out, you'll see."

Wizard Lenin scoffed but said nothing.

He was certain that this time, that strange nobility Lily harbored deep inside herself was going to bring her nothing but grief.

Lily closed her eyes, let her soul expand outwards, through the gold hidden the walls, up towards the sky, and finally to the bright sparks of life hidden away in the caverns.

There was the too bright flame that must be Ilyn, a flickering candle that—that had to be Annde, and every shade and intensity you could imagine in between.

"Here we go," Lily said, and pushed through time and space, pulling the others with her.

They landed on top of Ilyn who collapsed under their collective weight.

"Sorry," Lily offered as she scrambled off him (Elizabeth and Theyn too stunned to move), "We took the long way around."

10 THE ORIGIN OF WAR

In which a great battle with a fearsome beast takes place, Lily accidentally cheats the system, and an unlikely friendship or two blossoms.

"But how did you do it?!"

Lily didn't regret saving Elizabeth's life, but she was starting to regret that she hadn't simply hit her over the head and told her she'd hallucinated falling off a bridge in the first place.

The twelve hours had passed and thanks to Nhoj they'd finally made their way out of the maze of twisty little passages all alike that had so very nearly been their grave.

Personally, Lily would label it all very anticlimactic. The falling off the cliff bit had easily been the most terrifying part, and that wasn't supposed to have happened. The rest of it had just been silently falling Nhoj around and trying not to fall off cliffs.

He hadn't even had the decency to make it look hard or interesting.

The places that showed some sign of life, great carved columns and straight lines where there shouldn't have been any, he walked through so fast Lily barely got a look at them.

Lily only managed to catch the scorch marks staining the walls, the rubble of collapsed columns, and signs of something having happened out of the corner of her eye.

No signs of any people though, no food being made, no fires just put out, no graves even, or signs of any bodies either.

It was as if the place had built itself, left itself in this half-ruined state, and now it served as the set for an *Indiana Jones* film, where you could find holy grails but nothing more.

When they'd made it out into the early morning sunlight, Ilyn had taken pity on them, and they'd immediately set up camp. Despite the sunlight Lily had been more than ready to succumb to exhaustion.

Elizabeth, despite not having slept in nearly twenty-four hours now, hadn't.

"Iff, are you listening to me?" Elizabeth huffed.

There were horrific, dark, circles under her eyes. Elizabeth seemed immune to them as well as the bone deep exhaustion that had to be weighing her down.

Lily wanted to cry.

"No," Lily said wearily, wishing she'd just go away.

If they were lucky, Ilyn would let them spend the whole day at camp here. More likely, Ilyn would give them two hours, then march them on before they wasted an entire day loafing around.

She didn't know how it was possible, but he was so much worse than when he'd burned her house down.

"Elizabeth," Theyn, beautiful Theyn, tried to save Lily, "Maybe you could give her some space?"

Elizabeth was very clearly not going to give Lily space, "Your Highness, honestly—"

Oh, so Theyn got to be Your Highness while Lily had been promoted to a lowly 'Iff'.

"—What she did just isn't possible. I've never heard of any spells remotely like that!"

Theyn spared Lily a glance, a grimace, and tried his best, "But, Elizabeth—"

"It doesn't make sense!" Elizabeth cried out, hands gesturing despite herself, "I was there, Your Highness! I saw what she did! I know it happened! But it doesn't make any sense! Floating is possible, but only up to a certain height and couldn't have happened instantaneously like that! Transporting items through air is possible, difficult but possible, but you can only move one singular item at a time and certainly not four including the rabbit."

"Stop expecting the universe to make sense," Lily advised dully, "It'll make everything so much easier."

Of course, Elizabeth wasn't going to take that for an answer.

Elizabeth huffed, "You're dodging the question."

"I'm really not," Lily replied.

"You really are," Elizabeth said in turn, giving Lily a very challenging look, "I've never heard of anyone but an elf casting a spell not from one of the tomes. Even then, it's only their instinctive clan magic and that wasn't clan magic."

She pointed at Lily in accusation, as if she'd just caught Lily with both hands in the cookie jar, "But you don't use spell books for anything! Have you even read one?!"

The look on Lily's face must have said "no" for her.

Elizabeth brought out one of her books as evidence, waving it damningly in Lily's face, "Here!"

She shoved it at Lily, Lily fumbling and barely managing to catch it, nearly buckling under its weight.

There was something deeply, horribly, wrong with Elizabeth, Lily decided.

"Can I sleep, please?" Lily asked and couldn't help but notice Theyn giving her a very grateful look.

"Not until you answer the question!" Elizabeth barked.

Wizard Lenin didn't have to tell Lily that this meant supplying an answer that Elizabeth would like, not necessarily one that was true.

Lily stared at her for a long moment.

"I—found secret spell books in Tellestria," Lily said after a very long pause.

Elizabeth and Theyn stared at her.

"Really?" Theyn asked.

Elizabeth glared over at him, "Your Highness—"

She took in a breath, clearly to stop herself from snapping, "Your Highness, there are no spell books in Tellestria. There's no such thing as magic in Tellestria."

Right, because Elizabeth would supposedly know all about that.

"Uh—" Lily scrambled to think of something, her exhausted mind failing her, "I just did it, I don't know, it's a thing."

"It's a thing," Elizabeth said slowly.

"Can I please sleep?" Lily asked instead, she was almost at the point of begging. Why couldn't this girl just leave her alone? She'd had no problem doing that since they'd set out.

Elizabeth looked as if she was about to dig in her heels but, after a very deep breath, stopped herself.

"Fine," she said with a forced calm, "But you're answering everything when we start up again, I'm not taking no for an answer."

Oh, good, that would be so much fun.

Theyn shot Lily a look that was at once both apologetic and grateful, and guided Elizabeth away back to her sleeping roll where Lily could be left in peace. Without a word, Lily sent the book back into the safety of Elizabeth's bag where she could find it tomorrow and assume Lily had read it.

"You realize she's learned nothing and never will, yes?" Wizard Lenin cut in, thinking, of course, of Lily's very inspirational speech at the bottom of the cliff that Elizabeth apparently hadn't picked up on.

It was worth noting that, before this moment, he'd had a small amount of hope for Elizabeth. Oh, she was twelve, but she seemed bright enough and had time to learn from her mistakes and the curriculum. However, it appeared to him now that she was quite happy with her rote memorization and would never willingly step outside it. He was officially washing his hands of Elizabeth.

Lily chose to ignore that.

Lily looked about the camp, seeing if there was anyone to commiserate with her. As usual, there wasn't, no one was meeting her eye but—more than one was staring at her with an assessing look in their eye.

Lily tried not to pay it any mind, a sense of unease creeping through her.

"Blame your mother," Wizard Lenin offered.

Lily blinked in exhaustion, wondering if she'd somehow missed the context of that, *"What?"*

"That girl is going to badger you until you come up with an answer," Wizard Lenin explained, *"Either whack her over the head until she doesn't remember or blame your mother."*

"My mother?" Lily frowned, *"What's she got to do with anything?"*

"She was an extraordinarily powerful mage," Wizard Lenin said, *"They say she's the greatest seer the sun elves have ever had. The sun elves were very stingy when it came to their magic, they gave the humans next to nothing, a few parlor tricks. If you blame your mother, they might believe that it's just sun elf nonsense."*

Lily tried to hold onto that thought, understanding what it was supposed to mean, the odd feeling that it was more important than it sounded, but she was drifting fast. She was so tired that this time, she didn't remember if she met Wizard Lenin in her mind or not, she only had the feeling she'd missed something important.

***

Lily wasn't exactly what you'd call well-rested, two hours later when they were on their way again, but she had a renewed sense of energy.

So did Elizabeth.

"Well, Iff—"

Before she could start in, Lily looked over at Theyn (who had also drifted to the back of the group to hike with Lily and Elizabeth), "What's the next task?"

Lily was ready. This time, she'd be there to witness all of it, wouldn't accidentally fall off cliffs, and would be a key member of whatever they were doing.

She'd decided it was like the pilot episode of a TV series, the first task had been there just to get them all in the mood, give them a good idea of what the show was about, but in no way be the best episode in the series. Now that the quest had been renewed, so to speak, they could really get into the meat of things.

"That's a terrible metaphor."

And Wizard Lenin could just go to hell.

"You mean you don't know?" Elizabeth asked, unable to help the judgment in her tone.

"Why would I know?" Lily asked, "Nobody tells me anything!"

"They did tell you!" Elizabeth said, crossing her arms and glaring, "They told the entire kingdom in the ceremony before we left."

"They did?" Lily asked in dull horror.

"They said it dozens of times!" Elizabeth said, "The whole kingdom knows exactly what we'll be facing and how we'll be doing it. Everyone except you, apparently."

"How was I supposed to—"

"You were too busy gossiping with Ilyn to notice!" Elizabeth said, "And at least he knows what we're doing!"

Oh, that was not Lily's fault.

It'd been so hot and boring, and she'd been so tired, how was she supposed to know that they'd been saying important things?

She was about to say as much when she caught Theyn shaking his head desperately.

"Fine, I'm sorry," Lily huffed, hoping that'd make Elizabeth feel more cooperative, "Now can you please just repeat it now that I am paying attention?"

"It's the moon elf's task," Theyn cut in before Elizabeth could say anything to that, "According to the sun elves, he'll have to fight a fearsome guardian."

Lily—

Supposed that was the kind of thing you usually saw in a quest or series of tasks.

All the Greek heroes had to fight things with their swords, bare hands, or what have you. They usually had to do it multiple times, actually, so Lily shouldn't be surprised.

She still couldn't help her feeling of disappointment as she realized she would be zero help with that.

Lily understood she was twelve. Not only was she twelve, but she was also a girl, and she was scrawny. The fact that she was having the worst time keeping up with just the hiking was probably a sign that she wouldn't be of any use in a fight at all.

Her eyes moved to the moon elf, to his clearly defined muscles, ridiculously broad frame, and the broadsword, ax, and bow all strapped to his back at the same time along with his supplies.

It had never been more obvious to Lily in her life that someone did not need her help.

"Any, uh, more details on that?" Lily asked, feeling deflated again.

At Theyn and Elizabeth's silence, she looked over to see them giving her a funny look.

"I thought you said they told us exactly what we'd be facing and how we'd be facing it!" Lily protested.

"Yes, he's facing a guardian," Elizabeth said slowly, like Lily was the one who was stupid, "And then he's going to kill it."

"Yeah, but—" Lily desperately searched for justifications, "Is it a giant pig? A giant walrus? A giant bird? This could be important!"

"It's just the guardian," Elizabeth said, even slower than before, as if she thought that Lily had somehow sounded even dumber.

Theyn hastily cut in, "The sun elves didn't say, they probably don't know either. Sometimes, Ilyn says they only get the gist of things."

Well, that was useless.

"Anyways," Elizabeth said, brushing that aside, "You never answered my question. Don't think you can wriggle out of it this time, Iff."

She'd never dream of such a thing.

"Uh—" Lily tried to decide if she was going to take Wizard Lenin's advice or not.

It sounded reasonable, but something about it just didn't seem right to Lily, not when she didn't know anything about her mother herself.

"You must have some idea how you did it," Elizabeth said, "That wasn't an accident."

That would have been a better plan, wouldn't it? To have pretended to accidentally somehow saved them from certain peril. God, she wished she'd thought of that.

"I—really, really, wanted it," Lily blurted, "And when I really, really, want things—they happen."

Elizabeth and Theyn didn't stop walking, but they did stare, and not one of them said a word either.

All at once, Lily was aware that, like usual, they were the only ones talking. The elves made it a point to never talk to one another unless they had to. Annde only made those weird ringing noises everyone else swore were words when Theyn or Elizabeth talked to him.

This meant the entire party had heard every word of that.

"You're an idiot," Elizabeth concluded.

"I'm not—"

"You're an unfairly talented idiot," Elizabeth continued, "And I wish that I had the nerve to hit you."

Oh, did she? Well, if she wanted to—

No, she looked much stronger than Lily, Lily would die in that fight.

"Well, Your Highness, I think I'm done for the day," Elizabeth said to no one, staring out ahead of them with a thousand mile stare, "I need to seek out saner company,"

THE HEART OF THE WORLD

She started moving forward, clearly beelining for Annde of all people, like she'd rather talk to a ringing wineglass than to Lily. Lily looked over at Theyn who—that bastard—he gave her a sheepish little smile and hurried after Elizabeth.

"You did sound remarkably stupid," Wizard Lenin offered unsympathetically.

"I am not stupid!"

She wasn't, she just—

That hadn't been a stupid answer! That's what she did, if you thought about it. That's the way it always worked. She was sorry that wasn't how it went for other people but that didn't mean what she'd said had been wrong.

She sighed, looked down at the uneven ground she was traversing.

There was no road on this side of the mountains.

The exit had been small, there had been no door leading them out, and when they'd exited all Lily had been able to see for miles were trees. Endless trees without a hint of smoke, lumber, or anything else.

They'd been walking for some time now, their path determined by Ilyn and his pocket watch, cut out for them by the moon elf and his sword. For all Lily had never been hiking on Earth, she knew that this wasn't what most hiking was like.

There wasn't any trail to follow here, and they could only hope they were going in the right direction.

Lily wondered if this quest was strictly necessary. Maybe, if she wanted it, she could just teleport to wherever the Heart of the World really was. She knew where it would be, she'd seen it so many times before, it was just a matter of getting to it in the real world.

That felt wrong though, so wrong that even Wizard Lenin hadn't brought it up as an option, as if the journey itself was the key to unlocking the door.

Ilyn came to a sudden stop, the rest of them all bumping into each other in their haste to stop with him. He stowed his watch and looked over to the moon elf who nodded.

Ilyn stepped out of the way, letting the moon elf step forward. He took one step, two, then raised a hand and shouted.

A gust of wind blew out in all directions, rattling the trees and nearly blowing all of them over. Lily barely managed to stay upright, clinging to a nearby trunk, and watched as the wind rushed back in and returned to his hand.

"Just up ahead in a clearing," the moon elf announced in a low gruff voice that perfectly fit his appearance. He looked back at the rest of them, yellow eyes sharp, "Stay out of the way, or we'll all die."

He took the lead, Ilyn taking his advice and remaining several paces behind. The rest of them hung even further back, eagerly avoiding what was starting to sound like a death sentence.

The moon elf, though, with his wild grin and the way he hacked out the path for them, he looked eager for the fight.

"*He probably is,*" Wizard Lenin said off-hand, "*I imagine the last few years have been quite boring without any wars or rebellions. It's hard to pride yourself as a warrior when there are no wars.*"

This was the only legitimate use for his skills, beyond guarding human caravans in the provinces, slaying some beast or another troubling a village, or simply sparring that the moon elves had seen in years.

Lily supposed she was glad someone was looking forward to this.

Maybe Lily didn't have to have an integral part, a grand time, so long as someone was having fun.

As predicted, they suddenly found themselves in a clearing where before there had only been dense trees.

It wasn't just a clearing though.

Even though they'd exited the trees, it was still dark, darker somehow than before when there should have been afternoon sunlight. The air was colder than it had been, there was a bitter taste to it, and there was nothing visible up ahead or—

Lily turned around, knowing what she'd find.

There was nothing visible ahead and nothing visible behind them either.

If they'd passed through another door, it would have just closed.

Lily turned back around to face forward with the others. Out of the darkness, six red eyes opened, each more than a handspan apart from one another.

Nothing else of it was visible, not its teeth, not the size of its head, or the bulking size that had to be its body. Only those red eyes, barely recognizable as eyes, and certainly not shaped like any human's.

Except there was something else, something Lily couldn't see, something she was sure she should have no way of knowing but—this thing wasn't really a thing.

The monsters in legend had origins, they had purposes. Even if that purpose was to guard a treasure on behalf of a god, or to run rampant in a maze beneath a city, they all had a reason for existing and left corpses when they died.

This wasn't like that.

It was a clockwork monstrosity, nothing more than a windup toy, something that had been purposefully set in their path by someone or something but nothing more than that.

Lily was struck by the horrifying truth that this thing didn't really exist, it was only here because they were here, because someone or something had been waiting for them and had set together a collection of trials.

"So, you seek passage," a voice called out to them from the mist, it didn't even attempt to be a human voice.

The moon elf didn't respond, he kept his sword raised, his eyes narrowed, and waited. Lily caught movement from the others, saw the elves (save for the happiness elf, that sorry bastard) moving back towards the trees. Theyn and Elizabeth disappeared, too, they must have been pulled back by Annde who Lily still couldn't see for some reason—

"Do you know where you are?" the voice asked, trying and failing to sound gleeful, "These are unfinished grounds."

The moon elf muttered something under his breath, something Lily couldn't hear, and his sword began to glow.

Lily hastily looked around, trying to see where she should watch from. Everyone else had disappeared, except the happiness elf who looked content as usual. She panicked, realized she'd wasted enough time already, and darted into the bushes, dragging the happiness elf with her at the last moment.

To her relief, she didn't end up crouching next to Annde, she wasn't sure she could have handled that. Unfortunately, she ended up next to Nhoj the gold elf.

"Hello," Lily offered awkwardly.

The man glared at her, looked as if he was about to tell her and the happiness elf to get out, but caught himself.

At least he seemed intent on ignoring her, Lily thought, there were worse options. She sighed with relief, looked over at the happiness elf whose collar she was still clutching and—

God, he had no idea what was happening, did he?

He was staring blissfully out at the scenery, his head tilted so he was looking up at the canopy overhead and nothing else, complete with a little smile on his face.

Lily let him go with some annoyance, unable to help noticing that he hadn't even thanked her for saving his life.

She set Rabbit on the ground as well, cracking her neck, and letting out a sigh of relief. Well, maybe she should be glad that she wasn't getting involved with this one.

She settled in to watch the fight.

Obviously, she didn't know anything about medieval sword fighting. The moon elf looked impressive, though. His hair was crackling with electricity, there was a strange glow about him, and he was meeting something blow for blow at the edge of the fog.

Every movement looked efficient, easily gliding into the next, and his legs never buckled beneath him, and his arms didn't falter either.

He looked really good at this.

"It's quite the sight, isn't it?"

Lily's head swiveled to look next to her.

To her shock, Nhoj had addressed her. He wasn't looking at her or the happiness elf, though, but instead watching the man in the clearing.

There was a strange half-longing in his eyes, something distant, bitter, and resigned all at once.

"My people have never been capable of anything like that," he said quietly.

"Well," Lily said hesitantly, watching Nhoj to see if he really had been talking to her, "We can't all be that—tall."

The moon elf disappeared into the fog, even his bright hair no longer visible. Something tried to laugh at him, it wasn't laughter though, for all the sound was malevolent it sounded recorded.

Whatever waited in there, while undoubtedly hideous, was even less of a concept than Rabbit.

Lily tried to force her attention back to the elf next to her.

He was done talking, though, his eyes still riveted on the fog the man had disappeared into. It was as if by staring at it long enough, he could part through it, see the man dancing inside.

Lily swallowed, her throat suddenly dry.

"Nhoj," she said quietly. He flinched at the sound of his name exiting her throat.

"Nhoj," she forced herself to repeat, closing her eyes and trying to just get through it, "Why do the elves hate each other so much?"

For a moment, he said nothing.

He didn't look at her, didn't move, and for a moment she was sure he wasn't going to say anything at all.

Then he looked at her.

It was an odd, assessing look, the kind he'd never given her before, not even when she'd first stepped into his parlor so many years ago.

He must have seen something new in her, she realized as his expression changed, something she wasn't sure she'd wanted anyone to see.

"You really have no idea, do you?" he asked.

"I—" Lily started but his look stopped her.

"You're playing a very dangerous game, Princess."

Lily blinked, spluttered, feeling like she'd completely lost the conversation, "What are you talking about?!"

This time his look was easier, knowing, as if he'd seen through her very stupid act, "When the night elves find out they'll eat you alive."

Oh.

Oh, that son of a—

Seven years, seven years he went without realizing, without questioning, handing her money so easily and now—

He was going to do this now?!

"I don't know what you're talking about," Lily said, desperately looking elsewhere.

"The resemblance is uncanny," he said, looking her over, "Not just the face, the mannerisms as well, though she was always a little older."

There was a terrible, awful, feeling of Wizard Lenin thinking 'I told you so' from the depths of her mind. She could just feel his smug, overbearing, shadow in her head, luxuriating in all the memories where he had told her so.

"Who put you up to it?" he asked.

"Nobody!" Lily spluttered.

"Nobody?" he asked in turn, clearly suspicious.

"You did!" she said, throwing a hand at him, glaring when he looked confused and even wounded, "I just walked in, and you were the one who threw me her money! I just thought—well, if somebody thinks I'm this Lily Jones person!"

Then Frank had of course shown up and the rest was history.

"You had dyed your hair," he said slowly, like that was somehow her fault.

Lily held up her hair towards him, her damning red hair, "Oh, like I could have walked around with this? Hello, everybody, pleasure to meet you! I've just wandered in from Tellestria, can anybody get me a taxi home?!"

He stared at her dumbly, then his eyes moved over her shoulder.

God, the happiness was sitting right there, wasn't he?

He'd heard all of that, she was sure, and now Lily was sitting next to Nhoj and the happiness elf, having confessed to not really being Lily Jones.

—She was sure neither of them would tell Frank.

"Are you going to answer my question?" Lily huffed, desperately changing the subject.

He didn't say anything, just looked past her into the fog, then, "They say that the first murderer was a night elf. That he ate the firstborn son of the sun elf, and that this was just his first murder."

Lily couldn't see the night elf through the fog, but she could imagine her, pale and dark-haired, so very proud and beautiful even in the light of day when there was so little of her.

Nhoj's lips curled downwards, teeth bared, "They have always been demons.

"When it comes to the others, there was war for some time between all of us, we separated from one another," Nhoj continued quietly, the fight gone out of him, "My people retreated into the mountains, we used them as our shield, our mines, and carved out wonders for ourselves."

He looked down at his hands for a moment, "We made ourselves respected for our art, necessary to each of them, and that spared us the worst of it. At least, until it didn't."

He fell silent, and even though they were only words, words he himself had uttered, they seemed to hurt him like a physical blow.

"We aren't like the others," he said quietly, "We had no talent, no gift, for warfare. We could forge the finest blades but never wield them. When the night elves rose like a shadow, when they came for the mountains, there was nothing we could do."

Xhigrahi, Lily remembered.

Frank, Wizard Lenin, Death, had all mentioned the empire that ruled the other side a thousand years ago. Frank had spoken of it with fondness and bitter regret, Wizard Lenin talked about it as if it were ancient history, Death an unfortunate misstep in human destiny no different than any other.

Nhoj talked about it like it was the shadow hanging over his head.

Suddenly, Lily saw their journey through the mountains in a new light. She remembered all the scorch marks, the ruined architecture, and how she'd thought it was a city empty even of ghosts. He hadn't walked quickly out of skill, efficiency, or a readiness to be done with it, but because he could hear and see the memories that Lily couldn't.

Lily, all at once, felt not only ignorant but vulgar and crass.

She'd walked through that place thinking it was nothing. She'd met with this man, unwittingly dressed like a night elf, and had thought it was nothing.

It wasn't so much that Lily had never believed she was wrong, she'd been wrong about many things, but there had been no one to wrong.

The Tylors were the Tylors, everyone else had been more distant than even that, and so long as she kept out of their way they kept out of hers. She hadn't realized it wasn't the same here.

Her stomach churned and her face caught fire, everything twisted inside her, and Lily knew this must be what shame felt like.

"They made us build their cities, their palaces, forge their swords, and cut their jewels while they fed off the blood of our children for a thousand years," he continued in that quiet, aching voice, "We traded gold, silver, precious jewels, art, weaponry, anything we could think of for the sanctity of our own flesh and the survival or our people. We could do nothing."

He looked over at her, eyes landing on her red hair with a pronounced frown. He took a lock of it in his fingers meaningfully, shaking it at her, "Only they escaped. They bided their time in their own mountains for a thousand years, while the rest of us were enslaved and devoured!"

He dropped her hair, offering her a smile that wasn't quite apologetic.

Lily tried to smooth it out unconsciously, as if she could make it a little less red.

"There isn't a night elf empire anymore though," she pointed out, his look turned amused and knowing.

"Thank god for that," Nhoj agreed, only to sigh as he looked at her,

"But we paid the price for that as well."

"What do you mean?" Lily asked.

He nodded towards her, "There was a human king. His was a very small kingdom, harmless, at the very edge of civilization. The night elves paid them no mind at all. They had no magic, no great talents or knowledge, there was nothing noteworthy about them."

Lily tried to picture it, comparing it to the capital city that they'd come from, how opulent and grand it had all been.

"They sent messengers to each of the clans, asking to form an alliance. There had been rebellions before, all failures, but this time a sun elf went with them."

He gave her another meaningful look, "We were desperate, and we took it as the only chance we might ever get. We gave them everything. We taught them our magic, anything that might help in battle or even just survival, we built them forges and weapons, we told them how to build armies and win battles."

He smiled bitterly, "The sun elves—they gave them nothing. They taught them how to light candles and fireplaces.

"It was the sun elves who tore apart Xhigrahi, not the rest of us, certainly not the humans. They could have done it anytime they'd liked; they could have done it in the very beginning. They simply chose not to."

He paused, looked straight into Lily's eyes without flinching, and said, "You asked why we hate each other. The others, in truth, I do not mind so much. They suffered as we suffered, they lost what we lost, and for all we might envy each other, I do not hold their gifts against them.

"The sun elves, though, they deserve the same level of hell that the night elves do for that."

He smiled then, looking at her with bitter fondness, "Then the humans took their borrowed magic and turned it against us. We never returned to the mountains, we found ourselves working once again as impoverished artisans, and we became a quiet mockery of our talents.

"It's the same story everywhere, except, of course, for the sun elves."

He sighed, turned his attention back to the mist. The night elf stumbled out of it. He looked battered, there were bruises where none had been before, his face was swollen, and blood was gushing out of his left shoulder. He hunched over his sword, leaning on it, clutching at his ribs as he stared into the black mist.

"Still," Nhoj said looking quietly at the man, "For how defenseless my people are, I often think we chose better than them."

"Why's that?" Lily asked, watching as the man straightened, forced himself to lift his sword. He flung himself back into the mist with a great cry, it swallowed him whole.

"We will always be wanted," Nhoj said, "By the humans, the night elves, it doesn't matter. They will always covet our work and want for great memorials dedicated to themselves. We will bend like reeds in the wind, even when all the others crumble. But what use does a kingdom of demons or human mages have for swordsmen?"

The moon elf was shot back out, this time with a new wound in his stomach. It looked deep, a horrifying burgundy that spread quickly. He was thrown to the grounds, skidding backwards near the edge of the clearing. His legs twitched and he shuddered as he forced himself first to sit up, then kneel, then stand.

The blood trickled down his legs.

"So, it ends here," Nhoj commented quietly.

"What end?" Lily asked him desperately.

"This quest," Nhoj said, as if it meant nothing to him, "If he can't do it, with all his gifts, then none of us can."

The moon elf shuddered, fell to his knees again, unable to support himself even against his sword. The wind was whipping around him, clearly his own magic desperately trying to cling to something, but it couldn't bat away the mist.

"That can't happen," Wizard Lenin's voice, which until now had been absent, rang through her head loudly.

"Do something!" he commanded, *"We can't go back empty handed!"*

Lily watched in terror as the fog stalked forward, moving with the unseen beast, inching closer towards the bleeding man.

Lily jumped to her feet and sprinted forwards, ducking Nhoj's hand before he could pull her back. She flung herself to the moon elf's side.

She tried and failed to lift the sword next to him, gritting her teeth and yelling, begging it to just lift upwards.

It didn't move.

Instead, the sword stuck in the ground, she turned to look at the thing stalking towards her. She saw its six red eyes, each the size of softballs, staring at her in wide-eyed terror.

It had stopped moving, stopped laughing, stopped saying anything at all. Facing her, it was reduced back into whatever it really was.

Lily stepped forward, dragging the sword with her, overturning the grass as she went like a plow. She dashed into the fog, willing her arms to lift, but before they did—

There was a flash of light then the fog was gone.

There was no monster, no body, no nothing, just a clearing and a man bleeding out behind her.

Lily let the sword fall to the ground, her arms numb from holding it, everything shaking from exertion and the aftermath of terror. She sank to the ground, laughing, staring up at the clear blue sky.

Well, she'd done it after all, hadn't she?

She hadn't been able to lift a sword but here she was.

She'd saved the quest after all.

She felt a hand tug at her jacket. She looked over to find herself staring at the moon elf, who had managed to drag himself towards her. He'd left a bloody trail in his wake.

"You saved my life," he said, jerking her closer.

"Oh," Lily said lamely, trying to look anywhere but his face, "Yes."

He grinned at her, as before it was a sharp grin, fanged. He paid no mind to Elizabeth hurrying towards him with a text book and a small metal box, likely containing medical equipment.

"We are blood brothers now, you and I," he told her.

"Oh," Lily said, only to then flush, "Oh, I mean, that's a bit much. Really, I just—"

He cut her off, pulled her towards him again, ignoring Elizabeth's admonishments. He pulled her close enough to whisper in her ear, his blood now soaking through her uniform as well, "You, Iff, will be the first and only human queen the clan will recognize."

He shoved her off and Elizabeth immediately took her place, flipping through her books and yelling poetry to close his wounds. Lily numbly took Rabbit from Nhoj, unsure what to think.

She had the sudden thought, utterly unbidden, that somehow, in some way, she'd just cheated.

11 THE ONCE AND FUTURE KING

In which Lily finds herself facing consequences, Wizard Lenin hints at his mysterious past, and Lily has a vision featuring the strange, ineffable, terrifying truth of Rabbit.

"Iff, can I—um—talk to you for a few seconds?" Theyn grimaced, paused, then valiantly pressed on, "It's about Ailill."

Lily looked at him with all the dumb, aching, exhaustion she felt. They'd started walking immediately after the fight with the clockwork monster. As usual, Lily was lingering far behind the others.

Lily didn't even bother to ask, she knew they wouldn't stop until sunset, as usual. The question was if they'd reach the mind elf task before that point, and worse, if Lily would be required to do anything for it.

At some point, she'd realized that she'd now walked more than she ever had in her life.

"Oh, honestly," Elizabeth huffed, because she was here too of course and as energetic as ever, "Don't you know everyone's name yet?"

Lily just continued looking at them both. She wasn't sure she wanted them to go away, that wouldn't stop her feet from hurting, but she wished they'd be a little quieter.

"Ailill is the moon elf," Elizabeth said slowly, once again clearly implying Lily was stupid, "Your new devoted knight."

Right, him.

He was walking up ahead, hacking at the foliage as usual, giving no indication that his vow to her had ever happened. Lily had been hoping they could just ignore it.

Apparently not.

"It's just—" Theyn glanced at Elizabeth, who only gave him a look. Theyn wilted, "He said that he, the moon elves, will only support you as the next ruler. Well, he said as much to Annde—"

"Oh, Your Highness, just spit it out already!" Elizabeth commanded, whacking him on the arm.

Theyn rubbed at it with another painful grimace, looking like he'd rather be anywhere else, even at the bottom of a cliff.

"He can't—do that," Theyn finally said weakly, "Iff, he really can't do that. You know that, don't you? You have to say something to him."

Lily gave him another look, "What am I supposed to say to him?"

"Anything," Elizabeth commanded, "Remind him that you're not crown princess, you're not going to inherit, and he should be swearing fealty to the crown and not you."

Lily had thought of that.

She'd tried to say as much to him before they'd started walking again, but he'd charged ahead, not waiting to hear a word she said.

It was almost refreshing, in a terrible way. She was so used to these people not treating her like a princess that to see someone actually refer to it was a little nice. Strange, and misguided certainly, but nice.

"You don't understand—" Theyn started, but he was cut off by Elizabeth.

Lily was struck by the sudden thought that when Theyn grew up, it'd be his advisors who ended up ruling because they'd walk all over him like a doormat.

"You should have said something right then," Elizabeth concluded, "It wasn't your place and look at the mess we're all in because of it."

"I was busy!" Lily pointed out, in case they had forgotten she'd saved all their lives and this quest thing, "And what do you mean it wasn't my place? I saved his life! He would have been eaten if I hadn't done anything!"

The rest of them certainly hadn't done anything to stop it.

"You can't seriously be suggesting I should have left him to die," Lily concluded, giving them both very skeptical looks.

If Elizabeth was suggesting as much, then she and Wizard Lenin had a lot more in common than Lily had thought.

"I'd never make a pretense that I was suggesting anything else," Wizard Lenin cut in, which Lily supposed was true, Wizard Lenin had a very refined sense of shamelessness that Elizabeth certainly didn't possess.

Wizard Lenin liked to view it as a kind of integrity, he was certainly deplorable but never pretended he wasn't.

"No! Of course not, but I—" Elizabeth cut herself off, gave a small hum of annoyance, and started again, "You could have gotten yourself killed! Should have gotten yourself killed, if we're being honest, it's a miracle you're even alive!"

"I'm very talented at not dying," Lily dryly offered.

Of course, without knowing any of Lily's history or even what had happened the night Wizard Lenin had blown up, neither got the joke.

"Not dying isn't a talent, Iff," Elizabeth scoffed, she did soften then somewhat and said, "Regardless, I'm glad you're alive, even if you are an idiot."

"Thanks," Lily responded blandly.

"And Iff, remember, just—talk to him, please," Theyn pleaded again.

Lily eyed him, thought it over.

It wasn't a hard thing to do, easy even, and she really owed Theyn much more than that. And she'd always thought, if she ever did find friends, friends that lived in the mortal plane, she'd make it a habit not to disappoint them. If she could have something true, something real, then she wanted to do more than live up to expectations.

"You are—" Elizabeth's voice cut into her thoughts. Looking over, Lily found the girl lost in thought, looking ahead rather than at Lily or Theyn, "You are talented though."

It didn't quite look like it pained Elizabeth to admit this, but it looked like it was harder to say than she'd have liked. Theyn always admired everyone's talents so easily, even laughing about it. Maybe it was because that's what it meant to be Theyn, easily, hopelessly, talentless.

Lily suspected that Elizabeth had made it a point to never come second in anything. She was the type who, back on Earth, would have been a three-time spelling bee champion.

"I don't know why or even how you do it—" Elizabeth cut herself, and almost looked over at Lily shyly, before looking away again, "Well, you're going to give me a run for my money at the academy."

Lily realized in sudden horror what her future at this academy was going to be like, she wouldn't just be attending, she and Elizabeth would be vying for valedictorian in a cutthroat competition over manipulating the universe every day for the rest of Lily's life.

Lily was going to die.

"You can't die," Wizard Lenin cut in with his usual lack of sympathy and excess amount of biting wit.

"Why are you so happy?" Lily asked, *"You're going to be suffering right along with me!"*

"If I don't have a body by then, then I'll be making a point of making you suffer right along with me."

"You're going to have to get rid of the rabbit though," Elizabeth said, side eyeing Rabbit on top of Lily's head, "No instructor's going to put up with that thing on your head."

"They'd better put up with it," Lily huffed.

"I'm telling you, they're not—"

"Well, then they'd better say goodbye to the capital city, because it'll be in Rabbit's stomach," Lily said, jerking her thumb up at him.

Elizabeth actually had the nerve to roll her eyes, "The rabbit doesn't eat cities, Iff."

"How would you know?" Lily asked, "And I told you, he's not actually a rabbit, he just looks like a rabbit."

"Oh, what's he supposed to be then?" Elizabeth asked.

"I don't know!" Lily said, if she did then she'd have said as much, wouldn't she.

"You don't know because he's just a rabbit," Elizabeth concluded with a hum.

He was not just a rabbit, he didn't even look like a rabbit. Lily had looked up pictures in loads of encyclopedias, and not one of them looked like Rabbit did. Oh, he was rabbit shaped and everything, had the ears, the face, but rabbits weren't expressionless and perfectly still the way he was.

"Calm down," Theyn urged them both desperately, stepping between them and holding up his hands in defense, "I'm sure the rabbit, I mean Rabbit, will be fine."

Oh, Rabbit would be fine, it was the rest of them she was worried about.

Elizabeth and Theyn soon got distracted by their own conversation about the academy. They discussed certain instructors, different branches of mage craft, and the difference between Ilyn as an instructor and Ilyn as a quest companion (apparently, there was very little).

Lily let her mind wander, trying to picture what it would be like.

Maybe, in time, Lily would get used to this place. She'd go to this academy, everyone would call her Iff (they certainly wouldn't be calling her Your Highness), she'd occasionally check in on Frank, visit Uncle Death, and this would become her world in a way she'd never quite been able to before.

Then again, Lily wasn't sure any world would ever belong to her. She'd been an outsider wherever she went.

Lily's eye fell on the mind elf, whose task was next.

He had his nose stuffed in a book, the same way he had for every day they'd walked so far. There was a practiced ease to the way he walked while reading, even the way he carefully but swiftly turned the page, as if it'd been ingrained in him ages ago.

She had no idea how he thought those books were going to help him here.

"I wouldn't take him lightly," Wizard Lenin chastised.

Though, she supposed 'chastised' wasn't the word for it, this was closer to a warning, something that Lily wasn't supposed to simply brush aside.

Lily stiffened, trying to stifle down her annoyance, *"I wasn't taking him lightly—"*

"What you're seeing is not the extent of what he's capable of," Wizard Lenin noted darkly.

"What he's capable of?"

Lily hadn't said anything about what the man was or wasn't incapable of, she never had. Wizard Lenin, though, had been the one to say that anyone who wasn't the sun or night elves were small potatoes.

Not just Wizard Lenin but Frank, Nhoj, and Ilyn too. It was the only thing everyone seemed to agree on.

"I—" Wizard Lenin uncharacteristically stopped.

His unspoken thoughts raged like a river inside her head, each barely glimpsed before it was out of sight.

There was a tall man, proud, with blue-black hair, and a cruel smile.

"I made the acquaintance of a mind elf once," Wizard Lenin said, *"I've met others since then, I even attempted to recruit them. It was a lost cause, they had no interest in seeing something like me topple the monarchy and I had no interest in relying on them. That first man though—"*

He cut himself off, purposefully not defining him, not naming him. Lily was left with the impression of something far more than a colleague or even acquaintance, but something he didn't want to admit even to her.

Perhaps, Lily thought with some fascination, especially to her.

"He made it all too clear that while he lacked the raw power of the sun or night elves, that he could be exceedingly clever and callous," Wizard Lenin finished, *"In their eternal quest for knowledge, callousness is almost a tool to the mind elves."*

There were more images that Lily couldn't catch, not only because of how fast they moved but because of a great shadow of emotion hanging over them.

Whatever had happened with that man, with a young Wizard Lenin, it had been scarring enough that it could only be seen as the shadow of a memory.

The aftertaste of a feeling.

Lily felt her mouth go dry, her thoughts racing.

Wizard Lenin rarely, if ever, revealed any information about himself and especially not about his youth. She wanted to ask, she wanted to ask desperately, but her thoughts were caught in her throat.

Instead she asked, *"Do you know this one?"*

"No," Wizard Lenin said easily, *"But I know how they work and I know he has no interest in pleasing the monarchy or playing along with a prophecy. He's here for his own purposes, and whatever those are, they will be anything but pleasant for the rest of us."*

Lily especially was in trouble if the man put enough clues together.

The important thing was that these people, Wizard Lenin strongly felt, were not to be trusted.

***

Several days later the forest had transformed. The trees slowly turned from towering pines into mangroves, the firm ground beneath their feet turned into marsh. Unlike the mountain, this place was not abandoned.

It felt as if eyes were watching them from every shadow, eyes that didn't belong to silent birds or lurking alligators, but something else that wasn't supposed to be here.

They hadn't reached the task yet, but Lily couldn't shake the feeling that it'd be something very unpleasant.

She didn't want to think that; it wasn't the kind of attitude you should have on a life-changing quest, but after the last time she just couldn't muster the same enthusiasm. It was beginning to occur to her that this quest wasn't what she'd been led to believe it would be.

Up ahead of her, the mind elf came to a sudden stop, he snapped his book shut. His lips contorted into a self-assured smile and his eyes glittered with some joke the rest of them were too ignorant to understand.

Ilyn and the moon elf turned back toward him, both stopping in their tracks, the moon elf still having his sword raised to hack through the vines.

"It's time?" Ilyn asked, but there was no enthusiasm in his question, only a dry sort of judgment.

He didn't say it, but Lily had the feeling what he really wanted to say was that the mind elf was getting ahead of himself.

"Isn't that your job?" the mind elf asked in turn, his smile only growing, relishing Ilyn's nerve at questioning him.

Ilyn's face darkened, he didn't respond.

"I can't say whether it's here or not," the mind elf said, clearly implying that this was Ilyn's job, "But I am fully prepared for it."

(Lily's eyes darted to the moon elf, sure that had been some kind of dig at him, at the last task that he had failed to fulfill himself but—

He wasn't responding either.)

"We'll see," Ilyn said, turning back to the way ahead.

The mind elf only smiled and started walking ahead.

While the rest of them were just standing there, watching, he made his way to the front of the group, just behind Ailill. He motioned for the moon elf to get on with it, to continue clearing the path, looking like he didn't have a care in the world.

Like he, somehow, was far more suited for his task than Nhoj, Ilyn, or any of the rest of them ever could be.

"I really don't like this guy," Lily noted.

God, even though it would cost Lily the Heart of the World, even though it was so needlessly petty, she couldn't help but want to see him fail.

It said a lot that Wizard Lenin wasn't vehemently disagreeing.

The path forward got worse.

With every step she took, her feet made a disgusting squelching noise as the ground became muddier and muddier. Soon, there was no chance of avoiding the puddles, and Lily's well-insulated boots started leaking.

Looking ahead, Lily saw in dread that it only got worse, the ground disappeared into algae filled water.

"No," Lily thought, her eyes looking forward and tracing out possible paths, all of them leading into opaque water of unknown depth.

"No!" Lily repeated when the mind elf didn't change direction, didn't even flinch at the thought of all the snakes, crocodiles, piranhas, bacteria, and who knew what else was in that water.

To Lily's horror, he walked straight in, with Ilyn unblinkingly following behind. Everyone else hesitated for one second, two, but then dutifully stepped in behind him.

Lily, last as always, hesitated the longest before she ran in, hoping getting it over with would make it easier.

It was uncomfortably cold, but not damningly cold, not cold enough to ward off the swamp monsters that had to exist. Ahead of her, Elizabeth was cringing, pretending she was perfectly fine with swamps while Theyn was doing nothing to hide his discomfort.

"He couldn't have made a raft?" the love elf asked under her breath.

"That would make him look dependent on the likes of us," Nhoj responded wryly, shuddering as he sank into the unseen mud.

God, that showed how awful this was, these people were actually talking to one another.

None of this was helping Lily feel as if she wasn't being watched by something that didn't have her best interests at heart. She looked up at the dense cover of trees, but she couldn't see anything beyond the hints of sunlight peeking through the leaves.

Lily could have built a boat. She could have built a boat, a bridge, parted the swamp, done anything, but something was stopping her. It wasn't just Wizard Lenin's constant disapproval of her flagrant abuse of magic, it was the very feeling of this place.

A wild land, someone had called it, and Lily was starting to believe it.

On the other hand, she was cold, wet, and feeling more creeped out by the minute. She was far past the limit of her own discomfort, and something was going to have to give.

She was just going to go for it.

She pulled herself out of the water and on top of its surface. She wobbled a bit as she tried to keep her balance, feet sliding everywhere, but managed to keep from falling back in. It was almost like walking on ice, the same lack of traction, but instead of a hard sheet it bent under her like a thin trampoline.

"What are you doing?!"

"I can't do it," Lily responded, walking forward, passing each and every

flabbergasted elf staring at her like she'd scored the winning field goal for the opposing team, *"This place is gross, creepy, and wet."*

She might have to put up with some of it, but she wasn't going to put up with all of it.

"Do you listen to a word I say?!" Wizard Lenin asked, *"Do not hand any of these people free information!"*

"They've already seen me teleport," Lily pointed out. The cat was entirely out of the bag by this point. She'd been breaking the rules left and right, as Elizabeth had reminded her on so very many occasions.

That, according to Wizard Lenin, was not nearly a good enough excuse for this latest batch of lazy idiocy.

"Iff, you can't walk on water!" Elizabeth cried out from somewhere behind Lily. She didn't just sound offended, but despairing. Lily was sure, deep in her mind where she would never admit it, Elizabeth was wishing she could be a rule breaking magical princess too.

"Well, I can today," Lily called back, not looking over her shoulder for fear of losing her balance.

She looked down at the murky, awful, water she didn't have to wade through and felt very grateful for her bullshit abilities.

Before she could really get the hang of walking on water, though, she ran into Ilyn's back. He gave her an annoyed look and caught her just before she fell backwards into the water by grabbing her collar. It was there, hanging from her jacket, that Lily noticed they'd reached it.

No one asked if this was it, no one had to, it was obvious.

Right in front of them, standing upright in the middle of the water, was an isolated marble statue.

There were no other buildings or statues, no temples, no paths, just the statue.

However, despite rising out of the water, there was no hint of erosion. Like the pedestal on Death's Island, it looked as if it had been placed there only a few seconds ago, like it existed on some other plane than theirs and they could only see its three-dimensional shadow.

It was large, towering over their heads and almost reaching the canopy. However, that wasn't what caught Lily's attention. It wasn't even how it was placed in the middle of nowhere, in this strange swamp, without any sign that it was supposed to be a part of the swamp.

It was the fact that it was a sculpted white, obsidian-eyed, unblinking rabbit.

Theyn looked over at Lily, looked at Rabbit held against her head with one hand, then back to the statue in confusion.

He opened his mouth, closed it, then looked at the others.

They looked equally stupefied.

No one said anything.

"Why am I filled with a sudden sense of dread?" Lily asked Wizard Lenin, but he didn't answer either.

Rabbit's weight against her hand felt heavier than it ever had, suffocating for all that he was the one nearly tumbling into the water, and even though he wasn't moving she felt as if she was barely keeping hold of him.

Then the mind elf hauled himself up onto the platform that served as the statue's base. He didn't even look at Rabbit, didn't even glance in Lily's direction, and instead was grinning like an idiot.

He knelt at the base of the statue, without any hesitation, looking as if he was prostrating himself before a god.

That feeling of dread spread from her stomach down to her toes.

Then the statue spoke, "What is hard to find but easy to lose, worth more than gold but costs less than a coin?"

Lily started, nearly dropping Rabbit into the water.

Like the guardian's, it was a voice that wasn't a voice. It didn't just lack human emotion but some defining human characteristic that made a human's voice more than a robot's.

Lily felt as if small creatures had just raced up and down her spine.

The mind elf answered without hesitation, "A friend."

"When you know what I am, then I am something. When you know what I am, then I am nothing. What am I?"

Rabbit, Lily wanted to answer unthinkingly. Except, no, that wasn't the right answer.

That was Bilbo Baggins blurting out "time!" in his riddle game with Gollum. It was the unwitting, yet somehow not unfounded, answer to a question that hadn't been about that.

No, even that was too much, this was like the riddle "what have I got in my pocket?"

The answer was something else, but the answer should be Rabbit.

"A riddle," the mind elf supplied calmly, easily, evidently correct as the statue asked the next question.

"You can run but cannot walk. You have a mouth but cannot talk. You have a head but never weep and have a bed but never sleep. What are you?"

"It's a riddle game," Lily realized.

His task must be to win the riddle game, or they'd all be killed or the way forward would be lost. Looking at him, seeing how easily he answered, Lily felt some disappointment that the man was suited for it after all.

Certainly, better than Lily would have been.

She felt the same irrational disappointment she'd felt when she realized she'd be no help to Nhoj or to Ailill in their tasks.

She was going to just have to sit this one out again.

A hand fell on her shoulder and she found herself yanked away from

Ilyn, "Princess."

Lily found herself staring at Ailill, the moon elf, whose intimidating yellow eyes were even more intimidating than usual.

"Yes?" Lily asked.

"It's time to train," he said, as if Lily had any context for that.

"Train?" Lily repeated like a parrot.

"While the mind elf is busy regurgitating ancient facts and clever word games."

Well, wasn't it nice that they all respected one another. Truly, they'd all learned the meaning of both teamwork and friendship in their short time together.

She couldn't believe that, somehow, Nhoj was taking the lead because he'd said he didn't hate everyone, just a few people.

"Training," Lily repeated, "To do—"

He unsheathed his sword, holding it in front of Lily's face.

Oh.

She could see her terrified reflection in its gleaming surface. She looked around, hoping someone might intervene but—

Ilyn was sitting on the pedestal, polishing his watch like he didn't have a care in the world, Nhoj was nowhere to be found, and Theyn—was looking at her imploringly.

It wasn't disapproval, not betrayal, not yet, but he was so clearly asking why she hadn't talked with this man yet. The sight of his eyes, the very idea of them, was enough to make it feel like a knife was twisting inside Lily's heart.

He had been nothing but kind to her, nothing but patient, and the seeds of friendship had only just started to flower.

She had to do something.

Lily winced, "Alright, sure, let's go talk somewhere."

The moon elf easily carried her out into the swamp, away from the rabbit statue, the trial, and Theyn. Lily couldn't help but wonder how light she was, that it was this easy to haul her around.

When he came to a stop, he threw her without prelude into the water, then threw his sword on top of her. Lily flailed desperately, breaking the surface, then diving back in for Rabbit, then having to dive in again for the sword she couldn't lift.

When she surfaced with Rabbit, he looked as immaculate as ever, not even a droplet hanging off his fur. She ended up standing half bent over, one hand holding Rabbit against her head, the other gripping the handle and terrified of letting it go, staring at the man across from her.

"I don't think this was made for someone my height and weight," she said slowly.

He didn't look sympathetic.

"Maybe there are—things I'm just not supposed to be good at," Lily said. It was strange admitting as much, but everyone had their talents. Lifting heavy objects didn't appear to be one of Lily's.

"You're weak," the man said.

"Yes, I'm aware of that," Lily said, her smile strained.

"Swordsmanship is good in a queen," Ailill said with his own smile, like he was a teacher who saw great potential but a lot more attitude.

"Oh, I'm sure it is," Lily laughed awkwardly, ducking down to prevent the sword from slipping, her feet sliding in the mud, "The thing is—I'm not going to be queen."

"You will," the man said easily.

"No, I really won't," Lily corrected, her words a bit more strained than she meant them to be, "See, there's this thing called the rite of succession. The way it goes, Theyn's first in line, I'm second, and since nothing's going to happen to Theyn then I don't get to be queen."

"If nothing happens to Theyn," Ailill said, grinning ear to ear.

She let the sword drop to stare at him.

"What do you mean?" Lily asked slowly.

"Did they tell you the moon elves supported the Usurper?" Ailill asked, inclining his head towards her.

"No," Lily said breathlessly, and that was true, she'd heard elven clans but neither Wizard Lenin, Questburger, nor anyone else had mentioned which specific ones. That had, Lily now realized, made it all seem less real.

All at once, she wondered if the moon elf could see Wizard Lenin's shadow in her head.

"We've never been fond of the humans," Ailill offered, as if this was something he could just say, "We never even made a show of tolerating them, I don't know why they ever forgot that."

The sword flew out of the water and into his hand, he pointed it at her, water running off its gleaming surface, "They will not make you queen, Iff, you'll make yourself queen."

It wasn't Theyn's place she'd be taking, she realized in growing fear, but Wizard Lenin's.

This wasn't a discussion of succession, but usurpation.

Questburger's words, his prediction of what would have happened if Lily hadn't been sent to Earth, if the elves had found her, came back to her suddenly.

The idea of it horrified her.

"I don't—" Lily spluttered, taking a step backward, "That's—That's not my role here."

Ailill stepped forward, the blade still pointed at her.

"They fear you because of your mother," he continued, eyes never wavering, never letting her look anywhere else, "They sent you to Tellestria and willfully forgot your existence. They intend to put that shaking sorry excuse of a mage on the throne because they're terrified you'll take it from him."

"No!" Lily protested, unable to come up with anything else, anything firmer to protest him, but having to say something.

"And you will take it from him," he prophesied, his sword tapping against her shoulder, resting there, so heavy it caused her to sink into the mud.

"And I," he said with a smile, sheathing his sword back into its scabbard, "Will present you his head as a coronation gift."

Lily turned and ran.

"Where are you going?!"

Lily didn't know, didn't think, she only sprinted on top of the water faster than the moon elf or anyone else could think to follow. She ran faster than her own thoughts, memories of Theyn, that battle with the guardian, blood brothers, and Wizard Lenin.

Just before she hit a tree, she skidded to a stop, sliding on top of the water and only barely managing to catch herself.

She breathed heavily, leaned against it, and distantly realized she'd left Rabbit behind somewhere.

"Shit."

She looked around for any sign of impossibly white fur, but there was nothing.

She didn't even know if she'd left him with Ailill, even if she had, she doubted Ailill would watch him.

She'd have to retrace her steps, she realized with an overwhelming feeling of exhaustion. She'd find Rabbit somewhere along the way then— then she'd manage to find the others.

She sighed, preparing herself for it, for seeing Ailill again, Theyn, and trying to explain—something. God, what was she going to say? She couldn't tell Theyn that Ailill now intended to kill him, that he really wasn't going to take no for an answer.

She couldn't let that happen, either, she just—

She opened her eyes and stared down at her reflection. It was the first time she'd seen it since they'd set out.

A small, twelve-year-old, red-headed girl stared back at her with too green eyes.

It was worse than staring in a mirror, somehow, the water made her eyes even greener, even less human despite being inside a human face.

Lily could believe that they'd been plucked out of a god's head and placed in her eye sockets.

Before she could look away, the water shifted. She leaned forward, eyes narrowing. The water rippled, Lily's reflection rippling with it, and then it wasn't her reflection at all.

"Death?" Lily asked, because it was him, or someone eerily like him.

It was still her eyes staring back, Death's eyes, but the face wasn't right. This face was more like an approximation of a human face, something too symmetrical to be truly human, sculpted out of stone with dark feathers for hair. The eyes were the only hint of color in him.

The water grew dark, pitch black, like all the light had just been sucked out of the water's surface. Her reflected stranger held a hand above his head, looking at it in concentration, and a brilliant white light appeared inside it.

The darkness scattered, brilliant light chasing it out. Lily shielded her eyes, found herself tumbling forward into the water.

There, as she fell, she watched the light and dark chasing after one another. A pattern began to emerge. The man still held up his star, but the rest of the darkness had transformed itself into a set of dark eyes.

The statue's eyes, Lily realized, Rabbit's eyes.

The light turned into Rabbit's fur, his maw opened into a great black abyss with no teeth and no tongue. He leaned forward and devoured the man, his star, and Lily as well.

Lily found herself screaming, flailing underwater as if she was still being swallowed. She pulled her head out, took a deep breath, and wiped soaked curls away from her face.

"What the hell was that?!"

Wizard Lenin was unusually quiet, just as unnerved as she was, and didn't appear to have an answer.

His only guess was that there were reasons no one crossed the mountains. This was where the gods lived.

"I hate this swamp!" Lily thought, forcing her heart into a steadier rhythm, *"God, I hate this swamp!"*

She waited until her breathing was calm, until she felt half sane again, before she picked herself up.

Then she stopped.

There, floating on top of the water like a little boat, was Rabbit. He looked at her with those dark, soulless, unblinking eyes.

Lily picked him up, clutched him to her chest, and with her heart racing once again teleported them back to the statue in his likeness.

There, of course, the mind elf had smugly beaten the riddle game, completed his task without any idea that there were riddle games worse than his had been.

THE HEART OF THE WORLD

12 WHAT ARE WE GOING TO DO ABOUT RABBIT?

In which Lily tries and fails to get to the root of the Rabbit problem and Wizard Lenin reveals some interesting though momentarily unimportant history.

Lily lost track of time after the mind elf's task.

The swamp had disappeared with the statue. Just as they'd passed it, the trees, the water, everything had suddenly vanished. They'd all winced in the open sunlight, held up their hands against it, and been greeted by endless fields of grass extending into the horizon.

It made for easy marching, but it meant that there was more marching than ever before, Ilyn had taken the lead and with him all hints of any breaks had disappeared.

He'd been staring unerringly at that compass ever since they'd left the swamp.

There was no hint of the love elf's task anywhere in sight.

Maybe it was that lack of a sign, of anything, but Lily could tell that the party was starting to lose their energy. Nhoj's clothes were ragged at the edges in a way they hadn't been at the start, the mind elf had stopped reading his books, Ailill had sheathed his sword to bat away at the grass with his hands, the night elf had wrapped her clothes over her head to shield herself from the sun, even the happiness elf walked slower than he once had. Elizabeth had lost all energy to talk, even to nag at Lily or Theyn, and collapsed every time they stopped to make camp. Her French braids, which had started the journey looking so perfect, now looked worse than they had in the swamp.

And Lily was still thinking about Ailill, Rabbit, and the unfamiliar dread that hadn't left her.

She hadn't spoken to Ailill since, hadn't dared, and Rabbit—

She'd barely been able to look at him.

She believed Ailill, that was the thing. She absolutely believed him when he said that he would—

That he would murder Theyn and make her queen whether she liked it or not.

Was it just a matter of convincing him that she didn't want the throne? She never had, not ever, even before Theyn, Wizard Lenin had wanted it and—She tried not to think about that either.

Maybe she could make him think that it wasn't important. It didn't matter whether Lily was sitting on it or Theyn or anybody else. Maybe then he'd go and do something else.

Maybe it was a matter of offering something else of equal value. He couldn't place her on the throne but he could make her—Lily didn't know—queen of the dolphins or something.

There had to be some way out of this.

"I wouldn't concern myself over it," Wizard Lenin cut in.

Lily felt herself grow colder at the easy way he said that.

"Why not?"

"He's made up his mind," Wizard Lenin said with amusement of all things, *"He wants what he wants. Neither you, nor I, nor anyone else can talk him out of it."*

Why not?

And why was Wizard Lenin so at ease with this, when he prided himself in talking anyone into anything he wanted?

"Not them," Wizard Lenin said with a laugh.

"He said they were on your side," Lily reminded him, her stomach churning.

"That had nothing to do with me," he told her with a hum, *"It was a simple matter that they hated the monarchy more than they hated me. I offered them a better deal, and if I start again, I can offer them the same deal."*

And when they asked to place Lily on the throne, as he was sure they would, then Wizard Lenin would find some way to deal with that.

It was no skin off his nose if Theyn died young.

"We can't—"

"I didn't say anything," Wizard Lenin interjected, for all he'd certainly thought it, *"My point was that you'll save yourself a headache not getting hung up on it."*

Yes, well, it was her headache now.

She'd have to watch Theyn. She didn't think he'd make a move now, not when there was still Wheyn to deal with, and not when Lily was so young, but in a few years, he'd certainly do something. She would just wait, watch, maybe try to give Theyn some warning while she tried to convince Ailill that there was no need to murder her cousin.

That, at least, was an outline of a plan, a lot better than nothing.

She kept frowning as she stared ahead, something else nagging at her.

The Ailill problem was as solved as it was going to get, Wizard Lenin had offered as much advice as he was willing to give, but something about what he'd said bothered her. What was it?

"Was it the murdering your cousin bit?" Wizard Lenin asked dryly.

No, she almost expected that at this point, it was very on brand Wizard Lenin.

Yes, she knew what it was, it was how easily Wizard Lenin had accepted the moon elves' changed loyalties. If this stuck, if this spread to the rest of the clan, then they'd be loyal to Lily and certainly not to Wizard Lenin. As much as Wizard Lenin pretended that didn't bother him—it should have bothered him.

It didn't though.

There was a quiet truth he hadn't wanted to speak freely, admit out loud, and it was that he didn't need the moon elves.

If he could get back Ilyn, gifted sun elf that he was, then that man was worth the weight of the entire moon elf clan and more. If Wizard Lenin could have him, if he could have Lily, then he didn't have to care about the moon elves.

Even then, Wizard Lenin felt he could go it alone if he had to. There was nothing left of the human resistance and he could easily wipe out the Elizabeths and even the Questburgers. It'd just be annoying if he had to deal with Ilyn on the opposite side. Lily and her bullshit cosmic abilities, he could just sit in a corner somewhere out of the way if he had to.

Perhaps, Lily thought, Wizard Lenin didn't care about anybody.

She wondered if this just made Lily a slightly more useful, unique, tool in Wizard Lenin's toolbox.

She didn't want to think about that.

If the Ailill problem was as solved as it was going to get that left—

That left the Rabbit problem.

He was perched on her head again, as always, and giving her the usual kink in her neck. To everyone else, it was a familiar and perhaps even comforting scene. To Lily—they could be right.

There'd been no indication of anything else Rabbity since the swamp. No appearing out of nowhere, no vivid hallucinations, no floating on top of water, or giant ominous statues defying the elements.

While everyone had noticed the statue, no one had talked about it, and everyone else seemed to be over it already as if it was just another quirk of the quest.

The trouble was that Lily wasn't.

She'd said it often enough to anyone who would listen. She'd tell them that Rabbit was this monstrous abomination, from somewhere outside of time and space, who would devour them out of reality if given half a chance.

Everyone, and she did mean everyone, had written it off. Somewhere along the way, maybe since the very beginning, Lily had written it off too.

It was now this standard disclaimer she gave offhand, this thing to justify bringing Rabbit everywhere, and not something she expected anyone to listen to.

She'd left Rabbit in the swamp.

In her panic, her petty emotional distress, she'd left him somewhere and hadn't thought twice about it.

All these years, she hadn't been carting him around out of a sense of duty or fear, but out of inertia. She put him on her head and marched on because that's what she'd been doing for seven years.

And now she was reckoning herself with that.

"Since when are you concerned about the foundations of reality?"

Oh, Wizard Lenin could say what he liked, he was trapped in her brain and clearly above Lily's concerns for the foundations of reality.

Wizard Lenin scoffed, *"I seem to recall you insisting at the age of five that reality was simply falling apart and that there's nothing us lowly mortals can do about it."*

"Well, I don't know," Lily thought irritably, *"There's reality falling apart then—there's reality falling apart."*

"You're going to have to spell that one out for me," Wizard Lenin said dryly.

That was the trouble, she didn't know how to put it.

It was true, reality was falling apart. Lily believed that down to the marrow of her bones. The proof was in everything, these magical portals appearing all over the place, magic that relied on rhythmic chanting and interpretive dance, and everything in between.

Reality was ridiculous.

It wasn't her fault that no one else seemed to be able to see it.

They took the world as it was, assumed that it must be working the way it was supposed to, and Lily just couldn't. Whatever it was Lily saw, she felt as if the reality they all knew was made of more than a few happy accidents.

This place, whatever it really was, wasn't as purposeful or stable as everyone kept assuming it was.

It was in its nature, she was sure, to fall apart. As unfortunate as that was, there was nothing Lily or anyone else could do about it.

The only question was when it happened.

Rabbit was different. Rabbit wasn't a natural decline, a slow unraveling of a tapestry or the erosion of a cliff face, he wasn't declining at all. Whatever the death of the universe was, Rabbit was something far worse, far more concerning.

Rabbit wouldn't rewrite reality to his own desires like your standard mage. He wouldn't mangle threads here and there or fray them for his own purposes either. The threads would simply disappear as if they'd never been there.

Reality, for Rabbit, would become even less than a dream dreamt by no one.

"Why do you insist on being melodramatic at every possible moment?"

And Lily completely lost her train of thought.

She shifted Rabbit from her head into her arms, taking the opportunity to crack her neck again, *"I am not being melodramatic! This is very serious stuff here!"*

"You just accused your pet rabbit of being responsible for the utter annihilation of the universe," Wizard Lenin pointed out, sounding like he could hardly think that sentence with any seriousness.

"Well, he is!" Lily protested, *"You saw that whole swamp fiasco!"*

Wizard Lenin hadn't been impressed.

In retrospect, he suspected some kind of swamp gas was responsible.

"I think I'd know if I was drugged, Lenin!" Lily said though—

That would make sense, she supposed, would certainly explain the vivid hallucinations as well as the terror. It didn't explain the rabbit statue though or things just disappearing whenever she wasn't looking.

Wizard Lenin still wasn't impressed and wasn't convinced that anything had disappeared when he wasn't looking.

"When I'm proven right, and we both know I will be, you're going to eat your words!" Lily promised (while internally wishing, of course, that she'd never face a moment where she was proven right).

Wizard Lenin did not believe she'd ever be proven right about anything.

"I am right—"

"Then tell me, Lily," he cut her off, beyond his limit of bickering for the day, *"What did he eat this time?"*

Lily stared forward dumbly.

"You took your eyes off him, for quite a while too, so what's missing?"

Lily—

Lily had absolutely no idea.

She looked left, right, up, then down, but nothing immediately obvious was gone. There was still a sky overhead, still ground beneath her feet, and all eleven party members were accounted for.

Everything looked like it was in order.

Maybe Rabbit hadn't eaten anything, Lily thought to herself with some unease.

Maybe this time, Rabbit had just haunted Lily with terrifying dreams and impersonated a sphinx with the mind elf.

"Or maybe he hasn't eaten anything because he doesn't eat anything," Wizard Lenin said.

"What about the bridge club?" Lily asked, referring to Carol Tylor's bridge club which had vanished into thin air.

"I don't know," Wizard Lenin said, sounding like he certainly didn't care, *"Maybe your adoptive mother lost all her friends but was too embarrassed to admit as*

much."

That—

It was possible, Lily supposed, but then why block off the time on the calendar? Why pretend that something, anything, was happening when she could just have pretended that she never went to bridge at all or didn't even like bridge?

"Alright, I'll humor you," Wizard Lenin said, *"In the event that he has eaten something, what can you personally do about it?"*

Nothing.

Whatever he'd eaten, if he'd eaten anything, Lily had no idea what it was, much less what she could personally do about it. The only thing she could do was what she'd always done—keep an eye on him.

She sighed and looked down at Rabbit hanging limply in her arms. His large unnaturally dark eyes stared unblinkingly up at her. There wasn't anything in them, not a spark of thought, emotion, or even a hint of a soul. He was just a shell that enticed the viewer into believing it was more than it really was.

With a louder sigh, Lily placed him back on his head, and only hoped that whatever he'd eaten (if he'd eaten) hadn't been important.

She also hoped that Ailill would return to his previous indifference and leave Lily alone, and that her strange prophetic swamp vision of a dark-haired Death didn't have any spark of truth to it.

Maybe it was time to stop thinking about anything.

"Finally," Wizard Lenin breathed with relief.

(Not that he'd been doing anything better with his time, but Lily wasn't petty enough to say that out loud.)

"So, this love elf business," Lily said instead, looking ahead to the love elf, *"What do you think her task is going to be?"*

Lily was torn between picturing a fantasy beauty pageant or else having to seduce some hideous stone-hearted gargoyle.

"I'm sure I have no idea," Wizard Lenin said.

Wizard Lenin didn't care too much about the tasks in and of themselves, the journey wasn't all that important to him, what mattered to him was the end goal. They'd reach the Heart of the World and either the elf in question or Lily would muddle their way through the tasks to get there.

"Me?" Lily asked.

That didn't sound right.

They weren't supposed to be Lily's tasks, no, they *weren't* her tasks. After three of them having come and gone she'd reconciled herself to the fact that she must have been invited by accident.

Whoever, whatever, had put this all together had clearly not had Lily in mind.

"That's the point," Wizard Lenin said pointedly, *"If they can't do it, then you*

can surely magically bullshit your way through, as you're so fond of saying."

Well, Lily supposed she could, and that she had. That was exactly what she'd done with Ailill for all she hadn't thought to help make Nhoj's job a little easier. God, she could have skipped past the caves, avoided Ailill's injuries, and—

No, the arrogant mind elf had had the time of his life. He could keep his riddle games and Rabbit impersonating monoliths.

Still, if it really was a beauty pageant then Lily doubted her ability to win even by cheating.

"It will not be a beauty pageant," Wizard Lenin insisted flatly, *"If you're so curious, ask that chattering little girl who bothers you so much, she'll know."*

"Elizabeth?" Lily asked, glancing forward at the uncharacteristically silent Elizabeth.

Lily was hit by a sudden premonition that, if she asked Elizabeth, she'd just harp on her about the moon elves or magic again.

It wasn't worth it.

"You'll find out soon enough," Wizard Lenin agreed.

Lily wasn't sure that she felt better about that. She wasn't sure if having warning about the Rabbit statue would have helped but—

Maybe it would have helped.

Well, moving past the love elf task, Lily had no idea what the happiness elf task would be.

She spared the man a glance and he—

Was the same as ever, still smiling, always smiling, not in the least bit disturbed by rabbit statues, creepy swamps, or endless fields of nothing.

He probably would be happy walking until he died.

Just what the hell was he supposed to do?

"Ilyn once told me that in Xhigrahi the other clans would practically throw the unresisting happiness elves at their overlords to spare themselves," Wizard Lenin observed, *"The night elves got so tired of the taste, that they imposed a tithe specifically on each of the clans."*

Lily stumbled, almost landing flat on her face.

"Are you saying they got together and drew straws—"

"And that someone always picked the short straw and never noticed," Wizard Lenin finished for her.

Now all Lily could see was Nhoj, Ailill, and all the rest of them some thousands of years ago, huddled in a bleak cell, gleefully pushing the happiness elf out the door and into Frank's arms.

"And he doesn't even hold it against them," Wizard Lenin tsked, taking in the happiness elf's complete lack of animosity towards the other clans.

The happiness elf hadn't said much to anyone but—

That was more because it seemed like he didn't have much to say.

"Well, I guess they must have survived," Lily said slowly, they couldn't all have

been eaten by night elves.

Maybe there was something to it, even. Everyone else was so busy bickering, holding onto resentment, that they weren't living in the moment. The happiness elf wasn't mired in his own unhappiness, bitter about the past, but seemed genuinely content with what he had.

He was certainly more content about his lot in life than Lily was.

Aristotle would violently disagree, but to Lily, the happiness elves really might be living the best kind of life. Despite everything, they were the only ones who seemed perfectly content with who they were and what they were doing.

"That's the problem," Wizard Lenin cut in, *"They're always happy, they're even happy when they're miserable."*

Lily supposed that was a problem.

"What about the love elves?" Lily asked, taking in the woman who still seemed so at odds with the journey.

She was, frankly, too pretty. Not just pretty, either, but beautiful in the way that reminded you that beautiful was a word that had to be reserved. She looked as if she was made for palaces, for worlds that glittered, and not the open road.

She'd never complained about it, she was certainly dressed for the task, but her face just wasn't suited for a quest.

"I'm rather fond of the love elves," Wizard Lenin said plainly.

If Lily had been drinking her water, she would have choked.

She took in the woman's figure, her adult curves, her dark hair shining lustrously in the sun, the curve of her eyelashes—

It had never occurred to her to think of Wizard Lenin as a sexual creature, as a man predisposed to certain activities, but now she couldn't get the idea of Wizard Lenin, Wizard Lenin and multiple elves, tangled together—

"Not like that," Wizard Lenin retorted wearily, knowing exactly what Lily was getting at, *"I mean that they, above all others, have always been generous supporters of my cause."*

She was sure that didn't mean what she thought that meant.

"They fought alongside me," Wizard Lenin spat in clarification, just daring her to interpret one more thing the wrong way.

"Her?" Lily asked in surprise, wondering why Wizard Lenin hadn't said as much.

"Not her," Wizard Lenin said, as if Lily was being willfully stupid, *"I don't know all love elves, Lily."*

Before Lily could respond that he'd clearly been implying he knew somebody, he continued, *"Certainly more than the moon elves, Ilyn the stray sun elf, and the few night elves I collected, they were my greatest supporters."*

Lily looked closer at the woman, as if just by looking at her, she could find some hint of why the love elves would do that.

Ilyn she didn't understand, but Wizard Lenin had admitted he didn't understand that one either. Ilyn had just shown up one day and that was it.

The moon elves she certainly understood, Wizard Lenin had been the lesser of two evils.

She hadn't known any night elves worked with him, but it hadn't been Frank and sounded like it hadn't been the night elf from the quest either.

"They love elves sympathized with my personal circumstances," Wizard Lenin offered, *"They saw in me an example of what could be done by one man alone. We have always had a great mutual respect for one another."*

A respect that Wizard Lenin hoped had survived the years since his passing.

"They arguably fared the worst of the great elven clans," Wizard Lenin continued, *"The gold elves have their artistry, their trades, and their ability to create status symbols for the wealthy. The moon elves, for all they've been driven out of the cities and replaced by human mages, can defend themselves. The happiness elves have their heads so high in the clouds they can't tell what their circumstances even are. The mind elves seclude themselves in their towers and care nothing about the outside world. The sun elves retained everything. The night elves live in miserable poverty, but power is theirs if they have the means to take it again. The love elves, though, theirs is a bitter fate."*

"What happened to them?" Lily asked.

"What do you think happened, Lily, to a clan whose reputation is to be notoriously beautiful but little else?"

He didn't say it, but as he noted, he didn't have to.

He didn't even have to picture it, not under the night elves, nor under the humans.

"As I said, we understood one another," Wizard Lenin concluded bitterly.

Lily felt herself freeze, a horrible, unthinkable, conclusion fermenting in her head, *"You don't mean—"*

"No," he corrected easily, *"Simply that—I am no stranger to adversity, obstacles placed in my way simply because of who I am and where I came from."*

She felt herself sighing in relief, feeling almost boneless.

That hadn't explained much, not anything, but at least—

She was willing to let things lie here.

She looked back up at the woman. It was hard, just staring at her back, but she tried to see the smallest hint of what she was really after and what she was doing here.

Was she looking for battle, like Ailill? Was she performing an expected duty like Nhoj, surpassing expectations like Elizabeth, or was her reason something else?

"Iff."

Lily started, turned her head, and caught sight of Nhoj who had slowed his pace to match hers.

His golden hair was matted with sweat, dark shadows beneath his eyes, and although he was managing better than Elizabeth, he'd clearly reached some milestone of exhaustion.

"Yes?" Lily asked.

Nhoj nodded to the front of the group, to the barely visible Ilyn leading the way, "The bastard sun elf, you seem to know him—"

"Know is a strong term," Lily corrected.

He'd burned down her house one time, if that's what Nhoj meant. She supposed there was a certain intimacy that came with your relationship when a man burned down your house in broad daylight then kidnapped you to another dimension, but 'knowing' was still a strong term.

Nhoj wasn't impressed, "You seemed friendly enough on stage with him—"

"They wouldn't stop talking and I had no idea what the hell was going on," Lily justified, wondering why everyone was so hung up on that episode, "It wasn't like the rest of you were volunteering—"

Nhoj didn't give Lily time to finish, "Go and ask him when the hell we're reaching this night elf task."

Well, Lily could certainly do that—

"Wait, the night elf task?" Lily asked, blinking in confusion, "No, you mean the love elf task."

They had two more to go until the night elf task, or at least, Lily thought they did. She supposed no one had said the exact order, but Lily had thought it was implied.

It was gold, moon, mind, love, happiness, night, and sun: just like in Frank's story.

"What are you talking about?" Nhoj asked impatiently, "There is no love elf task. Just go and—"

"No, wait a second!" Lily said, holding up her hands in defense, "Of course there's a love elf task, there's a task for everybody. That's why you're all here, isn't it? You have a task, Ailill has a task, that guy has a task, everybody gets a task!"

Lily pointed to the happiness elf, staring happily up at clouds, "Even that guy gets a task!"

"No," Ailill shouted over his shoulder, loud enough that the whole party heard and stared at him. He grinned back at Lily, clearly not having forgotten her at all, "That one doesn't get a task."

"What?" Lily shouted back, looking at him then Nhoj, feeling even more out of sorts, "But—You mean there's only five?! But—"

Hadn't there been this whole thing of every clan, every one of them, having some vital piece of the puzzle only they could put together? Hadn't that been a whole thing? Lily hadn't made that up, she just knew she hadn't!

Nhoj didn't seem to care, he rubbed at his face and pointed at Ilyn, "Just go ask—"

"Why are they even here?" Lily snapped, waving a hand at them, "Seriously, I am sure that someone, at some point, said that they definitely had—"

And then it hit her, the explanation, and exactly what Rabbit must have eaten.

"You can't be serious," Wizard Lenin scoffed, but he wasn't as confident as he should have been.

Rabbit had eaten the love and happiness tasks.

Slowly, unwillingly, Lily looked at Rabbit hanging over the top over her head.

"I'll go see," Lily said, sounding distant even to her own ears.

She moved forward, sprinting faster than she had in days, until she was at the front with Ilyn. She wheezed, her lungs burning, trying to catch her words as Ilyn looked down at her with raised eyebrows.

Lily coughed, nodded towards him, and as soon as she had her breath asked, "There are love and happiness tasks, aren't there?"

"No."

God, not a yes, not even a maybe, but just a no.

"Doesn't that—oh, I don't know—not make much sense?" Lily asked, trying to smile but stretching it too far so that her cheeks hurt.

Ilyn shrugged, as if making sense of the universe was above his pay grade, "I don't write the prophecies."

Lily pressed, "Yes, but bear with me here—"

"I don't write the—"

"I know you don't write the prophecies!" Lily snapped, "You've been very clear on that!"

She took a breath in, let it out, and forced herself to relax.

Well, Rabbit had eaten two tasks.

There was nothing for it, it had happened, and now they were in a world without those two tasks.

Lily should be happy, grateful even, he'd just saved her a lot of time and potentially a lot of heartache. Now, there were only two tasks to go, then they'd find the Heart of the World.

Wizard Lenin was that much closer to being a real boy.

"Lily, don't ever use that phrasing again."

This was fine. Everything was fine.

Lily was blood brothers with an elf who wanted to lop off her cousin's head, she'd had a terrifying vision of Rabbit eating Death, Rabbit had clearly eaten some very important things from the universe, and no one cared about any of it.

Lily was cool as a cucumber.

Staring ahead into the infinite horizon, Lily said, "Nhoj wants to know when we get to the night elf task."

"Three hours."

And that, apparently, was that.

13 FATE IS WRITTEN THIS WAY

In which Lily wanders down someone else's memory lane and begins to realize that some things can't be mended.

"Well, this is—" Lily didn't finish that sentence.

No one else finished it either.

Lily lamely cleared her throat and shifted Rabbit from her head into her arms. It didn't help her feel any more comfortable with the situation.

Stretching in front of them, dominating the horizon, was a black reflective wall. Except, of course, that it wasn't a wall. It was a black film, glossy and thin like the outside of a bubble, but entirely opaque. Lily couldn't see anything except her own oily reflection on its surface.

Looking left and right revealed that there was no obvious way around it, it stretched further than Lily could see in both directions.

Nhoj lifted a hand, turned it over, and a six-foot hole appeared at the base of the film. Perhaps as expected, the film extended underground, deeper than Nhoj's hole.

It wasn't worse than the Rabbit statue, but it had a disquietingly similar feeling to it. It was as if, whoever or whatever had put these little tasks together, had stopped pretending this was a quest.

No more finding the right path, slaying monsters, or winning riddle games—just this.

Lily found herself hoping she wouldn't have to intervene with this one.

"What is it?" Theyn breathed to Elizabeth.

"It's some kind of ward," Elizabeth said, equally awed by the black substance, "Only, I've never heard of one this large or this—"

"Ominous?" Lily finished for her.

It was flat, so their reflections weren't warped, but due to its oily texture, barely visible colors mixing together, the Lily reflected back didn't look right. There was a wash of the barest hint of red sweeping through her right eye, moving slowly, mixing with an off-purple extending from her neck.

"Yes, that," Elizabeth agreed dully.

Theyn surreptitiously looked at the night elf, or tried to anyway, he was a little too obvious about it to be subtle. As usual, the night elf wasn't even looking. No one in the quest could really be called chatty, but of all of them, she had to be the most stubbornly silent.

She looked grimmer than usual, and not just because of the afternoon sunlight bringing out the worst of her features. Hers was the expression of someone meeting their long-anticipated destiny and having this one last moment to turn back, knowing, of course, that turning back wasn't an option.

"What do you think she's supposed to do?" Theyn asked Elizabeth quietly.

"I wouldn't know, Your Highness," Elizabeth snapped before reigning in her temper, "She probably has to go in, find a way to dismantle it, and disable whatever magic is keeping it going."

And however she did that, it was supposed to be in a way that only she could manage.

"Elizabeth is right, Your Majesty."

Lily jerked out of the way as Annde appeared right between her and Theyn. Standing this close to him, closer than she'd ever been, it somehow made the Annde effect that much worse.

Lily found herself inching away without even realizing it, her feet moving before her brain could stop them.

Elizabeth's hand caught Lily's collar in an iron grip, preventing her escape. The look in her eyes very clearly stated that Lily would not be rude or there would be consequences.

"And I expect it won't be easy," Annde added, either not noticing or not caring about Lily's thwarted escape attempt.

Lily waited for him to say something else, but he didn't. That, it appeared, was the end of that thought.

"It's likely some kind of ward," Annde said, his voice barely audible over the murderous ringing in Lily's ears.

Again, Lily waited for him to expand on that, but he didn't.

"Yes, exactly!" Elizabeth said, her voice climbing a pitch in excitement, "It's some kind of ward! It must be some sort of blood magic that only the night elves use."

Yes, they'd both said that now already.

"Very good, Elizabeth," Annde agreed, "It's likely some sort of blood magic that only the night elves use."

Another pause, then, "The night elf likely has to enter and find a way to dismantle it."

Lily blinked slowly, looking at Elizabeth and Theyn, checking to see if they were participating in the same conversation. However, neither seemed to notice anything amiss, Elizabeth looked, in fact, beyond ecstatic at this point.

"Yes!" Elizabeth said quite triumphantly (even shooting Lily a dirty look for all Lily hadn't said anything), "She'll have to go in and dismantle the ward from the inside. It's the only way!"

Were they just–

Repeating each other?

"It's the only way with blood magic," Annde agreed sagely.

What the hell was happening?

"She's trying to impress him," Wizard Lenin, who apparently wasn't confused but only mildly annoyed, cut in.

Lily didn't understand.

"He's a grown man, one who had presumably studied some magic and graduated the academy," Wizard Lenin explained, *"Elizabeth's the type who's just dying for validation. I don't know what his problem is, I can only assume he's an idiot who's trying to look impressive."*

But he was only repeating what Elizabeth had already said.

"They're repeating each other," Wizard Lenin corrected, *"They both read the same books."*

Needless to say, Wizard Lenin didn't find said books very impressive. He also didn't think this was going to end any time soon either.

Lily shot a look at Elizabeth who–

Still didn't seem to be realizing what was happening.

Lily tried to escape again, only to be held fast by Elizabeth.

Lily was going to die, this was going to cause her very soul to wither, there would be nothing left of her.

"Blood magic," Theyn said quietly, looking at the wall with wide eyes, "I've never seen blood magic before."

"That's because the night elves didn't record their spells when the tomes were first made," Elizabeth stated with authority, "It also requires too much raw power, nothing a human mage could pull off. Even the night elves can't do it all the time, they have to feed on—"

Elizabeth halted abruptly, eyes wide, and face slack with horror. She turned slowly to look at Annde, the resident night elf victim.

Yes, Lily wondered, how was Elizabeth going to finish that sentence?

No one said anything, not Theyn, not Lily, not Elizabeth, and oddly not Annde either. Not being able to look at his face, Lily couldn't tell if he was shocked, horrified, offended or—or if he'd forgotten his own backstory.

Elizabeth flinched, something about Annde's demeanor having changed for the worse, and let go of Lily as she mumbled, "I'm sorry, I wasn't thinking."

Lily quickly escaped before Theyn and Elizabeth could start comforting the man.

Nhoj raised an eyebrow when Lily ended up bumping into him, but looking over to where she came from, didn't ask any questions.

Instead, he casually noted while staring at Annde, "It really is terrible what happened to that man."

He looked over and addressed the woman, expression dark, "I thought you were supposed to be keeping a leash on that. Such bold promises."

The woman didn't turn, didn't say anything at all, she was still focused on the wall ahead of her.

"Are you getting on with it?" Nhoj pressed unsympathetically.

Her frown tightened, "After the sun sets."

"Ah yes, the sun," Nhoj said, tilting his face upwards to stare at the dying light with a bitter smile, "We can't expect you to contend with that, can we?"

No, it was more than bitterness.

It was hatred in a concentration and form that Lily had never seen. It wasn't dismissive contempt, bland indifference, tolerable dislike, but the kind of loathing that ate away at your own soul. It was the kind of loathing that said you had never forgotten, would never forgive, and that this had carved out the foundations of your soul.

"You forget," the woman said coldly, "That you need me."

Nhoj said nothing to that and made no pretense of smiling. From the look on his face, he hadn't forgotten for a moment.

Lily looked up at the sky.

The sun was maybe three-quarters of the way across, a duller orange not quite shifting into the hazy red of twilight. They had at least an hour or two until it would be dark.

That was different from the other tasks. Those had happened when they happened, there'd been no anticipation of them, no waiting around to see what would happen next.

For all it would get her off her feet far earlier in the day than normal—she wasn't sure she preferred this.

It also meant she had several hours to kill.

Lily thought about walking back to Theyn and Elizabeth, setting up camp next to them but Annde was still over there. She didn't know why, couldn't justify it to herself, but the idea of going anywhere near him made her nauseous.

She just couldn't stomach the idea of willingly standing near him.

She supposed she could continue to talk with Nhoj, he seemed to like her well enough after their Come to Jesus moment ages ago. Before she could open her mouth, she noticed Ailill moving towards her, a hungry smile on his face.

Lily sprinted to the one person that everyone agreed to hate but no one had the nerve to confront.

"Oh, please no," Wizard Lenin despaired.

It was too late though; Lily was about to have another heart to heart with the loveable kidnapping arsonist.

Ilyn was sitting away from the rest of the group, having taken off his pack and even his boots. He'd set his watch down next to him. Lily felt fascinated despite herself, it was her first time getting a good look at it.

It was plainer than she'd thought. It was gold, but looking closer it didn't look like it was actually made out of gold, but some brass or an even cheaper metal. It looked banged up and scuffed, not enough to stop it from gleaming, but nothing like something that had come out of a factory. There were no carved decorations, nothing fancy about it, and—and it wasn't a watch at all.

Oh, it was round and shaped like one, had the kind of gold exterior you expected from a pocket watch, but it had only one needle and it wasn't pointing at any hour or minute. The black needle (a little too thick at the base and a little too thin at the tip) spun wildly, like a compass needle placed next to a magnet.

"Is it a compass?" Lily asked, it was her only guess for all that it clearly wasn't pointing north.

He opened his strange, opaque, eyes.

There was no expression on his face, not annoyance, nostalgia, or any hint of emotion as he looked at her. It was more like he was looking at a puzzle he had no personal stakes in, indifferently dissecting the pieces with no intention of putting them back together.

Lily looked over her shoulder.

Ailill was definitely giving her an unamused look, but he wasn't following. Nhoj had certainly noticed but seemed bemused more than anything else. Elizabeth and Theyn—

Were still sitting with Annde.

Lily turned back to Ilyn.

"Hello," she offered, she probably should have started with that.

Ilyn said nothing, did nothing, his eyebrows didn't even raise a fraction.

"It's like talking to a stone wall," Wizard Lenin mused almost fondly, recalling his own painful attempts to have any conversation with Ilyn.

Wizard Lenin had quickly learned that it wasn't worth bothering with.

Lily's smile fell.

She contemplated just sitting across from him, saying nothing until Ailill got bored and lost interest. She squirmed in the silence, feeling horribly uncomfortable, and ended up just speaking anyway.

"So, we've had a few moments," Lily ended up saying, "You lit my house on fire, dragged me to a different dimension, but we had a conversation at that ceremony—"

Lily cut herself off at his complete lack of response.

God, she really had no idea what he was thinking. He gave nothing away; she couldn't even guess what was going on in his head.

His eyes were also very unnerving. Beautiful, a very striking color, certainly memorable, but like Lily's eyes they looked wrong in his face if for different reasons. Her eyes were too vibrant, his were too washed out.

Lily shook herself and pointed down at the compass, "So, is this the north pole?"

His eyes moved to its surface, took in the spinning needle, and for a moment Lily swore she saw a hint of something. Then he said, "No."

That non-negotiable no again.

Lily grimaced and tried again, catching sight of Ailill and motioning towards him, "So, have you heard about my blood brother?"

She was sure Ailill was still grinning at her, planning all the ways to decapitate Theyn.

"That's been an interesting development," Lily huffed, "I really don't think I'm the warrior queen he's looking for, too twelve at the moment. Do you—What do you think about all that?"

"Nothing," he said easily, closing his eyes and leaning back against his pack, a clear dismissal.

"Nothing?!" Lily blurted, "You know he wants me on the throne, right?"

He'd said as much to Annde and Theyn, which meant everybody had to know. Lily knew the entire party knew about it, for all they didn't talk about it much or seem to care.

The only thing people didn't seem to know was just how far Ailill planned to go to make it happen.

"I told you, the moon elves think with their swords," Ilyn said matter-of-factly, almost bored.

"But isn't that your job?!" Lily asked.

"My job?" he asked in turn, the barest hint of irritation coloring his words.

"You work for the monarchy," Lily pointed at him in accusation, "You're Theyn's personal tutor! I'd think it'd be in your job description to care whether or not Theyn sits on the throne."

Lily then caught herself and laughed awkwardly, "For the record, I'm all for it, Theyn being crowned king I mean."

"I have no loyalty to the crown prince," Ilyn dismissed, opening his eyes to stare at her again. They weren't necessarily cold, but they were hard and sharp, there was no room for compassion in them, "The boy's the most useless mage I've ever seen."

Lily had noticed somewhere along the way, that for all Theyn seemed to respect Ilyn's opinion, he'd never sought it out. Theyn spent most of his time with Elizabeth, Annde, or Lily, and when it came to magic—he always spoke to Elizabeth.

Now she knew why.

"Then why are you teaching him?" Lily asked, all hints of pleasantness dropping from her voice.

"It was in my job description," he said dully, echoing her own words, "I was to teach the boy as well as the next generation of human mages."

"But you don't believe in them either," Lily said for him, "You don't even think Elizabeth has any real potential."

Elizabeth, who so clearly knew what she was talking about, and was so confident in her abilities that they'd sent her here at the age of twelve.

Lily didn't know if she was far and away the best there, if she had to work her fingers to the bone, or if it was some mix of the two. She also didn't know if Elizabeth had the slightest idea that no matter how hard she worked, how much she read, she'd never meet Ilyn's standards.

"She has talent and work ethic, she's especially gifted considering her age," Ilyn conceded, nodding towards the oblivious Elizabeth, "But she lacks imagination and any true understanding of the principles of magic. She will never be great, only ever good."

Lily silently took in that statement, wondering if Elizabeth had already heard it, had already railed against it.

"That's not much of a reason to teach," Lily commented.

"Fate seems to have been written this way," he said with gravitas belied by his leaning against his bag.

He didn't elaborate, letting the words hang in the air for Lily to digest.

Fate, he'd said, as if he had nothing to do with it.

***

When the last rays of sunlight disappeared, everyone's eyes turned to the night elf. She looked more natural in the dark, her hair no longer such a flat color, her skin no longer sickly looking, and her eyes luminous. At night, she was quite beautiful.

For a moment she stood perfectly still, hands pressed against the oil. Then a breath, a step, and she pushed against the wall and disappeared into it, leaving small ripples in her wake.

Just like that she was gone, not a hint of her on the other side, or any sign that she'd even been a part of their party. It was as if she, along with the love and happiness tasks, had been swallowed whole by Rabbit.

"It's alright, she'll be back."

Lily started, turning her head to the happiness elf who'd been standing next to her.

Had she ever heard him talk? She didn't think she had; he'd always seemed too at ease to bother saying anything. She'd started wondering if he even could talk.

He'd said this so easily too, with the same cheerful smile he always wore.

The camp died down quickly, everyone exhausted, and no one in the mood to stay up any later than they had to.

No one but Lily, at any rate. She found herself laid out on her bedroll, staring up at the sky, feeling restless.

Her thoughts were on the wall.

The night elf wasn't back yet. She didn't know how long it'd been, but it'd been enough that she should have made it back. Nhoj had taken twelve hours, but he'd made visible clear progress and known how long it would be. Ailill's task hadn't taken very long at all. She had no idea how long the mind elf's had taken but—it couldn't have been too long, not more than a few hours.

It'd be sunrise soon, and there was no hint she'd gotten anywhere.

For all they knew, they could be waiting here forever for her to come back.

Lily sighed and turned towards the wall.

What was on the other side of that thing anyway? What was it hiding? It was so ominous looking that Lily couldn't imagine it'd be anything good. In fact, it might just be the worst task yet.

"That's not your concern," Wizard Lenin noted.

He wasn't wrong.

It wasn't Lily's concern so long as the woman made it back and pulled down the wall with her.

Lily could very easily sit here, just like everyone else, and let her continue on her merry way. No one was asking for Lily's help, expecting it, or even wanted it.

But what if she didn't come back?

How would they know if she would or wouldn't?

They'd watched Nhoj, seen Lily, Theyn, and Elizabeth fall off a cliff. They'd watched Ailill too, seen him nearly die. For all Lily hadn't personally watched the mind elf, everyone else had. This time, no one knew what was happening to the night elf and if things had gone wrong.

If the night elf needed Lily's help, then Lily would never know.

It wasn't just that though.

As ominous as it was, Lily felt a growing curiosity, an insatiable need to know just what was there. If she didn't go now, this moment would pass her by, and Lily had the feeling whatever she could have learned she'd need desperately someday.

"Haven't you heard that curiosity killed the cat?" Wizard Lenin asked.

It was also dangerous to pass up information even if you had to take risks to receive it.

He also was ignoring the fact that if he really wanted the Heart of the World, if he wanted that body, then the night elf couldn't fail. If failing wasn't an option, then Lily had to go see for herself and probably should have gone in at the beginning.

Wizard Lenin didn't refute that.

She sat up quietly, looking to see if anyone had noticed. It didn't seem like it.

She placed Rabbit back on her head and stalked towards the barrier.

She looked behind her, searching every sleeping face, then pressed forward.

***

Her first thought was that the air was made of liquid, the same dark oil that had coated the wall. It stung her eyes and tears blurred her vision as she stumbled forward. Each breath was suffocating.

Then, blinking, breathing through it, she realized it was more than just the air. Smoke was everywhere, foul smoke that wasn't from burning wood, but things that shouldn't be burning.

In the distance, through the smoke and thick air, she could hear screaming.

She was standing on a hill, looking down over a great unfamiliar city. It was composed of dark windowless spires, curving and twisting like dragons as they rose into the sky. It looked foreboding, purposefully so, as if someone had built this city to be terrifying.

Every building, every last one of them, was burning.

"What is this place?" Lily asked.

"If I had to guess—" Wizard Lenin cut himself off uneasily, not wanting to guess. Eventually, he found his words, *"I would guess that this is the siege of Xhigrahi. This was when the humans and elves sacked the last stronghold, the imperial city, and murdered the emperor Yaghiroshnik and his family."*

An act the night elves had never recovered from, Wizard Lenin thought to himself. A thousand years in the aftermath, and they still were fractured, with no single leader guiding them and no one rising out of the ashes.

Lily made her way down the hill towards the city, cutting her way through the smog and oil, keeping a firm grip on Rabbit.

With every step, the screaming became louder, the roar of the flames deafening. When her feet hit the pavement, people began to stream past, desperately shoving past each other but oddly indifferent to her.

She saw a red-headed man set fire to a building with a single gesture, a dark-haired woman fell back into the shadows only to reappear behind him, lunging for his jugular. Half a second later, before she could get anywhere near him, she burst into flames.

Red-eyed children ran through the streets, screaming, darting into shadows and scrambling over rubble as fiery arrows flew after them. Most, Lily noticed in numb horror, were hit and stopped moving.

There was more than just smoke in the air, she realized in a daze, there was also the thick iron scent of blood.

"It's an illusion," Wizard Lenin assured her, *"The wards are striking where it hurts the most, where it will hurt her the most, we're just uninvited guests."*

"But it was real," Lily thought distantly.

She'd watched many violent movies, too many at too young an age for most people's tastes, and she'd always been fond of them. Lily had always had a special place in her heart for action movies with the rugged maverick hero hacking and slashing his way to the ending.

This wasn't anything like that.

Wizard Lenin didn't refute this, didn't offer that it'd been a long time ago, or that there was no changing what had already happened.

Instead, he offered, *"If you want to shut it down, you should travel to the center and cut the power supply."*

The center—

Lily looked up, took in the largest, highest, tower in the center of the city.

Like all the others, it was windowless, made from an obsidian black stone. Like all the others, it too was on fire, and looking near the point of collapse. Chunks of stone fell as red-headed elves and men pushed towards the single entrance, kept away only by rings of oily black walls not unlike the one Lily had just passed through.

This must have been the palace.

Lily edged past them wordlessly and took in all the hints of people she knew in their faces.

There, skin streaked with dirt and soot, silver hair in disarray, was a hint of Nhoj. There, sword drawn, stained in blood, standing despite the wounds on his arms was Ailill. There was the love elf in the thin face of a man, the happiness elf sitting in a daze on the steps of the palace, smiling and utterly unconcerned about anything, Frank in the last few guards defending the gates, and in the man at the front, dark red hair and eyes a glowing green, was Ilyn and Lily.

The sun elf lifted his hand and said a single, clear, word, "Shatter."

Light of every color burst from his plan, racing out towards the wards in a shimmering rainbow. On impact, the wards shattered just as commanded, breaking apart like glass and dissolving a second later.

For a moment, his comrades simply stared at him, eyes dark and baleful. Holding swords, bows, axes, that for a second looked like nothing more than cheap toys.

Then they raced ahead with the night elves retreating inside the tower.

Lily stepped inside after them.

They acted quickly. The night elves were tearing up the stairs, the others wasting no time in chasing after them. Vases broke, tapestries caught fire, paintings started melting, and fleeing servants were struck down from behind, left dead and bleeding on the ground.

Within seconds, it was just Lily and the corpses left.

Numbly, Lily moved towards the stairs, but stopped when she felt a prickling at the back of her neck.

Turning her head, she saw that one had been overlooked. There was a dark-haired little girl, a few years younger than Lily, staring at her from underneath a table. She was so small, curled up so tightly, that she was almost unnoticeable.

At Lily's attention, she took a quick and terrified breath.

"Remember, Lily, it's not real," Wizard Lenin cautioned.

Lily stepped forward, stopping when the girl flinched. Slowly, Lily extended a hand, "I won't hurt you."

"She's not real," Wizard Lenin repeated, *"This is only a memory, a memory that died a thousand years ago. Nothing in this place, Lily, is meant to help you."*

"I promise," Lily repeated forcefully, "I won't hurt you."

Tentatively, shaking with fear, the girl got up and walked towards her. On reaching Lily safely, on not having been gutted or lit on fire, she collapsed into Lily's arms with a jerking sob.

"I can't find anyone!" she cried, "I can't find mother, father, Frieghiweig—everyone's gone! I don't—"

Lily didn't say anything, couldn't say anything.

"She's a trick, a product of the wards meant to distract you," Wizard Lenin insisted, *"Leave her."*

But Lily found she couldn't care what the girl was or wasn't.

It might be a memory, Lily might not have ever been here when it really happened, but she couldn't turn away.

There was something familiar about the girl's face.

"The city's being sacked," Lily said, her throat raw, "I suspect your family's—"

She didn't finish that sentence.

It was obvious what had happened to the girl's family, what was going to happen to her shortly.

"No!" the girl tried, pushing Lily back, "No, you're lying! My father's the emperor, my older brothers are princes!"

She swallowed, jerked backwards, and lifted her chin proudly, even with tears streaming down her face, "I am Hajigihr, youngest daughter of the emperor or Xhigrahi, the only empire in the world, and you're lying!"

Her face crumpled, "Tell me you're lying!"

And Lily realized—

"*She's me.*"

"*What on earth are you talking about?*"

"*Look at her! Look at where we are!*" Lily said, eyes darting around the burning palace, "*Doesn't this look familiar?*"

A burning place, an invading force, and a lone surviving princess who was never meant to inherit.

Wizard Lenin, of course, did not like that thought, "*You came here for a reason. If that woman does manage it with you trapped inside the wards it will not end well for us. Leave the girl.*"

The girl, however, was looking around desperately, as if just now reconciling herself with the fact that everything was on fire. She darted towards the stairs.

Lily sprinted after her.

"You're going the wrong way!" Lily called after her, "There's nothing up there!"

Lily tried to catch her but she was too fast, flying forward up the stairs with Lily only just keeping her in sight. Everything felt slow, like a dream, that thick oily air physically preventing her from moving any faster.

She couldn't stop the girl from hurtling into the throne room.

As soon as she entered, the girl skidded to a halt, stopping in horrified disbelief.

There, sitting on an ornate onyx throne, was a dark-haired corpse with a crown of golden laurels on his head. He was slumped to the side, eyes and mouth both open in a soundless scream.

A man was standing above him, holding the corpse's heart in one hand, burning it away into ashes. It was the red-headed man, the sun elf, from earlier, Lily's ancestor.

With his other hand, he summoned the crown from the emperor's head. The body fell onto the marble floor with a deafening thud.

The girl shook, mouth opening wordlessly, as the man stalked toward her. He placed the bloodstained crown on her head.

He looked down at her for a moment, smiling at some private joke only he could hear, then tilted her chin upwards with bloody fingers, "Long live the king."

She didn't take her eyes off the body, not even as the sun elf pushed past her, like a hurricane that had just hit.

Her father, Lily couldn't help but notice, looked just like her. Even when his handsome face was distorted in pain and death, he looked so much like her.

Slowly, as if in a trance, the girl moved forward, step by stilted step, until she collapsed on the throne. There was a sound behind Lily, she turned, and instead of the red-headed man it was the night elf from the quest, the

THE HEART OF THE WORLD

one from the present.

A woman who, Lily suddenly realized, greatly resembled the little girl and the man on the floor—her father.

"Why are you here?" the woman asked, expression thunderous and her hands curled into fists.

"She's you," Lily said, pointing at the girl then back at the woman, "You're her, you're the heir to—"

The woman brought her hands together, and as she pulled them apart, a blade formed out of smoke. Suddenly, she was right in front of Lily, the blade resting against Lily's throat in a clear threat, "You don't belong here."

Lily eyed it warily, but asked, "What happened?"

Xhigrahi had fallen, everyone said that, and Lily had distantly known it for years. Xhigrahi had fallen and somehow Frank and the others had found themselves working for a girl named Lily Jones, others had worked for Wizard Lenin, and she—

She was supposed to have been a princess.

So, what had happened?

"They died," Wizard Lenin said soberly, *"The alliance killed everyone with any hint of capability of taking the throne. Not just then, but for years afterwards. Without leadership, the clan fractured."*

The girl, this woman, hadn't been enough to keep it together.

The woman didn't remove the sword, was now looking at Lily with an odd tilt to her head, considering, "Do you know where you are, Iff?"

The woman answered for Lily, the blade pressing a little closer, "You're in a world with no witnesses, no protectors, in a place made out of blood and sacrifice. You're in my world."

She grinned, "No one would ever look for you."

The sword started to draw blood, "Our people have always been two sides of the same coin, the sun and night elves. Certainly, everyone treats them the same way. It was so easy to put you out of sight and mind, for over ten years—I don't think they'd miss you at all."

"I am not your enemy," Lily said, looking down at the blade.

"I don't see why not," the woman said easily, "You're the descendant of my enemies."

"That doesn't make me your enemy," Lily insisted, lips curling downwards as she thought of Frank and the fact that—

The fact that he didn't really know who she was, thought she was someone else entirely.

(All at once, suddenly and fervently, Lily missed Death. She missed the island that wasn't an island, she missed his gentle smile, and she missed the way she could tell him everything.

God, she wished she could see him.)

Before the woman could strike, Lily forced the sword back into nothingness, leaving the woman empty handed.

She stepped back, looked down at her empty hands, then back up at Lily.

"I'm not your enemy," Lily repeated tiredly, knowing she wouldn't listen.

Lily looked towards the throne, to the girl still sitting there, absolutely dwarfed by it.

"Why did you come here?" Lily asked quietly.

"It's my task!" the woman balked.

"No, I mean, why did you come on this quest?" Lily turned back to look at her, searching her face.

"Nhoj is here for politics, Ailill's here for a good fight, Ilyn's here because someone told him to be here, the mind elf is here for—bragging rights, maybe, and the happiness elf just happened to come along. Why are you here?"

The woman was shaking with fury, no doubt dying to draw a sword again, "I'm here to reclaim my dignity, to make the world remember us as more than we are now."

She laughed then, looking at Lily, "N.E.L.F.," the word was said with a menacing air, something she'd clearly ruminated on in the weeks since Lily had brought it up and written her off, "You think you can buy me, my kingdom, off with Jones and N.E.L.F.? You, the daughter of those that destroyed my kingdom?"

"I don't see you doing anything better," Lily snapped but—

What she meant was that she hadn't seen the woman doing anything at all.

Lily knew night elves, she didn't know everything, but she knew Frank and he'd never once made it seem as if the royal line was out there doing anything for anyone. He'd always, always, spoken as if everything would have to be done on their own.

"We're not all Jones's lackeys!"

And that was her problem, wasn't it?

She was too proud.

She was burdened by a legacy stretching back a thousand years, shackled by expectations she'd placed on herself. That was why she couldn't accept Jones or N.E.L.F. or anything but this quest.

She had always been trapped in this very room, seated on that throne, wearing a crown too heavy for her head.

She could never move forward unless the path brought her back to this place, nowhere else, even though there was nothing left of it.

Lily couldn't help her.

"Lenin," Lily asked, *"How do we leave this place?"*

"Isn't it obvious?" he asked, but it was quiet, sober, as if he didn't want to

say it.

"You have to remove the source of the illusion through blood and sacrifice," he said, *"What, Lily, has been the most reactive part of this place?"*

Lily's head unwillingly turned to the girl seated on the throne.

"To break through, you have to kill the girl."

That's why it'd taken so long, wasn't it?

The woman must have known that. She must have known that from the start—she couldn't do it.

Lily stared at the girl sitting there, staring at nothing, and tried to bring herself to move. She couldn't though, she just couldn't.

Instead, she pulled deep within herself, past where she'd ever gone, and sent her power outwards. Light raced through the palace, the kingdom, to the very walls of the illusion. On touching the dark film separating them from the outside, the illusion shattered, the wards crumpled into shards of dark glass.

And above them, Lily saw so many stars.

"Or I suppose you could always cheat," Wizard Lenin groused, *"As you're wont to do."*

Lily turned to the woman, a grin on her face, about to say something to put all of it behind them, but the woman didn't look at her.

The woman walked forward, ignoring the sound of shouts of surprise and relief as the others realized it was over.

Lily was sure, to the rest of them, it'd looked like nothing had happened at all.

.

14 THE BLIND PROPHET

In which Lily has an identity crisis and Ilyn reveals some of the truth about what he is and how he lives.

"Lenin," Lily thought quietly, "I'm not sure I want to find out what happens next."

At some point since that last task, with everyone but Lily unaware of who Hajigihr really was and how it didn't matter anymore, Lily found herself coming to a realization.

She wasn't enjoying this.

In the beginning, there had been parts she'd disliked, but it'd been an adventure. It'd been the point at which her life would start being about something. If she hadn't met Death, if she hadn't met Wizard Lenin, if she'd only been Ellie Tylor living her mundane life, then she wouldn't have had any reservations at all.

Now, though, Lily was left with a bubbling sense of dread, and the certainty that she didn't want to see where this was going.

It just kept building up on itself.

The first task hadn't been so bad, the hard part had been falling off a cliff and convincing Elizabeth and Theyn to give her a chance. The second had been unnerving, but Lily didn't regret saving Ailill's life, even if it had come with unfortunate consequences. The third was when things had started to take a turn for the worse, not so much in the task itself, but those tangential moments only Lily had witnessed. And the last one—

Lily didn't like thinking about the last one, she didn't want to, but she couldn't seem to stop herself.

Had Frank been in that burning city? Had he been a child or a young man? Or had there been no one left but Hajigihr, the last princess, inexplicably spared in the pillaging of her city?

Was that sun elf still alive somewhere? What had he intended by letting her live? Had he known then it would make no difference? Had he done it to spare her or to make her suffer?

Did Hajigihr still have her father's crown? Did she wear it, telling herself that someday—

"Then don't," Wizard Lenin cut in.

"Don't what?" Lily asked in confusion, finding herself back in the present moment, where they were walking to the very edge of the world.

The place looked unfinished, as if this was as far as God had gone in making this place. It was like he'd never counted on anyone making it this far, and slapped endless golden fields on the rest of it and called it Sunday.

"Don't find out what happens next," Wizard Lenin repeated, referring to what she'd said earlier, *"If anyone can get through without your meddling, it's Ilyn."*

That was a lot of faith in one man, a surprising amount given it was Wizard Lenin.

Wizard Lenin meant every word of it though.

He might not understand Ilyn, might not like him, but if there was one thing he did trust, it was the man's stubborn competence. If Ilyn put his mind to it, he could damn near well accomplish anything.

Lily could sit this one out.

"Oh," she breathed, feeling at once relieved and—

And guilty.

"Why would you feel guilty?" Wizard Lenin asked, *"It's not your responsibility. As you pointed out, they're not even your bloody tasks."*

Lily knew that.

She wasn't taking back her words, but for all she hadn't enjoyed these trials she knew the others had liked them even less. The caves had meant nothing to Lily but everything to Nhoj, Ailill had nearly died, and that wasn't even getting to Hajigihr.

Only that smarmy bastard the mind elf had had a decent time, and if he'd had any sense he'd realize you don't find statues of rabbits in swamps.

Whatever Ilyn was about to do, even if it was something only he could do, it wasn't going to be pleasant.

"I can't believe I'm saying this," Wizard Lenin noted with more than a little disbelief, *"But you're too noble for your own good."*

Noble? Lily had never thought of herself as particularly noble before.

Wizard Lenin had reminded her often enough that Lily Jones had not been a force of good in the world, that Lily's stepping into her shoes wasn't good either. Moreover, for all that Lily was and would always be on his side, Lily recognized that Wizard Lenin wasn't a force of good either.

Helping him, restoring him to any plane of mortal existence, would be condemned not just by Death but many others.

Lily didn't linger on it, didn't let herself linger on it, but sitting here she'd admit that these were actions that would be questioned.

Lily had never lived for the approval of others, she'd never thought to prove herself valiant or noble to anyone. That said, there'd never been anyone to be noble for.

"Yes, that's your trouble," Wizard Lenin said with a hum of discontent, *"The second you recognize someone as worthy of possessing a human soul, whether they exist beyond your plane, inside your head, are cannibals, or something even stranger than that, you start bending over backwards for them."*

"I don't—"

"Remember Elizabeth and Theyn?" he asked, cutting her off.

"Oh, come on, no one would just leave them to die down there. That's just—"

"Remember the moon elf, your blood brother?"

Lily scoffed, "If you'll remember, you were the one who told me to jump into the fray—"

"And the gold elf clan head, Nhoj, what about him?"

"What about him?" Lily asked dully, "I don't remember doing anything for him."

"You consider him a friend," Wizard Lenin said, *"You're planning to visit him in the future, not simply for your own gain, and if he asks a favor or two I'm more than sure you'd grant it."*

Lily backtracked, "He's not a bad guy, I like him, he won't ask for anything—"

"And your hired help Frank, who would do more than simply kill you if he was aware of what you're doing," Wizard Lenin interjected mercilessly, *"You're prepared to help him found a country. You'd help Ailill if his goal wasn't putting you on the throne and decapitating your cousin. You certainly helped the night elf, Hajigihr, even after she threatened you. You saved her the grief of destroying herself by breaking out of the memory for her."*

Lily would laugh if he wasn't so serious, "I think you're looking into this a little too closely, Lenin—"

"And what about me?" he asked, the question echoing inside her head, *"I gave you no reason to trust me. You have no reason to trust me, to help me, given what I am and what I want. Yet, simply by acknowledging your existence enough to insult it, you've gone this far for me and are prepared to go further."*

What was she supposed to say to that?

She'd never thought of it that way, she'd never taken what he'd done to her family personally. That didn't matter, would never matter, what mattered was that he was here and always had been.

"You don't have to say anything," he said, a note of wry fondness entering his voice, *"I certainly have no complaints on my account. Ilyn, though—don't waste your compassion on the likes of him."*

Wizard Lenin thought of those eyes, the eyes that reflected nothing back.

"Like all sun elves, he serves a greater goal he can't fully see."

With that thought, Lily bumped into Theyn. She found the entire party at a complete standstill. Lily, taking a step back, blinked and asked, "What? What is it? Why are we stopping?"

Theyn didn't answer, didn't look like he could hear her. Lily stepped around only to find herself stopping too.

It wasn't a wall this time, not a veil either, instead it was as if they really had reached the edge of the world.

Lily had thought the fields would go on forever. In theory, she knew that the Heart of the World rested elsewhere, but there'd been no sign of how they would get there. However, the fields had abruptly stopped in a single straight line, like they were standing on the edge of a piece of paper or the corner of a cube. Looking out, there was only the black void of space and distant stars.

God, Lily thought to herself, hadn't made it this far.

"How are we supposed to get past this?" Lily breathed, realizing that this—this had to be Ilyn's task, "Is there even anything past this?"

Could they reach the Heart of the World?

Maybe the prophecy had been wrong, maybe this was the part everyone got to, but were stopped by. Maybe there was nothing out there.

God, she'd never considered that—

She couldn't afford to fail, not with Wizard Lenin's body on the line, but she wasn't seeing how it could be avoided.

She looked over at Ilyn. He was balanced precariously over the void, the toes of his boots hanging over the edge. She couldn't see his face, only his back and his rose-gold hair floating in the wind.

Without a word, he stepped forward, and dropped off the face of the earth.

The rest scrambled after him, looking over, and seeing only a black pit where Ilyn's hair should have been.

"Where did he go?" Lily asked, peering over the edge, keeping hold of Rabbit to stop him from tumbling back into the nothingness from whence he came.

There was nothing down there, only black interrupted by distant glittering stars. There wasn't any sign of him.

"God only knows," Nhoj said quietly, staring down with the rest of them, "But I suppose that's why we brought him along."

He stepped away from the edge with a bitter smile, but he didn't say anything, just moved a healthy distance away to set up camp. Slowly, the others trickled away as well, setting themselves up for another long wait.

Theyn lingered with her, giving her a smile that tried too hard, "He'll be back, don't worry. Everyone always says he's the best of the best."

Lily just kept staring out into the darkness.

"Don't do it," Wizard Lenin cut in.

"I wasn't," Lily protested, but her eyes didn't leave the abyss beneath her.

She couldn't even see a hint of him down there, nothing at all except the endless void.

"You were thinking about it," Wizard Lenin retorted, *"And I told you, you don't need to concern yourself over him."*

That was probably true, everyone had said as much, but it didn't dispel the uneasiness rising in her.

"Weren't you contemplating how little fun you had with the last one?" Wizard Lenin asked, *"And she hardly needed your help either."*

The night elf would have gotten through with or without Lily, and while Lily had sped up the process and made it less painful, it wasn't something that had been strictly necessary.

"The only one who's needed your help was the moon elf," Wizard Lenin pointed out, *"And that made itself obvious."*

If Ilyn was down there for a week then perhaps they could acknowledge that he was in trouble. Five minutes, though, wasn't nearly enough time to be concerned about.

Even if what he was going through was truly awful.

"Did you forget he burned down your house?" Wizard Lenin asked, *"That he did it explicitly so you would have nowhere to return to? That he did it for as little reason as Questburger telling him to?"*

Ilyn would have let her get eaten by sharks if he'd been in her position. He wouldn't have lifted a finger to help her and probably would have been glad to wash his hands of her.

"And, as you've said yourself more than once, you are not the hero of this story," Wizard Lenin concluded, *"No one's expecting you to save the day, no one wants you to, and every time you've gone and stuck your nose into things it has upset everyone around you. He wouldn't want your help even if you were to offer it."*

All of this was true, Lily couldn't really argue against a single point he was making.

It was true that the night elf's task had been horrifying and she knew this one would be worse. It was true that Ilyn probably didn't need her help, that most of the elves hadn't. It was true that Ilyn didn't deserve her help and worse didn't want it, that no one did. It was even true that he'd probably resent her if she tried.

All of this was undoubtedly true.

But she still found herself standing on the ledge.

"Oh, for God's sake—"

Before she could regret it, she shoved Theyn out of the way and leapt into the abyss.

She felt, for a moment, as if time ceased to exist.

Her hair floated upwards, and the world above disappeared, like a cardboard set abruptly rushed off stage. There was only the vague sensation of falling into something endless.

"What is wrong with you?!"

She could imagine falling into this forever, forgetting there ever was an Earth or a dimension parallel to it, perhaps even forgetting there was a girl whose name was Ellie and Iff but called herself Lily.

"Lily!"

He wouldn't understand.

It simply wasn't in his nature the same way it apparently hadn't been in her nature not to jump.

"Sorry," Lily offered, hating herself a little for thinking it, and knowing it would only make things worse.

Wizard Lenin didn't answer, but she wasn't here for him. She was here for someone else.

With that thought, she stopped her descent, touched her feet down on a surface that didn't exist, and watched it ripple like water. She walked forward on a sheet of stars, feeling them bend ever so slightly with each step.

Finally, she found him.

He was sitting cross-legged with hunched shoulders, glowing in the dark, holding his compass and looking down at its spinning dial.

"Ilyn."

At the sound of his name, he looked up. His eyes were different this time, they were wide and full of fear, the first blatant emotion she'd ever seen from him. It made him look so vulnerable and so human.

He looked back to the compass, swallowed, and in a hoarse voice stated, "It won't stop spinning."

Lily sat down next to him, looked over his shoulder at the compass that was still spinning. She looked back up at him, "Why does that matter?"

He didn't answer, didn't look at her.

"You can see the future, can't you?" Lily pressed, "You should just—"

He laughed, a small, short sound that Lily almost didn't catch. He let go of the compass, letting it float freely against the backdrop of stars, "I'm blind."

"Blind?!" Lily squawked, raising a hand in front of his face, watching his eyes clearly track the movement.

"Close enough to it," Ilyn corrected, an odd, half-smile appearing on his lips, "You can put your hand down."

"But you said you were—"

"I don't see things like I'm supposed to," Ilyn corrected, pointing to his eyes, "They don't work, they never have."

He picked up the compass, dangled it in front of her, his expression more desperate by the moment, "This—this was a gift from your mother, Lilyanna. She made it herself, kept it secret, so it could be my eyes when she couldn't. It points me where I'm supposed to go, tells me what I'm supposed to do. But we've gone further than even she could see."

Wizard Lenin was hanging on every word, feeling a profound sense of disbelief, and a growing sense of betrayal. He imagined Lilyanna (an odd spark of emotion, rage, regret, contempt swirling together at the thought of her) letting Ilyn con everyone, con Wizard Lenin himself, into believing that he could see the future.

She'd built an item so impossible no one would ever have dreamed of it, didn't even think to covet it, not even when Ilyn stared at it constantly, unabashedly. She'd recklessly given away her own visions to a man who couldn't even protect them.

All those years, all those years he'd spent believing Ilyn could see something, anything, and it'd been all of them dancing to her tune.

(It was just like her, he thought to himself, just like her, and he hated her for it.

The way he'd always hated her for it.)

Ilyn threw the compass back onto the water-like surface of stars.

"You know," Lily said slowly, shaking her head to clear Wizard Lenin's thoughts, "There's no shame in not being able to see the future, most people can't. And everyone seems to respect and or fear you anyway, so it's not—"

"He's a farce!"

"You wouldn't understand," Ilyn said bitterly, "You're your father's daughter."

Lily wasn't sure she agreed with that.

For all her parents had been royalty, known by everyone, she knew nothing about them. She found it hard to imagine that she was like either of them, like anyone at all.

He did have one point though, she didn't understand, Lily had never seen the future.

(As usual, she was ignoring the swamp episode.)

She looked at him quietly, watching as he stared blankly into the void, searching for something he'd be able to see with mortal eyes.

He looked the same as he had when he'd shown up at her house, but so very different, as if this was what always rested beneath that stone-faced determination he always wore.

"The only thing I've ever seen for myself," Ilyn said quietly, so quietly Lily wondered if he was talking to her or just confessing to himself, "Was the thing all of us see."

"What's that?"

"My death," he said plainly, as if it was the most natural statement in the world.

"The others believe they can live forever, if they play their cards right, but we know better," he told her, "We're bound by our prophecies, each of us comes into this world knowing that for all our tricks, all our veneers of immortality, we die along with everyone else.

"There is no such thing as immortality.

"Knowing that and everything else, that's the curse the rest of them are convinced we avoided."

He smiled, looking down at his hands, curling his fingers and causing small sparks to emit from them, "But that's the only thing I've ever seen, a vague acceptance of my own demise, a betrayal that I don't foresee. Instead, I have this, this great raw magical talent, to compensate."

"Do you know who?" Lily asked, "I mean, do you know who betrays you?"

"Then it wouldn't be a betrayal," he told her, laughing somewhat.

"No, not who, nor how, nor when, nor even why. I only know that it will happen, someday, and despite knowing it all my life I won't expect it."

His smile turned bittersweet, something that both suited him and didn't all at once. It was the kind of smile that Death often wore.

"I have always been adrift in a world where everyone I've ever known and loved knows exactly where they're going."

Including, Lily knew without a doubt, Lily's mother.

Lily picked up the compass, looking down at the spinning needle and her own dim reflection in the glass.

She covered it with one hand, looking over at him, "You know, I think there might be something to that."

"To what?"

"To not seeing the future," Lily said.

He raised a dubious eyebrow.

"Think about it," Lily persisted, "If you could see everything, or almost everything, then what's left for you? You know the best path to take, and even if you hate it, you have to do it. It's not your choice anymore, you just go through the motions you've already laid out for yourself. You stop being anything, you're just your own puppet. If you can't see anything, though, then you can do anything. You can up and join Len—I mean, the Usurper's rebellion at a moment's notice, then join up with the monarchy in the next breath."

She pointed a finger at him, digging it into his chest. She grinned and concluded, "You're free."

He was giving her an odd look, like he'd never seen her before, or she'd just gone and shattered every preconception he'd had of her.

"Who told you that?"

"What?" Lily asked.

"She said that to me, an age and a half ago, when we were still children—" he reached out with trembling hands, brushed the hair away from her face, staring into her eyes, "Are you repeating her or was she—

was she repeating you?"

"I don't—"

"Your mother must have said this to him," Wizard Lenin said, quiet and bitter, vindicated only by the fact that Lilyanna hadn't chosen Ilyn either. No, for all it'd looked like she'd chosen, she must have chosen death.

"Look," Lily said, grabbing his wrists in her hands and offering a sheepish grin, "What I meant to say was that—"

She trailed off, looked down and noticed the compass had stopped spinning. Its needle was pointed directly at Lily.

Ilyn brushed her hands away and took the compass from her. He moved it from side to side, watching as the needle unerringly pointed at her.

"Lilyanna thought it would be a son," Ilyn said quietly, "It was the only time she was ever wrong."

"A son?" Lily asked, not sure what he was getting at.

"He means you, you were supposed to have been a son," Wizard Lenin said, his mind racing, remembering the prophecy, the fact that it'd been so explicit about a king—

"You were supposed to be the crown prince," Ilyn said with a sad smile, "Someone who could unite all of us under one banner and make it stick this time."

He looked over at her, "Even if you were a son, I never thought the humans would stand for it, any more than they would have stood for a Tellestrian on the throne."

"Well, they did leave me in a dumpster," Lily joked with a small huff, it was starting to be an almost funny thing to her, "And they only remembered to send you to light my house on fire when it was convenient."

"Necessary," Ilyn corrected, "I was sent to find you because it was necessary."

"Some necessity I've been," Lily scoffed, but he only gave her a look, something both fond and exasperated, something she'd never have expected from him.

"Iff, haven't you realized it yet?" he asked.

"Realized what?"

"This task isn't mine," he said, his smile growing as he tapped her once on the forehead, "It's yours."

"Mine?"

"Just as this quest is yours," he added, sounding confident, more confident than she'd ever heard him before, "And the Heart of the World is yours."

"Deny it! Dammit, Lily, deny it!" Wizard Lenin screamed in her head, Ilyn was stumbling far too close to the truth for Wizard Leni's comfort.

"I—don't know what you're talking about," Lily said lamely, but his smile just became fonder.

"They may never admit it, perhaps not even to themselves, but even a blind man can see it."

"Finish this, Iff, and then let's go home."

He held out his hand towards her and with a small smile she took it in hers.

Somehow, finding the way through and building a bridge for the rest of them was the easiest thing she'd ever done.

.

15 THE ENDLESSNESS OF ETERNITY

In which Lily finally reaches the Heart of the World and discovers a terrible secret.

The thin bridge of light arched over the great abyss to the far side of existence. They made their way across in a single file line and one by one stopped off onto the surface of a small moon that Lily knew so well, the place she'd known this journey would end.

It was exactly the same as when she'd first arrived seven years ago, before Death had made his appearance and added a table and tea. At the outer edges was the sand which had deceived her into thinking it was a beach and an island. Inside were the softly glowing plants, still unfamiliar, not native to Earth or to the other side.

She'd always thought that whenever she died, she entered a metaphor of sorts, a place that wasn't supposed to be a real world. Oh, it'd been very scenic, beautiful, and so very empty, but it had never meshed with what she knew on Earth.

Standing here, though, she wondered if she hadn't truly ended up here every time she died. Or, maybe, the party had passed the bounds of where they were supposed to go and ended up in this place.

Death was nowhere in sight.

Lily looked for him, unable to help herself, but there wasn't any sign of him. Not his cloak, his boots, gloves, or even his red hair. She found herself missing him again. It'd been weeks now, maybe even months, she hadn't seen him since before she'd started this journey. She hadn't dared while on the journey, when someone might miss her if she died for a few hours, and she'd felt so rushed and busy—there were times that she'd genuinely forgotten or told herself that she'd see him when everything calmed down.

That was a mistake, she now distantly realized. He'd know what to do about the moon elf, Theyn, the night elves, and the entire quest. All that time Lily had spent running herself in circles and he'd surely have known what to do.

She would have to fix that, when everything was over, she would have to see him again.

And the Heart of the World—

Just in front of them, where the pedestal should have been, was a seemingly immaterial gate made of light. Like the veil in the night elf's task, it stretched high over their heads, a localized aurora borealis, formed in a perfect circle obscuring its center from view.

It was the most beautiful thing Lily had ever seen.

She didn't know why, couldn't possibly explain it even if Wizard Lenin had asked, but it made her think of homecoming. Homecoming in a way she'd never really felt before, not even when she came to this place to find Death.

It must have been different this time, somehow, because—

Because she knew this place, truly knew this place, and was glad to be here.

"So, we really did make it," Nhoj said breathlessly, unable to look away from the veil.

"But what kind of magic is it?" Elizabeth asked in excited wonder, stepping close enough to touch it, "It's not a blood ward, it's not a normal ward either. I have no idea how someone could even make something like this—"

She reached out with shaking fingers, ignoring Theyn as he stumbled forward to stop her, and pressed against it.

Nothing happened.

With a frown, she tried pushing against it with both hands, but what looked like nothing more than shimmering light was evidently solid.

"What the hell do you think you're doing?" Ilyn asked with the look of a man who'd just watched his supremely stupid cat ram its head into the wall for the tenth time in a row.

"Oh, sir, I—" Elizabeth flushed, stumbled back in embarrassment, "I just thought, well, that maybe we could get—"

"It's not for you," Ilyn said with his usual lack of tact and compassion.

Elizabeth flushed the shade of red usually seen in stop-signs, dark eyes burning with humiliated rage, and stomped away from the gate to stand next to a nervous but relieved looking Theyn.

"Well, I just thought someone should stop standing around and try something!" she bit out, clinging to her crumbling dignity, "I don't see you doing anything, sir!"

Ilyn didn't look bothered by this, simply put his compass away and noted, "My part in this is finished."

Elizabeth looked confused for a moment, looked towards the rest of her elven companions, then seemed to catch on. Her eyes brightened and she grinned, "Oh, oh, this is because of the prophecy!"

She looked over at Theyn standing just behind her, "Theyn, this must be why you're here, because you're the only one who can get through!"

"Me?!" Theyn asked, motioning to himself in alarm.

"Him?" Wizard Lenin echoed in alarm and confusion.

Theyn started nervously babbling, "But I'm not good for anything! I can never, could never—"

Elizabeth grabbed his hands, grinning as she got over her embarrassment and saw Theyn's golden opportunity, "Of course you can! That's why you came, Your Highness! Maybe nobody thinks I should be here, but you're actually supposed to be here!"

She squeezed his hands tightly, paying no mind to his increasing discomfort, "Theyn, something saved the kingdom from the Usurper, something that clearly cares about you deeply and bent the laws of magic to do it. Something sees you as much more than just our next king. You're destined for great things, Your Highness, and I know that this—this is just the first of them. You can do this. You're meant to do this!"

Theyn looked over at Annde for confirmation.

As usual, Lily couldn't even look in the man's direction, so whatever expression he gave Theyn was a mystery to her. (She couldn't imagine anything about that man being reassuring, encouraging, though, even here, maybe especially here he seemed—wrong). It must have been enough, though, as Theyn next looked over towards Ilyn with a growing smile.

Ilyn—did not look encouraging.

His expression, if possible, grew even less impressed.

However, that look must have been so familiar to Theyn that it had no effect anymore. Theyn took a step forward to stand next to the veil.

"There's no chance in hell," Wizard Lenin scoffed.

Lily wanted to disagree, she really did, but she couldn't help but think how terribly human he looked in front of it. Whatever his abilities, his gift, this wasn't a place mankind was meant to touch.

Death had said it the first time she'd ever met him, humans didn't come to this place.

They watched with bated breath as he stopped in front of it, drew a large breath, and reached out in front of him.

Predictably, he met something solid.

"What?" Theyn asked, pressing against it. Just like with Elizabeth, it didn't budge an inch.

"It's not—" Theyn turned and looked at them with wide disbelieving eyes, "I can't—I can't do it."

He tried to smile, to laugh it off, but his smile was stretched too wide and didn't meet his eyes. His laughter was choked, as if his throat was closing in.

"I can't do it!" he said, louder this time, rubbing the back of his head and staring out into the emptiness of space, "Sorry, I just—I guess I can't do it after all. Even though we came all this way, went through everything, I can't—"

He glanced at Elizabeth, took in her stunned and heartbroken expression, and jerked his eyes away again.

"I guess I just can't do it!" Theyn concluded, throwing his hands in the air, unable to look at any of them, "Just like I can't do anything else right either!"

"We know," Ilyn interjected, "You were never meant to be here either."

"Ilyn," Theyn said, whipping his head towards the sun elf, a look of devastation on his face, but Ilyn was no longer looking at him.

Ilyn reached out to take Lily's hand in his, squeezed it gently, and looked down at her with the oddest and fondest smile.

Oh, Lily had a bad feeling about this.

"Iff," he said gently, "Do you remember what I told you?"

And with every word out of his mouth, that look of unbreakable faith he was giving her, a nail was being hammered into her cousin's heart.

"So, even the sun elf thinks the girl should be queen," Ailill laughed, grinning jaggedly over at his fellow supporter.

The night elf pointedly said nothing, looking out into empty space and dreaming of a crown placed on her head. The happiness elf was still smiling, as if this would all work itself out somehow. The others, though, while they didn't say anything they were each giving Lily an assessing look.

Like Wizard Lenin had said, they'd seen more than enough, and forgotten none of it.

"You showed your hand," Wizard Lenin agreed, *"There are consequences to that."*

"Iff?" Theyn asked, his voice shaking.

All at once, Lily realized she had a choice.

She could refuse. She could stand here, laugh it off, or go and pretend to try and fail and say she couldn't do it either. She'd allow Theyn to save face and maybe something even more important than that. She'd come back later, somehow, and grab it when the rest weren't looking to pass off to Wizard Lenin.

She could lie to everyone, lie for her cousin, and let things remain the way they were supposed to be.

Or she could do it here and now, confirm everyone's suspicions. And acknowledge that something had gone awry in ways that none of them had suspected.

"What should I do?" she asked Wizard Lenin even as she stared at her cousin.

For a moment, he didn't answer. Then he said, *"Do it."*

She was surprised, she thought he'd tell her to lay low, to take the spotlight off herself and let Theyn return in glory.

"The moon elves will follow you, Ilyn will follow you, if you do this perhaps the rest will as well," Wizard Lenin explained, *"Lily, you and I are not in competition with one another. When I return, we'll be hand in hand. Your enemies will be my enemies, your friends my friends. I'd rather show the world what you are than have it believe in a scared little boy."*

Lily felt like her heart had just stopped.

She'd never known how much she wanted that.

She didn't want Wizard Lenin's future or glory, not the throne, he could keep that for himself, but the idea that when he was out of her head she would have more than just a place in his world—

She'd never let herself believe it.

She closed her eyes, took a breath, and took one step forward then another. She kept walking until she felt a patch of cool mist pass over her.

When she opened her eyes, she found herself inside the ring of light, the Heart of the World placed on the pedestal exactly where she'd expected it to be.

As always, it looked so ordinary.

Nothing more than a reflective orb, the kind you might find in a cheap magic shop on Earth. There was nothing that seemed special about it, nothing that ever had beyond the fact that it'd always been here.

Maybe it was having seen it every time she died, she'd gotten used to it when she had found it eerie at first, but—

She just couldn't believe that this was what she'd waited seven years to find. She couldn't believe she'd seen it, or something like it, every two weeks and had never just—taken it then.

She looked down and stopped in her tracks.

Stretching beneath her was a shadow that shouldn't be there in this bright lighting, far taller and broader than Lily.

Lily watched as with each step she took it grew larger. When she neared the Heart of the World, it started to rise inch by inch out of the ground, into the shadowy form of a man.

It rose to a height far taller than Lily, Death's height, and the closer Lily drew the more details formed.

Dark hair sprouted like feathers from his head, the same texture as hers, the shadows settled into the folds of a tunic and a cloak, and a thin neck rose to support a mask-like face with painted and finely carved features.

However, even when she came to a stop right in front of the orb, he had no eyes. There were no eyes, no empty sockets, only dark bottomless pits where they should have been.

"Death?" Lily asked, her heart pounding, but the man didn't respond.

THE HEART OF THE WORLD

Of course he didn't, it wasn't him, it looked nothing like him. He might have been the same height, but he wasn't the same build, didn't have the same hair, and certainly didn't have the same face. There was too much symmetry in his face, too little color in his hair, and those eyes—

This was the other Death, Lily suddenly realized, the one from Frank's story, the one who'd given his eyes away.

Lily reached up with shaking fingers, touching her cheek, hovering just under her own impossibly green eye.

The man across from her slowly, silently, smiled.

"Who are you?" Lily asked, "Are you another Ellie Tylor—Iff, I mean?"

He wasn't.

She didn't know what he was, but if Death was what she could become, what she might have been in some other world, then this man wasn't that at all.

He didn't answer, just reached out towards her. Lily leaned back, holding Rabbit desperately against her head. His hands hovered over where her face had been only a moment before. He quietly implored her, "Please."

His voice was like everything on this quest, the Rabbit statue, the guardian—it wasn't a voice that sounded human at all. It was pleasant enough in tone, understandable, and maybe even beautiful—but it wasn't human.

"Please," he repeated, "I need to see you."

Lily leaned forward until his fingers brushed against her cheeks. She waited, deathly still, not even breathing as he carefully mapped out her features beneath his hands.

He smiled, a small boyish thing, as his thumb brushed against her jaw, "Ah, I thought you would look different."

"You were expecting me?" Lily asked warily.

"Yes," the man responded easily, he removed his hands but his smile didn't fade.

"You're Death, aren't you?" Lily asked slowly, "You're that other Death, I mean, the one from the story, the one with the Heart of the World."

"Yes," the man answered.

Lily frowned, looked down at herself, at her now shabby uniform stained and worn from the journey. She felt as small, unassuming, and just as mortal as her cousin.

She looked back up at him, "But I thought—I thought I was supposed to be Death."

"Yes," the man agreed.

"But," Lily pointed at him, "If you're Death, and I'm Death—We can't both be Death, can we?"

Because he wasn't Iff, she knew that, she knew it in her heart. He hadn't come from some other reality and neither had she. They couldn't both be here.

"Time," the man said, tilting his head upwards as if he could see the small circle of stars above them, "Does not exist in this place."

"What's that supposed to mean?"

He smiled, still looking upwards. The light caught on his cheekbones, painting them blue, green, red, and purple, "It means that I am here in all my forms tonight. I have come as you and as your memory."

Lily stared at him, that feeling of unease growing.

"Did you follow any of that?" she asked Wizard Lenin.

"I think," Wizard Lenin said carefully, very purposefully avoiding thinking too deeply on any of this, *"That we should take the Heart and leave."*

"You're so beautiful," the man said, his smile moving from boyish into something heartbreaking.

Inky tears welled at the corners of his empty sockets, streaking down his face like thick and viscous mascara.

"Yeah," Lily thought to herself, *"We're leaving."*

Lily reached forward towards the orb only to pause as she noticed the man's hands reaching in time with hers. She retracted her hands, he did the same, and when she brought them forward again his followed.

He was mirroring her every action.

"Can you stop that?" Lily asked.

He didn't answer, he was still smiling, crocodile black tears still rolling down his face and falling in giant inky globs onto his clothing.

He was looking at her, Lily thought with some alarm, the way Lily had been looking at the rainbow gate earlier.

As if she was something heartbreakingly familiar and precious.

"Look, you seem nice and all," Lily continued, inching her hands closer and watching in nauseating horror as he did the same, "But I need this thing. I have this friend in my brain who doesn't want to be in my brain anymore. I can only get him out if I have this thing, so I really need it."

He didn't stop.

"Seriously," Lily threatened, her heart pounding, "I may look small but I'm very powerful."

He still didn't stop.

"Just grab it!"

Lily lunged forward, ignoring the fact that the man was moving just as fast as she was, and grabbed hold of the orb. Only, even as she triumphantly laughed and snatched it from the pedestal, she found that the strange man was no longer standing across from her.

He'd been replaced by someone who couldn't possibly be standing there.

"Lenin?!" Lily balked, nearly dropping the orb in surprise.

It was definitely him, though. Him in all his tall, dark-haired, pale-eyed, and disturbingly handsome glory.

He was dressed a little different than usual, not in Tellestrian wear or the dark tunic she'd first met him in. It was shabbier than he usually imagined himself in, the kind of thing Lily saw in markets and not in any stores. He also looked a lot younger than he usually did, a little lankier than he normally was, his face not quite grown into itself yet.

But it was certainly him.

Had she done it already?

She looked down at the orb in alarm. God, that thing had worked fast. At this rate, she didn't even have to give it to Wizard Lenin. She could hand it over to Theyn, no questions asked, and—

"Lily?" Wizard Lenin breathed, stumbling towards her, his expression of shock turning into one of overwhelming joy, "Lily, is it really you?"

Lily grinned in turn, caught up in the joy of the moment, the feeling that after seven years she'd somehow managed it, "We did it! Lenin we—God, we really did it!"

He lunged towards her, drew her into a hug, and squeezed far too tightly, far tighter than she'd ever imagined given his pride.

She laughed even as she tried to free herself, "A little too tight, Lenin."

He just squeezed harder, shoulders shaking, hiding his face in her hair so she couldn't see him. He was murmuring something, something she could barely make out, her name interchanged with something like "you really did come".

"Lily," A familiar voice, small and horrified, echoed inside of her head, *"That's not me."*

Lily jerked back, looked at the man, the boy, who most certainly was a much younger Wizard Lenin. Except—the boy grinned, a smile that Wizard Lenin would never have given simply because it showed too much feeling. It was a smile that he would think made him vulnerable.

The other Wizard Lenin didn't seem to notice Lily's distraction, "I knew you'd come, you promised you would. It took you long enough but—you're here, you really came."

"—Sure," Lily said lamely after a lengthy pause.

He laughed, laughed merrily in a way she'd never seen Wizard Lenin laugh, not a hint of anything bitter, caustic, or cynical inside it.

"Oh, I'm being rude," he said after getting a hold of himself, "Do you want tea?"

To their left, a small wooden table, two chairs, and a quaint little English tea set appeared.

"Of course you want tea," he said for her as he made his way to a chair, "You always want tea. How could I forget that?"

Lily hadn't thought it was possible, but this was weirder and worse than the mind elf task and the night elf task.

"Um," Lily started, not knowing where to start at all.

The Wizard Lenin who wasn't Wizard Lenin pushed her into a seat with that stupid smile on his face.

Lily was meeting too many people today that weren't the people they were supposed to be. First the Death who wasn't Death, now this Wizard Lenin doppelganger who had appeared out of thin air.

"Not out of thin air," Wizard Lenin corrected, a feeling of dread and understanding blossoming inside him, *"Lily, listen, there's something I need to tell you—"*

He was interrupted by the other Wizard Lenin. He looked at her with a strange, soft, smile as if he wouldn't want to stare at anybody else.

"Forgive me if I'm overeager, Lily," he said, "But I don't know how long I've been waiting, I lost track a long time ago. Moreover, expectations, well, they have a way of building up."

Lily opened her mouth to blandly agree or give some small hum of acknowledgement, but he just kept going, like he was trying to fill every quiet moment with noise.

"Of course, I wasn't sure I was going to see you again, even in the far-off future," he contradicted himself, "To tell the truth, I'd almost given up on the idea. I thought about it though, more often than I'd care to admit, I thought about how we'd meet again someday."

He paused, considered her with a worried frown. He gave Lily just enough time to catch her breath, to open her mouth, but not enough to get a word in edgewise.

"I thought you'd be a little older, not—" his brow furrowed, his head tilted, "Are you younger?"

His frown became more pronounced, even a little annoyed, "Yes, you're younger than you were. I know your face so well I could carve it blindfolded, you're younger than you should be."

Lily opened her mouth again, but he cut her off with a shrug, "Well, I suppose it doesn't really matter. We're here, after all these years and—And am I the only one who can't think of anything to say?"

He laughed again, then stopped, looked at her teacup in accusation, "Do you not like the tea?"

Lily looked down at the teacup, at her bewildered reflection, then back at him. With some trepidation, she picked it up and took a sip.

There was a thought, for a moment, that one should never eat or drink the wine and food of other worlds.

It didn't taste like tea, not even the tea Death served in the reflection of this place. It tasted like the memory of tea, not quite watered down, but lacking something integral that she couldn't place.

"It's—great tea," Lily said lamely, smiling weakly as she raised the cup towards him as if in toast.

Something must have been off about her response.

The younger Wizard Lenin's smile slipped, his eyes widened, and he noted without inflection, "You don't know who I am."

"Well—" Lily started, trying to think of a way to explain it. She couldn't find the words.

"Lily, I think I know who he is, what he is, and why he's here," Wizard Lenin said hurriedly, *"I even know who, what, that man earlier was—"*

The younger Wizard Lenin's face relaxed though, as if he'd just figured something out. He smiled at her fondly, "Ah, we haven't met yet, have we?"

"I—no?" Lily answered.

"That's just like you," he said with a grin, "Showing up in a place like this even when you have no idea who I am. I really have missed you, Lily."

"Right," Lily said as she looked down at the Heart of the World resting on her lap, then back at the teenage Wizard Lenin, "About that, why and how exactly are you here?"

He stiffened, body suddenly entirely too still, eyes burning through her. For a moment, Lily thought he might do something to her, but the moment passed and he relaxed once more. A strange sort of melancholy washed over him, "I made a bargain with a god."

"What?" Lily asked.

"When I was younger, his age, I summoned a god to barter for the immortality and power denied by the human half of my heritage," Wizard Lenin explained, that fear unease only growing as Lily stared at his younger self.

There was an image in her head, a memory of this teenaged Wizard Lenin standing in a chalk circle of foreign characters, incense and candles burning around him. A shadow loomed over him in a blindingly white room, too bright for Wizard Lenin to look at it properly.

"He took something from me in exchange, something of my humanity, but I never thought I lost anything."

Lily's eyes widened as she took in the boy across from her as Wizard Lenin concluded, *"I never noticed anything missing."*

"It's nothing," the younger Wizard Lenin, the price of Wizard Lenin's bargain, said stiffly, "Nothing for you to worry about."

He laughed again, his mood suddenly bright, leaving Lily with emotional whiplash. Was this supposed to be normal?

"How long has he been here?" Lily asked.

Wizard Lenin didn't answer.

"At first it wasn't so terrible being trapped here," the younger Wizard Lenin confessed, "I could do, be, anything I wanted. If I wanted tea, I could have it. If I wanted to be a king, I could do that too. Everything's possible here, and for a while, that wasn't so bad. The other me, the one on the outside, he could do what he needed now that the toll had been paid, and I would live my life as I saw fit."

He placed his hands behind the back of his head, leaning back and looking at his surroundings with a contemptuous smile, "That said, having complete control over your existence, your entire reality, being a god as it were, loses its appeal quickly. There's no point to this place, no time, no matter, no existence, just John Jones and the endlessness of eternity."

He looked back at her.

She'd never realized how captivating Wizard Lenin's eyes could be. She'd always thought they were striking, good for dramatic effect, and she'd even felt trapped in them from time to time—she'd never drowned in them before.

She found herself unable to look away and he, for whatever reason, didn't look away either.

"I used to pretend," he continued, "I lived in fake memories I built for myself, dreams of my glorious future. Then I stopped being able to tell the difference between what had really happened and what I'd only imagined, it became dangerous."

He looked away from her, frowning again, "There were consequences, and now, now I have to really think about what occurred and what didn't, and have no idea how long I've been trapped here."

He laughed, raking a hand through his hair, and gave her a wry look, "I thought it was a bargain, did you know that? I'd been prepared to sacrifice nearly everything, and all it'd asked for was nothing at all. Yet he got the immortality, he got the world, and what did I get?!"

His face contorted with rage and nearly too late Lily realized that hadn't been rhetorical.

"Tea?" Lily spluttered, grabbing her cup out of instinct, "You got— watered down tea?"

He laughed, burying his head in his arms, shoulders shaking with mirth.

"Yes, Lily," he agreed in amusement, "I have tea."

Lily tried to smile when he looked back up at her, it wasn't her best. Still, it seemed to bring an amused smile to his face.

It was funny for all his mercurial fits, right now he really did look like Wizard Lenin.

"We can't leave him here," Lily thought to Wizard Lenin.

She didn't know what Wizard Lenin had bargained for, exactly, and what he'd thought he'd sacrificed, but whatever had happened, this abandoned piece of Wizard Lenin didn't deserve this place.

Wizard Lenin, for everything he must have gained from the other Wizard Lenin's suffering, didn't disagree.

"Look, I just came for this thing," Lily said, motioning to the Heart of the World, "But I'll get you out of here."

He laughed, "I don't know how you got in here, Lily, but it's not so easy getting out."

He glared at the walls surrounding them, not looking angry so much as irritated and resigned.

"Sure it is," Lily insisted, she placed the Heart of the World on her chair and motioned for him to follow her to the wall.

He humored her, stood, and walked with her until she was just in front of it.

She reached out, placed a hand against it, then parted it as if it was a curtain of water.

"Look," she told him, "You can walk right through."

He stared, looking comically dumbfounded as he peered through to the other side, "How did you do that?"

"Magic," Lily said with a grin.

Elizabeth would have punched her in the face for that answer, but the younger Wizard Lenin just looked at her for a moment then laughed again.

"Now, go on, get going," Lily said, shooing him out of the circle, "I've got places to be and people to see."

"Yes, the world is waiting, isn't it?" he asked, a grin splitting his face from ear to ear, a smile that oddly tugged at her heart for all she'd never seen Wizard Lenin wearing it, "I'll find you on the other side, Lily, wait for me!"

And with that, he darted through, leaving Lily, Rabbit, the Heart of the World, and the immaterial Wizard Lenin.

She stood there, waiting for something else to happen, for Death to show up and put a cap on everything, but nothing else happened. That really seemed to have been the last of it.

"Well, this has been an experience," Lily summed up.

Wizard Lenin agreed.

They stood in perfect silence for another moment, waiting for the younger version of him to pop his head through the curtain or the eyeless Death to make another appearance.

It seemed, though, that they were finally on their own.

"So, your body," Lily thought, clapping her hands together as she moved back to the Heart of the World on the chair, *"We should get you a body."*

"That would be nice," Wizard Lenin agreed wistfully, still a little dazed.

"Not just any body, the greatest body. You'll look as capable, confident, and young as—"

"No," Wizard Lenin interrupted, *"No thank you, I do not need to be a teenager again."*

Wizard Lenin didn't look back fondly on his youth.

Lily picked up the orb, felt something buzz through her fingertips.

It struck her, now, that they'd never be like this again. Where before, they were always one, they'd now be two. He wouldn't be watching every moment of her life with her, wouldn't be having his running commentary in her head. Things would change, and maybe he really would leave her behind.

Except—

Except this was the only thing he'd ever really asked of her, the only thing he'd ever wanted. He had waited patiently for seven years, watched himself become irrelevant in the eyes of his home world.

How could she possibly say no?

Lily smiled to herself, holding the Heart of the World close, and gave one last thought to the greatest friend she'd ever had, *"I'll see you on the other side."*

She poured power into the ball, felt her hair rising above her head, the air disappear around her and—then it stopped.

Lily was standing there, a ball in her hands, feeling like the world's biggest idiot.

Belatedly, she realized she had no idea how this thing was supposed to work.

"Any—um—instructions on how to do this?" Lily asked.

He didn't answer.

"Lenin?"

Then came the thought, the one that Wizard Lenin hadn't wanted to admit to, hadn't wanted to confront for all the possibility had certainly occurred to him along the way.

He had no idea how this thing worked.

No one had any idea how it worked or if it even could work.

The Heart of the World, the miraculous object they'd waited seven years to obtain, the thing she'd gone on this journey for, was a paperweight.

16 A RABBIT BY ANY OTHER NAME

In which Lily proves to be a terrible con-artist, Wizard Lenin and Lily choose a guinea pig, and Ilyn relays an ominous warning.

"What do you mean you don't know how it works?!" Lily asked, dropping the useless orb to the ground.

"Perhaps because until a short while ago it was only a thing of ancient legends," Wizard Lenin spat back shamelessly.

The way he saw it, it would have been a minor miracle if he'd understood how it worked in the first ten minutes. It would have been nice, of course, if Lily had somehow gotten it to work in the first few seconds but she couldn't go and blame him for not having an instruction manual.

"You used me!" Lily accused, but it wasn't even that, she'd known that, it was the fact that he'd gone and used her poorly.

He'd taken all her energy, her talent, to retrieve something that would just sit on their shelf and remind them of all the good times they hadn't had on this field trip. He'd made her wait seven years, seven years waiting for a sign, had said that this was supposed to be it only to get stuck at the very end of it all.

"This is not about you!" Wizard Lenin shouted back at her.

"I don't know, Lenin, maybe it is about me!" Lily retorted, "Maybe, if I'd just given it another try, I could have done this years ago!"

"You make a human body?" Wizard Lenin laughed, "After the Rabbit disaster? Aren't you the one who thinks he eats planets?"

"Well, it looks like it has a better chance of working than this thing!" Lily waved towards the orb at her feet as damning evidence. At least, last time, Lily had made something even if it was horrible.

"Exactly," Wizard Lenin said with contempt, "You'd make some ghastly error and I'd have to live with it."

"You don't know that!"

"I do know that," Wizard Lenin cut her off, *"I've been stuck in your head for years. Who do you think has had a front row seat to every one of your cosmic disasters?"*

"And for seven years you've been too afraid to take any real risks!" Lily shouted back, *"You've been too afraid to trust that I can handle this!"*

"Prove it," he said suddenly, no longer shouting inside her head but thinking at a normal volume.

"Prove it?"

"Do it, here and now," he said, *"It's your second go around, should be easy."*

Lily felt something bubbling in her stomach. She knew he was doing this just to prove her wrong, to spite her, but she couldn't back down either.

Trouble was, she didn't have anyone to make a body for besides Wizard Lenin. Now that Death the Cryptic had disappeared along with the younger mercurial Wizard Lenin, it was just Lily in this place.

Well, Lily and Rabbit.

She lifted him off her head, and held him out in front of her.

He was—something, wasn't he? Something that could be changed into a human body if she wanted to.

"You can't be serious," Wizard Lenin said, somehow insulted that Lily's guinea pig for his body was going to be a rabbit.

Not that Rabbit had to be a rabbit, Lily had always thought that was just a coincidence. That was just what she'd wanted to pull out of a hat, ergo a rabbit he was.

Technically, he didn't have to be a rabbit.

Lily took in a breath, locked eyes with Rabbit.

Somehow, the soulless pits that made up his eyes conveyed less emotion than Death's empty eye-sockets.

"Alright, Rabbit," Lily said, "Get ready for some strange changes."

She closed her eyes and envisioned a world where Rabbit wasn't a rabbit, but instead inhabiting a human body. For a moment, the furry creature in her hands felt the same as always, in the next he was too heavy to lift.

Something heavy fell to the ground with a thud.

Lily hesitantly opened her eyes.

The first thing she saw was that it had worked. Where seconds before there'd been a white rabbit, there was now an equally pale boy around Lily's age collapsed at her feet.

The second thing she noticed was that she hadn't made him clothes.

Maybe that wasn't important, but looking down at him as he stared passionlessly back up at her made her uncomfortable.

Lily created the first outfit that came to mind, the fantastical tunic and trousers she'd just seen the younger Wizard Lenin wearing, and tossed them at his feet.

Rabbit neither looked at them nor bothered to blink. He stared at her sightlessly with the same expressionless dark eyes he'd had as a lowly bunny.

God, he was—

He was the most symmetrical looking being she'd ever seen. Somehow, even more so than the Death who wasn't Death.

It wasn't just the symmetry though.

There were no marks on his skin, no veins, no freckles, nothing. He looked like he'd been carved from stone. His eyelashes were long and black, impossibly so against his colorless skin. His hair, a soft curling white, was the same blinding shade it'd been when he was a rabbit. His limbs were too thin and his face too proportional for an adolescent's. There was no hint of growth, of noses and ears that were too large in a face that had yet to grow into itself. His was an eerily perfect face placed on a child's body.

It made for a hauntingly perfect young man, the kind of perfection that somehow stopped being beautiful at all.

He hadn't taken his eyes off hers.

"Did it work?" Lily hesitantly asked Wizard Lenin.

It looked like it had, all the moving pieces had been put together, and that was definitely a human body sitting in front of her, but—

Wizard Lenin was so beyond reasonable feelings he couldn't even respond.

"Maybe we should turn you back," Lily said slowly.

Rabbit gave no response to that either.

She closed her eyes, tried to think of him as a rabbit again, opened them and—

Nope, still an enchanted fairytale prince.

"Hm," Lily hummed, feeling less confident about all this than she had before. Was it just Rabbit that was the problem or was making a body just a bad idea?

She tried again, this time keeping her eyes open and willing it to work, but he didn't even twitch. There was nothing any more rabbit-like about him now than there'd been two seconds ago.

"So, you—want to stay like this?" Lily asked Rabbit slowly.

He said nothing.

"Still not a talker, I see," Lily said out loud, "Uh—do you know how to put on pants?"

Rabbit didn't respond to that either.

Lily stared and took him in. He wasn't much taller than her, maybe the same height actually, but Lily couldn't carry her own weight. He also wasn't nearly as small anymore, Lily wouldn't be able to cart him around in her arms, on her head, or set him down on a counter. He was now people-sized, people-looking, and—

How was she supposed to handle this?

"Perhaps you should have thought of that before you acted," Wizard Lenin commented dully.

Oh, as if he hadn't goaded her into this!

No, she wasn't going to go there, she now had—new problems.

She had an orb that didn't do anything, that everyone wanted, and she had a rabbit that wasn't a Rabbit anymore.

And he wasn't wearing clothes yet.

"Well, you could always kill him," Wizard Lenin noted in indifference, now assured that Lily would fail to make him a body and the Heart of the World was still their best choice.

"We can't kill him!" Lily squawked out loud, only to look desperately at Rabbit.

He—

Didn't seem to care.

Maybe he didn't speak English.

"You can't take him out with you," Wizard Lenin said, *"He'd be walking out of a god's realm, they'd think he's some kind of demon."*

That wasn't entirely wrong.

She just—

She wasn't sure she could kill Rabbit, even if she wanted to. Death didn't seem to touch him in the way it did everything else.

She'd have to come up with some sort of backstory.

"A backstory?" Wizard Lenin asked.

"Sure, I happened to find him—somewhere and uh—he's traumatized and that's why he's doing that."

'That' being what Lily would very generously call an eggplant impersonation.

"That you found right next to the Heart of the World," Wizard Lenin said slowly.

"Oh, I know!" Lily thought with glee, *"He was from the last party! The party that failed to get the Heart of the World. They made it all the way here, shoved him in, and—"*

"They didn't make it all the way here," Wizard Lenin said dully.

"Huh?" Lily asked in turn.

"None of them made it further than the mountains," Wizard Lenin told her. They'd also all been grown men and women, only this bunch had thought it was a great idea to bring children along for the ride.

Lily tried again, *"Uh—he's a refugee."*

"In what conflict?" Wizard Lenin asked, *"He's too young for it to have been my work and he certainly doesn't have the right look to him."*

"What look?"

"He's obviously not human," Wizard Lenin said, bringing up Rabbit's,

well—very clearly not human features. Wizard Lenin hadn't bothered the elves much in his campaign.

"Some other conflict then," Lily dismissed.

"There hasn't been a major conflict since I blew up," Wizard Lenin reminded her harshly, *"There haven't even been minor skirmishes."*

In his humble opinion, things had gotten hopelessly dull after he'd been forced to leave, likely because both sides had exhausted one another. It'd take a good while for any decent conflict to start brewing again. A while or, of course, Wizard Lenin's return.

"Even if there was some border upset," Wizard Lenin continued, *"That wouldn't bring him all the way out here."*

He wouldn't get out here, no one did, but if he had then it'd be because something so big was happening it'd gone and upended the very laws of reality.

And then Lily had it.

"No," Wizard Lenin said, reading it from her mind.

He didn't have any better ideas, and the way Lily saw it—

Well, it was free advertising, wasn't it?

***

"Everyone," Lily cleared her throat, trying to look authoritative, "This is Lepus Rabbitson, a N.E.L.F. refugee."

Lily motioned to her audience, each staring at her with varying shades of disbelief, "Lepus, this is everyone."

Rabbit, of course, didn't respond to that. However, he was now wearing clothes and staring out with a very dead-eyed look at the other party members.

It was Ailill who broke the silence, "What the hell is a nelf?"

"I can't believe you've never heard of N.E.L.F., everybody's heard of N.E.L.F.," Lily cried out, as if utterly aghast, she even put a hand against her forehead.

No one said anything.

"I'm embarrassed for you."

Lily cleared her throat again, ignoring Wizard Lenin, "N.E.L.F. is um—the night elves—the Night Elf Liberation Front, a very dangerous group of individuals who are—building—um—farming communes in—Xhigrahi."

She really should have come up with a more detailed outline for this speech. As it was, she wasn't entirely sure what Frank planned on doing and how he planned to do it. She'd just told him to branch out a bit, get out of the thumb of the monarchy. That alone would be enough to upset people even if nothing dangerous was happening because of it.

At the dead eyed looks of her audience Lily added, "And they're sacking villages! Tons of villages! Left and right and—and Lepus here was in one of those villages. He was in one of those villages, only survivor, ran all the way out here and has forgotten how to speak or wear pants."

Slowly, everyone turned to stare at the night elf princess. She glared back at them, hair standing on end with crackling electricity, and hissed, "There's no such thing as a nelf!"

"Just N.E.L.F.," Lily corrected, "No article, it's an acronym."

Elizabeth frowned, "I've never heard of—"

"Elizabeth," Lily gaped, shocked and appalled at Elizabeth's blasé attitude, "Are you going to ignore poor Rabb—I mean Lepus's suffering just because you can't keep up with politics? Is the suffering of poor human villages not interesting enough for you?"

"That's a human?" Nhoj asked dully, eyes landing on Rabbit's incredibly white hair.

Lily threw her arm around Rabbit's shoulders, "Look at these eyes, these dark, soulless, expressionless eyes. These are the eyes of a little boy who was forced into eating his own grandmother by evil N.E.L.F. operatives. Would you doubt eyes like these?"

Rabbit, naturally, neither flinched, moved, nor blinked as Lily manhandled him. Did it help him look human? No, but it did help him look very traumatized.

"And you found him with the Heart of the World?" Nhoj asked, eyebrows now up to his hairline, "In a place where no man, mortal or immortal, can reach."

Lily stared blankly for a moment, "Yes."

No one said anything to that either.

Theyn pointed to Lily's head, where Rabbit had been when she'd entered, "Where did your rabbit—"

"Rabbit did not survive the journey to the Heart of the World," Lily hastily cut in, "Such a tragic loss, may he rest in peace."

No one seemed terribly upset about that, Lily supposed she couldn't blame them.

Then Ilyn pointed to Rabbit and asked, "Can you put him back where you found him?"

Lily decided to pull an Ilyn and give the least sympathetic and helpful answer she could, "No."

Lily forced herself to smile and held out what they assumed was the Heart of the World to Theyn.

(The real one, of course, was with Lily in a place where no one would find it.)

"Ta da," she said, when it was clear she had to say something.

Theyn nearly crumpled with relief. The tension lining his shoulders disappeared, his knees buckled and nearly gave out, and a wobbling smile appeared on his face.

"He thought you were going to keep it," Wizard Lenin explained, keep it or else fail to retrieve it. Theyn had been well aware that he'd been entrusting everything to Lily because he'd failed to do it himself.

It suddenly seemed both worse and better than Lily was only giving him the illusion he'd won. In retrieving the Heart of the World, even if he hadn't gotten it himself, he'd proven himself a worthy prince. No one would question him, even though it hadn't really happened.

"Thank you," he said breathlessly, darting forward to take it from her.

He looked down at it in awe, carefully taking it from her, and for a moment just stared at it as if entranced.

He then held it out to Annde.

"Annde, you're the one who's supposed to carry this, right?"

What?

"Ah, yes, of course," Annde said, as much as Lily could make out what he was saying.

Lily could only watch his hands out of the corner of her eye, watch as they reached out to take the orb from Theyn, and the way he nearly dropped it when he tried to lift it.

"You're giving it to him?!" Lily squawked in horror, "Isn't he cursed?!"

"Of course he is," Elizabeth scoffed, "That's why Annde came, he's the appointed royal courier who, along with Theyn, will present the Heart to the king."

Elizabeth then paused, clucked her tongue, and noted, "And he's only— slightly cursed."

"Slightly cursed is still cursed!" Lily didn't think 'slightly' made whatever had happened to Annde any more palatable.

Annde, the slightly cursed man, was too cursed to stand up for himself. He was instead patting Theyn affectionately on the shoulder, to congratulate him on the hard task of putting an orb in Annde's pack.

"Oh, honestly, if you'd—" Elizabeth's eyes happened to meet Rabbit's. She flushed brightly, quickly looked at the ground as if it was very interesting, "I mean, if you'd been paying any sort of attention—"

She cleared her throat, tried to look at Rabbit again, "Lepus is your name, isn't it? You know, it's funny, there's an old language in Tellestria where that means 'rabbit'."

Yes, that was because Lily had picked it. Rabbit Son of Rabbit hadn't had the same ring to it.

"Did Iff really find you in the—"

Lily cut her off, "You know he ah—doesn't speak English, right?"

Elizabeth bristled, brow furrowing, "Iff, you dolt, why would that matter? We're not speaking English!"

"Huh?" Lily asked.

She—supposed she'd never thought of it. It'd seemed natural that everyone would just happen to speak the language she spoke. Sure, it'd been a bit odd, but this was a parallel dimension to hers and they must have happened into English the same way.

"You're not speaking English," Wizard Lenin chimed in, sounding, of course, incredibly English when he said it.

"I think I'd know if I wasn't speaking English," Lily shot back, but maybe she wouldn't.

Maybe, at some point early on, she'd made the switch without even realizing the difference.

That didn't seem right.

God, maybe Rabbit had eaten the English language.

"Don't be daft," Wizard Lenin said.

It wasn't stupid, this was a very real issue that—oh, who was Lily kidding? It didn't matter now, the universe was falling apart anyway, and she'd just have to get over this the same way she did everything else.

"Well, whatever we're speaking right now," Lily said dully, jerking a thumb at the tall cup of tasteless water that was Rabbit in human form, "He doesn't sprechen."

"Honestly, Iff, why do you always have to be so—"

Lily pointed in front of her dramatically, to where Ilyn was looking down at his compass again, "Oh, look at that, I think Rab—I mean Lepus, his name is Lepus—should spend some quality time with the other emotionally constipated lump of a person over there. Ilyn, hello, teach Lepus how to be a better person!"

"Iff, don't you—"

It was too late, Lily pushed Rabbit ahead towards Ilyn.

Ilyn was still frowning down at the compass, paying neither her nor Rabbit any mind.

"Please tell me we're getting out of here," Lily implored him.

"With your rabbit familiar turned man?" Ilyn asked without looking up.

Lily froze, the hair rising on the back of her neck, not sure what to do at having been caught out so fast.

"Your Rabbit is missing and you walked out of a place of miracles with a boy that looks like that," Ilyn explained, eyes still on the compass, "Any idiot can put it together."

Well, she probably should have expected that.

That meant—well, that meant everyone except maybe Elizabeth and Theyn knew.

"Uh, yes, he's coming," Lily said lamely, giving up, "But are we leaving?"

Lily couldn't put off Elizabeth forever, and she had the feeling that her sudden interest in Rabbit's face wouldn't spell anything good.

"I don't know," Ilyn said.

"You don't know?" Lily balked and looked down at the compass.

"It's not spinning," Lily pointed out. It was true, it wasn't mindlessly spinning. Instead, it was lazily oscillating between the bridge they'd come on and curiously enough—

Yes, it was pointing at the love elf.

"That woman's going to do something needing my attention," Ilyn said with a sigh, "The question is if it will be now or after we cross."

Lily looked down at it again, at the needle slowly moving between the bridge and the woman, "Can it be a little more specific?"

"It's been years since Lilyanna died," he said with a raised eyebrow, "We're lucky it still works at all."

Lily looked back toward the woman, trying to imagine what she was going to do.

She looked back at Ilyn, trying to guess what he had planned.

"So, are you—"

"It could be she'll do something stupid," Ilyn said, "Or it could be that we'll need her to make it back."

Well, wasn't that useful?

Lily was about to point out as much but Ilyn was already moving towards the bridge, apparently having made up his mind. Everyone, seeing his movement, desperately scrambled to pick up their things and get out of this place.

God, it was finally over.

They'd done it, Lily had done it, the hardest part was now over and all that remained was the journey back. It felt increasingly surreal, even with the task of making Wizard Lenin a body still lay ahead of her.

Lily tugged Rabbit along with her as she made her way towards the bridge.

The question was, how close was Lily really?

Rabbit was—

She didn't know if she'd succeeded or not. He hadn't been human to start with, which could have led to his—well Rabbit-like behavior. What Lily needed to prove was that stuffing Wizard Lenin into some new body wouldn't leave him brain damaged or twelve.

Or maybe if she could just prove that she could fix someone past the point of no return, that way, if she did mess up, then she could prove to Wizard Lenin that she could fix whatever had gone wrong.

Nobody was dying or injured though.

Ailill's injuries had healed on the way, could have been much more severe than they were. No one else had been injured on the trip at all.

She couldn't just wait for someone to trip off a cliff again, God, would she have to wait until they were back or—

She stopped, her mind stuck on the man whose face she'd never gotten a good look at.

She didn't know if Annde was dying or not, cursed or not, but everyone agreed that something was very wrong with him.

Wizard Lenin needed proof that Lily really could do what she said she could, either with the Heart of the World or without it. Lily needed someone who was already in poor health, maybe on death's door, and Annde needed to stop being cursed by night elves.

If Lily did it right—

Everyone got what they wanted.

17 AN INEVITABLE BETRAYAL

In which Lily questions her experiments on Annde and their results, the love elf makes her move, and Lily tells a truth and a lie.

The Heart of the World had made Annde much worse.

Lily had started at night when they'd broken for camp, after they'd crossed the bridge. There'd been no sign of the night elf's wall, no sign of anything but the golden fields.

She didn't know what she'd been thinking, maybe that he'd have the night to get used to it if it worked.

She'd thoughtlessly taken out the Heart of the World, made sure no one was watching, then poured her power into it. She mentally pictured that power going into Annde, entering through his ears, his mouth, anything it could and lift the curse.

For a moment, once again, there'd been nothing. No sound, no flashing lights, no sign that anything at all had happened beyond Lily rattling a paperweight.

And then he'd started screaming.

He'd started screaming, and in the hours since, he hadn't stopped. Instead, Elizabeth and Theyn had rushed to him, Elizabeth darting out for her med kit and announcing he had a high fever.

Lily still couldn't look at him, nearly vomited at having to listen, but couldn't help but notice that every half hour, Theyn would come running out with rags spotted with blood.

Lily, it seemed, had been wrong and now Annde was going to die.

She wondered if there was a way she could take the moment back.

If she'd never used the Heart of the World, he'd have stayed the same, maybe he would have died but—not like this. Lily had been counting on it to work, certain it would work. She'd never really thought something like this could happen.

And now Theyn would remember the night Annde died for the rest of his life.

"He doesn't have to," Wizard Lenin noted.

Lily blinked.

"Rewriting memories is common magic among the mind elves," Wizard Lenin explained, *"It's not easy, there's a certain art to it, but it can be done. If they can do it, you certainly can."*

The thought being, of course, that Lily somehow managed to dabble in everything she wasn't supposed to.

"Rewriting memories?" Lily repeated.

"Rewriting memories, illusions, even possession in a few rare cases," Wizard Lenin said, *"I told you, they're not to be taken lightly."*

Lily supposed so, though she hadn't thought that they could do anything like that.

God, if she could do that—

Then she really could make it so this night never happened. If Annde ended up dying, she could make it so that everyone thought he just died of a heart attack or in an accident. He'd have an easy, quick, death and while everyone would grieve him at least they'd know it could have been worse.

They wouldn't have to live with this.

She'd never done it before, wasn't sure how she'd do it, but it didn't seem like something that should be difficult. No one would thank her, as no one would remember to, but she was sure that if she asked then—

There was a sound next to her.

She looked over and found herself staring at the happiness elf, of all people. She looked to her other side but it was just Rabbit sitting there, staring dully at nothing, forgotten amidst the screaming.

She looked back at the happiness elf.

He looked as unaffected as always, smiling at the fire and warming his hands in contentment. The others—they weren't invested in Annde, clearly, but even they looked a little disturbed and no one had made any mention of when they'd leave camp next morning.

Lily looked back at the fire, warming her own hands, and tried to think of how she'd do it and when. Obviously, she'd have to wait to see if Annde pulled through or not, if he did—

Then maybe she should erase everyone's memories anyway. They didn't need to remember the horrible night he'd nearly died choking on his own blood.

So, she'd wait one way or another then, either until the fever passed or he died from it.

"It'll work out."

Lily looked over to the happiness elf who was still—smiling.

Lily tried and failed to smile back before looking back at the fire.

"It'll work out," the man insisted, "Things always work out."

Lily frowned, nearly ignored it, but then sighed and asked, "Like they've worked out for you?"

Maybe that would get him to leave.

He'd never spoken to her before, aside from that other time he'd assured her everything would be fine. She didn't see why he was breaking the pattern now.

The man didn't leave, though, didn't even look offended. Instead, he noted, "We're both still here, aren't we?"

"Is that what you call working out?" Lily asked slowly, the fact that they weren't both dead yet. She considered him then noted, "Annde's not going to be here much longer."

"He's here for now," the happiness elf said.

"And having a miserable time of it," Lily finished for him, daring him to disagree.

"He still has this moment, though," the elf pointed out, "And having something is a lot better than nothing."

Lily wasn't sure Annde would agree with that. It was hard to listen to him, hard to make out words, but she wouldn't have been shocked if he'd asked someone to kill him.

"Well, maybe you should tell him that," Lily said slowly, hoping the man would get up and go sit by Annde's bedside or something. Maybe his good cheer would have a beneficial effect.

The happiness elf was still staring at her though, not quite expectant but not leaving either.

"What is it?" Lily asked.

"Mind elves can steal memories, you know," the happiness elf said in lieu of answering.

Lily nearly jumped out of her skin. Had he—could he read her mind? How had he known that Wizard Lenin had just told her—Had he guessed?!

Even in her head, Wizard Lenin was a little disturbed.

"That's—an interesting fact," Lily said hesitantly, he didn't look away or take his words back.

He didn't accuse her of thinking about it, but he didn't have to.

He placed a hand on her shoulder, "Remember, Iff, even the darkest of moments is still a moment. Sometimes, moments are all we have left."

Her mouth was dry, a word didn't come out, but before she could ask anything else or even for his name he stood up and wandered elsewhere, still looking as happy as a clam.

"What was that?" Lily asked Wizard Lenin, he didn't answer though.

That morning, Annde survived, Lily didn't overwrite anyone's memories.

The trouble was—

She wasn't sure if he'd come out the other side right.

***

"Iff," Elizabeth said, hovering over Lily's shoulder. Lily had just knelt down to unpack her things, leaving Rabbit mindlessly sitting beside her. She'd been staring at Annde's back as he unpacked his things on the other side of the fire.

It'd been three days since the fever broke. They were days away from the swamp, maybe weeks, and Annde was doing—

He was doing well, that was the thing.

For the first time since she'd started the quest, she could look at him. She no longer felt the need to avert her eyes, no longer felt any nausea, any ringing in her ears, nothing.

It turned out, Annde looked like anybody else. He was certainly human, maybe looked vaguely like Theyn, but he was the kind of person you'd see anywhere walking down any street. There wasn't much that was notable about him, aside from the fact that after all of that he wasn't notable. There were no signs left of his fever, his curse, where all the blood must have come from, he looked perfectly fine and as healthy as anyone else.

It was just—

She couldn't shake the feeling that it'd worked a little too well. Maybe that was the Heart of the World for you, but she didn't think he was supposed to have recovered this well this fast.

"I just know, after that performance, you're not stuffing me into a body any time soon," Wizard Lenin chimed in. He was forcing it, though, his thoughts were elsewhere, something about Annde bothering him too.

Whatever it was, though, he was keeping it from her.

As if he'd heard her thoughts, Annde glanced behind his shoulder at her. He offered her a grin and a small little wave as he unpacked his sleeping roll.

God, Lily hated to agree with Wizard Lenin, but she had to agree with Wizard Lenin. She couldn't make Wizard Lenin a body.

She was going to have to do this again and pray, pray, that next time it worked.

"Iff," Elizabeth repeated in a huff.

"Yes, what, what is it?" Lily asked, trying to redirect her attention (she had the eerie feeling that Annde was watching).

"Don't you think you should be doing something?" Elizabeth asked, hands on her hips, looking down at Lily in judgment.

Lily stared up at her, frozen, feeling like the bag her hand was in had just turned into a cookie jar.

How the hell had Elizabeth figured out that Lily had anything to do with Annde's miraculous recovery? Annde had stated that it must have been carrying the Heart of the World in his pack that had done it and laughed it off. The elves had looked over at Lily, but none of them had said anything and Elizabeth hadn't been one of them.

Elizabeth nodded her head meaningfully at Rabbit, who as usual was staring at nothing, "Don't you think that maybe, instead of manhandling Lepus everywhere, you should be trying to talk to him?"

Lily blinked, mind scrambling to figure out what that meant or what it possibly had to do with Annde.

"No?" Lily ended up asking.

"No? Really, Iff?" Elizabeth asked, making it clear that had been the wrong answer. She motioned to Rabbit, "You said it yourself, he's traumatized! And you've spent the past several days doing nothing about it!"

Lily looked over at Rabbit, "I—uh—think he enjoys doing nothing."

"I can't believe—" Elizabeth sighed angrily, pinched the bridge of her nose, then sat down next to the pair of them. After a moment, she clapped her hands together as if in prayer, "Iff, I truly do think you mean well. You've always helped me and the prince, even when you're—you. However, you have to see that you're not helping him! He needs—"

Elizabeth looked over at Rabbit with all the tenderness that one would an adorable but neglected creature desperately in need of assistance. Rabbit did not even notice her gaze.

If Elizabeth finished that sentence with 'a woman' or 'me', Lily was going to vomit.

"He needs," Elizabeth restarted, flushing violently as she imagined the end to the sentence. She ended up chickening out, "A friend."

Rabbit had no friends.

"Iff, please," Elizabeth pleaded, "Can't you see how lonely he is? Have you even tried to talk to him?"

Lily wondered if she should just confess to him being the rabbit after all. Everyone else knew, Ilyn did at least but—

"Don't you dare," Wizard Lenin said, if she'd wanted to take that route then she should have killed him inside the rainbow gate.

"I don't think—"

Elizabeth's pleading expression became a righteous glare.

Lily turned to look at Rabbit.

Even as a human, he defied dirt. Days on the road without a shower, and he looked as pristine as ever. Lily, in the meantime, had only gotten worse.

"Lepus," Lily said slowly, feeling very stupid, "Elizabeth would—ah—like us to talk about our feelings."

Lily, for example, felt this was awkward and terrible.

At Elizabeth's furious expression, Lily added, "Can we talk about our feelings?"

Lily wondered when Elizabeth would give up. The words 'give up' didn't seem to be in her vocabulary, but at some point, she'd have to go to sleep and be reasonable. Maybe, if Lily could cut out herself as the middleman, then Elizabeth could waste her time trying to teach Rabbit as much as she wanted—

Rabbit gave a small nod.

It was barely noticeable, barely even enough to be called a nod, but he'd made it and his eyes hadn't left hers.

Lily's stomach dropped.

"Good!" Elizabeth beamed, like she'd personally brought Rabbit out of his shell, "See, Iff, you just have to ask!"

Lily had seen snuffling, she'd seen sitting, lying down, stumbling along when she dragged him behind her.

He'd never given any sign that he was intelligent or understood a word she said.

"Well, Elizabeth, great talk," Lily said abruptly, magically shoving Elizabeth away from her and Rabbit, "But I'm tired, you're tired, and poor Rabbit's very tired. So we should all sleep, okay? Goodnight."

Lily rolled on her side and pretended to sleep.

Elizabeth tried to protest, but she found herself suddenly and miraculously exhausted, and ended up crawling back to her own sleeping roll and passing out.

Lily breathed a sigh of relief.

She just—

Wasn't going to think too deeply about this.

The adventure was over, wasn't it? They'd found the Heart of the World, they were making the return trip. If this was a movie, the credits would have been rolling by now.

So, Lily could just pretend that—

That everything was going to be fine.

Lily found her mind drifting and soon enough she was somewhere else.

She didn't know if it was her or Wizard Lenin, but one of them was trying too hard today. They were inside a great hall decorated with a red carpet and a single gilded throne at the very end.

Wizard Lenin was seated on the throne looking far too comfortable for his own good.

"Aren't you getting a little ahead of yourself?" Lily couldn't help but ask him.

He didn't even have a body yet.

"Perhaps," he acknowledged with a rueful smile, "Certainly, if your experiments on that Annde fellow are to be relied upon.

He wasn't going to forget that, was he?

Lily frowned, shoved her hands in her pockets, and made her way over to him. When she was standing just above him, she noted, "You know, technically, he looks—fine."

Wizard Lenin gave her an entirely warranted look.

Lily sighed and sat on one of the arm rests. She looked out at the rest of the hall with him. It was funny, when it was empty, it looked like nothing more than a hall in a museum.

"I don't know what went wrong," she confessed, "I don't even know if anything is wrong. He looks fine."

Wizard Lenin didn't say anything. She looked over at him, but he looked—pensive.

"Lenin?"

He was looking to the side, at one of the large windows, tapping his fingers against the armrest.

"Illness like that isn't always caused by night elves," Wizard Lenin said abruptly.

Lily blinked, then she started laughing.

"Wait a second, you mean we've been blaming the night elves for months and—"

"Often, yes, night elf victims suffer horrific and sometimes inexplicable side effects," he continued as if he hadn't heard her, "They can vary wildly, sometimes they even curse a person and then just about anything's on the table. However, they're not the only ones who can do something like this."

Wizard Lenin finally looked back at her, eyes narrowed, lips curled into a frown, "There can be gruesome side effects to possession, that's something only the mind elves can do."

Lily looked at him, trying to put it together.

"You don't mean—"

Annde was the royal courier, he was the one who was carrying the Heart of the World, everyone had known that long before Lily.

"You mean the mind elf, from the very start—"

"I'm not saying anything," Wizard Lenin said abruptly, as if this suddenly wasn't his concern, "Merely considering possibilities."

Except Wizard Lenin didn't say things he didn't mean. He always kept some things to himself. If he'd said this, he meant to tell her, and he wanted her to think this over—

Lily suddenly woke up.

She sat up, dazed, blinking in confusion as she tried to figure out why she'd woken up.

There was nothing around, everything was right where she'd left it. Rabbit was lying next to her, staring unblinkingly up at the stars. The rest were slumped in on themselves, either sleeping or lost in deep thought.

It took her a moment to realize that this shouldn't be the case, someone was always awake. She'd never seen everyone asleep at the same time—

"Hey!" Elizabeth shouted, "What do you think you're doing?"

Lily scrambled to her feet. Turning her head, she found Theyn and Elizabeth both scrambling to their feet as well, moving towards Annde and the beautiful woman standing over him, the love elf.

The woman looked over at them as if just remembering their presence, "It's always weaker against children."

Well, that was ominous.

It was enough information for Elizabeth though.

"She's using a seductive illusion!"

Oh, Lily hoped that wasn't what it sounded like.

She looked over at Ilyn, looked closer at his face, and by the lovesick, dopey, expression it was exactly what it sounded like.

"Is that what your books call it?" the woman asked before sighing, and looking down at Annde, unconcerned by his listless smile and dull gaze, "I suppose it hardly matters."

"You're after the Heart, aren't you?!" Theyn asked, stepping forward, balling his fists.

"Clever prince," the woman said, rummaging through Annde's supplies as if she had no concern in the world, "Not clever enough though, you should have realized from the beginning."

"Maybe we did," Elizabeth said, a fire burning in her dark eyes, "You said it yourself, seductive illusions don't work on children, and they sent me!"

With that, she brought her hands together, and in a single eloquent motion produced a fireball and shouted, "May the righteous fire of my vengeance burn!"

The fire flew out from her hands and raced towards the woman, who immediately pulled her hands out, made a fancy blocking motion, and shouted, "Shield and counter!"

The fireball raced back towards them, hotter and faster than before, almost too fast for Elizabeth to hold up her hands, cross them, and shout, "Deflect the wrath of my enemies and let them taste the fruit of the seeds they have sown!"

The fireball ricocheted off the invisible shield Elizabeth had summoned around them. It flew back towards the love elf who watched it crash against her own shield. Both Elizabeth and the elf held their position, neither flinching as the fire volleyed back and forth, both waiting for one of them to break first.

"Little girl," the woman said, Elizabeth snarling at being called that, "These aren't your people, why are you fighting so hard for them?"

"You don't know anything!" Elizabeth shouted, sweating under the pressure of the fire hurled against her shield. Hairline cracks were starting to appear on its surface, the flames licking through.

"Elizabeth?" Theyn asked nervously, edging backwards, bringing his hands up into what had to be a starting stance of any spell.

The woman, however, just laughed and said a single word, "Desire."

Elizabeth's hands dropped, her eyes grew wide, and slowly, almost unwillingly, she turned to look at Rabbit, beautiful, traumatized Rabbit. The shield shattered and Lily hurled Elziabeth and Theyn down to the ground and out of the way of the fireball whizzing over their heads.

"Elizabeth!" Theyn shouted, shaking the girl. It was no use, Elizabeth looked as dazed and useless as the rest of them.

Theyn looked back at the woman and shouted, "Why are you doing this?!"

"Why?" the woman asked, returning to Annde's pack and pulling out the false Heart of the World.

As she lifted it and stood upright, she looked different than she had before. For all she'd been beautiful, she'd been barely noticeable, an afterthought at best. She'd been so beautiful, her first impression so overwhelming, it'd seemed like there couldn't possibly be anything more to her. So, Lily hadn't looked any further, not even when Ilyn had told her she'd do something.

When she was holding even a fake Heart of the World, there wasn't any overlooking her.

"You truly have forgotten, haven't you? It wasn't so long ago that we made it very clear we were not and were never on your side, yet here you are asking why. Or did you think that we had somehow forgotten?"

She was talking about Wizard Lenin.

The love elves, he'd said, more than any other had supported his revolution. Even when everyone else had turned their backs on him, when Ilyn had jumped sides entirely, they hadn't.

"They're still waiting for me," Wizard Lenin thought in stunned amazement.

Oh, they probably thought he was dead, but they hadn't abandoned him or compromised in his absence. No one else had done that.

It'd always been him and Lily against a world that had been so ready to put the past behind them.

Lily stared at the woman and realized—

If she left now, even with a fake Heart of the World, the others would come to and they'd go after her.

She was going to die, if not tonight, then tomorrow when they ran her down.

She had to have known that, known the chance of success was so small, but she'd still tried.

"I won't let you do this!" Theyn shouted.

He breathed in, began hand movements for a spell even as the woman lifted her hands. The woman would die, and if Lily did nothing, Theyn would die first in the ensuing fight.

"Wait!" Lily darted between them, hands spread wide.

"What are you—"

Lily looked at the woman, really looked at her.

She was beautiful, yes, she'd always be uncommonly beautiful. Right now though, holding the item she must have been waiting for this whole time, she looked more real than she ever had before. This was her moment, why she'd come, maybe even her missing task that she had no choice but to succeed or die trying.

Except Lily wouldn't accept that.

"He's alive," Lily blurted, "John Jones, he's still here and he's coming back."

The illusion didn't shatter, everyone except Theyn was still in that listless daze, but it felt as if something had.

Lily had said words she wasn't supposed to say.

"I appreciate the gesture," Wizard Lenin said carefully, *"But this woman means nothing. Think of what you're saying and who you're saying it to."*

"How—" the woman started, but Lily summoned the fake Heart of the World into her own hands.

"You don't need this yet," Lily told her.

"Iff," Theyn asked, a hopeful yet fearful look in his eyes, as if he too was seeing her for the first time.

"Go back," Lily told the woman, pointing ahead of them, "Go and tell them that word is coming."

Wizard Lenin wouldn't forget this, he'd come back for them, and if Lily had her way he'd do it sooner rather than later.

The woman opened her mouth, closed it, and Lily wondered what she saw. It must not have been a little girl, even a princess, because by the look on her face she believed Lily.

She believed her more than she'd ever dared to believe in anything.

She offered a small, short, bow, then took off.

Next to her, exhausted and terrified, Theyn dropped to his knees as they watched the woman disappear into the fields. She'd be out of their reach soon, without the Heart Lily doubted anyone would bother to pursue her.

She'd live.

"Iff," Theyn said quietly, "Was it—was what you said true?"

Lily looked down at him, at his wide brown eyes, and lied.

"Of course not."

18 A DISQUIETING REDUNDANCY

In which Lily gets a history lesson, an ominous reminder about the man who lives inside her head, and remembers whose side she's on.

Ilyn paced dramatically, trampling over golden fields, moving back and forth like a pendulum. For once, he wasn't looking at his compass.

Finally, he stopped dead in his tracks, not looking at any of them, "We will not hunt down the woman."

Lily breathed a sigh of relief. She'd guessed as much when she'd chased the love elf off, but it was reassuring to hear it in the aftermath.

"She took nothing and we've already lost too much time," Ilyn said, turning stiffly as he took out his compass, preparing to hit the road again. Before he took a step though, he glared back over his shoulder and noted, "And she will not be the last."

Theyn opened his mouth in alarm, tried to say something, but Ilyn was already walking. Theyn hastily packed up the remainder of his things as the rest of the party filed out.

Lily found herself stuck in place, staring dumbly after the man, two seconds from asking him to repeat that. She didn't, he didn't have to, she knew exactly what he'd just said.

There was going to be at least one more by the time they were through.

It shouldn't have been surprising, wasn't, not when the elves had nothing to gain from this venture. Lily hadn't realized as much on the way but she couldn't have been the only one to think of switching the Heart of the World out for a fake, she'd just had the first opportunity.

She sprinted forward, caught up to Theyn at the tail end of the group, and found her eyes wandering over each of them.

She wondered who would be next.

Would it be golden Nhoj?

No, she didn't think it'd be him.

He was looking worse for wear, his hair was matted, dulled, and dark shadows were blossoming beneath his eyes. There was nothing in him that screamed any kind of determination of scheming.

He wouldn't risk it, he wasn't the type, not when there was too much riding on the good will of the monarchy. She was sure of it, and it wasn't just because he quietly tolerated her. She was sure it wouldn't be him.

Ailill, the moon elf, looked the least changed by the quest. This was probably because this sort of thing, heroic quests to rescue fair maidens, slaying white deer, or retrieving the Heart of the World was exactly what he'd been made for. The others were all inconvenienced by their summer of extreme hiking, Ailill had never broken a sweat. Every time he was in action, he seemed exhilarated by it, gnawing at the bit at a chance to cut down poor Theyn.

Ailill—might, he might. It might have been why he'd come along in the first place. He'd probably cut Annde and everyone else down and run off with the Heart of the World while laughing his head off. Given his very vocal opinions on Theyn, she couldn't see him caring one bit about helping a mortal prince retrieve a legendary object. Except, even if that had been his plan, he hadn't done anything about it yet and he seemed to have shifted his focus to Lily. So long as they were blood brothers and she wasn't ready to take the throne, he probably wouldn't do anything.

Probably.

The happiness elf was back to staring at clouds like all was right with the world and he hadn't just spent the night enchanted or was going to be stabbed in the back any moment. Lily was going to go on a limb and say that he wasn't going to do anything.

Then there was Ilyn.

Lily stared at the back of the man she never thought she'd consider a friend. She wasn't sure if they were friends now, but they'd had a moment, perhaps a few moments, and all those little moments were starting to accumulate into something greater. She didn't think it was her imagination, she thought they meant something to him too.

In the void, there'd been something special, something that had maybe existed before she'd even met him for all she hadn't noticed. Whatever it was had solidified into a steadfast faith on both their ends. It was the feeling that even with burned down houses and different loyalties, they could trust one another.

He hadn't wavered, hadn't doubted for a second, that she could do what no one else could when they'd needed a bridge and when someone had to pass through the rainbow gate. In turn, maybe because of that feeling, she was finding it impossible to doubt him.

Besides, if he wanted the orb, he'd just have taken it from the beginning.

He'd have lit Lily on fire the moment she'd exited the gate, killed the rest of them, and there wouldn't be a thing any of them could do about it. Lily was starting to believe that he had no pretenses.

Now, she didn't know exactly what he wanted, why he was Theyn's tutor, what he was doing with the monarchy, or even what he'd been doing with Wizard Lenin, but whatever the answers to those questions were they didn't involve the Heart of the World.

"Why the concern?" Wizard Lenin asked, interrupting Lily's thoughts, *"You have the true Heart and you know it. Let them take the fake, it's of no consequence to us."*

No consequence to Lily and Wizard Lenin, sure, but to Theyn, Theyn and whoever took it—

"They know what they signed up for," Wizard Lenin wryly pointed out.

If they couldn't handle a gruesome death or two at Ilyn's hands, then so much the worse for them.

Well, when he put it like that—

"What if it's the Usurper?"

Lily jumped, stumbling forward a few steps. She looked over to find Theyn walking next to her, not having sped up when she was lost in thought. Ahead of them, Elizabeth and the rejuvenated Annde were talking energetically about something or another. Rabbit was the only one stumbling behind Lily as she dragged him along with an iron grip.

Theyn gave her a truly terrified look.

"What?" Lily asked, trying to look like she had no idea who or what that even was. People had mentioned him here and there, Questburger had brought him up in a roundabout way, Theyn had too, but no one had spent much time actually talking about him. It was always about the movement, the rebellion, and not John Jones himself.

"You said he's not gone, Iff, that he—"

"Theyn," Lily interjected, forcing herself to laugh brightly and smile tightly, "Please, I made all that up. I barely even know who it is, I've just heard the name here and there and it sounded—well—intimidating."

Theyn gave her, if possible, an even more alarmed and wide-eyed look than before.

"Lily, you moron, you didn't use me as a threat," Wizard Lenin curtly reminded her, *"You used me as the leader her people have been waiting for!"*

"—And I heard from Ilyn that the love elves were on his side back during the rebellion," Lily caught herself, "Given what she said—I figured it was worth a shot."

Inside her head, Lily swore she could hear the sound of Wizard Lenin slowly clapping.

Theyn said nothing for a moment, swallowed, and when he did talk he didn't sound reassured, "But what if it is him?"

"He's dead, Theyn," Lily said, the words heavy on her tongue, "He's dead as a doornail."

Theyn didn't look at her.

"I know you weren't here for it, that you were sent away to Tellestria, but he was—we thought he was human," he said quietly, "We think he was human, but if he was, then he was the most powerful human mage in—maybe he was the greatest human mage who ever lived. He entered the place, Iff, and burned it to the ground by himself even with everyone guarding it. Then he was just—gone, he was just gone."

He sounded mystified, like he couldn't believe it either, even when he'd only grown up knowing the aftermath. She could suddenly picture the surreal daze the kingdom and Wizard Lenin's rebellion had found themselves in afterwards. It was like the ending of a story in which you discovered it was only a dream, that none of it had ever happened.

"She's not alone," Theyn said darkly, clenching his fists and looking away from Lily, "Some people don't think he's really dead, just imprisoned somewhere or in hiding. It doesn't matter that it's been years, that we showed them a body, that the rebellion scattered without him, they just don't—And some people think he'd crawl out of hell itself. I know Questburger believes it."

"He won't," Lily insisted, voice dead even to her own ears.

He made her wish the Usurper would never return, that Theyn would continue to live and eventually rule in peace.

If Wizard Lenin did get his body—

He'd become the Usurper again, he'd always intended to, and then he'd do everything in his power to finish what he started.

Wizard Lenin had said as much already, but it wasn't until now that Lily agreed and realized—

By returning Wizard Lenin to the real world, the land of the living, she'd be signing her cousin's death warrant.

Now, with the possible tool of Wizard Lenin's resurrection in her hands, it suddenly became very real.

Theyn was going to die.

But if Lily had to weight Theyn and Wizard Lenin on a scale, if she had to choose—

Then there was no question of which she had to pick.

"We're still recovering," Theyn said with a bitter laugh, "Wheyn, our cousin, he wasn't anywhere close to the throne. He was just the oldest survivor they could find. Ilyn was brought in to instruct ages ago, before it was only humans, and he's still on the staff because they can't replace him. I mean—"

"He really did a number on you," Lily bleakley finished for Theyn.

Theyn smiled weakly, "Yeah, he really did a number on us."

He looked ahead at Elizabeth and Annde chatting away, "I don't think we can go through that again."

Lily could lie.

She could say something comforting about lightning not striking twice, or that it was hard enough for Wizard Lenin the first time and he surely couldn't manage it all again.

Except, this sort of thing had happened before. There was always Napoleon and Elba. They hadn't dared let Napoleon try a third time, poisoned him before it could happen, but he'd still marched on Europe twice.

If Wizard Lenin got his way—

Theyn was more right than he could ever be allowed to know.

"We won't," Lily forced herself to say, "And if we do, then maybe he'll mysteriously explode again."

Theyn laughed even as inside her head Wizard Lenin bristled. The important thing was that, for now, it didn't matter.

"Maybe," Theyn agreed with a smile, then looking her in the eye said, "Thanks, Iff, for everything I mean."

"Everything?" Lily asked, wondering what she'd done.

"The cliff, that monster Ailill had to fight, getting the Heart for me, and yesterday when that woman—If it weren't for you, if you weren't here, I don't know what would have happened," Theyn confessed.

That wasn't fair, not when Lily had stolen the Heart for her own purposes.

Wizard Lenin had been wrong, Lily was anything but noble.

She forced herself to smile and said, "I try."

That, at least, was always true.

She patted Theyn on the arm and started walking ahead of him, ignoring his mouth opening to call her back. She made her way steadily to the front, practically jogging to do it, where they wouldn't bring up things like gratitude, shadows that were best left buried, or anything else Lily didn't want to talk about.

A hand grabbed her collar and pulled her back.

"Ah, Princess, I was hoping we'd have a chance to chat."

A chill slid down Lily's spine, as if someone had just poured a vat of slushies down her shirt. She didn't have to turn, didn't even have to look, she knew exactly had interrupted her thoughts this time.

"Annde," Lily greeted, "You're looking—good."

He was.

Annde, out of all of them, had come out of this quest looking—well, like a person she could actually look at. It was like he'd become a weight loss advertisement, or an ad for miracle vitamins, where the before picture had been so horrific it'd been pixelated for your viewing pleasure.

Somehow, even though she could see his face—he looked unnatural.

Like he'd broken a bone somewhere, and while it'd healed, it hadn't healed correctly.

He smiled, in a manner that was supposed to be warm but left Lily cold.

He'd dumped Elizabeth, it seemed, as she'd gone back to talk to Theyn. Lily wondered if he'd done that on purpose or if Elizabeth had gotten bored of him at the exact right moment Lily had been passing by.

"I believe I have you to thank for that," he said, smiling with all his teeth bared.

Then his words hit her.

"Me?" Lily asked, trying not to look and see who was listening in this time, "I think you mean that cancerous, overpowered, mysterious orb you're carrying."

He just smiled, a horribly polite and charming smile, and said, "If you say so, Your Highness."

She shouldn't have been surprised.

As Wizard Lenin constantly reminded her, she'd shown her hand. Everyone had seen Rabbit go in and some boy named Lepus Rabbitson come out, everyone had seen Lily perform strange miraculous magic more than once and enter the gate Theyn was supposed to, at this point she was probably more obvious than she'd thought.

Except—

No, not this time. She'd given Theyn the orb, the orb everyone thought was the Heart, and no one had questioned that. The love elf had gone after Annde's pack, not Lily's, and for all anyone knew Lily had no reason to hold onto it. Lily never knew what was happening, who anyone was, or what they were doing—why would she know about the Heart of the World?

If it hadn't been for Wizard Lenin, they'd be absolutely right.

If Annde thought Lily had never given him the Heart of the World—wouldn't he have accused her earlier or tried to steal it back?

"Or he thinks it wasn't the Heart and that you miraculously fixed him," Wizard Lenin cut in, but his heart wasn't in it. His thoughts were elsewhere as he watched Annde for signs of—

Of something Lily didn't know how to put into words.

"Speaking of, Princess, there's something I've been wondering," Annde said, as if he hadn't just accused her of miraculous healing powers.

"I wonder things all the time," Lily said lamely, feeling something in her stomach plummet, which—

There was no obvious threat, no undertone of a threat, but standing this close to him had every hair on her head standing on end. Something about him, in a way she couldn't possibly point to, just oozed malice. Every smile, gesture, everything about him was wrong and gruesome without even a fatal curse to point to.

It could be something left over from the curse but—

No one else seemed to see it.

"What are you planning to do next?" he asked.

"Next?" Lily asked in turn. That hadn't been the question she'd been expecting.

"We're heading back to the capital," Annde explained, never taking his eyes off her, "If all goes according to plan, you'll be put in the academy with your cousin and Elizabeth."

"Right, yes," Lily said quietly, not sure what he was getting at, "I guess that's what I'm doing."

"Why?"

Lily's brow furrowed, and for a moment, she forgot the unpleasantness of talking to Annde as she retorted, "You're the one who said—"

He smiled even as he cut her off, "If all goes according to plan, Questburger's and the king's, but we both know it doesn't have to."

Lily looked around to see who was listening, if anyone was listening, but no one was looking at them. Everyone seemed lost in either their own conversations or their own thoughts, staring past Lily and Annde as if they weren't even there.

"Don't worry, they can't hear us," Annde said.

He'd cast a spell, Lily realized, the kind Lily hadn't realized anyone could cast. He hadn't said a word, hadn't even twitched, hadn't done anything. She—she hadn't thought that was possible for anyone but her.

Even Ilyn and the love elf last night had done something.

"In a perfect world, Iff, where would you be and what would you be doing after all this?" he pressed.

She opened her mouth then closed it. Suddenly, her throat felt dry, her feet tingling with the desire to run, to be anywhere except here.

Slowly, she asked, "Why do you think I wouldn't go to school?"

He gave her a look, as if he could see through every disguise she'd ever thought to make, "You have no reason to go there."

"I could learn things," she insisted.

"They have nothing to teach you," he dismissed easily.

"Ilyn, perhaps, could teach you something, but we both know you could graduate tomorrow and find yourself sent to an outpost," he nodded towards the oblivious others, "And each and every one of them knows it, even the girl and your cousin."

Lily blurted what Death had told her, what he'd said before she'd even left, "What about friendship?"

"Friendship," he said, his smile almost as sharp as his eyes, "Are you talking about the prince and Elizabeth? Forgive me, you don't seem very close."

"Close enough," Lily countered.

"But not that close," Annde smoothly corrected, "Elizabeth seems to be under the impression that you're an idiot savant. Oh, I'm sure she's polite enough not to say it to your face, to give you the benefit of the doubt in public, but at the end of the day she knows that she's right and you've lucked into talent you don't deserve. It will take more than dying to convince her that she's wrong."

His smile grew wider, and Lily couldn't help her eyes drifting to Elizabeth's fair French braids, the confidence in every step she took.

"She may think she's your friend, may even believe it," the man concluded, "But we both know that friendship is something much more than that."

Lily forced her eyes back to his and asked, "And Theyn?"

The air around them seemed to stiffen at his name, as if the world had taken its breath.

Annde's smile thinned, stretched itself past the point of breaking, "Theyn, the prince, is more desperate for friendship than friendship with you. Push him too far, show him what you truly are, and he will go elsewhere."

Lily eyed him, watched as he eyed her back, and said, "I liked it better when I couldn't even look at you."

He had the gall to laugh, "You know, it wasn't always like that."

"Yes," Lily agreed with narrowed eyes, "Your run in with the night elves, right?"

"Well," he said with an amused smile, "We both know I ran into something."

"So, you're admitting it wasn't night elves," Lily said slowly, "Why are you telling me? Why do I get a backstage pass?"

He hadn't said as much before, not to anyone, and no one had questioned it either. Even Lily hadn't been entirely certain, not when everyone kept saying how it was possible.

She didn't expect him to laugh.

"There's something wrong with him," Wizard Lenin noted as they watched Annde's laughter continue, moving past the point of laughter into a hysterical breakdown.

"You think I don't know that?"

Wizard Lenin was stating the obvious. What he didn't want to state, what he didn't want to think, was that he had no idea what was wrong with him.

The Heart hadn't worked, or if it had, then it'd only been superficial. The shell of Annde was healthier than ever, but just beneath the skin he was rotting.

She wasn't even sure if this was Annde anymore.

"Strange, I never imagined you'd be so—" Annde trailed off, looking at her through tears of mirth before settling on, "Perceptive."

"People usually settle on strange," Lily said.

He waved off her comment with a chuckle, "Yes, strange, undeniably so, but for a twelve-year-old girl—As for your question, I can't help but notice you didn't answer mine."

"You answered it," Lily reminded him, "I'm going to the mage academy because everyone expects me to."

"Was that so hard now?" he asked in turn, looking almost fond, sending another round of shivers down her spine.

"And my answer?" she pressed.

"Let's just say that, perhaps, I think you deserve a backstage pass."

Moreover, for whatever reason, he felt safe enough to let her and her alone know.

It was because he knew no one would ever believe her, she realized.

Their conversation seemed to be over, though, as the noise around them became louder and everyone seemed able to look at them again. Lily let herself fall back, back to where Elizabeth and Theyn were arguing about some mutually despised classmate.

***

Making it out of the fields and to the swamp did not make Lily any happier.

No one had done anything, Annde hadn't spoken to her since, and she felt like she was stepping on eggshells waiting for someone to try to gut her and run off with the Heart of the World. Were they waiting for the swamp? The mountains? Until they made it all the way back to the castle?

Annde was going to do something, she could feel it, she knew it, but he thought he had the Heart of the World already.

"Oh, just go and ask Ilyn already," Wizard Lenin spat, fed up with her disquieted monologue.

"What?"

"The man may be useless," Wizard Lenin was clearly not over the revelation that Ilyn couldn't see jack shit of the future, *"But he clearly knows something. Go and ask him which of these worthless bastards does it already."*

Well—

Yes, Lily supposed she could have done that days ago.

Somehow, that had never occurred to her.

Making up her mind, she stepped forward, eyes trained ahead to where Ilyn was leading the way. Except, he wasn't there.

Stopping in her tracks, Lily looked around.

No one was there, not even Rabbit whose hand she'd just been holding.

"Hello?" Lily asked, turning all around.

There was no sign that anyone had even passed through here.

"Theyn?" she called out, louder this time.

There was no response.

"Ilyn?

"Rabbit?!"

Nothing, only Lily and the perfectly empty swamp.

She closed her eyes, breathed out, willing herself not to panic.

"Don't look down," she reminded herself, remembering last time she'd looked down into this water, "Don't look down, don't look down—"

After a deep breath, she opened her eyes.

The swamp was still empty.

Something had happened.

Rabbit had been right there, she'd been holding his hand the whole time. He'd been right there and there wasn't a chance in hell she'd have made that same mistake twice in the same exact place.

Lily had been removed from them, or them from her, and—

"Or it's an illusion," Wizard Lenin said, *"The mind elves are notorious for crafting illusions."*

The mind elves—

"Yes, I think he's made his move."

Of course he had.

Lily felt her panic give way to annoyance then genuine anger. The one person she'd overlooked, that arrogant hack who'd won a riddle contest and thought it meant something, of course it'd be him.

She should have known.

"Couldn't he have even bothered to be slightly original?" Lily asked.

They'd just been through this song and death with the love elf. He was even pulling the same type of trick, using an illusion to distract everyone while he snuck off with the orb.

"Why be original when he can do what works?" Wizard Lenin asked, *"He managed to catch you this time, he must be well practiced."*

Lily didn't care if he was a genius, this was just—

God, here was something Rabbit could have eaten.

Forget those tasks that never happened, this second over dramatic betrayal, that she should have seen a mile off, was practically begging to be removed from the universe.

"Alright," Lily said out loud, "Alright, let's—Let's get this over with!"

She plunged into the water, closed her eyes, and pushed through the mud at the bottom then through to the other side of the illusion. Soaking wet, she stood and spluttered, pulling herself upright then blinked.

Her missing companions were all standing across from her.

Well, all of them except for the mind elf.

Ilyn's eyebrows rose, he lowered his compass and asked, "Iff, what the hell are you doing?"

She suddenly felt very self-conscious and confused.

"Stopping the mind elf?" Lily asked, voice cracking on the last word.

"The who?" Ailill asked with a tilted head.

"You know, blue hair, smarmy, after the Heart of the World?" Lily asked, looking at their utterly blank faces, "Just put us into an illusion so he could steal it?"

Unless, of course, Lily was still in the illusion. God, maybe she'd just escaped part of it and she had to keep going—

"Recursive illusions are near impossible," Wizard Lenin dismissed, *"Very finicky and prone to collapse at a moment's notice. Confining someone of your power would be impossible."*

That wasn't reassuring.

"Iff,' Theyn said awkwardly, wading towards her to whisper in her ear, "We didn't bring a mind elf, they didn't send anyone."

"What?" Lily asked, eyes popping out of her head, "Yes they did! He did that whole riddle thing with the giant rabbit statue. He—"

Her eyes drifted, almost unwillingly, to Rabbit standing among the rest of them.

She remembered thinking, only a few seconds ago, that Rabbit might as well have eaten the mind elf's betrayal.

He might as well have eaten the mind elf.

Rabbit had eaten the goddamn mind elf.

Lily cleared her throat, "Right, well—I guess it wasn't important anyway."

The swamp was still here, everyone else was still here, she could still feel the Heart of the World in extradimensional space. He couldn't have been that important.

That wasn't a comforting thought, the feeling that anyone could simply disappear at any moment and no one would notice. Worse, that Lily would be the only one who did notice, and she wouldn't care.

Lily didn't know how she felt about that.

19 ALL HAIL THE CONQUERING HEROES

In which nine of the eleven return home triumphant, Lily considers her immediate future and the consequences of the quest, and has her second meeting with Questburger.

There were no betrayals after the mind elf's. Perhaps Rabbit had eaten all of them along with the nameless man no one remembered, perhaps no one else had thought to try, regardless, the weeks that followed were subdued but ordinary.

Just as they met no more betrayals, they met no more trials, and just when it'd felt like the mountains would last forever, they exited the other side and caught sight of the capital gleaming under the summer sun.

She'd had to shield her eyes, it'd shone so brightly.

They'd all stopped for a moment, staring at it, as if it took that long for their vision to adjust back to reality and all its expectations.

The strange events of the quest, the raw, untamed, magic they'd met weren't quite gone, but they felt like a half-remembered dream. It was a flavor of thought that, in the light of day, grew fainter and fainter.

The castle in the distance, home only to a few and beloved by even fewer, served as a visible mark that it was nearly over.

And it felt—

It felt strange, that for once in her life, Lily felt like she had been changed by something. She'd always felt untouchable, unnoticed, like the world was just this thing that would always pass her by. That hadn't happened this time.

She'd touched something out there, something she couldn't describe, and she knew she wasn't the same as when she'd left even if she was staring at the same castle.

They'd gone on to pass through the gates, met by an escort of uniformed guards. These were quickly followed by trumpeters and drummers hailing their return. Crowds of people ducked their heads out of windows, came out onto the street, and started cheering the name of the heroic prince Theyn.

No one cheered for Lily.

It was a harsh reminder, one she hadn't thought she'd needed, that she wasn't supposed to mean something here. Whatever she'd managed on the quest, it hadn't mattered, and there was nothing like watching the crowds and crowds of people to make her feel small.

Even the Tylors had never forgotten her quite like this.

At least she wasn't alone, no one cheered for the elves either. Ilyn especially seemed to be able to part crowds like the Red Sea simply from the force of his glaring.

Ailill then disappeared into the crowd before they were halfway through the city. He squeezed Lily's shoulder, whispered into her ear, "Send word," and then disappeared before Lily could protest.

Only eight of the original eleven made it all the way back to the palace.

Each elf looked as out of place as the next, only here by forced invitation from a prophecy. Kings and vassals stood before the regent to a monarchy they'd never embraced, and despite this great quest, this epic journey, nothing had changed for any of them.

A deep unspoken humiliation permeated the air.

The guards in the room, the regent on the throne, and even Questburger standing behind the throne paid the elves and the new addition Rabbit no mind. Their eyes were only on the prince, worn and weary, and the rejuvenated Annde standing next to him.

The room held its breath as Annde walked forward, knelt before the regent, and held the Heart of the World up to him with reverence, "Your Majesty, the Heart of the World belongs to mankind now."

"Annde, your illness, it's—" the regent whispered, visibly shaken. He reached out with trembling fingers for the Heart, "You've done it, you've really done it—"

His hand stopped just shy of the surface. For a moment, he was transfixed by his reflection, a terrible fear passing through his eyes. Though nothing in the room changed, Lily could feel some dark presence looming over his head, something that would overwhelm him entirely.

He pulled his hand back as if he'd been bitten. He stood off the throne and laughed joyfully, as if the moment had never happened. Annde was still kneeling in front of him.

Lily barely caught it, but she swore the edges of Annde's lips lifted into a cruel smile.

"We shall have a celebration!" the regent demanded, "A ball, in honor of the brave heroes. In your honor, my dear cousin."

Theyn flushed, stammered, broken out of the spell and returned to his awkward self, "Thank you, Your Highness, but it was really Princess Iff who—"

"And a great feast!" Wheyn continued, looking over to Questburger, as stoic and formidable as he'd been on stage when this all started, "You can put all of that together, can't you?"

Whether that was in his job description or not, Questburger simply dipped his head and said, "Yes, Your Majesty."

"Annde," the regent demanded, a wild grin still plastered on his face. He had the look of a man who had no idea what had happened to him but was desperately pretending he did, "Place the Heart in the treasury. We'll see to its use, its place in the kingdom, after the celebrations have ended."

Annde nodded, stood in an oddly graceful motion that he never should have been capable of, and echoed Questburger, "Yes, Your Majesty."

"Wait—" Lily cried out, a warning that anyone except him should store it trapped in her throat.

Before she could reach him, Elizabeth caught her and hissed in her ear, "Iff, what the hell are you doing?! Just stand here and be quiet!"

Lily turned to glare at her, but as she looked away from Annde, she realized the entire room was glaring at her.

It was like Lily had wandered into the set of the wrong movie, and now everyone noticed her here, speaking when she'd been given no lines.

For a moment there, Lily had almost forgotten these were the people who'd left her in a dumpster.

Nhoj left shortly after, bowing his head, and was rewarded with a small medal for his participation. He turned and looked at Lily. He stood perfectly still as he stared at her, and then, just for a moment, he offered her a smile.

When he walked out of the palace doors, he didn't even glance back at the throne room and the throne his people had undoubtedly created.

The night elf princess was given nothing, deliberately passed over. Her red eyes burned, she gritted her teeth, but said nothing as she faded back into the shadows and left the building.

The happiness elf had to be escorted out politely, in too much of a daze to realize he'd missed his cue to exit.

At the end of it, of the elves, only Ilyn remained.

And that was how the quest ended.

***

"You know, Lenin," Lily mused to her oldest and closest friend, *"I always thought Cinderella gave the wrong impression. When you're at a ball you weren't invited to, even if you look the part, it feels like the only thing worth doing is hanging out by the hors d'oeuvres."*

Lily placed a pastry in her mouth, still undecided on what the flavor was supposed to be.

The party had happened as promised and Lily was dressed to the nines, in a ball gown with too many laces in the back and was the most unflattering shade of yellow imaginable.

"I don't know why you're complaining," Wizard Lenin said with barely concealed mirth, *"Isn't it every little girl's dream to be a princess?"*

"I look awful in yellow," Lily frowned down at the dress, which wasn't so much yellow as it was that unflattering color trapped between yellow, green, and brown.

"Don't worry," Wizard Lenin chided, *"No one is looking at you."*

Funny, Lily had noticed that.

She was well aware that she was standing in a corner by herself with Rabbit and the punch bowl.

Theyn, on the other hand, dressed in a suit so white it almost glowed, was overwhelmed by attention from people of all ages.

Lily was feeling a bit like chopped liver.

"Iff, Lepus, there you are!"

Lily almost had to do a double take, "Elizabeth?"

It was definitely her, but she'd really cleaned up.

Gone were the strict braids that had kept her hair out of her face the entire quest. Gone, too, was her proud uniform. All of this had been replaced by a prim and modest blue dress, with her golden hair pinned up in a bun with an equally modest gold pin.

The fabric's quality wasn't anywhere close to Lily's, the undecorated pin her only jewelry, but the radiance of her smile more than made up for it. She looked ten times the little princess that Lily did.

"Have you been standing by the drinks this whole time?" Elizabeth asked, hands on her hips, giving Lily that 'you should know better, and I certainly know better, because I'm better than you' look she so adored.

"Yes," Lily said without any shame whatsoever.

"Honestly, Iff," Elizabeth clucked her tongue, "We're going to start classes in a few days and you haven't even tried to meet anyone."

Lily couldn't help but stare. Elizabeth seemed more–natural than usual, in a way she'd never been while on the quest. She was less on edge, less aggressive, and seemed comfortable with her surroundings in a way Lily just wasn't. This was clearly her territory in a way it would never be Lily's, and Elizabeth knew it.

Elizabeth motioned towards Theyn, towards some of the teenagers surrounding him, "Look, there's a few of them now, why don't you—"

"Thanks, but no thanks," Lily said, "I'm not exactly a people person."

It was best Lily put off meeting new people for as long as possible.

Lily remembered her days as a precocious social pariah at elementary school with extreme fondness. Like most film series, the world would thank her if she didn't rush to produce a half-baked and underfunded sequel.

"You won't be a people person if you don't even try," Elizabeth said, before nodding towards Rabbit, "And you shouldn't deprive Lepus of the chance to meet people just because you're a wallflower."

"Can she get away with calling a princess a wallflower?" Lily asked Wizard Lenin.

"A half-bred elf that the monarchy would dearly love to call a bastard if they could get away with it? Yes, yes she can."

"I think Rab—Lepus is just fine," Lily commented, looking over at Rabbit. He'd been staring into the red depths of the punch bowl since they'd arrived (he'd originally been looking across the ballroom at nothing in particular, but Lily had felt uncomfortable and tilted his head to at least look at something).

"And I think you better shape up when you enter the academy," Elizabeth stopped, paused, and glanced over at Rabbit with a flush on her cheeks, "Is—ah—Lepus going to the academy?"

"Yep," Lily said, because if he wasn't, then Lily could not be held responsible for her actions.

Either Rabbit was going or Rabbit was going, that was final.

"Oh, that's wonderful!" Elizabeth said, clapping her hands together, "I wasn't sure, I had to take an entrance exam, but it might be different for—Anyways, you'll have a great time once you're caught up to speed, I promise. It took me no time at all, I'm sure you won't have any trouble either—"

Elizabeth prattled on, unconcerned by Lily's swiftly dulling expression and clear lack of attention. It was clear though, more than anything, that Elizabeth really did love this academy. More than being selected for the quest, certainly more than being on the quest, Elizabeth loved whatever this school was. She was practically glowing, she loved it so much.

"Ilyn's not the only instructor," Elizabeth continued, a smaller, prouder smile on her lips, "He's certainly the—toughest, I suppose, but there are many instructors with all sorts of specialties. They've all been very encouraging, said I was the greatest mage they've seen in ages, even at my age."

The greatest since John Jones, she meant, since Ilyn had nearly wiped out the human magee forces and taken the kingdom.

Elizabeth was the shining star of what was left of the kingdom.

Lily was struck by the sudden, chilling thought that Elizabeth might not be so singularly good, so easily recognized, if it hadn't been for the Usurper. Lily was hardly an expert, but while Elizabeth was hardworking, and she seemed powerful, she hadn't lasted two seconds against the love elf. The world was filled with Elizabeths, in ordinary circumstances, but here there was only one.

Except, Elizabeth didn't know it because she was from Earth.

"Elizabeth," Lily cut in, ignoring Elizabeth's glare at being interrupted, "How did you get here?"

"What do you mean?" Elizabeth huffed, crossing her arms and narrowing her eyes, like she just dared Lily to say something.

"I mean you're from Earth, aren't you?" Lily asked, "So how did you end up here? How did you end up in the academy?"

Elizabeth's face darkened, her pout transformed into a true frown, and she stiffened, "What are you getting at? You think someone from Earth can't—"

"I'm saying that I'm from Earth and I know that you don't just end up in a place like this," Lily spoke over her.

For a moment, Elizabeth held her ground, then lacking opposition she slumped.

"You know, no one's asked that in ages," Elizabeth admitted with a wry smile, "They only asked when I first got here—"

For a moment, she simply stared out onto the dance floor, watching the elegantly dressed people twirling about. She looked conflicted, her expression torn and hesitant, then in the blink of an eye she was as resolute as ever.

"It doesn't matter," she said with forceful confidence, "I'm here, when I got here and the academy saw my talent I was accepted as a student just like anyone else."

Her voice rose in volume, not enough to be noticeable over the din, but enough to ensure she had Lily's full attention.

She looked like an actor in the first dress rehearsal, rehashing lines she'd memorized long ago, meant to be spoken to anyone who dared ask her to justify herself.

Except, Lily was certain that she was the first and only person who had ever bothered to ask.

"Better than everyone else," Elizabeth continued, "Good enough to join a quest for the Heart of the World! Not you, not Theyn, not anyone ever gets to ask me where I came from. All that matters is where I'm going."

There was a very long pause. Elizabeth and Lily stared at one another, both listening to the way Elizabeth's last statement echoed.

"And what did you leave behind?" Lily asked.

Elizabeth's determination broke, "What?"

"People don't just fall through holes in worlds," Lily pressed, "They always leave something behind in their wake."

Even Lily had left the Tylors, hollow as they were, behind.

Ilyn had ensured that she could never look back, never return, but she'd left them just the same.

She'd left the cinema, the literature, all the world she'd ever known to come to this place.

"Well, maybe you did," Elizabeth said softly, looking away again, "But I—I didn't really have anything. No family, no future really—"

She trailed off, looking at Theyn, "Even if I did, would I have traded everything, magic, for Earth?"

Yes, Lily had thought so.

Elizabeth was Luke Skywalker in her own way too, except, not quite. An orphaned lonely girl, probably in the foster system Lily had miraculously avoided, who one day slipped into a wondrous world filled with magic, magic she had a great talent for.

And it was because of that that she couldn't see what this place really was.

"Look," Elizabeth said firmly, crossing her arms again, "I don't want to talk about it and you're not going to get any more information by badgering me. Besides, if you want to talk about Earth, Tellestria, I'm the last person you should talk to. I haven't been to Tellestria in ages."

"I got that much," Lily said blandly, that wasn't why she'd asked.

Elizabeth was never going to sit down and talk Star Wars with her.

"Well, in that case, we should talk about something else," Elizabeth finished, physically unable to stop herself from getting the last word in.

"Such as?" Lily asked with raised eyebrows.

"Oh, I don't know," she huffed, "What kind of magic are you looking forward to learning?"

'The—uh—magic kind," Lily said, knowing immediately that was the wrong answer.

"You're going to have to stop doing that," Elizabeth said with a dull look, "No one likes a smart aleck."

Before Lily could say anything, Elizabeth continued, "Magic comes from all kinds of sources and can be used for all kinds of things. The ancient sun elf prayers, for example, are great fire and light spells."

"I guess I haven't put that much thought into it," Lily admitted.

"Oh, I know you haven't," Elizabeth said insufferably, "But you can't get away with it forever!"

Lily was pretty sure she could, but she didn't say as much.

Elizabeth must have seen it on her face, though. With an aggravated and over dramatic sigh, Elizabeth gave up, "Oh, I just can't deal with you. Lepus, I don't know how you put up with her!"

"Hey!" Lily protested, Rabbit of course giving no indication he'd heard her as he continued to stare into the punch bowl's mysterious depths.

"I'll see you later," Elizabeth offered, turning on her heel and walking over to Theyn and Lily's future classmates with the kind of controlled stride that made it clear she wished she could stomp her way across the ballroom.

"Oh god," Lily suddenly realized, "I'm going to be attending class with that every day."

There was a small, harsh, laugh next to her, "Try teaching that for the past four years."

Lily looked behind her and immediately grinned at the new face, "Ilyn!"

He looked about as cleaned up as you could expect him to get.

His uniform was gone, replaced by layered, multi-colored clothing that looked like it'd been taken from the cover of a fantasy novel. His gold-red hair was loose, falling down his back in tight curls. Even more than Lily, he looked like he'd been invited to a party he never should have attended.

He tipped his head at her in acknowledgement, ladled himself some punch, and after pale eyes raked her over remarked, "You look terrible."

Well, he wasn't wrong, but she wasn't sure she liked him saying it.

On the other hand, you could always trust Ilyn to tell you when a dress made you look fat.

"Yes, well, given the short notice they had nothing else lying around," Lily said.

Ilyn gave a small hum of agreement and nothing more.

They fell into a strangely comfortable silence, that sense of kinship still there, even in a setting as different as this one.

She hadn't thought much about the future, but some part of her had assumed that when the quest was done, most things would fade back to normal. For whatever reason, whatever happened between her and Ilyn stood firm even without the quest as an excuse.

It was nice, she decided, having someone here. It was nicer to think that, in the future, she'd still have this when she'd never had anything like it before. Anything like him before, really, a—friend.

She felt a small, contented smile grow on her lips at the thought and let her attention turn elsewhere. Her eyes lingered on Theyn and Elizabeth as they chatted to each other. The others, those teenagers around him, seemed uncomfortable and even resentful of her presence. They glared at her, tried to talk over her, but she stayed exactly where she was. She was either utterly oblivious or, more likely, perfectly aware but choosing to rub their faces in her presence.

Elizabeth wasn't going anywhere and she was letting them know it.

Theyn, for his own part, seemed to actually be oblivious.

Lily's attention wandered again.

The regent was sitting on the throne, lounging really, his clothing more ornate and decorated than even Theyn's. The crown on his head seemed heavy, the weight of it tilting his neck forward, but there was a smile on his lips as he chatted with—

As he chatted with Annde.

"Why is Annde talking to the king?" Lily asked, feeling very cold.

Annde's head lifted. He met Lily's gaze and smiled across at her.

"I don't pay much attention to the regent," Ilyn said with no small amount of contempt, "I believe they're old friends. Anyone with a drop of noble blood is now an old friend of the monarchy, that's the world John Jones left to them."

"So, he's a friend," Lily said in growing horror as she saw it coming together, "An advisor too?"

"I suppose," Ilyn shrugged, "Mostly they listen to Questburger, he's the last of the old hands. Otherwise, the regent seems to listen to just about anyone."

Ilyn gave her an amused look, "Especially if they offer him objects of great power."

On finishing his drink, Ilyn ladled himself more punch, "But I don't concern myself with him."

Lily should probably think about that, wonder what the hell that meant.

She couldn't focus on that, though, instead her eyes locked on Annde hovering over the regent.

Wasn't the tilt of the regent's head beneath that crown a little like a marionette's? Gesturing here and there, his hands had taken on a jerking sloppy quality that Lily associated with the wine but could just as easily have come from the unexpected pulling of strings.

Annde's hands were nowhere near the king or his head, in one was a glass of wine, the other resting on the armrest of the throne, but she could just picture it—

"There's something wrong with him," Lily blurted.

It was too loud, but they were far enough away that no one should have heard it. Somehow, though, Annde's head tilted towards her, and his smile grew.

It was like he was just daring her to come out and say it.

"I mean—" Lily swallowed her words, trying to force them into something coherent as she met Ilyn's eyes, "He's changed. He's gone through some creepy metamorphosis, and I don't think he got better from whatever happened to him. He got worse, much worse. I don't think he's Annde, if he ever was Annde to begin with."

At Ilyn's silence, Lily pushed through, "And I think he's after the Heart of the World, if he hasn't stolen it already."

For a moment, Ilyn said nothing, he just looked at her. Then he quietly noted, "Iff, I can't kill him."

"What?" Lily asked, because that hadn't been what she'd been asking, not even what she'd been thinking.

He looked deathly serious though, those strange pale eyes burning as he stared down at her, as if he'd like to do nothing more than murder the man on the spot because of Lily's word alone.

"I am—" he paused, closed his eyes and swallowed harshly. When he spoke again, his voice was rough, "I am the monarchy's errand boy, desperately trying to piece together the visions Lilyanna left behind. If I murder that man, if I act on my own bloody initiative once again, then I take up John Jones's mantle and embark on the road that led to the place in flames. That's not why I'm here, Iff, and it's not why you're here."

"But—"

He held up a hand, stopping her before she could finish, "There are things, Iff, that you and I should never touch. There are fates we must allow fools to condemn themselves to."

"We can't do nothing!" Lily cried out, because that man would kill them all. He'd murder Wheyn, or worse than murder him, and turn him into some kind of thrall. Theyn, though, Theyn he'd simply kill to get out of the way.

"There is nothing—" he paused, cut himself off, and reached into his clothing to pull out the compass.

"Ilyn?" Lily asked, standing on her toes to peer at its surface and see where the needle was pointing.

It flew desperately between Annde, Lily herself, and somewhere out of the ballroom. Just as quickly, he put it away, and pulled her across the dance floor and out of the party. Lily only just managed to grab Rabbit's hand in time to pull him with her.

As he walked, he said without looking backward, "I will be no help to you in this, can't help you in this, but whatever remains of your mother thinks that Quesburger may help you."

"Questburger?" Lily asked.

"*Questburger?!*" Wizard Lenin echoed.

"If the order comes from Questburger," Ilyn continued, "If you can convince him that Annde is a traitor, a thief, possessed, or simply returned from the journey wrong, then even the regent won't question it. Then, only then, can the man be safely cut down."

Their pace didn't slow as he pulled her through corridors, away from the ballroom, and closer to the offices of government officials.

As she stumbled along, Rabbit shuffling even more unwillingly behind her, Wizard Lenin hissed her ear, *"Lily, just turn around. Trust me when I say talking to Questburger will get you nowhere, no matter how many open doors he's offered you.*

"In fact, it will take you to the place you least wish to go. Never attract that man's notice if you can help it. Just go to the party and let Annde do whatever he wants!"

"But he'll—"

"I don't care! Both your cousin and the regent are dead men walking anyway!"

No.

Not like that, not like this, she wouldn't write off Theyn like this.

She and Questburger had met once before, and she'd seen nothing of what Wizard Lenin feared in him. He'd offered to meet with her in the future, when would she do that if not now?

Feeling her resolve harden, she forced Wizard Lenin back in her head and moved faster to keep pace with Ilyn.

Finally, Ilyn stopped at a door and threw it open, revealing Questburger sitting at his desk, hunched over a pile of paperwork. Even in a setting like this, there was something in Questburger made from steel, something that hadn't dulled over the years.

Ilyn shoved Lily inside, bowing his head, "Iff has something to tell you."

Questburger put down his pen and looked at her with dark eyes. He looked—different today, different than that first day. He'd been formidable then too, but welcoming. He'd been softer, kinder, today he was looking at her as if she was already wasting his time.

Aware of how her dress clashed with the office, she slowly sat down, and tugged Rabbit forward to stand next to her chair. She cleared her throat and forced the words out, "Annde is going to steal the Heart of the World and murder the crown prince."

Her words hung in the air like heavy smoke.

Questburger's eyes moved from her to Ilyn standing just behind her.

"Is this a joke?" he asked.

Lily felt her hopes, the faith she'd placed in him, fall like a lead weight.

"She is her mother's daughter," Ilyn said coldly, his face darkening, "It would not be wise to dismiss her so easily."

"And what about the other one?" Questburger asked, his eyes falling on Rabbit.

"We're a package deal," Lily said with a forced smile, "He's a refugee from Xhigrahi, from the night elves and—"

Questburger's eyes turned back to her, dismissing Rabbit's tragic backstory entirely, and asked curtly, "Do you have any proof?"

"His recovery," Lily blurted, "He was—something was wrong with him, I don't know if he was ill or cursed but—everyone knew it. Now, though, he looks like he could run goddamn marathons—"

"And what would you know about magic?" the man asked. There was something about him, something about his attention, that made Lily feel uncomfortably small.

"What?" Lily asked in turn.

"You were sent to Tellestria for your protection," Questburger reminded her, lacing his fingers together with a sigh, "But Tellestria doesn't have magic, only the fantasy of it. You have no idea what it is or isn't capable of. You have no idea the horrors a human being can recover from."

"Then why send me?!" Lly spat, something inside her breaking, some dam she didn't know existed faltering and the floodwater rushing through.

That open door he'd promised was nothing more than a brick wall she'd rushed headfirst into.

"*Lily,*" Wizard Lenin cautioned, but she paid him no mind.

"Why send me there if you're just going to use it as an excuse to dismiss everything I—"

"Because we will train you soon enough," he cut in harshly, "And when you're trained, then we can talk.

"Until then, no matter how naturally talented you are, I see no point in humoring you. If there's something wrong with Annde, beyond the fact that against all odds he recovered due to the Heart of the World, then you can trust us to find it. I do not have to trust you to find it."

"And if Theyn told you this, Elizabeth?!" she demanded.

"Then I would take them far more seriously," he said, no hint of a smile, no hint of any compassion or understanding, "Because they have had the training you lack."

"*He's not going to help you,*" Wizard Lenin said, a flash of a younger Questburger in his mind, that same expression on his face, "*This man will never help you.*"

"Ilyn," Questburger said sharply, "Take the princess and her—friend back to the ball. See that this doesn't happen again."

Ilyn bowed his head, saying nothing, and pulled Lily and Rabbit back out the door and walked them back to the ballroom.

Lily felt like she was in a dream, being pulled through dark water to a bottom she couldn't see.

That was—

It was the first time she'd reached out to anyone, expecting something from them, and even though Ilyn had tried, the man above him had slammed that door in her face.

Everything Questburger had said in that first meeting, every assurance he'd made, it was all a lie. He'd never intended to listen to Lily at all, just make the offer, just placate her and make her feel—

Maybe he'd have made time to meet her when she was in the academy., Maybe he'd take time to explain something or another about magic, the royal family, but the moment she needed a few seconds of his time—

Wizard Lenin had been right.

This whole time, he'd been right.

Annde was still here, would still have to be dealt with, but it was Lily alone who would have to do it.

Just like she had to deal with everything else.

"*Don't overreact,*" Wizard Lenin said, "*You might not have to do anything. Even if you do, he'll still be here tomorrow and the day after that. There's no rush, without the Heart of the World in the treasury, he's not our priority, no matter what's wrong with him.*"

"Do you have any idea what's wrong with him?" Lily asked in turn.

Wizard Lenin paused. A whirring, sinking, doubt stretched from him down into Lily, straight into the pit of her stomach.

"An idea."

He didn't elaborate.

The ballroom glittered, the crystal chandelier painting rainbows across the golden hall. Lily wondered if Nhoj had had a hand in making any of them.

For an odd moment, it reminded her of Christmas. As if the rainbows created by the crystals were the colored lights found on dozens of trees. Even amidst the glitz and glamor, there was something warm about this place, about the warm glow of the candlelight.

It reminded her of Death.

Death—

She hadn't seen him since before the quest started.

There'd never been a good moment to bow out and take her exit. She felt like it'd been years since she'd seen him.

He hadn't heard about Elizabeth, Theyn, Nhoj, Ailill, Ilyn, or anybody.

It was the first time in her life, she realized, that he would have no idea what had happened to her.

Suddenly, she had to see him.

She had to see him now, tonight. It didn't matter that the last thing he'd said was to destroy the Heart of the World, never let it fall into Wizard Lenin's hands, she had to see him just the same.

She practically ran out of the ballroom, pulling Rabbit behind her. If anyone noticed, if anyone bothered to look in her direction, she'd give some flimsy excuse later. In the meantime, she had a joyful reunion to make and a tale to tell.

Looking back at Rabbit, she laughed, "Oh god, he hasn't even seen your pretty human face!"

20 JOHN'S BARGAIN WITH THE GODS

In which Lily has her reunion with Death, learns the truth about Wizard Lenin and his borrowed immortality, and chooses to go anything but gently into that good night.

She was running as soon as she'd died, sprinting across the grass, pulling Rabbit along as she shouted, "Death!"

It was like she'd never left, never disappeared back to the mortal world at all. He was still at his table, the one that hadn't been there in the real world, still staring out at the stars with a nostalgic melancholy.

At the sound of his name, he looked up with a smile on his lips. He stood and walked towards her, "Lily—"

She beat him to it.

She abandoned Rabbit's hand, threw herself at him, and pulled him into a hug. He stiffened, his hands fluttering like startled birds, before they settled on her back and pulled her deeper into his cloak.

Running a hand through her hair, he murmured, "Yes, I have missed you."

She laughed, the sound muffled in his clothing, but couldn't find words to express the feeling. She just squeezed him tighter and only when she could bear it looked up at his smile.

It was that same soft, sad smile he always had and always would have, a smile that felt like home.

She opened her mouth to say something, even just hello, but his attention moved past her, "Oh my god, it's human."

Lily looked behind her, caught sight of Rabbit staring into space as usual.

"Oh, right," Lily said lamely, "That's a new thing. Um—there was a very good reason for it at the time."

Even if that reason hadn't panned out even in the short term.

"I see you've been busy," Death murmured, one hand still twisting absently through her hair as he stared at Rabbit, as if waiting for it to decide to eat him.

It was nice to know that someone took the threat of Rabbit seriously.

"Very," Lily agreed with a grin, "I couldn't really contact you during the whole quest thing so—here I am."

"Here you are," Death echoed, ruffling her hair one last time before finally stepping back, "You'll have to tell me all about it."

"You still have tea?" Lily asked as she walked with him towards the table.

"I will always have tea, Lily," Death responded with an amused smile.

As Lily pulled out a chair, she noticed that Rabbit had awkwardly, as if he wasn't quite sure how legs worked, made his way over to the table as well. He slumped, practically fell, into the chair next to hers.

She found herself staring at him, heart pounding.

He wasn't supposed to do that, he'd never done that before. He'd never given any indication that—

That he was the kind of thing that would want to sit next to her.

She looked over to note it to Wizard Lenin, but he hadn't approached the table at all. He'd stayed right where they'd entered on the sand. At her attention, he wordlessly walked away, out onto the rest of the moon and out of sight.

Lily stood, opened her mouth to call him back, but closed it with a sigh.

"And he's as charming and dramatic as ever," Death commented as the tea appeared out of nowhere.

"I met Questburger again," Lily explained.

Death's red eyebrows rose higher as he stared after Wizard Lenin, "And that caused this?"

"He didn't think I had a reason to talk to him," Lily said with a sigh, feeling her previous bitterness return, "Maybe he's right, but—"

She cut herself off, shook her head, and watched as Death poured tea for himself, her, and after a moment's pause for Rabbit.

"Tell me about the quest, Lily," he said with a smile, "Did you make friends?"

"Shouldn't you know that already?" Lily asked with a raised eyebrow.

"I've told you, not everything is consistent," Death reminded her with a cheeky look on his face, "My friends might not be your friends."

Lily suddenly, painfully, was reminded of her last conversation with Annde. They, too, had talked about the friends Lily had and hadn't made.

"No, maybe," Lily conceded after a moment, "My cousin, Theyn came along, he's crown prince in my world at least and—it's complicated, but I like him, and I think he likes me."

She frowned at her tea, "There's also this girl Elizabeth, she's apparently the best mage there is right now, and she's—that's even more complicated."

To Lily's surprise, Death tilted his head back and laughed, a full belly laugh she'd never heard from him before, "I knew you two would butt heads!"

"Oh, come on!" Lily cried out, forgetting Annde entirely for a moment.

"Don't worry about Lizzie," he said, wiping away tears of mirth, "Give her half a chance, Lily, and she'll be one of the greatest friends you can find."

Then, with a mischievous smile, he leaned forward to whisper in her ear, "You know, in my world, I actually married Elizabeth."

Lily died.

She hadn't died to reach this place, no, this was what dying felt like. A horrible, spine tingling, nauseous sense of dread and betrayal that Death had—That Lily herself could—

She was going to puke.

Her expression must have said it all as he just laughed again and said, "Never mind the love of my life, what about everyone else?"

Never mind? Like Lily could just forget he'd suggested wedding bells were in her and Elizabeth's future?

She could see it now, Elizabeth in the dress, because of course she'd be the one in the perfect white dress without a hair out of place, and Lily stuffed like a dope into some suit. There'd be music as she slowly made her way down the aisle, but to Lily standing there it'd sound like the *Imperial March*, the kind of music to accompany the end of all good things.

With one last shudder, Lily forced her nightmare aside, "That's a mixed bag."

She thought it over, tapping her fingers, trying to figure out who to start with, "Nhoj, the gold elf clan head, he and I get along pretty well. Since he's local I plan on badgering him when I get a chance. He's a bit dubious of the Lily Jones thing—"

"You don't say."

"—But I think he likes me. I know he likes me."

Lily frowned, not willing to look at that too closely, not after her introspective wondering of whether she and Theyn were really friends or not. Death didn't look particularly convinced either, his eyebrows raised practically to his hairline.

"Ailill, the moon elf, is now my blood brother because of this thing that happened—"

Death spit out his tea, gaped at her like she'd just confessed to chopping off his head.

"—And I'm pretty sure if I sneeze the wrong way, he's going to assassinate Theyn and put me on the throne. Other than that, he's alright I guess."

Lily really hoped he didn't get any funny ideas now that the quest was over, though.

Death opened his mouth, clearly about to interrupt, and Lily hurried to beat him to it.

"The night elf princess, the heir, Hajigihr, and I—No, actually, she tried to kill me. That didn't go well."

Death closed his mouth, seeming to realize it was best that Lily just get it out all in one go.

"The happiness elf exists, we talked once, it was weird."

Nope, nothing else to add to that one. She idly wondered where he'd even gone, what he was doing, and if he'd even managed to find his way home.

"The love elf—well, she tried to take the Heart of the World. I stopped her by telling her John Jones was coming back someday, and then lied to Tyen about that."

She looked away for a moment, rubbing the back of her head, trying not to think too deeply on that either.

"Ilyn ended up letting her live, so I guess she's back home now, wherever that is."

She took a breath, "The mind elf—well, he doesn't exist anymore, Rabbit ate him."

"Rabbit ate—"

"Rabbit ate him," Lily finished for him, unwilling to go into any more detail.

"And Ilyn—" she paused, thought about the man and his strange eyes and his stranger smiles, "I guess we're close now. I don't know how it happened, not really, but he—"

"Ilyn?!" Death blurted, spilling tea all over himself.

"Yes?" Lily asked, eyebrows raising.

"You get on with Ilyn?!"

"Well—" Lily paused, trying to find a way to explain, but ended up lamely adding, "Yes."

Death actually threw his hands wide, his eyebrows furrowed, eyes wide as he asked, "How?!"

"I don't know," Lily huffed, "I helped him out with his task on the quest and—we had a moment I guess. Since then, we've really clicked."

Not that they hadn't clicked in the beginning, now that she thought about it. He'd burned down her house and all but—she had talked to him on the stage. She'd kept talking to him too, whenever she wanted to know something or wanted to get Elizabeth off her back.

Death looked at her like she'd just admitted she was Jesus. No, wait, she did the whole resurrection thing already. He was looking at her like she was Theyn admitting he was Jesus.

"I don't—" he cut himself off, gaped at her, and then of all things flushed, "In my world, Ilyn and I—I mean he—We didn't get on."

He looked wildly down at the table, confessed down to it, "I think I came on too strong, or touched a nerve. I asked him about my mother, about her being a sun elf too, and—"

Lily had never tried, so she couldn't say, but she somehow thought that'd be a bad idea.

"Yes," Death agreed with an almost neurotic laugh, "It never improved."

All she could do was drink her tea and try not to picture Ilyn pummeling her twelve-year-old male counterpart into the ground.

Lily hastily moved on, "That just leaves—"

Lily cut herself off, because the only one left was Annde.

Death seemed to know it too because that out of character embarrassment disappeared. His humanity dripped off him, like water on glass, and suddenly he looked like the god he pretended he wasn't.

There was no wavering in his voice as he said, "The royal advisor, courier, and mage Annde after his return from the wastelands of Xhigrahi."

Lily felt her stomach drop, "You know what's wrong with him."

Death stared at her. He hadn't looked like the man in the swamp, the clearing, before now. He'd been too human, had too many human expressions and memories corrupting him. Now, though, something had fallen away, and was left wasn't a man at all.

Now, even with his coloring, even with his eyes in place, he looked something like him.

"He's a host for the remnants of John Jones's indestructible spirit."

She felt as if something should have shattered. There was nothing, only the clinking sound of china as she set down her cup, "What?"

Death looked away, towards the stars, and as he did so the air around them warped and grew darker. Rather than the ethereal cleanliness of the island, Lily found herself staring into ash floating in the air like fog.

"Annde did travel to Xhigrahi before that quest," Death said quietly, "He'd been sent as an ambassador to the provinces."

And there, standing on the island quickly transforming into a desert, was Annde.

Except, standing there, whole and healthy, he looked nothing like he did now. The body was the same, but he wore it completely differently. There was none of that malice, that oozing confidence, no sharpness to him at all.

Annde looked over towards Lily and Death, unseeing.

"It wasn't the night elves who found him."

Annde's eyes widened, he took a step back, and a great shapeless shadow overtook him. Inside the smoke, his body disappeared, not even an outline of it visible.

"It was John Jones, what's left of him, a cursed thing that was neither mortal nor truly immortal," Death continued, "It infected Annde, eating at his mind and memories, and used him to influence the regent. When the sun elves made their prophecy, he used Annde to promote then infiltrate the quest, ultimately regaining his true form."

Death waved his hand and the vision disappeared, their surroundings returned to their previous state, and mused, "Of course, that was only how it happened in my world."

The indestructible spirit—

At her expression, Death's eyebrows raised, and he had a knowing look when he asked, "He's never told you, has he?"

"What?" Lily asked.

"He already knows," Death said, a bitter smile stretching across his face, "That's why he disappeared so quickly. He must have known for ages, and he's let you stumble about in the dark."

"What are you talking about?!" Lily asked, slamming her hands on the table.

Death considered her, his smile still bitter, and a sharp mirth flashed in his eyes, "Well, if he's not going to tell you, then I suppose it becomes my job, doesn't it?"

He snapped his fingers, and the island melted away once again, a memory taking its place.

Lily nearly fell out of her chair as this time, it wasn't Annde standing in front of them, but instead a younger Wizard Lenin. It was the same Wizard Lenin from the clearing, the same age, even wearing the same clothing.

The room they were in was dark, illuminated only by a few dying candles. There were inscriptions drawn on the floor, characters in a language she couldn't read, written out in intersecting circles. Heavy tomes lay open on a desk, piled on top of one another, giving the impression of a well-worn study.

In the corner, almost out of sight and unnoticed lay a human body.

Looking back at Wizard Lenin, Lily noticed dark liquid dripping from his hands.

"When he was a very young man, not much older than a boy, John Jones made a bargain with a god."

The young Wizard Lenin stepped into one of the circles. The chalk beneath his feet glowed an impossible white, banishing all shadows from the room.

"In return for the blood and soul of his murdered father, John Jones asked for the heritage his human half had denied him."

Death smiled even as soundlessly, the young Wizard Lenin began screaming out some spell of summoning, drawing a shadow out of the light.

Lily stepped forward, unable to help herself, as the great shadow lifted to reveal that blind man from the clearing.

Wizard Lenin's eyes were closed, but Lily's weren't. She watched as that mask-like face, those empty eyes, turned towards her as if they could see her even through memory.

"But Death didn't want his father," Death continued, "Instead, he asked for John Jones's humanity, his human soul and blood. John, a fool, was happy to part with it."

"Wait!" Lily shouted, but neither actor could hear, or if they could, neither seemed to care.

That other Death, the one who wasn't an Ellie Tylor, reached forward towards Wizard Lenin's heart. He held his hand against the boy's chest for only a moment, then drew it back. Wizard Lenin bent over screaming as the god pulled a glowing star from his chest.

Then he disappeared back into the light, taking the star with him. The runes burned out on the floor and Wizard Lenin collapsed there, twitching, still clutching his chest.

"He gained exceptional magical ability as well as the immortality he craved, but he never questioned how," Death said contemptuously, watching beads of cold sweat break out on the boy's forehead.

"In truth, he stopped belonging to any world that day. So, when his body failed him, his spirit had nowhere to go. Death had already taken the best of him."

Slowly, with labored breathing, Wizard Lenin tried to pick himself up off the floor. In the effort, he knocked one of the candles over, extinguishing the flame as he tried to get back on his feet.

"Per his bargain, he cannot be destroyed, only grievously injured by something as brazenly stupid as attempting to murder a god," Death concluded, "So he wanders aimlessly, endlessly, and uses the magic he bargained for to possess his way into mortal forms, thinking that this will somehow end his suffering."

Death smiled, a cruel sharp thing, as the young Wizard Lenin's pale eyes opened sightlessly, "But he got his power, and I suppose to the likes of him that's all that ever mattered."

Wizard Lenin disappeared and the island was solid once again, Lily was desperately reaching towards nothing. Slowly, she turned back to Death. He was still seated, sipping his tea, as if none of this meant anything to him.

"It's what he's always been, Lily," Death said, holding his palm open like a peace offering, "And he knows it."

Lily, on shaking feet, stepped back towards the table, "But if Lenin's in my head, then—"

"He tried to murder a god," Death interjected, green eyes without sympathy, "It forced him to sacrifice what was left of himself to you, a second unwitting penance, and now what's wandering around in Annde is even less than that."

"Then Lenin's—"

"Scraps," Death finished for her, "Bits and pieces of John Jones and his memory thrown together until it makes something almost, but not quite, human."

"He's not scraps!" Lily spat back, "He has his own memories, his own goals, and—and he has me, dammit!

"It doesn't matter if he's not the real one, if he's not supposed to be here, if he was some—some stupid sacrifice that he didn't even know he'd made!"

She slammed her hands on the table, "It doesn't matter!"

She dared Death to say something, anything, but he didn't.

Lily pushed away from the table, grabbed Rabbit's head, and said, "I'm sorry but—There's something I have to do."

She took one step back, then another, and forced herself to look at him as she promised, "I'll be back."

She turned on her heel, dragging Rabbit with her, and sprinted through the foliage where Wizard Lenin had disappeared, "Lenin!"

She ran past the other Heart of the World, still on its pedestal, past where the party itself had gone, past anything she recognized.

"Lenin!"

Somehow, she came to the other side, and there was a bridge she'd never noticed in this place. It was the bridge she'd made for the quest, where on the other side, surely, was another world.

Wizard Lenin sat on the very edge, feet dangling off into the void.

Lily slowed and wordlessly sat next to him, her legs brushing against his. She was still wearing the dress, she noticed, and against his dark clothing—it didn't look quite so bad.

"If I wanted to be found," he said quietly as he stared out into space, "I would have returned to your little tea party."

"There's no tea party today."

He said nothing to that, just kept staring forward. Lily looked out with him.

It was beautiful, she hadn't had much of a chance to look when they'd been there in the real world, but it was beautiful in a way she didn't think a photograph could capture. It was—life, she thought, life itself beckoning in the distance, standing in defiance of the void.

She reached out a hand slowly, grabbed his in hers, and still looking out at the bridge said, "Death said that Annde is your puppet, the other you that got left behind."

He made some affirmative noise.

"He said something, when he first met you," Lily continued, "He said you were a copy, not even the original. I didn't know what that meant."

Here, a smile twitched on his lips, and he murmured, "Neither did I."

Finally, he sighed and looked down at her, "I suppose that makes three of us. Him, me, and that boy we found in this place. Funny, I didn't realize I'd left anything behind."

He stopped abruptly, clearly lost in thought, and Lily wondered if he was thinking about that memory Death had shown her.

"What do you think we should do about him?" Lily asked, "About Annde?"

For a moment, Wizard Lenin said nothing, then, "He would expect me to aid him, if he knew I existed. He'd expect me to hand over the Heart of the World. He must know his is a fake, that you took it for yourself, but—"

He stopped, swallowed, and his voice was raw with bitter anger when he continued, "But I don't want to be trapped here, to become nothing more than a memory of him, just another price he paid to be where he is. If he realizes what I am, what he made, he'll lock me—us—in the highest tower he can find and swallow the key."

With a crazed laugh, laughter almost swallowing his words, he looked at her and added, "After all, there is only one lord of the rings!"

He squeezed her hand too tightly, clearly unaware he was doing it, "I'll walk the world again. I've waited too long, come too far, to throw it all away."

"What should we do?"

His eyes met hers, his lost expression gone, that familiar fire in his eyes.

"Get rid of Annde."

Lily waited, but nothing followed. Slowly, she noted, "That's a vague plan."

Wizard Lenin didn't appreciate that, as he used his free hand to hit the back of her hand, "It'll be less vague when you give me a chance to think!"

He looked away from her, the gears in his mind turning, "If he is me, if he hasn't gone mad from all this, then he won't be easily outwitted or defeated. Ilyn wasn't wrong, Annde's not a man who can just disappear."

He looked back at her, rose to his feet and pulled her up with him, "Give me time, Lily, and we'll surely win."

21 THE PLAY

In which Lily and Annde engage in a high stakes battle of wits.

For a moment, she stood and faced the door to Annde's study.

It was an ordinary door, less ornate than some of its brothers, but nothing to draw the eye. It was the office of a bureaucrat, just like every other bureaucrat, a man important enough to need an office but not one you could easily find.

She'd had to wander labyrinthian halls, past mirrored hallways decorated with chandeliers, pleasure gardens, to this small hallway sanctioned for offices.

For the first time in a long time, Lily was in her clothing from Earth, jean shorts, flip flops, all the clothes she'd worn when she'd first been dragged here. She imagined that she didn't just look out of place, but alien, for all there was no one around to see it.

For better or worse, it was just her and Wizard Lenin's better half on the other side of that door, Rabbit the sole witness.

In her hands, she held a simple box sloppily wrapped in red and gold paper, a crinkled blue ribbon on top.

Taking a breath, she knocked, then shouted, "Merry Christmas, Annde!"

There was no answer for a long time, only a thickening miasma crawling out from underneath the door like smoke. Lily tried not to look at it.

"The cleanest ending is if he leaves of his own volition," Wizard Lenin had said as they'd quietly navigated the palace, following the thread of Wizard Lenin's wayward soul, *"He'll only do that if he has the Heart."*

She'd already created one false Heart of the World, one that had fooled everyone but Annde, she could do it again. If she gave him the right incentive, admitted to having stolen it in the first place, then maybe—

The door opened slowly, pushed open by the smoke rather than a human hand. Inside it was too dark to see, the windows shuttered, not a candle in sight. As she squinted into the darkness, she could barely make out the form of a human man and the white teeth of his smile.

"Princess Iff and Lepus Rabbitson," he greeted, his voice clearer than it'd ever been before, "I was hoping you'd stop by."

Lily felt her body slide across the floor, summoned inward by intangible strings. The door slammed shut behind her and Rabbit. Lily gripped the box tighter, pressed her lips together, but said nothing as he pulled her forward until she stopped just in front of him.

He didn't look like Wizard Lenin, not even with the dark hiding his features. He was too short, too plain, his eyes too dark. However, she could see something of Wizard Lenin hiding behind him. His eyes held none of Wizard Lenin's color, but all his expression.

Forcing herself to grin, Lily lifted the box up towards him, "Merry Christmas."

He stared down at it, a single eyebrow raised, and noted with a small smile, "You're such an odd girl, aren't you?"

Lily said nothing, just set the box down on the edge of his desk, slowly lifting her hands away from it.

Inside her head, Wizard Lenin was perfectly silent.

(*"We can't wait,"* he'd concluded in the afterlife, *"Waiting only gives him time to plan, more time than he's already had. He'll sink his roots so deep into this place that to remove him would be to remove the monarchy itself. He'll use his position to destroy you, us, if he thinks that will get him what he wants.*

"If he thinks he's been discovered, if he knows Annde's cover is blown, and he has what he came for—he'll disappear to lick his wounds.")

"Your Highness?" Annde cut into her thoughts.

Lily started, flinching instinctively.

"It's a gift," Lily clarified, "Since you're—since we're so close."

His eyebrows now both raised dubiously, a look that was devastatingly and patently Wizard Lenin.

"Close," the man said dryly, fingering the ribbon idly, "You've spent the summer trying not to vomit at the sight of me, cringing whenever I stepped within five feet of you, and having no respect for me whatsoever."

Well—

That was one way to make Lily sound like a complete dick.

Funny, though, how he'd never pointed it out before. Not even when they'd had their creepy chat after his miraculous recovery.

"I'm turning over a new leaf," Lily responded with equal dryness, "Trying to be a more charitable person and all that."

"For—Christmas," he finished after a significant pause, as if the word galled him. Although whether it was the idea of Christmas or Lily thrusting it upon him out of season was anyone's guess.

"God bless us, everyone," Lily finished with a winning grin that would have been right at home in any Christmas special worth its salt.

(Not that she was sure if Christmas specials were a thing in this universe. Everyone seemed to agree there was a God, a God singular, but it never felt like the God Lily was familiar with. There hadn't been any signs of any of the usual religious artifacts, no crosses, fish, stars, nothing. There hadn't been any mention of any familiar stories for that matter either. It was one of those things that had remained a pleasant mystery.)

He simply stared, expression perfectly blank. He returned his gaze to the box, taking in its glittering red paper and shining bow.

(*"I'd never believe it,"* Wizard Lenin had scoffed.

"If you handed it to me, if I had to find it in your belongings, even if I had to kill you—I'd never believe it'd be that easy. I'd invade your mind, I'd place you in an illusion, or I'd start by cutting off your limbs.

"I'd find a way to make you talk.")

Wizard Lenin was and had once been a very efficient and cruel man.

He went from Point A to Point B in the manner he felt best, no matter how much blood was shed along the way. He was a man who knew how to get what he wanted.

Lily was powerful, she knew that. She'd had that hammered into her head for years. However, Wizard Lenin was clever. If she gave him time—

If she waited, left him to his own devices, if she approached him the wrong way, if she failed, then there was a high chance that he'd somehow have her handing it over to him.

"Do I get to know what's inside the box?" Annde asked, tugging at the ribbon with a tilt of his head, watching as it came undone.

"I think you know what's in the box," Lily said, "We did travel a long way together to find it."

He barely moved, didn't blink, but his fingers, ever so slightly, twitched as the suspicions he'd barely allowed himself were confirmed. His eyes drifted over to the box, and now there was a spark of longing in them, anticipation, as well as suspicion and hesitation.

Was it really going to be this easy?

"And you decided to give it to me," he said softly, staring directly into her eyes.

She shrugged, as if it was nothing, "It's a paperweight. I have no idea how to use it and the one time I tried—let's just say it had interesting results."

The unholy resurrection of Annde, for example.

For a few seconds, there was complete silence. If there was a clock in the room, it'd be ticking, a slow and painful ticking that ate away at the space between words. Her eyes never left his.

And then he didn't take the bait.

(*"Well just give it to him,"* Lily had said before they'd found Annde's door, "A fake, I mean."

"I told you," Wizard Lenin hissed, *"That's not going to work."*

His thoughts had still been spinning, still trying to see the one thing he'd never see coming, the easy answer. He was standing too close though, he was playing a chess game against himself, Lily wasn't.

"Not the first time," Lily agreed, *"But you're trying to win the game before he even plays his pieces. You have to play to win, Lenin."*

"And then what?" he asked.

"And then it's his turn.")

He laughed.

It was the laughter of a man who'd been driven to the edge, perhaps even past it, and couldn't believe what he was seeing anymore.

"No, no, we're done with this," he sighed through his smile, "There's no point if we're both playing pretend."

An oddly genuine smile grew on his lips, "This isn't the Heart of the World."

"How would you know?" Lily asked, opening the box and summoning the orb into her hands, "It looks like it, feels like it, even gives off that ominous hum. What more could you want?"

He peered closer, as if unable to help himself, "You made this—"

He tilted his head one way, then the other, reached out to touch it, "It's incredible, flawless even—"

Slowly, he lifted his fingers away, gave her a chiding look (also too familiar), "But unfortunately, not good enough. You know nothing about subtlety, do you?"

Lily's smile thinned.

"Do you know who I am?" he asked simply.

It wasn't a threat, not a demand, almost a casual question.

When she didn't answer, he answered for her, "I think you do."

He considered her, "Strange, that it'd be you who puts it together when the regent, Questburger, Ilyn, and so many who knew me did not. Perhaps even stranger, I was hoping you would."

Some of the tension left his shoulders, a purposeful relaxation, and what little façade there'd been of Annde disappeared. He was finally free to play his own part. Judging by the shark-like smile, it'd been a long time since he'd felt that way.

The fingers of one hand began to lazily tap against his desk as he surveyed her.

"You realize I could simply kill you and search your belongings."

"You could," Lily responded evenly.

"Or I could torture you," he added, "Remember I've broken grown men far more willful than you."

"You could do that too," Lily agreed.

He leaned back against the desk, crossing his arms as he looked down at her, a furrow growing in his brow.

"But I have a limited timeframe," he reminded himself.

For all the nobility seemed to purposefully overlook her, she would be missed if she wasn't found the next morning. Theyn would notice, Ilyn certainly would.

Annde could try and cast an illusion, but how long could that last when it was a princess missing?

He only had a few hours to search for and produce the Heart, get rid of her body or spirit her away, torture her into compliance, and then somehow sneak back into the palace without anyone noticing.

He pushed himself off the desk. Lily tensed, her fingers white around the orb, preparing to form a shield, but he walked right past her. He rounded his desk and moved to a small closet in the back of the room.

"I didn't know what to think of you," he confessed as he opened the door, "I thought I might hate you, that I might despise you on principle. I thought, perhaps, Questburger would have already gotten his hands on you, just like he has your idiot cousin the future king."

He looked back at her, the closet door still open.

Lily waited.

"You're not what anyone imagined you'd be," he told her, "Strangely enough, I find that infinitely preferable."

He reached in and dragged something out.

No, not just something.

Lily watched as the man dragged a bound Elizabeth out of the closet and into the middle of the room. She was still in her dress, now wrinkled and stained, but her hair had fallen out of its bindings and the pin was lost.

Her eyes were wild, desperate, and swollen as she tried to look at Lily, mouthing something silently.

"Help me," Lily thought she was trying to say.

"That's not fair," Lily said quietly, but that just seemed to amuse the man.

"Life's rarely fair," he chided as he tugged on one of Elizabeth's golden locks, "Death, now death is almost fair, taking from the mortal race as he pleases."

He gave Lily a dull look, "Oh come now, we both knew you were coming tonight; it was written all over your face. You have absolutely no patience and no ability to trust anyone to do a task for you. And if you hadn't, well, then perhaps I would have come to you."

He looked down at Elizabeth again, considering, "Theyn, your cousin, would have been ideal when I realized you might need extra motivation. Unfortunately, as heir to the throne he's not so easily spirited away. So, I settled on the uppity Tellestrian instead, she's very dispensable."

He smiled at Lily again, "I thought about simply killing you, but you're clever enough to have made it difficult to find. That, and I remember the last time I tried to wipe you from this world. I thought about torturing you, but that's such a messy business."

He paused for a second, letting his words sink in, before continuing, "Then I remembered we once had a conversation about the merits of friendship and being close enough."

He bent down, a quick fluid motion, and gripped Elizabeth's chin. He turned her head so she was staring directly at Lily with terrified eyes.

"Well, Iff, are you close enough?"

And it was finally Lily's turn.

With nothing more than a breath, Lily returned the fake Heart of the World back into dust and light. Her eyes never left Elizabeth's, taking in the sight of her sweat, the dried blood matting her hair, and the desperation on her face.

"You were right," Lily acknowledged to Wizard Lenin, *"You do play hardball."*

"They'll look for her too, you know," Lily commented.

"She's Tellestrian, an orphan," he dismissed, "They'll miss her talent for two seconds. They'll assume she returned to the mother country, never mind that she hasn't been there in years. That's if they bother to assume anything at all. She's nothing."

Then, looking bored, he added, "Do try to come to a decision quickly, we're still pressed for time, Princess."

Lily spread her hands, prepared to create another Heart of the World, but before she could he said, "Not too quickly, of course. I don't think you understand the gravity of Miss Elizabeth's situation."

He grabbed one of Elizabeth's hands, ignoring her terror, her futile attempts to struggle against invisible bonds. He reached down for her fingers, looking at them almost musingly, "There are limits to human magic. Human mages are tied to their hands and their tongues, the spells they can recite and interpret. A mage who can't talk isn't a mage, limited at best to ancient rituals. That's not the worst thing, though."

She didn't know exactly what he'd say next, only whatever it was, it was the punchline to the worst joke in the world. In about two seconds now, whenever he opened his mouth, he'd let her in on the secret and it'd all make terrible sense.

He paused, unable to contain his grin, knowing there was nothing Lily could do about it.

"Tell me, Iff, what happens to a mage who has no hands?"

Lily opened her mouth, stepped numbly forward, but it happened in less time than she had to blink. For a moment, Elizabeth was there, struggling but still whole, only bruised and battered. Then, without a word, without a single gesture, her hands hit the floor.

Blood spurted from her wrists and her mouth opened further in terror and agony. Her body shook with the force of her screaming as she bent forward, trying to reclaim her rapidly cooling fingers.

"Stem," Annde commanded, small pale shields forming around Elizabeth's wrists, keeping her from bleeding out.

Tears streamed out of Elizabeth's eyes but Annde paid no notice. Instead, he calmly stared back at Lily, and reached out with a single hand, beckoning.

Without a word, Lily summoned another Heart of the World and tossed it to him. He immediately dropped Elizabet to the floor, turning the object this way and that in his hands.

"He doesn't—" Wizard Lenin started.

"I know," Lily cut him off before he could say it.

He was distracted though, and that was all Lily needed.

Lily looked over at Elizabeth, still shaking violently and falling into shock.

Lily had never considered her own age too deeply, twelve-years-old, but it suddenly struck her how young that was. An older Elizabeth might realize these things, these moments, could happen. At twelve, she hadn't been prepared at all.

If left there on the floor in her own blood, she'd end the night dead. Annde probably imagined it'd take a few hours, that they'd remove her tongue next, perhaps her ears. There'd be a bit of conversation about sacrifice, and finally, watching Elizabeth break, a broken Lily would hand over the real Heart of the World.

But Lily wasn't playing by those rules.

With Annde's back still turned, Lily removed Elizabeth from the game board.

(*"Have faith,"* she'd said to Wizard Lenin before this all started.)

She wasn't entirely sure where she put Elizabeth, somewhere only just out of time and reach, a place you could only glimpse out of the corner of your eye. Wherever it was, she was only just visible, desperately dragging her hands towards her while looking unseeingly at Lily.

With a nod of her head, Lily motioned for Rabbit to follow, and for once he complied. Without a word or even a nod, he left her side, fading into the shadows and joining Elizabeth in her forgotten corner.

Lily turned her attention back to Annde. He was still looking at the orb, inspecting it more critically now that the awe had worn off.

Slowly, he placed it on the desk, the box behind it preventing it from rolling onto the floor. He turned back to her, only to have his expression morph into one of frantic confusion as he realized both of his hostages had disappeared.

"Where—"

She cut him off, "I suppose I could sit here for a few hours while I watch you hack off bits of Elizabeth, but I didn't want to."

He blinked, then, slowly but surely, whatever hint of geniality had been there fell away. His eyes were hard and dark, made flat by cold fury.

"You're playing a very dangerous game," he said.

His voice was like Wizard Lenin's, when he was truly angry, when it got soft and quiet so you could barely hear it but couldn't help but listen. Like every word, every hate-filled syllable, drew you in.

She wondered what game he thought they'd been playing. It'd always been dangerous and the stakes had always been high.

"Where is she?" he asked.

"Gone," Lily said simply.

In the corner, outside of time and the bounds of Annde's detection, Elizabeth and Rabbit watched the scene unfold. Rabbit was holding her severed hands in his, but his focus wasn't on Elizabeth, instead both watched Lily and Annde.

Annde seemed to reach a decision. Resolve entered his expression and he stepped towards her.

He stepped so close that his face was inches from hers, his eyes unavoidable, and before she could move, he grabbed her face, "You bring this on yourself, you know."

"*Lily*—"

Then everything went dark.

There was something cold and sharp, something that fit between her eyes, diving into her skull. Then, suddenly, she wasn't one, or even two minds anymore, but three.

They were late for the start of the play, it was already in progress, but they had good seats and were nearing the climax.

"Of course, it's not a very interesting play," she commented to her companion, the man she almost knew but not quite. She wasn't sure how he'd managed to get a seat.

"What?" he asked, looking around (suddenly, he had a neck to twist and eyes to see with). He seemed very confused.

"The chosen one," she explained as she motioned to the actors.

There were two on the stage. One, a young girl wearing a yellow-red wig, the other, a taller, hunched man, who wore a mask that was secretly another mask. They seemed to be stuck though, both frozen in place.

"What is this?" her companion asked breathlessly.

"Well," she started, "Princess Iff, the protagonist, is only now having her final confrontation with the nameless villain. Only, she's just pretending to be Iff, she fulfills the basic requirements, but she's wearing a mask too.

THE HEART OF THE WORLD

That's the trouble with these plays."

"No," the man said forcefully, "What is this?"

He was growing more insistent, she noticed, struggling to take form. Hands had appeared as well as a mouth, each trying to find its place with the other bits and pieces, desperately trying to make a man out of the sum of its parts.

Well, if he wasn't going to understand it, then he shouldn't have asked. She gave him an unimpressed look, creating her own form to do it, spinning Princess Iff into the seat.

"If you would stop asking questions, they might start moving again," she said, nodding at the stage, "I, for one, want to see how it all turns out. Don't you?"

At the sight of her, something in him seemed to snap and he grabbed her, "Where is it? Where is the Heart? I know you have it! Where are you hiding it?!"

The form of the girl didn't answer, instead it fell limp, like a discarded doll. She answered all the same, "If you're after one of the props we're never going to get anywhere. The play will never finish."

He dropped the girl as if struck, watched her dissolve back into her seat. He stood, finding his legs, and began searching first in the row he was sitting in, then the rest of the theater, ignoring the two lifeless actors on stage.

"Sit down," she called out to him, motioning to the actors with a newly formed hand, "They want to get this over with just as much as you do."

He turned wildly, searched for the source of the voice, but failed to find it. He quickly abandoned the seats and moved towards the stage.

"Hey! This isn't Avant Garde," she called out, "You can't just interrupt the performance because you don't like the way it's going! Believe me, if you could do that, would I be sitting here?"

He didn't listen. He reached for the girl, the mask, and tore it from her face. It dropped to the floor, clattering, and he looked at what was behind it. Nothing, absolutely nothing, just a dream dreamt by someone without the capacity to dream.

He took a step back, then another, and bumped into the villain of the piece. The actor came to life, grabbed him, and in Wizard Lenin's voice said, "Get out."

Lily breathed in, sucking in air as if she'd never tasted it before, and found herself collapsed on the ground. Annde wasn't in much better shape, he was leaning on the desk again, hunched over, and staring at her in growing fear.

Not simply wariness or confusion, but genuine fear.

Neither said anything, both working on regaining their bearings.

The last Heart of the World, the one she'd given him for Elizabeth, still sat on the desk.

"You might as well keep the one you have," Lily croaked out with a laugh, picking herself off the ground, "It's the last one you'll ever get."

He smiled at her, a jagged awful smile.

"You will tell me where it is," he promised, raising his hands to cast a spell. Lily beat him to it, breaking his fingers as thoughtlessly as he'd ripped off Elizabeth's hands.

"Just take your damn orb, Annde," she said as he clutched his fingers to his chest.

There was a moment where they just stared at each other, where every possibility Wizard Lenin had foreseen played out before her.

He could put her in an illusion, hoping she didn't break it. He could compel her to tell him the truth, hoping Lily didn't know how to lie without lying. He could torture her the way he'd tortured Elizabeth, hoping that Lily didn't just tell him what he wanted to hear. He could go back in her head; waste more time he didn't have. He could try to kill her and blow himself up in the process.

Looking at him, she was sure he was seeing the same roads ahead of them.

Then he lunged.

He knocked her onto the floor, trapping her beneath him, ignoring his own mutilated hands as he struck her across the face.

"Where is it?!"

Her head was smashed into the floor, everything growing both painful and dull. Her eyes drifted to the corner, she saw Elizabeth, silently screaming, desperately trying to say something.

Something vital, precious, was leaving Lily's body. It was a slow, crawling, familiar sensation as she drifted from herself.

She'd been down this path before.

"Lily? Lily?! Stay awake! This is no time to die!"

Distantly, another blow, repeated questions.

"Lily? Lily!"

And then she wasn't there anymore.

She was sitting on an island, staring ahead at nothing.

"Lily!" Wizard Lenin knelt beside her, turning her towards him, desperately searching her face, "Are you alright?"

"He killed me," she said dumbly, the words almost nonsensical.

"Lily?" Death called from somewhere in the distance, quickly walking towards them, "What's happened? Is she alright?"

Lily didn't look at him, just kept staring ahead, past Wizard Lenin, "That son of a bitch bashed my head against the carpet until it killed me."

It wouldn't help him find the Heart of the World, he had to know that, but he'd gone and done it anyway.

They hadn't talked about killing Annde. It simply hadn't been an option, not for her or Wizard Lenin. She'd just wanted him gone.

He'd gone and killed her anyway.

"Who?"

"Annde, who else?" Wizard Lenin responded; words bitingly sarcastic.

Wizard Lenin looked tired, as tired as she felt.

There were deep shadows beneath his eyes, his hands were shaking even as they held her in place. He'd been so quiet, he'd left most of it to her, but even now there didn't seem to be anything for him to say.

His hands tightened on her arms, a grim look of determination replacing his anxiety, "Let's go back, Lily, and see how he likes dying."

Neither mentioned that, in some ways, perhaps in many ways, Wizard Lenin was advocating killing himself.

Lily looked back up at him, found herself pouring over his features as if seeing him for the first time.

Wizard Lenin had always made his priorities perfectly clear.

Wizard Lenin looked out for Wizard Lenin. The only reason he looked out for Lily, when he did, was because he liked having a place to live.

She'd always thought that, if they'd met under different circumstances, he'd either drop her like a sack of potatoes or cut her down with extreme prejudice.

She hadn't even minded, never thought about it too closely. She wasn't in it for what Wizard Lenin thought of her, what he would have done with her, their relationship went beyond that. Like it or not, they were in this together.

She never imagined, though, that he'd choose her over himself without hesitation. Annde wasn't him, not exactly, more like a warped reflection but—but here they were, and it was terrible that it took something like this for Lily to realize she did mean something to him after all.

"Sorry," Lily said, finally turning to look at the stricken Death, "But I'm afraid we have to go now."

She smiled, "I'll tell you how it ends."

Lily opened her eyes, her head wound healed, and out of thin air summoned a single steel knife. Annde was staring down at her, had probably only just killed her, and was too close to avoid the knife slammed into his throat.

He tumbled backwards, a guttural noise escaping him.

Lily lunged forward, plunging the knife into his chest, stabbing over and over until she was sure he had to be dead.

Then, all she could do was stare at him, at those almost familiar features and glassy dark eyes.

"You should have taken the orb," she found herself saying numbly to his corpse.

She dropped the knife, it fell with a soft thud onto the carpet, covered in blood just like everything else.

With a deep breath, Lily stood and turned towards her audience, pulling them back into the room. She removed Elizabeth's invisible gag, her bindings, catching her as she fell into Lily's numb arms.

"Iff—I—Iff—" Elizabeth was incoherent, shaking from pain and blood loss, barely standing upright.

Lily took her hands from Rabbit, and slowly began to knit the blood, bones, and skin back together. After it was done, Elizabeth flexed her fingers in disbelief.

She was still trying to speak through her sobbing, "Iff, I—"

"You should erase her memory."

It would be for the best. Elizabeth didn't need this night in her mind, didn't need what it would do to her.

They also had to get rid of the body, cover up Annde's disappearance. Then Lily would attend the mage academy with Elizabeth and—

And it would be like it never happened.

Wordlessly, Lily walked Elizabeth out of the palace, leaving Annde's body behind. Elizabeth was blathering, mentioning something about Questburger, the regent, anyone. Lily ignored her.

She teleported herself, Elizabeth, and Rabbit to Nhoj's front door.

"Nhoj will see you home," Lily said.

"Iff, wait!" Elizabeth cried out," Please, what—what happened?"

What happened?

Elizabeth had been right there, had all her memories, and she still asked what had happened.

Lily turned, slowly, and could only give her a bitter smile.

"I'm sorry."

Then Lily was gone, like she'd never been there in the first place.

ABOUT THE AUTHOR

Jane Doe writes words sometimes.

Printed in Great Britain
by Amazon